MY ÁNTONIA

MY ÁNTONIA

Willa Cather

edited by Joseph R. Urgo

broadview literary texts

©2003 Joseph R. Urgo

All rights reserved. The use of any part of this publication reproduced, transmitted in any form or by any means, electronic, mechanical, photocopying, recording, or otherwise, or stored in a retrieval system, without prior written consent of the publisher — or in the case of photocopying, a licence from Access Copyright (Canadian Copyright Licensing Agency), One Yonge Street, Suite 1900, Toronto, Ontario M5E 1E5 — is an infringement of the copyright law.

National Library of Canada Cataloguing in Publication

Cather Willa, 1873–1947
  My Ántonia / Willa Cather ; edited by Joseph R. Urgo.

(Broadview literary texts)
Includes bibliographical references.
ISBN-10 : 1-55111-491-7
ISBN-13 : 978-1-55111-491-0

  I. Urgo, Joseph R.   II. Title.   III. Series.

PS3505.A87M9 2003   813'.52   C2003-900863-0

Broadview Press Ltd. is an independent, international publishing house, incorporated in 1985. Broadview believes in shared ownership, both with its employees and with the general public; since the year 2000 Broadview shares have traded publicly on the Toronto Venture Exchange under the symbol BDP.

We welcome comments and suggestions regarding any aspect of our publications – please feel free to contact us at the addresses below or at broadview@broadviewpress.com.

North America
Post Office Box 1243, Peterborough, Ontario, Canada K9J 7H5
3576 California Road, Orchard Park, NY, USA 14127
Tel: (705) 743-8990; Fax: (705) 743-8353;
e-mail: customerservice@broadviewpress.com

UK, Ireland, and continental Europe
Thomas Lyster Ltd., Units 3 & 4a, Old Boundary Way,
Burscough Rd, Ormskirk, Lancashire L39 2YW
Tel: (1695) 575112; Fax: (1695) 570120
email: books@tlyster.co.uk

Australia and New Zealand
UNIREPS, University of New South Wales
Sydney, NSW, 2052
Tel: 61 2 9664 0999; Fax: 61 2 9664 5420
email: info.press@unsw.edu.au

www.broadviewpress.com

Broadview Press Ltd. gratefully acknowledges the financial support of the Government of Canada through the Book Publishing Industry Development Program for our publishing activities.

This book is printed on acid-free paper containing 30% post-consumer fibre.

Series Editor: Professor L.W. Conolly
Advisory editor for this volume: Michel W. Pharand
Typesetting and assembly: True to Type Inc., Mississauga, Canada.

Certified Eco-Logo
30% Post.

PRINTED IN CANADA

Contents

Acknowledgements

I am grateful to Ashley Craig and Lorraine Dubuisson, graduate students in the Department of English at The University of Mississippi, for their assistance in gathering materials and manuscript preparation.

I wish to thank the University of Nebraska Press for permission to reproduce the text of its Scholarly Edition of *My Ántonia*.

Costs incurred in the reproduction of images were offset by funding from The University of Mississippi, for which I am grateful. I acknowledge permission to reproduce images in Appendices G and H of this volume from The Nebraska State Historical Society, the State Historical Society of Missouri, and the Library of Congress. At all three organizations, archive staff members were most helpful.

Introduction

In Willa Cather's *My Ántonia* the reader enters a fictional world reflecting some of the most salient elements of American social thought and history, elements that continue to reveal essential aspects of American culture and which make the reading of this novel as rewarding today as it was in 1918, when it was published to enthusiastic reviews. While the all-inclusive definition of the term precludes any novel from achieving such status, *My Ántonia* comes about as close as any book to being "the great American novel," a text which locates in American culture an aesthetic that endures the vicissitudes of contemporary events and speaks to successive generations its truth about the United States as an historical and intellectual experience.

In Cather's novel we find the centrality of the immigrant process (including interior migration—what we call relocation today) to American cultural vitality, and we may chart the web of influence that the immigrant experience has on newcomers and established populations alike. We enter an America that serves as a kind of testing ground for new ideas and fresh perspectives, where identities are fluid, where gender roles are evolving, where the constancy of social and economic change puts pressure on the emotional lives of men and women, leading them to adaptive strategies. We read of the interplay of country and city, agricultural and urban lifestyles, the confident appeal of living close to the earth, and the sophisticated and worldly satisfaction of living close to other human beings. We witness the demands made by new kinds of knowledge, the effects of education, the resultant class stratification and the nostalgia that afflicts those who benefit by upward mobility. We see the importance of family in America and we see how its fluid social structure enables and encourages individuals to leave families behind. We feel Cather's deep love and awe for the landscape and for the tremendous forces of nature that shape and sustain it. Finally, we recognize how important history is to a people who have broken with it at some point in their lives, how important it is for a migratory people to have some way of recalling the past. Living far from origins, the only evidence possessed to demonstrate identity is memory, the stories told of whence, for what reasons, and to what effect.

Whether there will ever be a great American novel is as unknowable as ever, but if one wishes to know something of the narrative soul of the United States, if one wishes to see American culture cast as an aesthetic, to probe the art that is made of this experiment in human culture and society, one must read *My Ántonia* or one has to abide missing something beautiful and enduring.

Making Art from Experience

Cather's career as a novelist was well underway by the time she published *My Ántonia*. Nonetheless, she had not produced a masterpiece of form until she wrote it and went on, after its publication, to produce one great work after another. *My Ántonia* is a watershed in the career of Willa Cather, and it shores up a number of strands of promise displayed in works before it. Most obviously, the novel projects a more complex and intellectually complete representation of emigration to Nebraska and settlement on the American prairie than her earlier novel, *O Pioneers!* (1913). The strong concern for the development of narrative voice and the exploration of female agency, both of which contribute to the energy behind *The Song of the Lark* (1915), are less overt and thus much more effective in *My Ántonia*. And Cather's lifelong attention to form, beginning in her first novel, *Alexander's Bridge* (1912), where the idea of the bridge informs the novel's structure as well as its thematic content, crashes through conventional symbol-making in *My Ántonia* to produce one of the twentieth century's most distinctively structured novels. While *My Ántonia* is surely a breakthrough novel for Cather, the one that established her as an artist working at the height of her creative powers, it has a genealogy in her writing that extends back through each of its precursor novels and back even further, to ideas and impressions which appear in her earliest fiction, and indeed to her earliest experiences as a child on the Nebraska frontier.

A central incident in *My Ántonia*, the suicide of Mr. Shimerda, is based on an actual suicide in Cather's childhood, an incident that she narrated repeatedly. Her early short story, "Peter" (Appendix D), was first published when she was in college in the 1890s. The novel's titular character, Ántonia Shimerda, is modeled on an immigrant girl Cather knew in Nebraska (the suicide's granddaughter), Annie Sadilek (Appendix G.5). Many other details in the text are taken from Cather's memory of her Nebraska childhood. Foremost among these was her emigration from Virginia. The shock, awe, and erasure that Jim Burden experiences as his body is moved from the lush settled farmlands of Virginia to the bleak, treeless Nebraska prairie are taken directly from Cather's experience of the same migration in 1883, when she was nine years old. Incidents such as Jim's killing of the snake and the story of the bride who was thrown to the wolves are doubtlessly things Cather heard about as a child. The Shimerda family is taken from the Sadilek clan and other Bohemian immigrants in Nebraska. Jim Burden's grandparents are modeled on Cather's own. After spending a few years on a farm, the Burdens, like the Cathers, moved to town—Black Hawk for Burden, Red Cloud for Cather. The novel's dedication, "To Carrie and Irene Miner," name Red Cloud friends whose characters are the basis for Francis and Nina Harling.

Annie Sadilek, however, is the source of inspiration for Cather's novel in the same way that Ántonia Shimerda is what fires Jim Burden's imagination and drives him to write down, as we learn in the novel's Introduction, all that she recalls to him. Annie Sadilek was hired by the Miner family, as Ántonia was hired by the Harlings. Annie Sadilek came to encapsulate, in Cather's imagination, all that impressed her about the European immigrants that she came to know as a young girl in Nebraska. In Cather's hands, Sadilek reaches heroic proportions as both mother-figure and as the figure of a pioneer woman who refuses to allow circumstances to determine her destiny. Other characters and situations in the novel are drawn from Cather's memory: Larry Donovan, the father of Ántonia's first child, is drawn from a railroad worker named James William Murphy; Wick Cutter from a shady businessman in Red Cloud named M. E. Bentley; Blind D'Arnault, the piano prodigy, on two performers, Blind Boone (Appendix G.6), whom Cather heard in Red Cloud, and Blind Tom, whom she saw in Lincoln. As can be surmised from these few examples, much critical energy has been and may be expended on source-hunting in My Ántonia. For the most complete study of parallels between the fictional and the actual, one is advised to return to the first chronicler of sources, Mildred R. Bennett, and her work The World of Willa Cather. The study of the sources behind the novel, and the degree to which each is transformed according to the demands of art, offers an intriguing look into the creative process.

If the parallels between Willa Cather's life and the content of her novel account for her materials, they do not account for her intellect, or for the aesthetic energies which drive the novel. It was not the recollections themselves that troubled Cather enough to make art of them; she began writing of her Nebraska prairie experiences as early as her first years away from Red Cloud, when she was a student in Lincoln. In her second novel, O Pioneers!, she made her initial attempt to turn this material into serious art, with definite success, albeit not at the level reached in My Ántonia. What distinguishes My Ántonia is neither the recollections nor the parallels to real things that happened and to the actual people Cather knew, but rather the form of the novel, its structure and organization. Ironically, these are the qualities that Jim Burden, in the Introduction, claims the novel lacks ("I suppose it hasn't any form," he says), the first of many ironies that should alert the reader to the novel's subtleties. For if it were nothing more than Willa Cather's nostalgic memories of her childhood, the novel would have no shelf life and would join the thousands of books that record the memories of middle-aged men and women convinced that their past possesses significance to someone other than themselves. My Ántonia is many things and contains a multitude of significance and relevance—but it is not self-indulgent. In fact, a remarkable aspect of the novel is the extent to which, despite its ironies, subtleties, and mysteries, Willa Cather manages to put to such transparent use unvarnished memories of people she knew and incidents that occurred in her Nebraska youth. It did not seem important to her to mask these details. The emphasis of Cather's art is not on the facts, people, and things she includes in her writing, but on the form these phenomena take as a result of meditations.

The first aesthetic act in the novel is marked by its Introduction. Here the author places between herself and her reader a narrator named Jim Burden. In this signal act, Cather opened her novel to successive generations of critics who have probed and will continue to probe the significance of this structural move. In the Introduction we learn that Jim Burden and an unnamed narrator share memories of a Nebraska hometown, where they both knew and were fascinated by a girl named Ántonia. They decide that they ought each to write down their memories of her. Jim follows through; the narrator of the Introduction does not. Jim hands his manuscript to the narrator and he, or she, presents it to the reader "substantially as he brought it to me," and with the title he gave to it, "My Ántonia." Many novice readers have read the Introduction literally, and assumed that Cather did not write the novel, but was given it by Mr. Burden. Even more sophisticated readers have assumed that the narrator of the Introduction is Willa Cather— even if the character, Jim Burden, is a creation—and the Introduction as a whole a transparent framing device. Nonetheless, there is no identity given the narrator of the Introduction and no particular reason to assume that narrator to be Cather or anyone else who walked the earth or rode the train.

On the other hand, Jim Burden bears a good deal of resemblance to Willa Cather. He, like she, moved to Nebraska from Virginia as a child and he, like she, knew the immigrant girl they would eventually write about. If the narrator of the Introduction is Cather, it is she in a series of potential juxtapositions to herself as Jim Burden: the adult to the child, the female to the male, the present to the past, the train to the farm, the city to the country, the reader to the writer. In other words, in *My Ántonia*, Cather transforms herself into a fictional character just as she does with people she remembered from her childhood. If, as she claimed, her characters were composites, then she too, like Jim Burden, is a composite, just as she may have become to some degree part of the composite of every character she created, male and female alike. In the Introduction, the observing and remembering Cather comes face to face with the active, writing Cather, the one who will make art out of her memories. The idea of a divided self is thus embedded into the very structure of the text, and it may be that it was this idea, or some version of it, that provided Cather with the intellectual break-through she needed to create an aesthetic structure sufficient to prop up this material.

It is one thing to write from memory—how else does one write?—but it is something again to make of one's memory an aesthetic exploration into the processes of recollection, re-envisioning, and representation. When we remember, the person who remembers is no longer solely the present-person but is that person filled with the past. At the same time, the person (or persons) recalled is neither with the present person nor with the person of the past, but something between the two, created by the present, indebted to the past. The past is gone, and what is envisioned in memory is not it but our re-creation of it. The splitting of her narrators into the one who introduces and the one who wrote, juxtaposed against the memories they shared, may be read as Cather's initial gesture toward one major theme of the novel, captured in its final phrase: "the incommunicable past." It is not the past which communicates, it is the present; the Jim Burdens must create the past by recording what they saw and what they know. The past is always communicated in the present and it becomes a part of the present through narration, through memory. Willa Cather had indelible memories of Nebraska, memories she took with her when she left, memories she would pour into three novels and numerous short stories. But it was not simply the content of her mind which drew her creative powers. Cather was also deeply consumed by the processes of memory and recollection, and the relationship between what the mind could draw from its experiences and its capacity for creative expression.

Career Woman

By the time she wrote *My Ántonia*, Willa Cather had gone through numerous iterations of herself. The novel was published in 1918, the year she turned 45. She was born in 1873, in Back Creek Valley, near Winchester, Virginia. In 1883, her family moved to Nebraska, and settled in Red Cloud, a small agricultural town close to the Kansas state line. Much like her character, Jim Burden, Cather attended the University of Nebraska at Lincoln. There, in the 1890s, she proved herself a prolific writer and editor, and even as an undergraduate began writing professionally for the *Nebraska State Journal*. The University of Nebraska was founded in 1869 as a land grant college. University Hall, the first building, was completed in 1871, and the first class, with two members, graduated in 1873. According to Kari Ronning, by the time Cather arrived in 1890, the four square block campus consisted of four buildings and five hundred students. By 1895, when she left, enrollment had reached fifteen hundred, a new library was under construction, and the campus was enclosed by an iron fence (Ronning, 11). (See Appendix G.7 for a photograph of the University at the turn of the century.) The University had no dormitories, and students roomed with private families or in boarding houses. Greek organizations were popular, and were the basis of much campus rivalry among students. According to Ronning, Cather was a "barb," or a non-Greek. She belonged to the Union society, and had friends in Greek organizations. However, as managing editor of the student paper, *The Hesperian*, she sought to avoid the appearance of partisanship (Ronning, 13).

After graduation in 1895, Cather became an editor with the Lincoln *Courier*. A year later her career drew her out of Nebraska with an appointment as editor of the Pittsburgh *Home Monthly*. She took her journalistic and critical writing very seriously; Willa Cather was an ambitious woman. She continuously sought additional outlets for her work and was, in today's jargon, a woman on the make. Within a few months of arriving in Pittsburgh, despite the demanding schedule at the *Home Monthly*, Cather secured a part-time position at the *Pittsburgh Leader* as arts critic, and published twenty-six columns in her first year in the city. At the same time, she renewed her association with the *Nebraska State Journal*, sending them seventeen columns in the first half of 1897. This was not hack work; on the contrary, and unlike many great writers, Willa Cather seems to have worked through her aesthetic principles in public and in print, leaving a vast archive of youthful writing for critical inspection.

The *Home Monthly* was sold in 1897, and Cather went home to Red Cloud for the summer. In September, the *Pittsburgh Leader*, at that time Pennsylvania's largest newspaper, offered her a job. She returned to Pittsburgh thinking she was to become a full-time drama critic. Soon after she arrived, however, the office was in some turmoil because its overseas telegraph editor had resigned. Cather was asked to fill in, which she did so skillfully that the publishers decided to hire her to that position permanently, despite the unprecedented nature of appointing a woman to the post. In the fall of 1897, Cather was processing the foreign news by day, attending theater and concert productions in the evening, and writing her arts columns in the late nights and early mornings. She kept this schedule for the next year and into 1899, a period when her journalism eclipsed her fiction writing. An observer at the time would have identified this woman as a career journalist with a promising future. She could move from the opera house to international diplomacy to household advice for new brides, seamlessly, in a twenty-four hour period. It was simply a question of assuming the appropriate narrative voice.

In 1900, Cather signed on to a new publication called the *Library*, with, as its name implies, a more bookish and less ephemeral mission. The magazine lasted six months, collapsing with the century in 1900. The production was absorbed by *Index of Pittsburgh Life*, where she published her Washington, D.C., correspondence during her stay in the Capitol in 1900-1901. At this time, Cather was working as a translator for the United States Commission to the Paris Exposition, and she continued, in this period, to send columns to the *Nebraska State Journal* In March 1901, ready once again to assume another career and another identity, Cather was back in Pittsburgh. She accepted a job at the city's Central High School to teach Latin, Algebra, and Composition, work she took on in hopes that she would have more time for her literary and freelance writing ambitions. She stayed on the faculty at Central for two years, and then moved to Allegheny High School and taught there until 1906.

While teaching at Central High in 1901-1902, she wrote a series of columns for the *Pittsburgh Gazette*. In the summer of 1902, while touring Europe, Cather sent travel columns to the *Nebraska State Journal* as well as to the *Gazette*. In 1903, at the top of her form in Pittsburgh, she met S.S. McClure, the start of a professional relationship that would take her from that Pennsylvania city to New York and to the editorship of *McClure's Magazine*. Cather also published a book of poems in 1903, *April Twilights*, with a vanity press— a move she would soon regret (although later in her life, after she was a successful author, she allowed its republication). S.S. McClure published her first book of fiction, *The Troll Garden*, in 1905, and she went to work for him in 1906. The pattern continued, then, as Willa Cather pursued twin careers in journalism and literature (she would never teach again, although she was successful at it). Nonetheless, it was her work as a journalist and editor—not as schoolteacher or fiction writer—that brought her acclaim and brought opportunity to her desk. With her appointment at *McClure's*, Cather had reached the pinnacle of national success as a journalist—as a woman or as a man—when she became editor of one of America's most famous and influential magazines.

Two concerns were paramount in Cather's journalism: exposing mediocrity and insufficiency, and promoting the arts and imaginative enterprises of all kinds. "After all," she wrote in 1899, "in art imagination is the only verity, and the poet is more reliable than the statistician." In 1901-1902, with the *Pittsburgh Gazette*, Cather ventured into social issues, writing about such matters as illegal poultry production (in violation of state and federal standards) and the plight of children left to their own devices in hotels, by wealthy parents—the century's original latchkey children. Her evolving social consciousness, coupled with high standards in all endeavors and a strong advocacy of the arts, would add to the credentials she brought to *McClure's Magazine* when hired away from Pittsburgh to work with that prestigious publication in 1906. At *McClure's* she moved up quickly, to the position of Editor in 1908 and, in 1909, Managing Editor. She worked at *McClure's* until 1911, producing the muckraking magazine through various progressive causes and publishing triumphs. In 1911, she took a leave of absence to write *Alexander's Bridge* (1912), a novel that grew out of *McClure's* interest in men of power and influence. After its publication (it was first serialized in *McClure's*), Cather turned her energies to literary matters, ready, at 40, to become a full-time novelist. Although she did some work for the magazine after that, she never returned as a full-time editor for any extended period of time.

Alexander's Bridge was followed by *O Pioneers!* in 1913 and *The Song of the Lark* in 1915. In the intervening year she ghost wrote *My Autobiography* for S.S. McClure, experimenting and proving herself entirely successful creating a credible male voice. (Her authorship was not generally known when the book was published.) With this work, also serialized in the magazine, she completed her professional association with *McClure's* and ended her remarkable career as a journalist. Much is made in American literary history of Sherwood Anderson's resignation from his office job to become a writer. However, there is no biography as dramatic and no career choice as consequential as that of Willa Cather, when she decided to leave journalism and devote her energies to literature. She did so in a prototypically American way—she headed West and asked the desert, addressing ancient ruins much in the way her character Thea Kronborg does in *The Song of the Lark*. In fact, she took a trip to the Southwest and got lost in a national park (see Appendix B for her published account of the episode). In 1915, Cather undertook a professionally and personally transformative vacation when she traveled to Mesa Verde, Taos, and Santa Fe. Artistically, we can identify a pre-1915 and a post-1915 Cather: after 1915, Cather no longer wrote *about* dedicating oneself to art and to the muses, no longer merely defined characters who were transposed by the muse, because now she did so herself, beginning one of literature's most astounding 25-year careers as a fiction writer.

Cather was already a successful novelist. The critical reception of her first three novels assured that what she wrote would be read and reviewed by national critics. However, she had yet to stop clocks, as it were, with her art. She would return to the American southwest the next year, and upon settling again in New York, began writing *My Ántonia* in 1916. In 1917, while she was writing, Cather was called back to the University of Nebraska to receive an honorary Doctor of Letters. She was in the midst of a novel that would take her back creatively, and now literally, to her years as a student in Lincoln. During the composition of *My Ántonia* she also took up residence at the Shattuck Inn, in Jaffrey, New Hampshire, the location she would eventually choose for her gravesite. The novel was published in 1918. It was based on Cather's childhood in Nebraska but it was conceived in the Southwest, begun in New York City, and completed in New Hampshire, and during its composition the author traveled more than once across the country and back. In the deepest sense, *My Ántonia* is a transcontinental, migratory novel, written by a woman who had uprooted and reinvented herself periodically, and who had carried, and no doubt had been sustained by, memories of former selves which marked her soul like the traces of shed skin.

Because by 1916–1918, the period of My Ántonia's composition, Cather had lived many lives. She had been the daughter of migratory parents, moving from settled but war-weary and economically strapped Virginia (the family barn may have been targeted by arsonists who held a grudge against the Cathers for their Union sympathies) to the Nebraska frontier with classically American intentions of new beginnings. There, on the prairie, ironically, she acquired a cosmopolitan sensibility from central-European immigrants. Her home in Virginia was a provincial backwater compared to what she found in Webster County, Nebraska. She grew up in the sheltered freedom of a small agricultural town and went on to become a college student in an era when few women attended universities (and many who did would remain unmarried career women). While at college she became a drama critic, achieving a regional reputation for her tough critiques of passing shows and performers in Lincoln. After graduation she became the editor of a women's magazine in Pittsburgh, a Washington correspondent, a professional translator, and a high school teacher. She also became a published poet with her book, April Twilights. She did her most significant editorial work with McClure's Magazine, where she became managing editor of the nation's premier muckraking phenomenon. When she finished her work there, she had become a successful novelist, publishing three novels before turning to My Ántonia. One wonders, then, what Willa Cather thought of herself, of professional identity, what she thought made a person who that person was, and how she would have answered the question, "What do you do, Miss Cather?" It is almost impossible to associate the ideas of stability and a single-minded career path with Cather. Almost a century before it would become a commonplace idea, Willa Cather was adept at multitasking and was comfortably pursuing multiple career goals well into middle-aged adulthood.

Writing for Conservation

One thing is certain. By 1916, when she began writing My Ántonia, Nebraska was almost pure memory. Cather had been a New Yorker since 1906, and she had resided in Pittsburgh for ten years before that. In 1916, she had not lived in Nebraska for two decades. Indeed, she would never live in Nebraska again, and would visit

Red Cloud even less frequently than other locations on her regular travel routes. (Her trip to Red Cloud to receive her honorary degree from the University of Nebraska, was very short: she complained of the heat and went on to Wyoming.) In this way her life parallels Jim Burden's quite closely; although not a lawyer, the work she took on as an adult made Red Cloud increasingly remote. And, as its remoteness intensified, so did the effect of it on her consciousness. One reason why *My Ántonia* was so well-received in 1918 (it is one of the few great American novels to have been a commercial and popular success, as well as satisfying to critics and, later, scholars) was that it struck a national chord. It rang true to contemporary readers not because it concerned the frontier (there was no shortage of U.S. frontier novels in the early twentieth century), not because it featured a strong female character (this was the decade of woman's suffrage, won in 1919, a decade of feminist articulation), and not because of the beauty of its language—although all these qualities contribute to its power and effect. The national chord struck by *My Ántonia* had to do with its tone, with the perspective it took on the landscape, the people who settled it, and with the straining not to forget taken on by the narrator. The era in which Cather remembered and wrote about Nebraska, when she was making of its unlikely location a landmark of American settlement, transforming its obscure inhabitants into harbingers of the nation's future, was an era of wide-sweeping national efforts to remember the landscape, and to connect its natural settings to its national character and destiny. In part, *My Ántonia* is a great American novel because it raises to the status of "landmark" the human experience on the landscape it recounts. To understand the full significance of this, we must understand something more about New York, Washington, and the national culture of Cather's era. The national scene with which she had come to identify so closely as a journalist was marked by decades of debate about what should be preserved and remembered on the landscape of the United States, and how that memory was to be articulated and presented for the experience of generations to come.

When Cather began writing *My Ántonia*, at the historical moment of its conception, a conservationist movement was in full force in the United States. That year Congress passed the National Park Service Act, creating the National Park Service that exists today, an established arm of the federal government, present in every national park and monument across America. The Park Service was created to oversee those federal properties called national parks and monuments, to police the conservation of the scenery, the natural and historic monuments and wild life, so that the landscape would be available to later generations to know, explore, and experience. The teens were a decade of park and monument establishment. In 1916 Congress established Hawaii National Park and Lassen Volcanic National Park (California). President Wilson also issued Proclamations establishing Sieur de Monts National Monument on Mount Desert Island, Maine, and Capulin Mountain National Monument, New Mexico—located, coincidentally, in two of Cather's favorite states. Northeast Harbor, where she stayed later in her life, is the tip of Mount Desert Island. Three years later, in 1919, Lafayette National Park (renamed Acadia National Park [Maine] in 1929) was established by Congress. In 1917 Congress established Mount McKinley National Park (Alaska) and at the National Park Service conference that year, attendees explored the role of the parks in American life. In 1918, the year *My Ántonia* was published, Congress approved a Migratory Bird Treaty Act, which implemented a 1916 Convention (between the U.S. and Britain, acting for Canada) for the Protection of Migratory Birds, and assumed responsibility for international migratory bird protection. The next year Congress established Grand Canyon National Park (Arizona) and Zion National Park (Utah), while President Wilson issued a Proclamation establishing Scotts Bluff National Monument (Nebraska).

The era of *My Ántonia* was one of national landscape preservation. But national parks creation is no coincidental context for the novel. Among the book's points of genesis was Willa Cather's trip to Mesa Verde National Park in 1915. In addition, Cather was subtly influenced by the public debate over preserving natural lands— especially since some of those landscapes, in Maine, New Mexico, and Colorado, for example, were in places to which she would often return, and so would have wanted unchanged. The forty years between 1880 and 1920 were the years of genesis for American environmentalism—and as we have seen, these were Willa Cather's formative years as well. The milieu into which Cather offered *My Ántonia* was one where policymakers and technocrats, capitalists and intellectuals, were grappling with the right relation between human beings and nature. At issue was the question of how to preserve the American wilderness experience as an art form; how to transform carefully selected wildlands into sites of heightened experience, valued by virtue of the capitalist sacrifice of profit represented by preservation. And yet, the sacrifice of preservation is necessary to the imagination of men like Jim Burden and women like Willa Cather, whose source of inspiration is tied to the preservation of frontier and landscape-laden memory.

Jim Burden is emblematic of the conservation debate: he is both a legal counsel for the railroads (and so he profits by land development) and a preservationist, someone to be counted on for funding "big Western dreams" of uncovering secret canyons and lost parks. The Introduction identifies Jim's "interest in women" as the novel's creative spark, and just as the nation has set apart certain landscapes to allow its citizens to enjoy nature, Jim "set apart time enough to enjoy [his] friendship" with Ántonia. There's an equation at work there: Jim's connection with Ántonia does for him what the nation's connection to its landscape does for its people. The parallel evoked is an aesthetic experience, which for Cather is serious and vital business. After all, the "gift" in Jim Burden's portfolio, in the Introduction, is a novel. The novel, as it emerges from the national parks era, is an aesthetic projection of the will to preserve. What Jim gives his friend when he hands over his manuscript is indeed a gift—something worth saving.

Cather's direct encounter with National Parks is documented in her essay, "Mesa Verde Wonderland is Easy to Reach," originally published in *The Denver Times* on January 31, 1916 (Appendix B in this volume). Cather's experience at Mesa Verde had a profound effect on the shape of her fiction and on her aesthetic sensibilities. But one thing she may have realized right away: the preservation movement of the early twentieth century (Mesa Verde was established as a National Park in June 1906) applied not only to ancient ruins but should properly inform as well the way we think about the landscape we live in *now*. Mesa Verde—the National Park, the Anasazi use of landscape, the American act of preservation—is writ large in the structure and form of *My Ántonia*. In its historical context, the novel suggests that while we act to preserve our frontier heritage by setting aside wilderness landscapes, we also must work to remember the landscape of our own origins, to preserve the labor and the identities of those who have contributed to the making of the present. When Jim acknowledges "all the human effort that had gone into" the "flat tableland" of Nebraska, transforming what was once a wild landscape into an agricultural patchwork "broken up into wheatfields and cornfields" and changing "the whole face of the country," he creates an aesthetic experience of the latest American land-dwellers and their way of inscribing a civilization into the landscape. Mesa Verde Park saves not so much the Anasazi—they're long gone—but preserves the *idea* that landscapes embody the past. Preserving landscapes, in turn, is remembering: it is the aesthetic expression and the physical behavior of memory itself.

American Migrations / American Identities

The landscape that Cather attends in Nebraska embodies a remarkable history. Cather lived a charmed life, historically. She attended college in an era when universities were opening doors and opportunities for women. She arrived in New York when her generation of college-educated women were assuming leadership roles, when hers at the helm of *McClure's* was pioneering but at the same time, timely. Likewise, as a child, she arrived in Nebraska at a historical moment which both embodied the frontier experience of the past century and anticipated the immigrant experience of the next. Between 1865 and 1880, the population of Nebraska doubled; in the 1880s, when the Cather family arrived, it doubled again. In Webster County, where the family settled, there were only sixteen residents in 1870. In 1880, there were 7,000 people in the county. When Willa Cather arrived in 1884, she contributed to the 1890 census count of 12,000 and to the emergence of a thriving community on the verge of becoming almost urban. After she moved to Lincoln in 1890, she would live in cities for the rest of her life, living in the countryside only as a tourist, on frequent excursions and through her fiction.

The 1890 census lists only 29% of Nebraska residents as Nebraska-born, and 28% as born in the United States outside Nebraska. Non-U.S. born residents made up 43% of the population, and were characterized by a pan-European representation: 37.6% German; 12.1% Swede; 10.8% Irish; 7.8% Czech; 6.6% English; 5.7% Dane, and others from various nations and territories. Cather's urban American readers, faced daily with the growing presence of Italian, Greek, Irish, and other immigrants in their cities, would recognize both the struggle of Ántonia to learn the English language and the puzzlement experienced by the Burden family as they attempt to fathom the thinking, the foodways, and the behavior of their Czech-Bohemian neighbors (see Appendix H.1). Cather's cowboys—the domesticated ones who work for the Burdens—are equally perplexed and intrigued by these strangers, as intrigued perhaps as Jim Burden is with the cowboys' tales of exploits in regions and times before the farmers arrived. The 1880s was a phenomenal decade in United States population history, encapsulating a moment which would recur at different times in different places throughout the twentieth century: a rapidly shifting population, the civil confrontation of peoples who, in other parts of the world, might have been enemies or perhaps never would have encountered one another, the presence of immigrant populations altering the very definition of American culture. Willa Cather was there and she remembered, and lending her genius to these memories, she produced a novel that continues to articulate something vital and true about the United States of America.

Ultimately, what Cather remembered is not as important to readers today as the aesthetic cast of her memories. True, biographers are able to identify prototypes of Cather's characters and places (see photographs of the Pavelka farm and Anna Sadilek, Appendix G.4 and G.5) and draw parallels between her experiences and Jim Burden's—a good deal of Cather criticism involves the important work of source hunting, and most readers will find it interesting. However, readers are not drawn to the novel generation after generation primarily because Willa Cather put loud echoes of real people into its composition. It is the cast of Cather's aesthetic vision that hooks us.

The most distinctive fact about the narrative structure of *My Ántonia* is that it starts twice: once with the Introduction, and again with Book I, "The Shimerdas." The Introduction is both indispensable and puzzling. It occupied Cather's thinking about the novel, we know, because in 1926, in preparation for a new edition of the novel, it was the only portion of the novel revised heavily (see Appendix A). The Introduction is indispensable because it sets the narrative which follows as *memory*, and the peculiar workings of human memory define much of what the novel is about. Without its Introduction, the novel would be about Ántonia, and not about Jim Burden's memory of her and the role she plays in his sense of himself. The Introduction is puzzling, moreover, because of Jim Burden. The fact of the male narrator has been a source of much attention by feminist and gender critics, some of whom have found in Jim's voice evidence of patriarchy, objectification of women, and condescension. What does Jim Burden have to do with this? What effect does he have on this story? Why can't Ántonia's story be told directly?

At its most basic level of plot *My Ántonia* is about migration and settlement. Everyone in the novel, all the characters on the Nebraska prairie, are from somewhere else or on their way to somewhere else. And the original inhabitants, the Indians, are gone. Even the Introduction takes place on a cross-continental train. A dialectic informs the novel from start to finish, a dialectic between migration and settlement, and the contradictory yet combinatory effects of this great American paradox. Characters continuously negotiate a life that lies between their origins and their destination, and a common ailment among many is homesickness. Characters also reinvent themselves in their new surroundings—Ántonia's greatest resource may be the capacity to shed an old self and take on a new one, as her life circumstances demand. If we consider the novel as a poetics of migration, attending to the structures of mind that are concomitant to moving from one place to another, we will recognize a series of related effects common to a number of characters. What is apparent is that structures of living change rapidly and dramatically (reified in the stages of settlement Cather charts, from cave to sod house to farm house), such as when Ántonia moves into town as a hired girl, or when Jim leaves the farm to attend college in the city. There is a continuous recurrence of what recent critical theory has labeled as defamiliarization, where characters are confronted with unknown ways of living and experience, and expected to cope with challenges to ways which have become settled. Prescribed norms disintegrate with migratory tides, and what was considered sacred or sacrosanct in one context become irrelevant or impossible in another. As a child Jim Burden is not sure, for example, if his parents, who are dead, know that he has moved to Nebraska. There arises from the novel a sense of a migratory consciousness, a way of thinking rooted, paradoxically, in memories of being uprooted. Such consciousness knows ambivalence above all, knows what it is to hold contradictory values strongly and simultaneously.

As a college-educated career woman in the early twentieth century, one who had risen to the top of the world of journalism, who had done "man's work" and had proven, not by polemic but by example, that a woman could do these things and do them well—and then to give up her place to pursue a career as a serious artist, to become not a only major woman writer but among the two or three most important novelists of the twentieth century—in light of all this, why do we question the male narrator? The issue would seem not to be with it, or with her or him, but with us, with readers, or perhaps with readers of limited vision. Cather had already ghost-written S.S. McClure's autobiography, and readers assumed, and were right in their assumption, that the writing revealed

McClure's voice. To Cather, voice came from experience, not gender. To live a life in which a person did things traditionally assigned to males was to acquire, in a social sense, masculine aspects of character. These aspects, however, are social, not physical phenomena. Ántonia knows what it is to "work like mans," as she says. Jim Burden as well possesses feminine qualities, inevitably the result of his close friendship with Ántonia and the other hired girls in his town. The frontier immigrant experience had shown Cather how Virginians become Nebraskans, and together with Bohemians, Russians, and Swedes (among others) become Americans, and how a woman could dress like a man and successfully impersonate masculinity in social settings (she was a cross-dresser in high school and college). The frontier is a landscape of reinvention, and its transmutation into ideology makes it not more remote but more accessible to thinking men and women in cities, towns, and other settled areas, long after the pioneer era has passed and long after one's ancestors have made the crossing. Gender identification, in this sense, is among those ideas carried by migrants to new territories. Some of the ideas carried in suitcases settle; others don't.

In My Ántonia, identity is experience. In contemporary terms, the identities of those who migrate are deconstructed with the crossing and, through experience, reconstituted. The indispensable quality of the Introduction is that it opens the novel with this fact. Jim Burden is who he is because of the experiences he recounts in his memoir, Cather's novel. By the time she wrote My Ántonia, the Willa Cather of Nebraska was another person, perhaps as different from herself in New York as an Austrian is from a Ukrainian, or as a man is from a woman. Jim Burden's narration establishes that distance, establishes distance as an important component of memory, and in turn declares memory to be the vital, communicable ingredient of identity. Nonetheless, the suggestion that gender is malleable, that Cather may have gendered her own mind as male in order to tell this story, has broad implications that will continue to demand critical and scholarly analysis while we, as a culture, work out such issues in successive eras.

What seems clear is that the experiences of immigrant crossing, geographic migration, settlement in new lands, and encounters with different peoples produce a sense that identity is a fluid commodity. And as Americans continue to move—recent statistics reveal that on average, Americans relocate every five years—Cather's novel will continue to strike resonant chords. What postmodern critics suggest to be the salient features of contemporary life—fractured selves, fragmented experience, the absence of linear continuity—may be no more than the accumulated effect on consciousness of successive, generational migration. In telling this story, the story of how immigrant experience informs the American mind, and specifically how an obscure Bohemian immigrant-woman's biography in an equally obscure Nebraska farming county can be so centrally a part of a railroad lawyer's consciousness, Willa Cather accomplished something we might well be tempted to call the great American novel.

The Illustrations

The novel is divided into five Books, in addition to the Introduction, and contains eight illustrations. The Books get successively shorter. It takes more space to tell Jim's oldest memories and much less space to narrate fairly recent events—including the events of the Introduction, which take place in the novel's present, the shortest duration of all. The structure mirrors consciousness itself, which expands beneath the surface of present-tense experience; or it is like our experience of time, which moves slowest in childhood and youth, and accelerates with the aging process. There is a sense in the narrative of a leisurely but distant childhood, as if youth were a country to visit by those whose younger selves have migrated into memories.

The eight illustrations present another challenge to readers, and in themselves add to the fictionality established by the Introduction. (Jim Burden, when he presents his manuscript, makes no mention of illustrations.) Willa Cather arranged their inclusion herself, and contracted with W. T. Benda to draw pictures based on the novel. Illustrations are not common in fiction, except children's literature, and cheaper editions of *My Ántonia* have irresponsibly omitted them. They are, without question, an integral component of the novel, and considering them in succession provides a useful introduction to the book.

The placement of the illustrations parallels the structural pattern of the novel. Of the eight drawings, six appear in Book I, one in Book II, and one in Book IV, as if to suggest that picture-making occurs over long periods of time, with most pictorial memories persisting from our youngest days and oldest memories. The drawings have no captions, and are referred to in the text only obliquely, if at all. Captions are provided here for the sake of identification only.

1. *The immigrant family* (p. 53). Placed only a few pages into the novel, the scene illustrates Jim Burden's initial sighting of the Shimerda family at the Black Hawk train depot. The illustration draws on Jim's description of the woman with "a fringed shawl tied over her head," and of an old man, "tall and stooped." Jim also sees "Two half-grown boys and a girl," whom he sees standing and "holding oil-cloth bundles, and a little girl clung to her mother's skirts." Benda's illustration shows only one girl, and has one boy seated, and no one is holding oil-cloth bundles (although there is a bundle on the ground behind the stooped man). From the start, then, the reader encounters discrepancies between what Jim says and what the illustrations depict. In this first case, the variations are relatively immaterial, but they do suggest the existence of another perspective above or paralleling Jim's. The illustration depicts the family in a prototypically "huddled" immigrant arrangement (see Appendix H.2 and H.3), while at the same time the lack of any eye contact between any two members of the family implies a radically individual experience of dislocation. The first illustrations brings to the foreground the immigrant experience, and the idea of selective perspective or point of view.

2. *Mr. Shimerda and his rifle* (p. 72). Jim describes Mr. Shimerda in the sunset as "walking slowly, dragging his feet along as if he had no purpose." Benda's illustration depicts a glorious sunset, and a man walking, not so much "without purpose" as with fatality—a very clear and purposeful movement toward death. He walks directly toward the setting sun. The rifle on his shoulder is the tool he will use to end his life, and his death will lead to the family's rejuvenation. Benda's drawing tilts slightly, giving the impression that Mr. Shimerda is walking uphill, and his feet, hidden within the grasses, appear already to have entered the earth. The illustration echoes the most famous image in the novel, one that is not illustrated by Benda, that of the plow against the setting sun on the prairie. This second illustration stresses the costs borne by immigration, and the deaths of all sorts that were endured so that others might survive (See Appendix H.4).

3. *Gathering mushrooms* (p. 93). Mrs. Shimerda, who has almost nothing and whose family lives in a cave dug out of the prairie, gives the Burden family some precious, dried mushrooms which she brought to American from Bohemia. The Burdens destroy the gift, and Jim imagines that the mushrooms "had been gathered, probably, in some deep Bohemian forest ...." Benda depicts a woman, stooped and laboring intensely, with mushrooms in the

foreground. That the fruit of her labor will be so callously disre-garded, that what was valuable in the old world is of no value in the new, that value itself is contextual and not transportable—in all such connotations Benda evokes a great deal from the minor inci-dent. This third illustration makes clear the inevitable clash of val-ues among peoples whose suitcases contain such vastly different baggage.

4. *The Christmas tree* (p. 95). Jim recalls seeing "a dark spot mov-ing on the west hill" and, running to the pond, he saw Jake bring-ing home a cedar tree for Christmas. Benda's illustration is an elab-oration on this moving dark spot, the rider faceless (the horse's face is more intelligible), man and horse a black imprint against the whiteness of snow and sky. Benda's perspectival drawing calls atten-tion to the great distance Jake had to travel to find a tree for the Burden holiday. This fourth illustration displays the small acts of human kindness that make settlement possible. There is also a sad-ness evoked by the print (the horseman assumes the gesture of bringing home a dead body), a sadness not in Jim's recounting of the incident.

5. *Ántonia at the plough* (p. 117). There is an echo in this drawing of the earlier illustration, that of Mr. Shimerda against the sunset, although the substitution of plough for rifle makes plain Ántonia's assimilation into agricultural existence, and thus her survival. The illustration pointedly counters Jim's concern about her ploughing. He recalls that when she took on such work "she was ... grown up and had no time for me." While he mourns the loss of a playmate (his family is wealthy enough to hire out such work), we see her intense labor. Her face, unlike Jake's in the previous drawing, is illu-minated, and she stands erect behind the large work horses, appear-ing capable and confident, and if Jim feels sorry for her (bemoan-ing her labor, suspecting her father would disapprove), she clearly possesses no self-pity. This fifth illustration reveals a gap between Jim's perspective on Ántonia and her assessment of herself, and continues the thematic content of Benda's drawings, implying that Jim's perspective is far from authoritative.

6. *Jim and Ántonia outside in the summer* (p. 125). This drawing would seem to represent Jim's best memories of his youth with Ántonia, and may well be a commentary on those memories. There is nothing in the accompanying text that suggests the scene direct-ly. Furthermore, the boy and girl depicted appear to be teenagers, implying as well that the scene may constitute Benda's interpreta-tion of Jim's longings. By the time Jim and Ántonia (who is four

years older than Jim, but in this illustration that is not evident) are in their teens, they had become much less close than they had been as children. The drawing is placed at the end of Book I, where the separation of Jim's and Ántonia's destinies is made plain by their final exchange, where both desire an eternal summer, but each suspects that things are coming to an end. Indeed, although the drawing shows the two young people at sunset, their bodies are poised as if in anticipation of what is to come. This sixth drawing accentuates the interplay of circumstances and desire in the novel, suggesting that what constitutes memory is, in large degree, desire.

7. *Lena Lingard knitting in the field* (p. 140). The more time Lena Lingard spends outdoors, the whiter her skin becomes, according to Jim, "which somehow made her seem more undressed than other girls who went scantily clad." Benda's illustration stresses the voluptuousness of Lena and the role she plays in Jim's sexual awakening. Quite daring for 1918, Lena's breasts strain the fabric of her dress while she seems wholly oblivious to the reader's gaze—an attitude which in itself echoes her encounter with Ole Benson. This seventh illustration draws our attention to the sexual energies brought to their communities by the daughters of immigrants, and looking ahead to Ántonia's brood, suggests a connection between immigration and the nation's sexuality.

8. *Ántonia in the snowstorm* (p. 217). Benda depicts Ántonia on the day when she will give birth to her child, when Jim sees her "driving her cattle homeward across the hill." She holds a whiplash in her hand, and wears what Jim calls "a man's long overcoat and boots, and a man's felt hat." However, in the drawing her skirts are clearly visible, her face is discernibly female, and she does not appear mannish, as Jim suggests. As in the drawing of her at the plough, she looks strong and capable, and despite engaging in what Jim considers masculine activities, the figure is clearly female. What is not apparent in the drawing is her pregnancy, although its unremarkable presence is in keeping with her birthing when, "without calling to anybody, without a groan, she lay down on her bed and bore her child." This eighth drawing accentuates Ántonia's status as a physically exceptional woman who exists outside of prescribed roles and expectations, defining herself as she makes her way through the circumstances she encounters.

W.T. Benda's drawings, commissioned and selected by Willa Cather, constitute a parallel picture-story in the novel, sometimes affirming and sometimes contradicting Jim's memoir, and continuously reminding the reader of alternative perspectives. One thing is quite clear: these are not the most memorable scenes in *Jim Burden's* narrative. The images that Jim draws most memorably include such scenes as the plough at sunset, the throwing of the bride to the wolves, the killing of the snake, the frozen body of Mr. Shimerda, the fight with Ambrosch, the dates he enjoys with Lena Lingard in Lincoln—among many others. Benda's drawings imply a relationship between memory and selection which narrative sometimes obscures. The distance between subject and object, or the gap between remembering and memory, first suggested in the novel's Introduction, is picked up and carried across the text by Benda's illustrations. The drawings imply that there is another way to see this, another way to remember; that other media aside from narrative exist to structure art out of memory. In the very structure of the novel, then, memory merges into art. Something or someone as impressive and indelible as Ántonia may have inspired prose or drawing, poetry, music, drama, or sculpture. In 2000, for example, Emmylou Harris released a CD entitled *Red Dirt Girl*, including a track, "My Antonia," in which Harris sings of a man's memory of a woman he knew before his ambition for fortune compelled him to leave her. The singer's female voice, articulating the male narrator's memory, mirrors and (through twists in Harris's lyrics) interprets yet again the significance of the woman called Ántonia. All readers of Willa Cather's novel will engage in this exercise, assessing and reassessing Ántonia, making of Jim's Ántonia their own.

Reading *My Ántonia* Today

If anything, the social relevance of *My Ántonia* has increased since its publication in 1918. Written near the end of the first great wave of immigration to the United States (between 1870 and 1920 twenty million immigrants settled there), successive waves would take place throughout the century and into the twenty-first, so that we no longer speak of immigration as ebbing and flowing, but constant. After the central and southern Europeans came Asians, Indians, Middle-Eastern peoples, Mexicans, Central and South Americans. The processes of encounter and conflict, assimilation and the maintenance of original cultures depicted in the novel (Ántonia, at the end, has resisted Americanization) have become mainstays of the American social and intellectual experience. The anxiety of uprooting persists; it is as strong as the fear of becoming too entrenched. The idea of the United States of America, as a place where lives can be renewed and ancient stigmas overcome, still draws immigrants from around the world, seeking reinvention and craving new circumstances. The United States remains, moreover, the enemy of any set of ideas that are immutable. The national experience stands antithetical to any assumption that one people, one faith, or one historical experience is more valuable or should be privileged above another. Liberal tolerance (not without its own flaws) has allowed nations and creeds of the world to coexist in peace in America; it has also emerged as an ideology that stands in implicit challenge to fundamentalist worldviews. In some parts of the world, for example, the Catholic religious practice that Mr. Shimerda brings into the Protestant Burden household—when he crosses himself before their Christmas tree—would result in violence. In Cather's novel, it, like the struggle over where to bury the body of the suicide, is yet another occasion to establish new civil rules of behavior that allow tolerance.

Feminist and gender critics will continue to be drawn to the complex interplay of voice, observation, objectification, representation, and sexuality in the novel. Ántonia will, for the foreseeable future, present a challenge to readers; a strong, independent woman whose apotheosis, finally, comes as the mother of a large family of bilingual children. Readers drawn to Cather's biography will need to think and rethink her choice to narrate through Jim Burden's voice, and the myriad ways in which her own sexuality is projected onto the novel. Critics interested in social structures will find Jim's experiences as an upwardly mobile middle-class man compelling, especially his sense of the social dynamic among Black Hawk's economic classes. Postcolonial critics recognize the Nebraska settlements as a hothouse of colonial encounters, particularly salient in the relationship between the Burdens and the Shimerdas, and in the situation of the "hired girls" in Black Hawk. Other approaches to literary texts, such as ecological criticism, reveal fresh perspectives on the novel, especially with regard to Cather's attention to environmental factors and the effect of landscape on character and social processes. My Ántonia has reached canonical status, and any new critical approach will turn to the novel to test both the validity of the approach, and the capacity of the novel to yield renewed relevance. It is safe to say that as the past century has shown, My Ántonia will continue to speak in direct ways to readers of all sorts, migrants and settlers, men and women, wealthy and modest, laboring and owning, old and young.

Willa Cather was forty-five when My Ántonia was published and its author enjoyed a long and productive career after it. Her next book was a compilation of short stories, *Youth and the Bright Medusa* (1920). As nearly all Americans were, Cather was consumed by the legacy of World War I on her culture; she responded with *One of Ours* in 1922, the book that won her a Pulitzer Prize. A period of intense productivity followed, with one masterpiece after another increasing her fame and deepening the respect of other writers: *A Lost Lady* (1923); *The Professor's House* (1925); *My Mortal Enemy* (1926); and *Death Comes for the Archbishop* (1927). In the 1930s she published *Shadows on the Rock* (1931), *Obscure Destinies* (1932), *Lucy Gayheart* (1935), and *Sapphira and the Slave Girl* (1940). Cather's health began to fail in the 1940s, when she was in her late 60s, and her productivity slowed. She died in 1947, in her seventy-fourth year. Her novels have never been out of print and her reputation among scholars and critics has grown steadily since her death. Back in Red Cloud, the Willa Cather Pioneer Memorial and Educational Foundation is dedicated to the preservation of relevant historical sites in Webster County and to the promotion of Cather scholarship worldwide, including the sponsorship of international seminars and annual conferences dedicated to Cather's work. Information about this organization and links to important Cather internet resources may be found at <www.willacather.org>.

Willa Cather: A Brief Chronology

1873   December 7, Wilella Cather born, in Back Creek Valley, near
       Winchester, Virginia, to Charles Fectigue Cather and Mary
       Virginia Boak Cather, their first child. Named for maternal
       aunt. One year later Charles Cather moves his family to his
       father's sheep farm at nearby Willow Shade and manages the
       farm until 1883.

1877   Brother, Roscoe, born. Grandparents William and Catherine
       Cather relocate to Webster County, Nebraska, where their
       son George and his wife Francis are farmers.

1880   Brother, Douglass, born.

1881   Sister, Jessica, born.

1882   Begins to call herself Willa Love Cather and claims to have
       been named for her maternal uncle, William Seibert Boak
       (killed in the Civil War), and the man (Dr. Love) who
       attended her birth.

1883   The Cather sheep barn mysteriously burns down. Willow
       Shade is sold and the family moves to her grandparents'
       farm in Nebraska. The move was both traumatic and inspir-
       ing for Willa Cather, indelibly affecting her consciousness.
       She gradually adapts to frontier prairie conditions, and
       becomes interested in Scandinavian Russian, German,
       French, and Bohemian immigrant settlers in the area.

1884   Cather family moves to Red Cloud, the county seat, where
       Charles Cather opens a real estate office.

1885   Attends performances at the Red Cloud Opera House,
       which opens this year.

1888   Brother, James, born. Cather experiments with dissection
       and vivisection, sometimes calling herself "William Cather,
       M.D."

1890   Sister, Elsie, born. One of three graduates of Red Cloud
       High School in June; delivers speech in favor of scientific
       methods titled "Superstition vs. Investigation." Enrolls for a
       one year course of study at the Latin School, a University of
       Nebraska preparatory school in Lincoln.

1891   First publication, "Concerning Thomas Carlyle," in the
       Nebraska State Journal, leads to preference for literary over
       scientific study. Begins freshman year at the University of
       Nebraska. Second publication, "Shakespeare and Hamlet,"
       published in the *Nebraska State Journal*.

1892   Brother, John Esten (Jack), born. First short story, "Peter,"
       published in *The Mahogany Tree*, and first poem, "Shake-
       speare: A Freshman Theme," published in the *Hesperian*.
       Becomes literary editor of the *Hesperian*.
1893   Regular contributor to the *Nebraska State Journal* with
       drama criticism and a Sunday column. Becomes managing
       editor of *The Hesperian*. Gains reputation for "meat-ax"
       reviews.
1895   Sees opera in Chicago. Graduates from the university.
       Becomes associate editor of the Lincoln *Courier*.
1896   Moves to Pittsburgh to become editor of the *Home Monthly*.
       Sends drama reviews to Lincoln publications and to the
       Pittsburgh Leader.
1897   Leaves the *Home Monthly* and is employed by the *Pittsburgh
       Leader*.
1898   Spends time in New York City reviewing plays and opera, in
       Pittsburgh at the telegraph desk of the *Leader*, in Washington
       D.C. with a cousin, and travels to Red Cloud, the Black
       Hills, Wyoming, and Ohio.
1899   Meets Isabelle McClung and begins significant friendship.
1900   Publishes under the name "Willa Sibert Cather," which she
       keeps until 1920. Resigns from the *Pittsburgh Leader*.
1901   Begins job teaching Latin at Central High School in Pitts-
       burgh. Moves into the home of Isabelle McClung's parents.
1902   Travels to Europe with Isabelle McClung, later joined by
       Dorothy Canfield.
1903   Publishes *April Twilights*, a collection of poetry. Submits sto-
       ries to *McClure's* magazine and visits S.S. McClure in New
       York. Spends summer in Nebraska, meets Edith Lewis.
       Begins teaching English at Allegheny High School, in Pitts-
       burgh.
1905   Publishes *The Troll Garden*, a collection of short stories. Trav-
       els through the West, camps in the Black Hills, visits Red
       Cloud and New York. Attends Mark Twain's birthday dinner
       at Delmonico's.
1906   Resigns Allegheny High and joins editorial staff at
       McClure's.
1907   On assignment in Boston, researching and rewriting
       Georgine Milmine's biography of Mary Baker G. Eddy.
1908   Meets Sarah Orne Jewett in Boston. Travels to Europe with
       Isabelle McClung. Sets up household with Edith Lewis in
       New York, an association which lasts until her death. Pro-
       moted to managing editor at *McClure's*.

1909   Travels to London, on assignment; visits Red Cloud.
        Assumes full editorial responsibilities at *McClure's* when S.S.
        McClure is away.
1911   Travels in New England. Begins work on *Alexander's Bridge*;
        continues to work on the novel on a three-month leave of
        absence from *McClure's*. Writes "The Bohemian Girl" and
        "Alexandra," later incorporated into *O Pioneers!*
1912   *Alexander's Masquerade* serialized in *McClure's;* published in
        book form as *Alexander's Bridge*. Attends W.D. Howells's
        birthday dinner. Travels in the Southwest, visits ancient ruins
        and cliff dwellings; visits Nebraska and Pittsburgh; works on
        O Pioneers!
1913   *O Pioneers!* published. Moves into a large Bank Street apart-
        ment with Edith Lewis. Meets Olive Fremstad, source of
        inspiration for *The Song of the Lark*, begun this year. Visits
        childhood home in Virginia. Ghost writes *My Autobiography*,
        by S.S. McClure, serialized in *McClure's* and published as a
        book in the next year.
1914   Works on *The Song of the Lark*; travels to Maine, Nebraska,
        and the Southwest.
1915   *The Song of the Lark* published. Has extended visit with
        Isabelle McClung in Pittsburgh. Travels to Mesa Verde, Taos,
        and Santa Fe. Writes essay on Mesa Verde ruins for *The Den-
        ver Times*, published in January 1916.
1916   Isabelle McClung marries Jan Hambourg. Cather travels to
        Santa Fe and Taos, returns to New York to work on *My
        Ántonia*; commissions W.T. Benda to illustrate the novel.
1917   Receives honorary Doctor of Letters from the University of
        Nebraska. Visits Isabelle and Jan Hambourg in New Hamp-
        shire; works on *My Ántonia*.
1918   *My Ántonia* published. Travels to New Hampshire and
        Nebraska. Plans novel inspired by the death of a cousin in
        the World War.
1920   Signs with Knopf to publish *Youth and the Bright Medusa*,
        now as Willa Cather (dropping the "Sibert" on title pages
        from hereon). Travels to France to research World War I
        novel. Visits Italy.
1921   Travels to Toronto for five months and then to Grand
        Manan Island in New Brunswick, and visits Nebraska later
        in the year. Works on *One of Ours*.
1922   *One of Ours* published. Publishes "The Novel Démeublé" in
        the *New Republic*. Teaches at Bread Loaf Writers' Conference
        in Vermont. Visits Red Cloud for extended stay, and is con-

firmed (along with her parents) in the local Episcopal Church.

1923 *A Lost Lady*, serialized in *Century* and published later in the year. *April Twilights and Other Poems* published. Publishes "Nebraska: The End of the First Cycle" in *The Nation*. Travels to France to visit the Hambourgs. Awarded Pulitzer Prize for *One of Ours*. Returns to New York to work on *The Professor's House*.

1924 Agrees to edit a two-volume edition of Sarah Orne Jewett's fiction; publishes an Introduction to Daniel Defoe's *The Fortunate Mistress*.

1925 *The Professor's House*, serialized in *Collier's* and published later in the year. The movie version of *A Lost Lady* is released, resulting in Cather's vow to allow no more film versions of her work. Works on *My Mortal Enemy* and begins *Death Comes for the Archbishop*.

1926 *My Mortal Enemy* published. Abridges the introduction to *My Ántonia* for a new edition of the novel. Travels in the Southwest and visits Red Cloud on the way back to New York. Attends the MacDowell Colony in New Hampshire, and works on *Death Comes for the Archbishop*.

1927 *Death Comes for the Archbishop*, serialized in *Forum* and published later in the year. Travels to Wyoming. Suffers angina attack. Visits Red Cloud. Forced out of Bank Street apartment to make way for subway system; moves, with Edith Lewis, to Grosvenor Hotel. Lives in New Hampshire in the fall and returns to Red Cloud for the holidays.

1928 Father dies; travels to Red Cloud for his funeral. Suffers from influenza. Receives honorary degree from Columbia University. Travels to Grand Manan and visits Québec City. Begins work on *Shadows on the Rock*. Returns to Québec later in the year. At the end of the year, her mother suffers a stoke while visiting family in California.

1929 Travels to California to be with her mother. Works sporadically on *Shadows on the Rock*. Elected to National Institute of Arts and Letters; received honorary degree from Yale University. Returns to Québec and visits Grand Manan. Travels to New Hampshire and makes a fourth trip to Québec to research *Shadows on the Rock*.

1930 "Neighbor Rosicky" serialized in *Woman's Home Companion*. Visits mother in California sanatorium. Travels to

France, and returns via Quebec and New Hampshire. Awarded the Howells Medal by the American Academy of Arts and Letters for *Death Comes for the Archbishop.*

1931 *Shadows on the Rock* published. Visits mother for the last time. Receives honorary degrees from Berkeley and Princeton. Travels to Grand Manan. Is unable to arrange travel to attend mother's funeral. Visits Red Cloud for family reunion.

1932 "Two Friends" published in *Woman's Home Companion;* "Three Women" ["Old Mrs. Harris"] serialized in *Ladies' Home Journal; Obscure Destinies* (consisting of these two stories and "Neighbor Rosicky") published. Travels to Grand Manan and New Hampshire. Moves out of Grosvenor Hotel and into a Park Avenue apartment in New York.

1933 Begins work on *Lucy Gayheart.* Receives honorary degree from Smith College; receives *Prix Femina Américain* for *Shadows on the Rock.* Travels to Grand Manan and New Hampshire.

1934 Finishes *Lucy Gayheart.* Travels to Grand Manan and New Hampshire.

1935 *Lucy Gayheart* serialized in *Woman's Home Companion* and published later in the year. Visits the Hambourgs in Chicago; travels to Italy and France.

1936 *Not Under Forty,* an essay collection, published. Spends summer at Grand Manan.

1937 Works on Autograph Edition of her works. Begins work on *Sapphira and the Slave Girl.* Travels to Grand Manan.

1938 Travels to Virginia and New Hampshire. Elected to American Academy of Arts and Letters.

1939 In New York, working on *Sapphira and the Slave Girl.*

1940 *Sapphira and the Slave Girl* published.

1941 Visits San Francisco and Victoria, British Columbia. Begins work on a novel set in Avignon.

1942 Has gall bladder and appendix removed; never fully recovers strength. Travels to Williamstown, Massachusetts, for privacy and rest.

1943 Travels to Mount Desert Island, Maine. Answers letters from servicemen.

1944 Receives Gold Medal from the National Institute of Arts and Letters.

1945 Completes the third story that will form posthumous book, *The Old Beauty and Others,* published in 1948.

1946   Travels to Atlantic City to recover from influenza. Rejects
        Viking's offer to publish "The Portable Willa Cather," a pop-
        ular format of the time.
1947   April 24, cerebral hemorrhage causes death at home in New
        York. Makes last trip for final rest at Jaffrey, New Hampshire.

Her headstone, with its fictional birth date, reads:

WILLA CATHER
December 7, 1876 – April 24, 1947

THE TRUTH AND CHARITY OF HER GREAT
SPIRIT WILL LIVE ON IN THE WORK
WHICH IS HER ENDURING GIFT TO HER
COUNTRY AND ALL ITS PEOPLE.

"... that is happiness; to be dissolved
into something complete and great."
From *My Ántonia*

A Note on the Text

The text of *My Ántonia* reproduced here is taken from the University of Nebraska Press scholarly edition (1994), bearing the imprint from the Modern Language Association Committee on Scholarly Editions as an Approved Edition. We are grateful to the University of Nebraska Press for permission to reprint. The Approved Edition text is a reproduction of the first edition, published on September 21, 1918 by Houghton Mifflin. A second edition was published in 1926, with a revised Introduction (included as Appendix A in this volume).

My Ántonia

BY

WILLA SIBERT CATHER

Optima dies ... prima fugit—Virgil

WITH ILLUSTRATIONS
BY
W.T. BENDA

TO CARRIE AND IRENE MINER
In memory of affections old and true

Contents

INTRODUCTION

Last summer I happened to be crossing the plains of Iowa in a season of intense heat, and it was my good fortune to have for a traveling companion James Quayle Burden—Jim Burden, as we still
call him in the West. He and I are old friends—we grew up together in the same Nebraska town—and we had much to say to each
other. While the train flashed through never-ending miles of ripe
wheat, by country towns and bright-flowered pastures and oak
groves wilting in the sun, we sat in the observation car, where the
woodwork was hot to the touch and red dust lay deep over everything. The dust and heat, the burning wind, reminded us of many
things. We were talking about what it is like to spend one's childhood in little towns like these, buried in wheat and corn, under
stimulating extremes of climate: burning summers when the world
lies green and billowy beneath a brilliant sky, when one is fairly stifled in vegetation, in the color and smell of strong weeds and heavy
harvests; blustery winters with little snow, when the whole country is stripped bare and gray as sheet-iron. We agreed that no one
who had not grown up in a little prairie town could know anything about it. It was a kind of freemasonry, we said.

Although Jim Burden and I both live in New York, and are old
friends, I do not see much of him there. He is legal counsel for one
of the great Western railways, and is sometimes away from his New
York office for weeks together. That is one reason why we do not
often meet. Another is that I do not like his wife.

When Jim was still an obscure young lawyer, struggling to make
his way in New York, his career was suddenly advanced by a brilliant marriage. Genevieve Whitney was the only daughter of a dis-
tinguished man. Her marriage with young Burden was the subject
of sharp comment at the time. It was said she had been brutally jilt-
ed by her cousin, Rutland Whitney, and that she married this
unknown man from the West out of bravado. She was a restless,
headstrong girl, even then, who liked to astonish her friends. Later,
when I knew her, she was always doing something unexpected.
She gave one of her town houses for a Suffrage[1] headquarters, produced one of her own plays at the Princess Theater,[2] was arrested

1 Women's suffrage was a national political issue during the novel's composition. The Nineteenth Amendment, granting women the right to
   vote, was ratified in 1920.
2 A venue for experimental drama in New York City.

for picketing during a garment-makers' strike, etc. I am never able to believe that she has much feeling for the causes to which she lends her name and her fleeting interest. She is handsome, energetic, executive, but to me she seems unimpressionable and temperamentally incapable of enthusiasm. Her husband's quiet tastes irritate her, I think, and she finds it worth while to play the patroness to a group of young poets and painters of advanced ideas and mediocre ability. She has her own fortune and lives her own life. For some reason, she wishes to remain Mrs. James Burden.

As for Jim, no disappointments have been severe enough to chill his naturally romantic and ardent disposition. This disposition, though it often made him seem very funny when he was a boy, has been one of the strongest elements in his success. He loves with a personal passion the great country through which his railway runs and branches. His faith in it and his knowledge of it have played an important part in its development. He is always able to raise capital for new enterprises in Wyoming or Montana, and has helped young men out there to do remarkable things in mines and timber and oil. If a young man with an idea can once get Jim Burden's attention, can manage to accompany him when he goes off into the wilds hunting for lost parks or exploring new canyons, then the money which means action is usually forthcoming. Jim is still able to lose himself in those big Western dreams. Though he is over forty now, he meets new people and new enterprises with the impulsiveness by which his boyhood friends remember him. He never seems to me to grow older. His fresh color and sandy hair and quick-changing blue eyes are those of a young man, and his sympathetic, solicitous interest in women is as youthful as it is Western and American.

During that burning day when we were crossing Iowa, our talk kept returning to a central figure, a Bohemian[1] girl whom we had known long ago and whom both of us admired. More than any other person we remembered, this girl seemed to mean to us the country, the conditions, the whole adventure of our childhood. To speak her name was to call up pictures of people and places, to set a quiet drama going in one's brain. I had lost sight of her altogether, but Jim had found her again after long years, had renewed a

---

1 A native of Bohemia, and area of Europe now incorporated into the Czech Republic.

friendship that meant a great deal to him, and out of his busy life had set apart time enough to enjoy that friendship. His mind was full of her that day. He made me see her again, feel her presence, revived all my old affection for her.

"I can't see," he said impetuously, "why you have never written anything about Ántonia."

I told him I had always felt that other people—he himself, for one—knew her much better than I. I was ready, however, to make an agreement with him; I would set down on paper all that I remembered of Ántonia if he would do the same. We might, in this way, get a picture of her.

He rumpled his hair with a quick, excited gesture, which with him often announces a new determination, and I could see that my suggestion took hold of him. "Maybe I will, maybe I will!" he declared. He stared out of the window for a few moments, and when he turned to me again his eyes had the sudden clearness that comes from something the mind itself sees. "Of course," he said, "I should have to do it in a direct way, and say a great deal about myself. It's through myself that I knew and felt her, and I've had no practice in any other form of presentation."

I told him that how he knew her and felt her was exactly what I most wanted to know about Ántonia. He had had opportunities that I, as a little girl who watched her come and go, had not.

Months afterward Jim Burden arrived at my apartment one stormy winter afternoon, with a bulging legal portfolio sheltered under his fur overcoat. He brought it into the sitting-room with him and tapped it with some pride as he stood warming his hands.

"I finished it last night—the thing about Ántonia," he said. "Now, what about yours?"

I had to confess that mine had not gone beyond a few straggling notes.

"Notes? I did n't make any." He drank his tea all at once and put down the cup. "I did n't arrange or rearrange. I simply wrote down what of herself and myself and other people Ántonia's name recalls to me. I suppose it has n't any form. It has n't any title, either." He went into the next room, sat down at my desk and wrote on the pinkish face of the portfolio the word, "Ántonia." He frowned at this a moment, then prefixed another word, making it "My Ántonia." That seemed to satisfy him.

"Read it as soon as you can," he said, rising, "but don't let it influence your own story."

My own story was never written, but the following narrative is Jim's manuscript, substantially as he brought it to me.

BOOK I
THE SHIMERDAS

I

I first heard of Ántonia[1] on what seemed to me an interminable journey across the great midland plain of North America. I was ten years old then; I had lost both my father and mother within a year, and my Virginia relatives were sending me out to my grandparents, who lived in Nebraska. I traveled in the care of a mountain boy, Jake Marpole, one of the "hands" on my father's old farm under the Blue Ridge, who was now going West to work for my grandfather. Jake's experience of the world was not much wider than mine. He had never been in a railway train until the morning when we set out together to try our fortunes in a new world.

We went all the way in day-coaches, becoming more sticky and grimy with each stage of the journey. Jake bought everything the newsboys offered him: candy, orange brass collar buttons, a watch-charm, and for me a "Life of Jesse James," which I remember as one of the most satisfactory books I have ever read. Beyond Chicago we were under the protection of a friendly passenger conductor, who knew all about the country to which we were going and gave us a great deal of advice in exchange for our confidence. He seemed to us an experienced and worldly man who had been almost everywhere; in his conversation he threw out lightly the names of distant States and cities. He wore the rings and pins and badges of different fraternal orders to which he belonged. Even his cuff-buttons were engraved with hieroglyphics, and he was more inscribed than an Egyptian obelisk. Once when he sat down to chat, he told us that in the immigrant car ahead there was a family from "across the water" whose destination was the same as ours.

"They can't any of them speak English, except one little girl, and all she can say is 'We go Black Hawk, Nebraska.' She's not much older than you, twelve or thirteen, maybe, and she's as bright as a new dollar. Don't you want to go ahead and see her, Jimmy? She's got the pretty brown eyes, too!"

---

1 Ántonia: The Bohemian name Ántonia is strongly accented on the first syllable, like the English name Anthony, and the i is, of course, given the sound of long e. The name is pronounced Án-ton-ee-ah. [Author's note]

This last remark made me bashful, and I shook my head and settled down to "Jesse James." Jake nodded at me approvingly and said you were likely to get diseases from foreigners.

I do not remember crossing the Missouri River, or anything about the long day's journey through Nebraska. Probably by that time I had crossed so many rivers that I was dull to them. The only thing very noticeable about Nebraska was that it was still, all day long, Nebraska.

I had been sleeping, curled up in a red plush seat, for a long while when we reached Black Hawk. Jake roused me and took me by the hand. We stumbled down from the train to a wooden siding, where men were running about with lanterns. I could n't see any town, or even distant lights; we were surrounded by utter darkness. The engine was panting heavily after its long run. In the red glow from the fire-box, a group of people stood huddled together on the platform, encumbered by bundles and boxes. I knew this must be the immigrant family the conductor had told us about. The woman wore a fringed shawl tied over her head, and she carried a little tin trunk in her arms, hugging it as if it were a baby. There was an old man, tall and stooped. Two half-grown boys and a girl stood holding oil-cloth[1] bundles, and a little girl clung to her mother's skirts. Presently a man with a lantern approached them and began to talk, shouting and exclaiming. I pricked up my ears, for it was positively the first time I had ever heard a foreign tongue.

Another lantern came along. A bantering voice called out: "Hello, are you Mr. Burden's folks? If you are, it's me you're looking for. I'm Otto Fuchs. I'm Mr. Burden's hired man, and I'm to drive you out. Hello, Jimmy, ain't you scared to come so far west?"

I looked up with interest at the new face in the lantern light. He might have stepped out of the pages of "Jesse James." He wore a sombrero hat, with a wide leather band and a bright buckle, and the ends of his mustache were twisted up stiffly, like little horns. He looked lively and ferocious, I thought, and as if he had a history. A long scar ran across one cheek and drew the corner of his mouth up in a sinister curl. The top of his left ear was gone, and his skin was brown as an Indian's. Surely this was the face of a desperado.

---

1 A fabric water-proofed with an oil or resin, used for a variety of purposes, including table-cloths.

W. T. Benda

As he walked about the platform in his high-heeled boots, looking for our trunks, I saw that he was a rather slight man, quick and wiry, and light on his feet. He told us we had a long night drive ahead of us, and had better be on the hike. He led us to a hitching-bar where two farm wagons were tied, and I saw the foreign family crowding into one of them. The other was for us. Jake got on the front seat with Otto Fuchs, and I rode on the straw in the bottom of the wagon-box, covered up with a buffalo hide. The immigrants rumbled off into the empty darkness, and we followed them.

I tried to go to sleep, but the jolting made me bite my tongue, and I soon began to ache all over. When the straw settled down I had a hard bed. Cautiously I slipped from under the buffalo hide, got up on my knees and peered over the side of the wagon. There seemed to be nothing to see; no fences, no creeks or trees, no hills or fields. If there was a road, I could not make it out in the faint starlight. There was nothing but land: not a country at all, but the material out of which countries are made. No, there was nothing but land—slightly undulating, I knew, because often our wheels ground against the brake as we went down into a hollow and lurched up again on the other side. I had the feeling that the world was left behind, that we had got over the edge of it, and were outside man's jurisdiction. I had never before looked up at the sky when there was not a familiar mountain ridge against it. But this was the complete dome of heaven, all there was of it. I did not believe that my dead father and mother were watching me from up there; they would still be looking for me at the sheep-fold down by the creek, or along the white road that led to the mountain pastures. I had left even their spirits behind me. The wagon jolted on, carrying me I knew not whither. I don't think I was homesick. If we never arrived anywhere, it did not matter. Between that earth and that sky I felt erased, blotted out. I did not say my prayers that night: here, I felt, what would be would be.

II

I do not remember our arrival at my grandfather's farm sometime before daybreak, after a drive of nearly twenty miles with heavy work-horses. When I awoke, it was afternoon. I was lying in a little room, scarcely larger than the bed that held me, and the window-shade at my head was flapping softly in a warm wind. A tall woman, with wrinkled brown skin and black hair, stood looking down at me; I knew that she must be my grandmother. She had been crying, I could see, but when I opened my eyes she smiled, peered at me anxiously, and sat down on the foot of my bed.

"Had a good sleep, Jimmy?" she asked briskly. Then in a very different tone she said, as if to herself, "My, how you do look like your father!" I remembered that my father had been her little boy; she must often have come to wake him like this when he overslept. "Here are your clean clothes," she went on, stroking my coverlid[1] with her brown hand as she talked. "But first you come down to the kitchen with me, and have a nice warm bath behind the stove. Bring your things; there's nobody about."

---

1 Variant of coverlet; bedspread.

"Down to the kitchen" struck me as curious; it was always "out in the kitchen" at home. I picked up my shoes and stockings and followed her through the living-room and down a flight of stairs into a basement. This basement was divided into a dining-room at the right of the stairs and a kitchen at the left. Both rooms were plastered and whitewashed—the plaster laid directly upon the earth walls, as it used to be in dugouts.[1] The floor was of hard cement. Up under the wooden ceiling there were little half-windows with white curtains, and pots of geraniums and wandering Jew in the deep sills. As I entered the kitchen I sniffed a pleasant smell of gingerbread baking. The stove was very large, with bright nickel trimmings, and behind it there was a long wooden bench against the wall, and a tin washtub, into which grandmother poured hot and cold water. When she brought the soap and towels, I told her that I was used to taking my bath without help.

"Can you do your ears, Jimmy? Are you sure? Well, now, I call you a right smart little boy."

It was pleasant there in the kitchen. The sun shone into my bath-water through the west half-window, and a big Maltese cat came up and rubbed himself against the tub, watching me curiously. While I scrubbed, my grandmother busied herself in the dining-room until I called anxiously, "Grandmother, I'm afraid the cakes are burning!" Then she came laughing, waving her apron before her as if she were shooing chickens.

She was a spare, tall woman, a little stooped, and she was apt to carry her head thrust forward in an attitude of attention, as if she were looking at something, or listening to something, far away. As I grew older, I came to believe that it was only because she was so often thinking of things that were far away. She was quick-footed and energetic in all her movements. Her voice was high and rather shrill, and she often spoke with an anxious inflection, for she was exceedingly desirous that everything should go with due order and decorum. Her laugh, too, was high, and perhaps a little strident, but there was a lively intelligence in it. She was then fifty-five years old, a strong woman, of unusual endurance.

After I was dressed I explored the long cellar next the kitchen. It was dug out under the wing of the house, was plastered and cemented, with a stairway and an outside door by which the men

---

1 The name given to primitive prairie housing, literally dug out of the ground. See note on p. 57.

came and went. Under one of the windows there was a place for them to wash when they came in from work.

While my grandmother was busy about supper I settled myself on the wooden bench behind the stove and got acquainted with the cat—he caught not only rats and mice, but gophers, I was told. The patch of yellow sunlight on the floor traveled back toward the stairway, and grandmother and I talked about my journey, and about the arrival of the new Bohemian family; she said they were to be our nearest neighbors. We did not talk about the farm in Virginia, which had been her home for so many years. But after the men came in from the fields, and we were all seated at the supper-table, then she asked Jake about the old place and about our friends and neighbors there.

My grandfather said little. When he first came in he kissed me and spoke kindly to me, but he was not demonstrative. I felt at once his deliberateness and personal dignity, and was a little in awe of him. The thing one immediately noticed about him was his beautiful, crinkly, snow-white beard. I once heard a missionary say it was like the beard of an Arabian sheik. His bald crown only made it more impressive.

Grandfather's eyes were not at all like those of an old man; they were bright blue, and had a fresh, frosty sparkle. His teeth were white and regular—so sound that he had never been to a dentist in his life. He had a delicate skin, easily roughened by sun and wind. When he was a young man his hair and beard were red; his eyebrows were still coppery.

As we sat at the table Otto Fuchs and I kept stealing covert glances at each other. Grandmother had told me while she was getting supper that he was an Austrian who came to this country a young boy and had led an adventurous life in the Far West among mining-camps and cow outfits. His iron constitution was somewhat broken by mountain pneumonia,[1] and he had drifted back to live in a milder country for a while. He had relatives in Bismarck, a German settlement to the north of us, but for a year now he had been working for grandfather.

The minute supper was over, Otto took me into the kitchen to whisper to me about a pony down in the barn that had been bought for me at a sale; he had been riding him to find out

---

1 Name given to lung disease brought on by the inhalation of dust, a common ailment among miners in the Rocky Mountains.

whether he had any bad tricks, but he was a "perfect gentleman," and his name was Dude. Fuchs told me everything I wanted to know: how he had lost his ear in a Wyoming blizzard when he was a stage-driver, and how to throw a lasso. He promised to rope a steer for me before sundown next day. He got out his "chaps" and silver spurs to show them to Jake and me, and his best cowboy boots, with tops stitched in bold design—roses, and true-lover's knots, and undraped female figures. These, he solemnly explained, were angels.

Before we went to bed Jake and Otto were called up to the living-room for prayers. Grandfather put on silver-rimmed spectacles and read several Psalms. His voice was so sympathetic and he read so interestingly that I wished he had chosen one of my favorite chapters in the Book of Kings. I was awed by his intonation of the word "Selah." "*He shall choose our inheritance for us, the excellency of Jacob whom He loved. Selah.*"[1] I had no idea what the word meant; perhaps he had not. But, as he uttered it, it became oracular, the most sacred of words.

Early the next morning I ran out of doors to look about me. I had been told that ours was the only wooden house west of Black Hawk—until you came to the Norwegian settlement, where there were several. Our neighbors lived in sod houses and dugouts[2]—comfortable, but not very roomy. Our white frame house, with a story and half-story above the basement, stood at the east end of what I might call the farmyard, with the windmill close by the kitchen door. From the windmill the ground sloped westward, down to the barns and granaries and pig-yards. This slope was trampled hard and bare, and washed out in winding gullies by the rain. Beyond the corncribs, at the bottom of the shallow draw,[3] was a muddy little pond, with rusty willow bushes growing about it. The road from the post-office came directly by our door, crossed the farmyard, and curved round this little pond, beyond which it

---

1 Psalm 47:4. The word *Selah,* placed at verse endings, suggests musical pauses, or rests.
2 Initial, temporary housing on the Nebraska prairie, built into the side of a hill or over a hole in the ground, were called dugouts, or constructed out of blocks of earth, called sod houses. See Appendix G to this volume for a photograph of sod house construction. Once a wood-frame house was built, the dugout might be used as a cool, dry cellar for food storage.
3 A shallow valley.

began to climb the gentle swell of unbroken prairie to the west. There, along the western sky-line, it skirted a great cornfield, much larger than any field I had ever seen. This cornfield, and the sorghum patch behind the barn, were the only broken land in sight. Everywhere, as far as the eye could reach, there was nothing but rough, shaggy, red grass, most of it as tall as I.

North of the house, inside the ploughed fire-breaks,[1] grew a thick-set strip of box-elder trees, low and bushy, their leaves already turning yellow. This hedge was nearly a quarter of a mile long, but I had to look very hard to see it at all. The little trees were insignificant against the grass. It seemed as if the grass were about to run over them, and over the plum-patch behind the sod chicken-house.

As I looked about me I felt that the grass was the country, as the water is the sea. The red of the grass made all the great prairie the color of wine-stains, or of certain seaweeds when they are first washed up. And there was so much motion in it; the whole country seemed, somehow, to be running.

I had almost forgotten that I had a grandmother, when she came out, her sunbonnet on her head, a grain-sack in her hand, and asked me if I did not want to go to the garden with her to dig potatoes for dinner. The garden, curiously enough, was a quarter of a mile from the house, and the way to it led up a shallow draw past the cattle corral. Grandmother called my attention to a stout hickory cane, tipped with copper, which hung by a leather thong from her belt. This, she said, was her rattlesnake cane. I must never go to the garden without a heavy stick or a corn-knife; she had killed a good many rattlers on her way back and forth. A little girl who lived on the Black Hawk road was bitten on the ankle and had been sick all summer.

I can remember exactly how the country looked to me as I walked beside my grandmother along the faint wagon-tracks on that early September morning. Perhaps the glide of long railway travel was still with me, for more than anything else I felt motion in the landscape; in the fresh, easy-blowing morning wind, and in the earth itself, as if the shaggy grass were a sort of loose hide, and underneath it herds of wild buffalo were galloping, galloping ...

Alone, I should never have found the garden—except, perhaps, for the big yellow pumpkins that lay about unprotected by their

---

1 Dry moats ploughed around structures as protection against prairie fires.

withering vines—and I felt very little interest in it when I got there. I wanted to walk straight on through the red grass and over the edge of the world, which could not be very far away. The light air about me told me that the world ended here: only the ground and sun and sky were left, and if one went a little farther there would be only sun and sky, and one would float off into them, like the tawny hawks which sailed over our heads making slow shadows on the grass. While grandmother took the pitchfork we found standing in one of the rows and dug potatoes, while I picked them up out of the soft brown earth and put them into the bag, I kept looking up at the hawks that were doing what I might so easily do.

When grandmother was ready to go, I said I would like to stay up there in the garden awhile.

She peered down at me from under her sunbonnet. "Are n't you afraid of snakes?"

"A little," I admitted, "but I'd like to stay anyhow."

"Well, if you see one, don't have anything to do with him. The big yellow and brown ones won't hurt you; they're bull-snakes and help to keep the gophers down. Don't be scared if you see anything look out of that hole in the bank over there. That's a badger hole. He's about as big as a big 'possum, and his face is striped, black and white. He takes a chicken once in a while, but I won't let the men harm him. In a new country a body feels friendly to the animals. I like to have him come out and watch me when I'm at work."

Grandmother swung the bag of potatoes over her shoulder and went down the path, leaning forward a little. The road followed the windings of the draw; when she came to the first bend she waved at me and disappeared. I was left alone with this new feeling of lightness and content.

I sat down in the middle of the garden, where snakes could scarcely approach unseen, and leaned my back against a warm yellow pumpkin. There were some ground-cherry bushes growing along the furrows, full of fruit. I turned back the papery triangular sheaths that protected the berries and ate a few. All about me giant grasshoppers, twice as big as any I had ever seen, were doing acrobatic feats among the dried vines. The gophers scurried up and down the ploughed ground. There in the sheltered draw-bottom the wind did not blow very hard, but I could hear it singing its humming tune up on the level, and I could see the tall grasses wave. The earth was warm under me, and warm as I crumbled it through my fingers. Queer little red bugs came out and moved in slow squadrons around me. Their backs were polished vermilion, with black spots. I kept as still as I could. Nothing happened. I did not expect anything to happen. I was something that lay under the sun and felt it, like the pumpkins, and I did not want to be anything more. I was entirely happy. Perhaps we feel like that when we die and become a part of something entire, whether it is sun and air, or goodness and knowledge. At any rate, that is happiness; to be dissolved into something complete and great. When it comes to one, it comes as naturally as sleep.

III

On Sunday morning Otto Fuchs was to drive us over to make the acquaintance of our new Bohemian neighbors. We were taking them some provisions, as they had come to live on a wild place where there was no garden or chicken-house, and very little broken land. Fuchs brought up a sack of potatoes and a piece of cured pork from the cellar, and grandmother packed some loaves of Saturday's bread, a jar of butter, and several pumpkin pies in the straw of the wagon-box. We clambered up to the front seat and jolted off past the little pond and along the road that climbed to the big cornfield.

I could hardly wait to see what lay beyond that cornfield; but there was only red grass like ours, and nothing else, though from the high wagon-seat one could look off a long way. The road ran about like a wild thing, avoiding the deep draws, crossing them where they were wide and shallow. And all along it, wherever it looped or ran, the sunflowers grew; some of them were as big as little trees, with great rough leaves and many branches which bore dozens of blossoms. They made a gold ribbon across the prairie. Occasionally one of the horses would tear off with his teeth a plant full of blossoms, and walk along munching it, the flowers nodding in time to his bites as he ate down toward them.

The Bohemian family, grandmother told me as we drove along, had bought the homestead of a fellow-countryman, Peter Krajiek, and had paid him more than it was worth. Their agreement with him was made before they left the old country, through a cousin of his, who was also a relative of Mrs. Shimerda. The Shimerdas were the first Bohemian family to come to this part of the county. Krajiek was their only interpreter, and could tell them anything he chose. They could not speak enough English to ask for advice, or even to make their most pressing wants known. One son, Fuchs said, was well-grown, and strong enough to work the land; but the father was old and frail and knew nothing about farming. He was a weaver by trade; had been a skilled workman on tapestries and upholstery materials. He had brought his fiddle with him, which would n't be of much use here, though he used to pick up money by it at home.

"If they're nice people, I hate to think of them spending the winter in that cave of Krajiek's," said grandmother. "It's no better than a badger hole; no proper dugout at all. And I hear he's made them pay twenty dollars for his old cookstove that ain't worth ten."

"Yes 'm," said Otto; "and he's sold 'em his oxen and his two bony old horses for the price of good work-teams. I'd have interfered about the horses—the old man can understand some German—if I'd 'a' thought it would do any good. But Bohemians has a natural distrust of Austrians."

Grandmother looked interested. "Now, why is that, Otto?"

Fuchs wrinkled his brow and nose. "Well, ma'm, it's politics. It would take me a long while to explain."[1]

The land was growing rougher; I was told that we were approaching Squaw Creek, which cut up the west half of the Shimerdas' place and made the land of little value for farming. Soon we could see the broken, grassy clay cliffs which indicated the windings of the stream, and the glittering tops of the cottonwoods and ash trees that grew down in the ravine. Some of the cottonwoods had already turned, and the yellow leaves and shining white bark made them look like the gold and silver trees in fairy tales.

As we approached the Shimerdas' dwelling, I could still see nothing but rough red hillocks, and draws with shelving banks and long roots hanging out where the earth had crumbled away. Presently, against one of those banks, I saw a sort of shed, thatched with the same wine-colored grass that grew everywhere. Near it tilted a shattered windmill-frame, that had no wheel. We drove up to this skeleton to tie our horses, and then I saw a door and window sunk deep in the draw-bank. The door stood open, and a woman and a girl of fourteen ran out and looked up at us hopefully. A little girl trailed along behind them. The woman had on her head the same embroidered shawl with silk fringes that she wore

---

1 At the time of this scene (1883), Bohemia formed a part of the Austro-Hungarian Empire. Fuchs may well be referring to Czech nationalism, and Bohemian resentment against Austrian control.

when she had alighted from the train at Black Hawk. She was not old, but she was certainly not young. Her face was alert and lively, with a sharp chin and shrewd little eyes. She shook grandmother's hand energetically.

"Very glad, very glad!" she ejaculated. Immediately she pointed to the bank out of which she had emerged and said, "House no good, house no good!"

Grandmother nodded consolingly. "You'll get fixed up comfortable after while, Mrs. Shimerda; make good house."

My grandmother always spoke in a very loud tone to foreigners, as if they were deaf. She made Mrs. Shimerda understand the friendly intention of our visit, and the Bohemian woman handled the loaves of bread and even smelled them, and examined the pies with lively curiosity, exclaiming, "Much good, much thank!"—and again she wrung grandmother's hand.

The oldest son, Ambroz,—they called it Ambrosch,—came out of the cave and stood beside his mother. He was nineteen years old, short and broad-backed, with a close-cropped, flat head, and a wide, flat face. His hazel eyes were little and shrewd, like his mother's, but more sly and suspicious; they fairly snapped at the food. The family had been living on corncakes and sorghum molasses for three days.

The little girl was pretty, but Án-tonia—they accented the name thus, strongly, when they spoke to her—was still prettier. I remembered what the conductor had said about her eyes. They were big and warm and full of light, like the sun shining on brown pools in the wood. Her skin was brown, too, and in her cheeks she had a glow of rich, dark color. Her brown hair was curly and wild-looking. The little sister, whom they called Yulka (Julka), was fair, and seemed mild and obedient. While I stood awkwardly confronting the two girls, Krajiek came up from the barn to see what was going on. With him was another Shimerda son. Even from a distance one could see that there was something strange about this boy. As he approached us, he began to make uncouth noises, and held up his hands to show us his fingers, which were webbed to the first knuckle, like a duck's foot. When he saw me draw back, he began to crow delightedly, "Hoo, hoo-hoo, hoo-hoo!" like a rooster. His mother scowled and said sternly, "Marek!"[1] then spoke rapidly to Krajiek in Bohemian.

---

1 Possibly a reference to *Marek's disease*, named for the Hungarian veterinary surgeon, Josef Marek. Marek Shimerda does not have this disease (which infects poultry), but his name evokes agricultural hazards.

"She wants me to tell you he won't hurt nobody, Mrs. Burden. He was born like that. The others are smart. Ambrosch, he make good farmer." He struck Ambrosch on the back, and the boy smiled knowingly.

At that moment the father came out of the hole in the bank. He wore no hat, and his thick, iron-gray hair was brushed straight back from his forehead. It was so long that it bushed out behind his ears, and made him look like the old portraits I remembered in Virginia. He was tall and slender, and his thin shoulders stooped. He looked at us understandingly, then took grandmother's hand and bent over it. I noticed how white and well-shaped his own hands were. They looked calm, somehow, and skilled. His eyes were melancholy, and were set back deep under his brow. His face was ruggedly formed, but it looked like ashes—like something from which all the warmth and light had died out. Everything about this old man was in keeping with his dignified manner. He was neatly dressed. Under his coat he wore a knitted gray vest, and, instead of a collar, a silk scarf of a dark bronze-green, carefully crossed and held together by a red coral pin. While Krajiek was translating for Mr. Shimerda, Ántonia came up to me and held out her hand coaxingly. In a moment we were running up the steep drawside together, Yulka trotting after us.

When we reached the level and could see the gold tree-tops, I pointed toward them, and Ántonia laughed and squeezed my hand as if to tell me how glad she was I had come. We raced off toward Squaw Creek and did not stop until the ground itself stopped—fell away before us so abruptly that the next step would have been out into the tree-tops. We stood panting on the edge of the ravine, looking down at the trees and bushes that grew below us. The wind was so strong that I had to hold my hat on, and the girls' skirts were blown out before them. Ántonia seemed to like it; she held her little sister by the hand and chattered away in that language which seemed to me spoken so much more rapidly than mine. She looked at me, her eyes fairly blazing with things she could not say.

"Name? What name?" she asked, touching me on the shoulder. I told her my name, and she repeated it after me and made Yulka say it. She pointed into the gold cottonwood tree behind whose top we stood and said again, "What name?"

We sat down and made a nest in the long red grass. Yulka curled up like a baby rabbit and played with a grasshopper. Ántonia pointed up to the sky and questioned me with her glance. I gave her the word, but she was not satisfied and pointed to my eyes. I told her, and she repeated the word, making it sound like "ice." She pointed up to the sky, then to my eyes, then back to the sky, with movements so quick and impulsive that she distracted me, and I had no idea what she wanted. She got up on her knees and wrung her hands. She pointed to her own eyes and shook her head, then to mine and to the sky, nodding violently.

"Oh," I exclaimed, "blue; blue sky."

She clapped her hands and murmured, "Blue sky, blue eyes," as if it amused her. While we snuggled down there out of the wind she learned a score of words. She was quick, and very eager. We were so deep in the grass that we could see nothing but the blue sky over us and the gold tree in front of us. It was wonderfully pleasant. After Ántonia had said the new words over and over, she wanted to give me a little chased silver ring she wore on her middle finger. When she coaxed and insisted, I repulsed her quite sternly. I did n't want her ring, and I felt there was something reckless and extravagant about her wishing to give it away to a boy she had never seen before. No wonder Krajiek got the better of these people, if this was how they behaved.

While we were disputing about the ring, I heard a mournful voice calling, "Án-tonia, Án-tonia!" She sprang up like a hare. "Tatinek, Tatinek!"[1] she shouted, and we ran to meet the old man who was coming toward us. Ántonia reached him first, took his hand and kissed it. When I came up, he touched my shoulder and looked searchingly down into my face for several seconds. I became somewhat embarrassed, for I was used to being taken for granted by my elders.

We went with Mr. Shimerda back to the dugout, where grandmother was waiting for me. Before I got into the wagon, he took a book out of his pocket, opened it, and showed me a page with two alphabets, one English and the other Bohemian. He placed this book in my grandmother's hands, looked at her entreatingly, and said with an earnestness which I shall never forget, "Te-e-ach, te-e-ach my Án-tonia!"

IV

On the afternoon of that same Sunday I took my first long ride on my pony, under Otto's direction. After that Dude and I went twice

---

1 Father, or, Papa.

a week to the post-office, six miles east of us, and I saved the men a good deal of time by riding on errands to our neighbors. When we had to borrow anything, or to send about word that there would be preaching at the sod schoolhouse, I was always the messenger. Formerly Fuchs attended to such things after working hours.

All the years that have passed have not dimmed my memory of that first glorious autumn. The new country lay open before me: there were no fences in those days, and I could choose my own way over the grass uplands, trusting the pony to get me home again. Sometimes I followed the sunflower-bordered roads. Fuchs told me that the sunflowers were introduced into that country by the Mormons; that at the time of the persecution, when they left Missouri and struck out into the wilderness to find a place where they could worship God in their own way, the members of the first exploring party, crossing the plains to Utah, scattered sunflower seed as they went. The next summer, when the long trains of wagons came through with all the women and children, they had the sunflower trail to follow. I believe that botanists do not confirm Fuchs's story, but insist that the sunflower was native to those plains. Nevertheless, that legend has stuck in my mind, and sunflower-bordered roads always seem to me the roads to freedom.

I used to love to drift along the pale yellow cornfields, looking for the damp spots one sometimes found at their edges, where the smartweed[1] soon turned a rich copper color and the narrow brown leaves hung curled like cocoons about the swollen joints of the stem. Sometimes I went south to visit our German neighbors and to admire their catalpa grove, or to see the big elm tree that grew up out of a deep crack in the earth and had a hawk's nest in its branches. Trees were so rare in that country, and they had to make such a hard fight to grow, that we used to feel anxious about them, and visit them as if they were persons. It must have been the scarcity of detail in that tawny landscape that made detail so precious.

Sometimes I rode north to the big prairie-dog town[2] to watch

---

1   A species native to Nebraska; it grows to about four feet, and is so-named for its bitter juices.
2   Rodents that dig elaborate underground "towns," labyrinths that penetrate up to twelve-feet deep and may cover several miles, accommodating thousands of black-tailed prairie dogs. Subterranean-nesting owls create smaller holes and will save labor by moving into abandoned prairie-dog towns.

the brown earth-owls fly home in the late afternoon and go down to their nests underground with the dogs. Ántonia Shimerda liked to go with me, and we used to wonder a great deal about these birds of subterranean habit. We had to be on our guard there, for rattlesnakes were always lurking about. They came to pick up an easy living among the dogs and owls, which were quite defenseless against them; took possession of their comfortable houses and ate the eggs and puppies. We felt sorry for the owls. It was always mournful to see them come flying home at sunset and disappear under the earth. But, after all, we felt, winged things who would live like that must be rather degraded creatures. The dog-town was a long way from any pond or creek. Otto Fuchs said he had seen populous dog-towns in the desert where there was no surface water for fifty miles; he insisted that some of the holes must go down to water—nearly two hundred feet, hereabouts. Ántonia said she did n't believe it; that the dogs probably lapped up the dew in the early morning, like the rabbits.

Ántonia had opinions about everything, and she was soon able to make them known. Almost every day she came running across the prairie to have her reading lesson with me. Mrs. Shimerda grumbled, but realized it was important that one member of the family should learn English. When the lesson was over, we used to go up to the watermelon patch behind the garden. I split the melons with an old corn-knife, and we lifted out the hearts and ate them with the juice trickling through our fingers. The white Christmas melons we did not touch, but we watched them with curiosity. They were to be picked late, when the hard frosts had set in, and put away for winter use. After weeks on the ocean, the Shimerdas were famished for fruit. The two girls would wander for miles along the edge of the cornfields, hunting for ground-cherries.

Ántonia loved to help grandmother in the kitchen and to learn about cooking and housekeeping. She would stand beside her, watching her every movement. We were willing to believe that Mrs. Shimerda was a good housewife in her own country, but she managed poorly under new conditions: the conditions were bad enough, certainly!

I remember how horrified we were at the sour, ashy-gray bread she gave her family to eat. She mixed her dough, we discovered, in an old tin peck-measure that Krajiek had used about the barn. When she took the paste out to bake it, she left smears of dough sticking to the sides of the measure, put the measure on the shelf behind the stove, and let this residue ferment. The next time she made bread, she scraped this sour stuff down into the fresh dough to serve as yeast.

During those first months the Shimerdas never went to town. Krajiek encouraged them in the belief that in Black Hawk they would somehow be mysteriously separated from their money. They hated Krajiek, but they clung to him because he was the only human being with whom they could talk or from whom they could get information. He slept with the old man and the two boys in the dugout barn, along with the oxen. They kept him in their hole and fed him for the same reason that the prairie dogs and the brown owls housed the rattlesnakes—because they did not know how to get rid of him.

V

We knew that things were hard for our Bohemian neighbors, but the two girls were light-hearted and never complained. They were always ready to forget their troubles at home, and to run away with me over the prairie, scaring rabbits or starting up flocks of quail.

I remember Ántonia's excitement when she came into our kitchen one afternoon and announced: "My papa find friends up north, with Russian mans. Last night he take me for see, and I can understand very much talk. Nice mans, Mrs. Burden. One is fat and all the time laugh. Everybody laugh. The first time I see my papa laugh in this kawn-tree. Oh, very nice!"

I asked her if she meant the two Russians who lived up by the big dog-town. I had often been tempted to go to see them when I was riding in that direction, but one of them was a wild-looking fellow and I was a little afraid of him. Russia seemed to me more remote than any other country—farther away than China, almost as far as the North Pole. Of all the strange, uprooted people among the first settlers, those two men were the strangest and the most aloof. Their last names were unpronounceable, so they were called Pavel and Peter. They went about making signs to people, and until the Shimerdas came they had no friends. Krajiek could understand them a little, but he had cheated them in a trade, so they avoided him. Pavel, the tall one, was said to be an anarchist; since he had no means of imparting his opinions, probably his wild gesticulations and his generally excited and rebellious manner gave rise to this supposition. He must once have been a very strong man, but now his great frame, with big, knotty joints, had a wasted look, and the skin was drawn tight over his high cheek-bones. His breathing was hoarse, and he always had a cough.

Peter, his companion, was a very different sort of fellow; short, bow-legged, and as fat as butter. He always seemed pleased when he met people on the road, smiled and took off his cap to every one, men as well as women. At a distance, on his wagon, he looked like an old man; his hair and beard were of such a pale flaxen color that they seemed white in the sun. They were as thick and curly as carded wool. His rosy face, with its snub nose, set in this fleece, was like a melon among its leaves. He was usually called "Curly Peter," or "Rooshian Peter."

The two Russians made good farmhands, and in summer they worked out together. I had heard our neighbors laughing when they told how Peter always had to go home at night to milk his cow. Other bachelor homesteaders used canned milk, to save trouble. Sometimes Peter came to church at the sod schoolhouse. It was there I first saw him, sitting on a low bench by the door, his plush cap in his hands, his bare feet tucked apologetically under the seat.

After Mr. Shimerda discovered the Russians, he went to see them almost every evening, and sometimes took Ántonia with him. She said they came from a part of Russia where the language was not very different from Bohemian, and if I wanted to go to their place, she could talk to them for me. One afternoon, before the heavy frosts began, we rode up there together on my pony.

The Russians had a neat log house built on a grassy slope, with a windlass well beside the door. As we rode up the draw we skirted a big melon patch, and a garden where squashes and yellow cucumbers lay about on the sod. We found Peter out behind his kitchen, bending over a washtub. He was working so hard that he did not hear us coming. His whole body moved up and down as he rubbed, and he was a funny sight from the rear, with his shaggy head and bandy legs.[1] When he straightened himself up to greet us, drops of perspiration were rolling from his thick nose down on to his curly beard. Peter dried his hands and seemed glad to leave his washing. He took us down to see his chickens, and his cow that was grazing on the hillside. He told Ántonia that in his country only rich people had cows, but here any man could have one who would take care of her. The milk was good for Pavel, who was often sick, and he could make butter by beating sour cream with a

---

1 Bow-legged; legs curved so as to be wide apart at the knees.

wooden spoon. Peter was very fond of his cow. He patted her flanks and talked to her in Russian while he pulled up her lariat pin[1] and set it in a new place.

After he had shown us his garden, Peter trundled a load of watermelons up the hill in his wheelbarrow. Pavel was not at home. He was off somewhere helping to dig a well. The house I thought very comfortable for two men who were "batching."[2] Besides the kitchen, there was a living-room, with a wide double bed built against the wall, properly made up with blue gingham sheets and pillows. There was a little storeroom, too, with a window, where they kept guns and saddles and tools, and old coats and boots. That day the floor was covered with garden things, drying for winter; corn and beans and fat yellow cucumbers. There were no screens or window-blinds in the house, and all the doors and windows stood wide open, letting in flies and sunshine alike.

Peter put the melons in a row on the oilcloth-covered table and stood over them, brandishing a butcher knife. Before the blade got fairly into them, they split of their own ripeness, with a delicious sound. He gave us knives, but no plates, and the top of the table was soon swimming with juice and seeds. I had never seen any one eat so many melons as Peter ate. He assured us that they were good for one—better than medicine; in his country people lived on them at this time of year. He was very hospitable and jolly. Once, while he was looking at Ántonia, he sighed and told us that if he had stayed at home in Russia perhaps by this time he would have had a pretty daughter of his own to cook and keep house for him. He said he had left his country because of a "great trouble."

When we got up to go, Peter looked about in perplexity for something that would entertain us. He ran into the storeroom and brought out a gaudily painted harmonica, sat down on a bench, and spreading his fat legs apart began to play like a whole band. The tunes were either very lively or very doleful, and he sang words to some of them.

Before we left, Peter put ripe cucumbers into a sack for Mrs. Shimerda and gave us a lard-pail full of milk to cook them in. I had never heard of cooking cucumbers, but Ántonia assured me they

---

1 A lariat is a lasso, a rope for tethering animals, used by cowboys, which could be held fast to the ground by a pin.
2 Living as bachelors; living without women.

were very good. We had to walk the pony all the way home to keep from spilling the milk.

VI

One afternoon we were having our reading lesson on the warm, grassy bank where the badger lived. It was a day of amber sunlight, but there was a shiver of coming winter in the air. I had seen ice on the little horse-pond that morning, and as we went through the garden we found the tall asparagus, with its red berries, lying on the ground, a mass of slimy green.

Tony was barefooted, and she shivered in her cotton dress and was comfortable only when we were tucked down on the baked earth, in the full blaze of the sun. She could talk to me about almost anything by this time. That afternoon she was telling me how highly esteemed our friend the badger was in her part of the world, and how men kept a special kind of dog, with very short legs, to hunt him. Those dogs, she said, went down into the hole after the badger and killed him there in a terrific struggle underground; you could hear the barks and yelps outside. Then the dog dragged himself back, covered with bites and scratches, to be rewarded and petted by his master. She knew a dog who had a star on his collar for every badger he had killed.

The rabbits were unusually spry that afternoon. They kept starting up all about us, and dashing off down the draw as if they were playing a game of some kind. But the little buzzing things that lived in the grass were all dead—all but one. While we were lying there against the warm bank, a little insect[1] of the palest, frailest green hopped painfully out of the buffalo grass and tried to leap into a bunch of bluestem. He missed it, fell back, and sat with his head sunk between his long legs, his antennae quivering, as if he were waiting for something to come and finish him. Tony made a warm nest for him in her hands; talked to him gayly and indulgently in Bohemian. Presently he began to sing for us—a thin, rusty little chirp. She held him close to her ear and laughed, but a moment afterward I saw there were tears in her eyes. She told me that in her village at home there was an old beggar woman who went about selling herbs and roots she had dug up in the forest. If you took her in and gave her a warm place by the fire, she sang old songs to the

---

1   A katydid; a North American bush-cricket.

children in a cracked voice, like this. Old Hata, she was called, and the children loved to see her coming and saved their cakes and sweets for her.

When the bank on the other side of the draw began to throw a narrow shelf of shadow, we knew we ought to be starting homeward; the chill came on quickly when the sun got low, and Ántonia's dress was thin. What were we to do with the frail little creature we had lured back to life by false pretenses? I offered my pockets, but Tony shook her head and carefully put the green insect in her hair, tying her big handkerchief down loosely over her curls. I said I would go with her until we could see Squaw Creek, and then turn and run home. We drifted along lazily, very happy, through the magical light of the late afternoon.

All those fall afternoons were the same, but I never got used to them. As far as we could see, the miles of copper-red grass were drenched in sunlight that was stronger and fiercer than at any other time of the day. The blond cornfields were red gold, the haystacks turned rosy and threw long shadows. The whole prairie was like the bush that burned with fire and was not consumed.[1] That hour always had the exultation of victory, of triumphant ending, like a hero's death—heroes who died young and gloriously. It was a sudden transfiguration, a lifting-up of day.

How many an afternoon Ántonia and I have trailed along the prairie under that magnificence! And always two long black shadows flitted before us or followed after, dark spots on the ruddy grass.

We had been silent a long time, and the edge of the sun sank nearer and nearer the prairie floor, when we saw a figure moving on the edge of the upland, a gun over his shoulder. He was walking slowly, dragging his feet along as if he had no purpose. We broke into a run to overtake him.

"My papa sick all the time," Tony panted as we flew. "He not look good, Jim."

As we neared Mr. Shimerda she shouted, and he lifted his head and peered about. Tony ran up to him, caught his hand and pressed it against her cheek. She was the only one of his family who could rouse the old man from the torpor in which he seemed to live. He took the bag from his belt and showed us three rabbits he had shot,

---

1 See Exodus 3:2, where an angel reveals itself to Moses in this fashion.

looked at Antonia with a wintry flicker of a smile and began to tell her something. She turned to me.

"My *tatinek* make me little hat with the skins, little hat for winter!" she exclaimed joyfully. "Meat for eat, skin for hat,"—she told off these benefits on her fingers.

Her father put his hand on her hair, but she caught his wrist and lifted it carefully away, talking to him rapidly. I heard the name of old Hata. He untied the handkerchief, separated her hair with his fingers, and stood looking down at the green insect. When it began to chirp faintly, he listened as if it were a beautiful sound.

I picked up the gun he had dropped; a queer piece from the old country, short and heavy, with a stag's head on the cock. When he saw me examining it, he turned to me with his far-away look that always made me feel as if I were down at the bottom of a well. He spoke kindly and gravely, and Ántonia translated:—

"My *tatinek* say when you are big boy, he give you his gun. Very fine, from Bohemie. It was belong to a great man, very rich, like what you not got here; many fields, many forests, many big house. My papa play for his wedding, and he give my papa fine gun, and my papa give you."

I was glad that this project was one of futurity. There never were such people as the Shimerdas for wanting to give away everything they had. Even the mother was always offering me things, though I knew she expected substantial presents in return. We stood there in friendly silence, while the feeble minstrel sheltered in Ántonia's hair went on with its scratchy chirp. The old man's smile, as he listened, was so full of sadness, of pity for things, that I never afterward forgot it. As the sun sank there came a sudden coolness and the strong smell of earth and drying grass. Ántonia and her father went off hand in hand, and I buttoned up my jacket and raced my shadow home.

VII

Much as I liked Ántonia, I hated a superior tone that she sometimes took with me. She was four years older than I, to be sure, and had seen more of the world; but I was a boy and she was a girl, and I resented her protecting manner. Before the autumn was over she began to treat me more like an equal and to defer to me in other things than reading lessons. This change came about from an adventure we had together.

One day when I rode over to the Shimerdas' I found Ántonia starting off on foot for Russian Peter's house, to borrow a spade Ambrosch needed. I offered to take her on the pony, and she got up behind me. There had been another black frost the night before, and the air was clear and heady as wine. Within a week all the blooming roads had been despoiled—hundreds of miles of yellow sunflowers had been transformed into brown, rattling, burry stalks.

We found Russian Peter digging his potatoes. We were glad to go in and get warm by his kitchen stove and to see his squashes and Christmas melons, heaped in the storeroom for winter. As we rode away with the spade, Ántonia suggested that we stop at the prairie-dog town and dig into one of the holes. We could find out whether they ran straight down, or were horizontal, like mole-holes; whether they had underground connections; whether the owls had nests down there, lined with feathers. We might get some puppies, or owl eggs, or snake-skins.

The dog-town was spread out over perhaps ten acres. The grass had been nibbled short and even, so this stretch was not shaggy and red like the surrounding country, but gray and velvety. The holes were several yards apart, and were disposed with a good deal of regularity, almost as if the town had been laid out in streets and avenues. One always felt that an orderly and very sociable kind of life was going on there. I picketed Dude down in a draw, and we went wandering about, looking for a hole that would be easy to dig. The dogs were out, as usual, dozens of them, sitting up on their hind legs over the doors of their houses. As we approached, they barked, shook their tails at us, and scurried underground. Before the mouths of the holes were little patches of sand and gravel, scratched up, we supposed, from a long way below the surface. Here and there, in the town, we came on larger gravel patches, several yards away from any hole. If the dogs had scratched the sand up in excavating, how had they carried it so far? It was on one of these gravel beds that I met my adventure.

We were examining a big hole with two entrances. The burrow sloped into the ground at a gentle angle, so that we could see where the two corridors united, and the floor was dusty from use, like a little highway over which much travel went. I was walking backward, in a crouching position, when I heard Ántonia scream. She was standing opposite me, pointing behind me and shouting something in Bohemian. I whirled round, and there, on one of those dry gravel beds, was the biggest snake I had ever seen. He was sunning himself, after the cold night, and he must have been asleep when Ántonia screamed. When I turned he was lying in long loose waves, like a letter "W." He twitched and began to coil slowly. He was not merely a big snake, I thought—he was a circus monstrosity. His abominable muscularity, his loathsome, fluid motion, somehow made me sick. He was as thick as my leg, and looked as if millstones could n't crush the disgusting vitality out of him. He lifted his hideous little head, and rattled. I did n't run because I did n't think of it—if my back had been against a stone wall I could n't have felt more cornered. I saw his coils tighten—now he would spring, spring his length, I remembered. I ran up and drove at his head with my spade, struck him fairly across the neck, and in a minute he was all about my feet in wavy loops. I struck now from hate. Ántonia, barefooted as she was, ran up behind me. Even after

I had pounded his ugly head flat, his body kept on coiling and winding, doubling and falling back on itself. I walked away and turned my back. I felt seasick. Ántonia came after me, crying, "O Jimmy, he not bite you? You sure? Why you not run when I say?"

"What did you jabber Bohunk for? You might have told me there was a snake behind me!" I said petulantly.

"I know I am just awful, Jim, I was so scared." She took my handkerchief from my pocket and tried to wipe my face with it, but I snatched it away from her. I suppose I looked as sick as I felt.

"I never know you was so brave, Jim," she went on comfortingly. "You is just like big mans; you wait for him lift his head and then you go for him. Ain't you feel scared a bit? Now we take that snake home and show everybody. Nobody ain't seen in this kawntree so big snake like you kill."

She went on in this strain until I began to think that I had longed for this opportunity, and had hailed it with joy. Cautiously we went back to the snake; he was still groping with his tail, turning up his ugly belly in the light. A faint, fetid smell came from him, and a thread of green liquid oozed from his crushed head.

"Look, Tony, that's his poison," I said.

I took a long piece of string from my pocket, and she lifted his head with the spade while I tied a noose around it. We pulled him out straight and measured him by my riding-quirt;[1] he was about five and a half feet long. He had twelve rattles, but they were broken off before they began to taper, so I insisted that he must once have had twenty-four. I explained to Ántonia how this meant that he was twenty-four years old, that he must have been there when white men first came, left on from buffalo and Indian times. As I turned him over I began to feel proud of him, to have a kind of respect for his age and size. He seemed like the ancient, eldest Evil.[2] Certainly his kind have left horrible unconscious memories in all warm-blooded life. When we dragged him down into the draw, Dude sprang off to the end of his tether and shivered all over—would n't let us come near him.

We decided that Ántonia should ride Dude home, and I would walk. As she rode along slowly, her bare legs swinging against the pony's sides, she kept shouting back to me about how astonished

---

1 A short-handled riding-whip with a braided leather lash.
2 A reference to Genesis 3, where the serpent tempts Eve with fruit from the tree of knowledge.

everybody would be. I followed with the spade over my shoulder, dragging my snake. Her exultation was contagious. The great land had never looked to me so big and free. If the red grass were full of rattlers, I was equal to them all. Nevertheless, I stole furtive glances behind me now and then to see that no avenging mate, older and bigger than my quarry, was racing up from the rear.

The sun had set when we reached our garden and went down the draw toward the house. Otto Fuchs was the first one we met. He was sitting on the edge of the cattle-pond, having a quiet pipe before supper. Ántonia called him to come quick and look. He did not say anything for a minute, but scratched his head and turned the snake over with his boot.

"Where did you run onto that beauty, Jim?"

"Up at the dog-town," I answered laconically.

"Kill him yourself? How come you to have a weepon?"

"We'd been up to Russian Peter's, to borrow a spade for Ambrosch."

Otto shook the ashes out of his pipe and squatted down to count the rattles. "It was just luck you had a tool," he said cautiously. "Gosh! I would n't want to do any business with that fellow myself, unless I had a fence-post along. Your grandmother's snake-cane would n't more than tickle him. He could stand right up and talk to you, he could. Did he fight hard?"

Ántonia broke in: "He fight something awful! He is all over Jimmy's boots. I scream for him to run, but he just hit and hit that snake like he was crazy."

Otto winked at me. After Ántonia rode on he said: "Got him in the head first crack, did n't you? That was just as well."

We hung him up to the windmill, and when I went down to the kitchen I found Ántonia standing in the middle of the floor, telling the story with a great deal of color.

Subsequent experiences with rattlesnakes taught me that my first encounter was fortunate in circumstance. My big rattler was old, and had led too easy a life; there was not much fight in him. He had probably lived there for years, with a fat prairie dog for breakfast whenever he felt like it, a sheltered home, even an owl-feather bed, perhaps, and he had forgot that the world does n't owe rattlers a living. A snake of his size, in fighting trim, would be more than any boy could handle. So in reality it was a mock adventure; the game was fixed for me by chance, as it probably was for many a dragon-slayer. I had been adequately armed by Russian Peter; the snake was old and lazy; and I had Ántonia beside me, to appreciate and admire.

That snake hung on our corral fence for several days; some of the neighbors came to see it and agreed that it was the biggest rattler ever killed in those parts. This was enough for Ántonia. She liked me better from that time on, and she never took a supercilious air with me again. I had killed a big snake—I was now a big fellow.

VIII

While the autumn color was growing pale on the grass and cornfields, things went badly with our friends the Russians. Peter told his troubles to Mr. Shimerda: he was unable to meet a note which fell due on the first of November; had to pay an exorbitant bonus on renewing it, and to give a mortgage on his pigs and horses and even his milk cow. His creditor was Wick Cutter, the merciless Black Hawk money-lender, a man of evil name throughout the county, of whom I shall have more to say later. Peter could give no very clear account of his transactions with Cutter. He only knew that he had first borrowed two hundred dollars, then another hundred, then fifty—that each time a bonus was added to the principal, and the debt grew faster than any crop he planted. Now everything was plastered with mortgages.

Soon after Peter renewed his note, Pavel strained himself lifting timbers for a new barn, and fell over among the shavings with such a gush of blood from the lungs that his fellow-workmen thought he would die on the spot. They hauled him home and put him into his bed, and there he lay, very ill indeed. Misfortune seemed to settle like an evil bird on the roof of the log house, and to flap its wings there, warning human beings away. The Russians had such bad luck that people were afraid of them and liked to put them out of mind.

One afternoon Ántonia and her father came over to our house to get buttermilk, and lingered, as they usually did, until the sun was low. Just as they were leaving, Russian Peter drove up. Pavel was very bad, he said, and wanted to talk to Mr. Shimerda and his daughter; he had come to fetch them. When Ántonia and her father got into the wagon, I entreated grandmother to let me go with them: I would gladly go without my supper, I would sleep in the Shimerdas' barn and run home in the morning. My plan must have seemed very foolish to her, but she was often large-minded about humoring the desires of other people. She asked Peter to wait a moment, and when she came back from the kitchen she brought a bag of sandwiches and doughnuts for us.

Mr. Shimerda and Peter were on the front seat; Ántonia and I sat in the straw behind and ate our lunch as we bumped along. After the sun sank, a cold wind sprang up and moaned over the prairie. If this turn in the weather had come sooner, I should not have got away. We burrowed down in the straw and curled up close together, watching the angry red die out of the west and the stars begin to shine in the clear, windy sky. Peter kept sighing and groaning. Tony whispered to me that he was afraid Pavel would never get well. We lay still and did not talk. Up there the stars grew magnificently bright. Though we had come from such different parts of the world, in both of us there was some dusky superstition that those shining groups have their influence upon what is and what is not to be. Perhaps Russian Peter, come from farther away than any of us, had brought from his land, too, some such belief.

The little house on the hillside was so much the color of the night that we could not see it as we came up the draw. The ruddy windows guided us—the light from the kitchen stove, for there was no lamp burning.

We entered softly. The man in the wide bed seemed to be asleep. Tony and I sat down on the bench by the wall and leaned our arms on the table in front of us. The firelight flickered on the hewn logs that supported the thatch overhead. Pavel made a rasping sound when he breathed, and he kept moaning. We waited. The wind shook the doors and windows impatiently, then swept on again, singing through the big spaces. Each gust, as it bore down, rattled the panes, and swelled off like the others. They made me think of defeated armies, retreating; or of ghosts who were trying desperately to get in for shelter, and then went moaning on. Presently, in one of those sobbing intervals between the blasts, the coyotes tuned up with their whining howl; one, two, three, then all together—to tell us that winter was coming. This sound brought an answer from the bed,—a long complaining cry,—as if Pavel were having bad dreams or were waking to some old misery. Peter listened, but did not stir. He was sitting on the floor by the kitchen stove. The coyotes broke out again; yap, yap, yap—then the high whine. Pavel called for something and struggled up on his elbow.

"He is scared of the wolves," Ántonia whispered to me. "In his country there are very many, and they eat men and women." We slid closer together along the bench.

I could not take my eyes off the man in the bed. His shirt was hanging open, and his emaciated chest, covered with yellow bristle, rose and fell horribly. He began to cough. Peter shuffled to his feet, caught up the tea-kettle and mixed him some hot water and whiskey. The sharp smell of spirits went through the room.

Pavel snatched the cup and drank, then made Peter give him the bottle and slipped it under his pillow, grinning disagreeably, as if he had outwitted some one. His eyes followed Peter about the room with a contemptuous, unfriendly expression. It seemed to me that he despised him for being so simple and docile.

Presently Pavel began to talk to Mr. Shimerda, scarcely above a whisper. He was telling a long story, and as he went on, Ántonia took my hand under the table and held it tight. She leaned forward and strained her ears to hear him. He grew more and more excited, and kept pointing all around his bed, as if there were things there and he wanted Mr. Shimerda to see them.

"It's wolves, Jimmy," Ántonia whispered. "It's awful, what he says!"

The sick man raged and shook his fist. He seemed to be cursing people who had wronged him. Mr. Shimerda caught him by the shoulders, but could hardly hold him in bed. At last he was shut off by a coughing fit which fairly choked him. He pulled a cloth from under his pillow and held it to his mouth. Quickly it was covered with bright red spots[1]—I thought I had never seen any blood so bright. When he lay down and turned his face to the wall, all the rage had gone out of him. He lay patiently fighting for breath, like a child with croup.[2] Ántonia's father uncovered one of his long bony legs and rubbed it rhythmically. From our bench we could see what a hollow case his body was. His spine and shoulder-blades stood out like the bones under the hide of a dead steer left in the fields. That sharp backbone must have hurt him when he lay on it.

Gradually, relief came to all of us. Whatever it was, the worst was over. Mr. Shimerda signed to us that Pavel was asleep. Without a word Peter got up and lit his lantern. He was going out to get his team to drive us home. Mr. Shimerda went with him. We sat and watched the long bowed back under the blue sheet, scarcely daring to breathe.

---

1 A symptom of tuberculosis.
2 A harsh, painful cough.

On the way home, when we were lying in the straw, under the jolting and rattling Ántonia told me as much of the story as she could. What she did not tell me then, she told later; we talked of nothing else for days afterward.

When Pavel and Peter were young men, living at home in Russia, they were asked to be groomsmen for a friend who was to marry the belle of another village. It was in the dead of winter and the groom's party went over to the wedding in sledges. Peter and Pavel drove in the groom's sledge, and six sledges followed with all his relatives and friends.

After the ceremony at the church, the party went to a dinner given by the parents of the bride. The dinner lasted all afternoon; then it became a supper and continued far into the night. There was much dancing and drinking. At midnight the parents of the bride said good-bye to her and blessed her. The groom took her up in his arms and carried her out to his sledge and tucked her under the blankets. He sprang in beside her, and Pavel and Peter (our Pavel and Peter!) took the front seat. Pavel drove. The party set out with singing and the jingle of sleigh-bells, the groom's sledge going first. All the drivers were more or less the worse for merry-making, and the groom was absorbed in his bride.

The wolves were bad that winter, and every one knew it, yet when they heard the first wolf-cry, the drivers were not much alarmed. They had too much good food and drink inside them. The first howls were taken up and echoed and with quickening repetitions. The wolves were coming together. There was no moon, but the starlight was clear on the snow. A black drove came up over the hill behind the wedding party. The wolves ran like streaks of shadow; they looked no bigger than dogs, but there were hundreds of them.

Something happened to the hindmost sledge: the driver lost control,—he was probably very drunk,—the horses left the road, the sledge was caught in a clump of trees, and overturned. The occupants rolled out over the snow, and the fleetest of the wolves sprang upon them. The shrieks that followed made everybody sober. The drivers stood up and lashed their horses. The groom had the best team and his sledge was lightest—all the others carried from six to a dozen people.

Another driver lost control. The screams of the horses were more terrible to hear than the cries of the men and women. Nothing seemed to check the wolves. It was hard to tell what was happening in the rear; the people who were falling behind shrieked as piteously as those who were already lost. The little bride hid her face on the groom's shoulder and sobbed. Pavel sat still and watched his horses. The road was clear and white, and the groom's three blacks went like the wind. It was only necessary to be calm and to guide them carefully.

At length, as they breasted a long hill, Peter rose cautiously and looked back. "There are only three sledges left," he whispered.

"And the wolves?" Pavel asked.

"Enough! Enough for all of us."

Pavel reached the brow of the hill, but only two sledges followed him down the other side. In that moment on the hilltop, they saw behind them a whirling black group on the snow. Presently the groom screamed. He saw his father's sledge overturned, with his mother and sisters. He sprang up as if he meant to jump, but the girl shrieked and held him back. It was even then too late. The black ground-shadows were already crowding over the heap in the road, and one horse ran out across the fields, his harness hanging to him, wolves at his heels. But the groom's movement had given Pavel an idea.

They were within a few miles of their village now. The only sledge left out of six was not very far behind them, and Pavel's middle horse was failing. Beside a frozen pond something happened to the other sledge; Peter saw it plainly. Three big wolves got abreast of the horses, and the horses went crazy. They tried to jump over each other, got tangled up in the harness, and overturned the sledge.

When the shrieking behind them died away, Pavel realized that he was alone upon the familiar road. "They still come?" he asked Peter.

"Yes."

"How many?"

"Twenty, thirty—enough."

Now his middle horse was being almost dragged by the other two. Pavel gave Peter the reins and stepped carefully into the back of the sledge. He called to the groom that they must lighten—and pointed to the bride. The young man cursed him and held her tighter. Pavel tried to drag her away. In the struggle, the groom rose. Pavel knocked him over the side of the sledge and threw the girl after him. He said he never remembered exactly how he did it, or what happened afterward. Peter, crouching in the front seat, saw nothing. The first thing either of them noticed was a new sound that broke into the clear air, louder than they had ever heard it before—the bell of the monastery of their own village, ringing for early prayers.

Pavel and Peter drove into the village alone, and they had been alone ever since. They were run out of their village. Pavel's own mother would not look at him. They went away to strange towns, but when people learned where they came from, they were always asked if they knew the two men who had fed the bride to the wolves. Wherever they went, the story followed them. It took them five years to save money enough to come to America. They worked in Chicago, Des Moines, Fort Wayne, but they were always unfortunate. When Pavel's health grew so bad, they decided to try farming.

Pavel died a few days after he unburdened his mind to Mr. Shimerda, and was buried in the Norwegian graveyard. Peter sold off everything, and left the country—went to be cook in a railway construction camp where gangs of Russians were employed.

At his sale we bought Peter's wheelbarrow and some of his harness. During the auction he went about with his head down, and never lifted his eyes. He seemed not to care about anything. The Black Hawk money-lender who held mortgages on Peter's livestock was there, and he bought in the sale notes at about fifty cents on the dollar.[1] Every one said Peter kissed the cow before she was led away by her new owner. I did not see him do it, but this I know: after all his furniture and his cook-stove and pots and pans had been hauled off by the purchasers, when his house was stripped and bare, he sat down on the floor with his clasp-knife and ate all the melons that he had put away for winter. When Mr. Shimerda and Krajiek drove up in their wagon to take Peter to the train, they found him with a dripping beard, surrounded by heaps of melon rinds.

The loss of his two friends had a depressing effect upon old Mr. Shimerda. When he was out hunting, he used to go into the empty log house and sit there, brooding. This cabin was his hermitage until the winter snows penned him in his cave. For Ántonia and me, the story of the wedding party was never at an end. We did not tell Pavel's secret to any one, but guarded it jealously—as if the wolves of the Ukraine had gathered that night long ago, and the

---

1 That is, paid about half what the notes were worth, again taking economic advantage of his client.

wedding party been sacrificed, to give us a painful and peculiar pleasure. At night, before I went to sleep, I often found myself in a sledge drawn by three horses, dashing through a country that looked something like Nebraska and something like Virginia.

IX

The first snowfall came early in December. I remember how the world looked from our sitting-room window as I dressed behind the stove that morning: the low sky was like a sheet of metal; the blond cornfields had faded out into ghostliness at last; the little pond was frozen under its stiff willow bushes. Big white flakes were whirling over everything and disappearing in the red grass.

Beyond the pond, on the slope that climbed to the cornfield, there was, faintly marked in the grass, a great circle where the Indians used to ride. Jake and Otto were sure that when they galloped round that ring the Indians tortured prisoners, bound to a stake in the center; but grandfather thought they merely ran races or trained horses there. Whenever one looked at this slope against the setting sun, the circle showed like a pattern in the grass; and this morning, when the first light spray of snow lay over it, it came out with wonderful distinctness, like strokes of Chinese white[1] on canvas. The old figure stirred me as it had never done before and seemed a good omen for the winter.

As soon as the snow had packed hard I began to drive about the country in a clumsy sleigh that Otto Fuchs made for me by fastening a wooden goods-box on bobs.[2] Fuchs had been apprenticed to a cabinet-maker in the old country and was very handy with tools. He would have done a better job if I had n't hurried him. My first trip was to the post-office, and the next day I went over to take Yulka and Ántonia for a sleigh-ride.

It was a bright, cold day. I piled straw and buffalo robes into the box, and took two hot bricks wrapped in old blankets. When I got to the Shimerdas' I did not go up to the house, but sat in my sleigh at the bottom of the draw and called. Ántonia and Yulka came running out, wearing little rabbit-skin hats their father had made for them. They had heard about my sledge from Ambrosch and knew

---

1 Zinc oxide used as white pigment.
2 Bobs are runners, as on a bobsled, placed in this case underneath a large, empty merchandise container.

why I had come. They tumbled in beside me and we set off toward the north, along a road that happened to be broken.

The sky was brilliantly blue, and the sunlight on the glittering white stretches of prairie was almost blinding. As Ántonia said, the whole world was changed by the snow; we kept looking in vain for familiar landmarks. The deep arroyo[1] through which Squaw Creek wound was now only a cleft between snow-drifts—very blue when one looked down into it. The tree-tops that had been gold all the autumn were dwarfed and twisted, as if they would never have any life in them again. The few little cedars, which were so dull and dingy before, now stood out a strong, dusky green. The wind had the burning taste of fresh snow; my throat and nostrils smarted as if some one had opened a hartshorn[2] bottle. The cold stung, and at the same time delighted one. My horse's breath rose like steam, and whenever we stopped he smoked all over. The cornfields got back a little of their color under the dazzling light, and stood the palest possible gold in the sun and snow. All about us the snow was crusted in shallow terraces, with tracings like ripple-marks at the edges, curly waves that were the actual impression of the stinging lash in the wind.

The girls had on cotton dresses under their shawls; they kept shivering beneath the buffalo robes and hugging each other for warmth. But they were so glad to get away from their ugly cave and their mother's scolding that they begged me to go on and on, as far as Russian Peter's house. The great fresh open, after the stupefying warmth indoors, made them behave like wild things. They laughed and shouted, and said they never wanted to go home again. Could n't we settle down and live in Russian Peter's house, Yulka asked, and could n't I go to town and buy things for us to keep house with?

All the way to Russian Peter's we were extravagantly happy, but when we turned back,—it must have been about four o'clock,—the east wind grew stronger and began to howl; the sun lost its heartening power and the sky became gray and somber. I took off my long woolen comforter and wound it around Yulka's throat. She got so cold that we made her hide her head under the buffalo robe. Ántonia and I sat erect, but I held the reins clumsily, and my eyes were blinded by the wind a good deal of the time. It was growing

---

1 A gully, or watercourse.
2 Ammonia obtained from the antler of a hart, or a male deer.

dark when we got to their house, but I refused to go in with them and get warm. I knew my hands would ache terribly if I went near a fire. Yulka forgot to give me back my comforter, and I had to drive home directly against the wind. The next day I came down with an attack of quinsy,[1] which kept me in the house for nearly two weeks.

The basement kitchen seemed heavenly safe and warm in those days—like a tight little boat in a winter sea. The men were out in the fields all day, husking corn, and when they came in at noon, with long caps pulled down over their ears and their feet in red-lined overshoes, I used to think they were like Arctic explorers.

In the afternoons, when grandmother sat upstairs darning, or making husking-gloves, I read "The Swiss Family Robinson" aloud to her, and I felt that the Swiss family had no advantages over us in the way of an adventurous life. I was convinced that man's strongest antagonist is the cold. I admired the cheerful zest with which grandmother went about keeping us warm and comfortable and well-fed. She often reminded me, when she was preparing for the return of the hungry men, that this country was not like Virginia, and that here a cook had, as she said, "very little to do with." On Sundays she gave us as much chicken as we could eat, and on other days we had ham or bacon or sausage meat. She baked either pies or cake for us every day, unless, for a change, she made my favorite pudding, striped with currants[2] and boiled in a bag.

Next to getting warm and keeping warm, dinner and supper were the most interesting things we had to think about. Our lives centered around warmth and food and the return of the men at nightfall. I used to wonder, when they came in tired from the fields, their feet numb and their hands cracked and sore, how they could do all the chores so conscientiously: feed and water and bed the horses, milk the cows, and look after the pigs. When supper was over, it took them a long while to get the cold out of their bones. While grandmother and I washed the dishes and grandfather read his paper upstairs, Jake and Otto sat on the long bench behind the stove, "easing" their inside boots, or rubbing mutton tallow[3] into their cracked hands.

---

1 Tonsillitis.
2 Berries.
3 A hard fatty substance used in dressing leather, obtained from sheep fat.

Every Saturday night we popped corn or made taffy, and Otto Fuchs used to sing, "For I Am a Cowboy and Know I've Done Wrong," or, "Bury Me Not on the Lone Prairee."[1] He had a good baritone voice and always led the singing when we went to church services at the sod schoolhouse.

I can still see those two men sitting on the bench; Otto's close-clipped head and Jake's shaggy hair slicked flat in front by a wet comb. I can see the sag of their tired shoulders against the white-washed wall. What good fellows they were, how much they knew, and how many things they had kept faith with!

Fuchs had been a cowboy, a stage-driver, a bar-tender, a miner; had wandered all over that great Western country and done hard work everywhere, though, as grandmother said, he had nothing to show for it. Jake was duller than Otto. He could scarcely read, wrote even his name with difficulty, and he had a violent temper which sometimes made him behave like a crazy man—tore him all to pieces and actually made him ill. But he was so soft-hearted that any one could impose upon him. If he, as he said, "forgot himself" and swore before grandmother, he went about depressed and shamefaced all day. They were both of them jovial about the cold in winter and the heat in summer, always ready to work overtime and to meet emergencies. It was a matter of pride with them not to spare themselves. Yet they were the sort of men who never get on, somehow, or do anything but work hard for a dollar or two a day.

On those bitter, starlit nights, as we sat around the old stove that fed us and warmed us and kept us cheerful, we could hear the coyotes howling down by the corrals, and their hungry, wintry cry used to remind the boys of wonderful animal stories; about gray wolves and bears in the Rockies, wildcats and panthers in the Virginia mountains. Sometimes Fuchs could be persuaded to talk about the outlaws and desperate characters he had known. I remember one funny story about himself that made grandmother, who was working her bread on the bread-board, laugh until she wiped her eyes with her bare arm, her hands being floury. It was like this:—

When Otto left Austria to come to America, he was asked by one of his relatives to look after a woman who was crossing on the

---

1 See Appendix I to this volume for sheet music.

same boat, to join her husband in Chicago. The woman started off with two children, but it was clear that her family might grow larger on the journey. Fuchs said he "got on fine with the kids," and liked the mother, though she played a sorry trick on him. In mid-ocean she proceeded to have not one baby, but three! This event made Fuchs the object of undeserved notoriety, since he was traveling with her. The steerage stewardess was indignant with him, the doctor regarded him with suspicion. The first-cabin passengers, who made up a purse for the woman, took an embarrassing interest in Otto, and often inquired of him about his charge. When the triplets were taken ashore at New York, he had, as he said, "to carry some of them." The trip to Chicago was even worse than the ocean voyage. On the train it was very difficult to get milk for the babies and to keep their bottles clean. The mother did her best, but no woman, out of her natural resources, could feed three babies. The husband, in Chicago, was working in a furniture factory for modest wages, and when he met his family at the station he was rather crushed by the size of it. He, too, seemed to consider Fuchs' in some fashion to blame. "I was sure glad," Otto concluded, "that he did n't take his hard feeling out on that poor woman; but he had a sullen eye for me, all right! Now, did you ever hear of a young feller's having such hard luck, Mrs. Burden?"

Grandmother told him she was sure the Lord had remembered these things to his credit, and had helped him out of many a scrape when he did n't realize that he was being protected by Providence.

X

For several weeks after my sleigh-ride, we heard nothing from the Shimerdas. My sore throat kept me indoors, and grandmother had a cold which made the housework heavy for her. When Sunday came she was glad to have a day of rest. One night at supper Fuchs told us he had seen Mr. Shimerda out hunting.

"He's made himself a rabbit-skin cap, Jim, and a rabbit-skin collar that he buttons on outside his coat. They ain't got but one over-coat among 'em over there, and they take turns wearing it. They seem awful scared of cold, and stick in that hole in the bank like badgers."

"All but the crazy boy," Jake put in. "He never wears the coat. Krajiek says he's turrible strong and can stand anything. I guess rabbits must be getting scarce in this locality. Ambrosch come along by the cornfield yesterday where I was at work and showed me three prairie dogs he'd shot. He asked me if they was good to eat. I spit and made a face and took on, to scare him, but he just looked like he was smarter'n me and put 'em back in his sack and walked off."

Grandmother looked up in alarm and spoke to grandfather. "Josiah, you don't suppose Krajiek would let them poor creatures eat prairie dogs, do you?"

"You had better go over and see our neighbors to-morrow, Emmaline," he replied gravely.

Fuchs put in a cheerful word and said prairie dogs were clean beasts and ought to be good for food, but their family connections were against them. I asked what he meant, and he grinned and said they belonged to the rat family.

When I went downstairs in the morning, I found grandmother and Jake packing a hamper basket in the kitchen.

"Now, Jake," grandmother was saying, "if you can find that old rooster that got his comb froze, just give his neck a twist, and we'll take him along. There's no good reason why Mrs. Shimerda could n't have got hens from her neighbors last fall and had a henhouse going by now. I reckon she was confused and did n't know where to begin. I've come strange to a new country myself, but I never forgot hens are a good thing to have, no matter what you don't have."

"Just as you say, mam," said Jake, "but I hate to think of Krajiek getting a leg of that old rooster." He tramped out through the long cellar and dropped the heavy door behind him.

After breakfast grandmother and Jake and I bundled ourselves up and climbed into the cold front wagon-seat. As we approached the Shimerdas' we heard the frosty whine of the pump and saw Ántonia, her head tied up and her cotton dress blown about her, throwing all her weight on the pump-handle as it went up and down. She heard our wagon, looked back over her shoulder, and catching up her pail of water, started at a run for the hole in the bank.

Jake helped grandmother to the ground, saying he would bring the provisions after he had blanketed his horses. We went slowly up the icy path toward the door sunk in the drawside. Blue puffs of smoke came from the stovepipe that stuck out through the grass and snow, but the wind whisked them roughly away.

Mrs. Shimerda opened the door before we knocked and seized grandmother's hand. She did not say "How do!" as usual, but at once began to cry, talking very fast in her own language, pointing to her feet which were tied up in rags, and looking about accusingly at every one.

The old man was sitting on a stump behind the stove, crouching over as if he were trying to hide from us. Yulka was on the floor at his feet, her kitten in her lap. She peeped out at me and smiled, but, glancing up at her mother, hid again. Ántonia was washing pans and dishes in a dark corner. The crazy boy lay under the only window, stretched on a gunnysack stuffed with straw. As soon as we entered he threw a grainsack over the crack at the bottom of the door. The air in the cave was stifling, and it was very dark, too. A lighted lantern, hung over the stove, threw out a feeble yellow glimmer.

Mrs. Shimerda snatched off the covers of two barrels behind the door, and made us look into them. In one there were some potatoes that had been frozen and were rotting, in the other was a little pile of flour. Grandmother murmured something in embarrassment, but the Bohemian woman laughed scornfully, a kind of whinny-laugh, and catching up an empty coffee-pot from the shelf, shook it at us with a look positively vindictive.

Grandmother went on talking in her polite Virginia way, not admitting their stark need or her own remissness, until Jake arrived with the hamper, as if in direct answer to Mrs. Shimerda's reproaches. Then the poor woman broke down. She dropped on the floor beside her crazy son, hid her face on her knees, and sat crying bitterly. Grandmother paid no heed to her, but called Ántonia to come and help empty the basket. Tony left her corner reluctantly. I had never seen her crushed like this before.

"You not mind my poor maminka,[1] Mrs. Burden. She is so sad," she whispered, as she wiped her wet hands on her skirt and took the things grandmother handed her.

The crazy boy, seeing the food, began to make soft, gurgling noises and stroked his stomach. Jake came in again, this time with a sack of potatoes. Grandmother looked about in perplexity.

"Have n't you got any sort of cave or cellar outside, Ántonia? This is no place to keep vegetables. How did your potatoes get frozen?"

"We get from Mr. Bushy, at the post-office,—what he throw out. We got no potatoes, Mrs. Burden," Tony admitted mournfully.

---

1 Mama.

When Jake went out, Marek crawled along the floor and stuffed up the door-crack again. Then, quietly as a shadow, Mr. Shimerda came out from behind the stove. He stood brushing his hand over his smooth gray hair, as if he were trying to clear away a fog about his head. He was clean and neat as usual, with his green neckcloth and his coral pin. He took grandmother's arm and led her behind the stove, to the back of the room. In the rear wall was another little cave; a round hole, not much bigger than an oil barrel, scooped out in the black earth. When I got up on one of the stools and peered into it, I saw some quilts and a pile of straw. The old man held the lantern. "Yulka," he said in a low, despairing voice, "Yulka; my Ántonia!"

Grandmother drew back. "You mean they sleep in there,—your girls?" He bowed his head.

Tony slipped under his arm. "It is very cold on the floor, and this is warm like the badger hole. I like for sleep there," she insisted eagerly. "My *maminka* have nice bed, with pillows from our own geese in Bohemie. See, Jim?" She pointed to the narrow bunk which Krajiek had built against the wall for himself before the Shimerdas came.

Grandmother sighed. "Sure enough, where *would* you sleep, dear! I don't doubt you're warm there. You'll have a better house after while, Ántonia, and then you'll forget these hard times."

Mr. Shimerda made grandmother sit down on the only chair and pointed his wife to a stool beside her. Standing before them with his hand on Ántonia's shoulder, he talked in a low tone, and his daughter translated. He wanted us to know that they were not beggars in the old country; he made good wages, and his family were respected there. He left Bohemia with more than a thousand dollars in savings, after their passage money was paid. He had in some way lost on exchange in New York, and the railway fare to Nebraska was more than they had expected. By the time they paid Krajiek for the land, and bought his horses and oxen and some old farm machinery, they had very little money left. He wished grandmother to know, however, that he still had some money. If they could get through until spring came, they would buy a cow and chickens and plant a garden, and would then do very well. Ambrosch and Ántonia were both old enough to work in the fields, and they were willing to work. But the snow and the bitter weather had disheartened them all.

Ántonia explained that her father meant to build a new house for them in the spring; he and Ambrosch had already split the logs for it, but the logs were all buried in the snow, along the creek where they had been felled.

While grandmother encouraged and gave them advice, I sat down on the floor with Yulka and let her show me her kitten. Marek slid cautiously toward us and began to exhibit his webbed fingers. I knew he wanted to make his queer noises for me—to bark like a dog or whinny like a horse,—but he did not dare in the presence of his elders. Marek was always trying to be agreeable, poor fellow, as if he had it on his mind that he must make up for his deficiencies.

Mrs. Shimerda grew more calm and reasonable before our visit was over, and, while Ántonia translated, put in a word now and then on her own account. The woman had a quick ear, and caught up phrases whenever she heard English spoken. As we rose to go, she opened her wooden chest and brought out a bag made of bed-ticking,[1] about as long as a flour sack and half as wide, stuffed full of something. At sight of it, the crazy boy began to smack his lips. When Mrs. Shimerda opened the bag and stirred the contents with her hand, it gave out a salty, earthy smell, very pungent, even among the other odors of that cave. She measured a teacup full, tied it up in a bit of sacking, and presented it ceremoniously to grandmother.

"For cook," she announced. "Little now; be very much when cook," spreading out her hands as if to indicate that the pint would swell to a gallon. "Very good. You no have in this country. All things for eat better in my country."

"Maybe so, Mrs. Shimerda," grandmother said drily. "I can't say but I prefer our bread to yours, myself."

Ántonia undertook to explain. "This very good, Mrs. Burden,"—she clasped her hands as if she could not express how good,—"it make very much when you cook, like what my mama say. Cook with rabbit, cook with chicken, in the gravy,—oh, so good!"

All the way home grandmother and Jake talked about how easily good Christian people could forget they were their brothers' keepers.

"I will say, Jake, some of our brothers and sisters are hard to keep. Where's a body to begin, with these people? They're wanting in everything, and most of all in horse-sense. Nobody can give

---

1 A strong, durable, striped linen or cotton.

'em that, I guess. Jimmy, here, is about as able to take over a home-stead as they are. Do you reckon that boy Ambrosch has any real push in him?"

"He's a worker, all right, mam, and he's got some ketch-on[1] about him; but he's a mean one. Folks can be mean enough to get on in this world; and then, ag'in, they can be too mean."

That night, while grandmother was getting supper, we opened the package Mrs. Shimerda had given her. It was full of little brown chips that looked like the shavings of some root. They were as light as feathers, and the most noticeable thing about them was their penetrating, earthy odor. We could not determine whether they were animal or vegetable.

"They might be dried meat from some queer beast, Jim. They ain't dried fish, and they never grew on stalk or vine. I'm afraid of 'em. Anyhow, I should n't want to eat anything that had been shut up for months with old clothes and goose pillows."

She threw the package into the stove, but I bit off a corner of one of the chips I held in my hand, and chewed it tentatively. I never forgot the strange taste; though it was many years before I knew that those little brown shavings, which the Shimerdas had brought so far and treasured so jealously, were dried mushrooms. They had been gathered, probably, in some deep Bohemian for-est.......

XI

During the week before Christmas, Jake was the most important person of our household, for he was to go to town and do all our Christmas shopping. But on the 21st of December, the snow began to fall. The flakes came down so thickly that from the sitting-room windows I could not see beyond the windmill—its frame looked dim and gray, unsubstantial like a shadow. The snow did not stop falling all day, or during the night that followed. The cold was not severe, but the storm was quiet and resistless. The men could not go farther than the barns and corral. They sat about the house most of the day as if it were Sunday; greasing their boots, mending their suspenders, plaiting whiplashes.[2]

---

1 The capacity to know things or to catch on.
2 Braiding; making whiplashes.

On the morning of the 22d, grandfather announced at breakfast that it would be impossible to go to Black Hawk for Christmas purchases. Jake was sure he could get through on horseback, and bring home our things in saddle-bags; but grandfather told him the roads would be obliterated, and a newcomer in the country would be lost ten times over. Anyway, he would never allow one of his horses to be put to such a strain.

We decided to have a country Christmas, without any help from town. I had wanted to get some picture-books for Yulka and Ántonia; even Yulka was able to read a little now. Grandmother took me into the ice-cold storeroom, where she had some bolts[1] of gingham and sheeting. She cut squares of cotton cloth and we sewed them together into a book. We bound it between pasteboards, which I covered with brilliant calico, representing scenes from a circus. For two days I sat at the dining-room table, pasting

---

1 A measure of rolled fabric.

this book full of pictures for Yulka. We had files of those good old family magazines which used to publish colored lithographs of popular paintings, and I was allowed to use some of these. I took "Napoleon Announcing the Divorce to Josephine" for my frontispiece. On the white pages I grouped Sunday-School cards and advertising cards which I had brought from my "old country." Fuchs got out the old candle-moulds and made tallow candles. Grandmother hunted up her fancy cake-cutters and baked gingerbread men and roosters, which we decorated with burnt sugar and red cinnamon drops.

On the day before Christmas, Jake packed the things we were sending to the Shimerdas in his saddle-bags and set off on grandfather's gray gelding. When he mounted his horse at the door, I saw that he had a hatchet slung to his belt, and he gave grandmother a meaning look which told me he was planning a surprise for me. That afternoon I watched long and eagerly from the sitting-room window. At last I saw a dark spot moving on the west hill, beside the half-buried cornfield, where the sky was taking on a coppery flush from the sun that did not quite break through. I put on my cap and ran out to meet Jake. When I got to the pond I could see that he was bringing in a little cedar tree across his pommel. He used to help my father cut Christmas trees for me in Virginia, and he had not forgotten how much I liked them.

By the time we had placed the cold, fresh-smelling little tree in a corner of the sitting-room, it was already Christmas Eve. After supper we all gathered there, and even grandfather, reading his paper by the table, looked up with friendly interest now and then. The cedar was about five feet high and very shapely. We hung it with the gingerbread animals, strings of popcorn, and bits of candle which Fuchs had fitted into pasteboard sockets. Its real splendors, however, came from the most unlikely place in the world— from Otto's cowboy trunk. I had never seen anything in that trunk but old boots and spurs and pistols, and a fascinating mixture of yellow leather thongs, cartridges, and shoemaker's wax. From under the lining he now produced a collection of brilliantly colored paper figures, several inches high and stiff enough to stand alone. They had been sent to him year after year, by his old mother in Austria. There was a bleeding heart,[1] in tufts of paper lace; there

---

1   The Sacred Heart of Christ, shown bleeding with love for human
    beings.

were the three kings, gorgeously appareled, and the ox and the ass and the shepherds; there was the Baby in the manger, and a group of angels, singing; there were camels and leopards, held by the black slaves of the three kings. Our tree became the talking tree of the fairy tale;[1] legends and stories nestled like birds in its branches. Grandmother said it reminded her of the Tree of Knowledge.[2] We put sheets of cotton wool under it for a snow-field, and Jake's pocket-mirror for a frozen lake.

I can see them now, exactly as they looked, working about the table in the lamplight: Jake with his heavy features, so rudely moulded that his face seemed, somehow, unfinished; Otto with his half-ear and the savage scar that made his upper lip curl so ferociously under his twisted mustache. As I remember them, what unprotected faces they were; their very roughness and violence made them defenseless. These boys had no practiced manner behind which they could retreat and hold people at a distance. They had only their hard fists to batter at the world with. Otto was

---

1 Probably "The Fir Tree" by Hans Christian Anderson.
2 The tree in the Garden of Eden, in Genesis 3.

already one of those drifting, case-hardened laborers who never marry or have children of their own. Yet he was so fond of children!

XII

On Christmas morning, when I got down to the kitchen, the men were just coming in from their morning chores—the horses and pigs always had their breakfast before we did. Jake and Otto shouted "Merry Christmas!" to me, and winked at each other when they saw the waffle-irons on the stove. Grandfather came down, wearing a white shirt and his Sunday coat. Morning prayers were longer than usual. He read the chapters from St. Matthew about the birth of Christ, and as we listened it all seemed like something that had happened lately, and near at hand. In his prayer he thanked the Lord for the first Christmas, and for all that it had meant to the world ever since. He gave thanks for our food and comfort, and prayed for the poor and destitute in great cities, where the struggle for life was harder than it was here with us. Grandfather's prayers were often very interesting. He had the gift of simple and moving expression. Because he talked so little, his words had a peculiar force; they were not worn dull from constant use. His prayers reflected what he was thinking about at the time, and it was chiefly through them that we got to know his feelings and his views about things.

After we sat down to our waffles and sausage, Jake told us how pleased the Shimerdas had been with their presents; even Ambrosch was friendly and went to the creek with him to cut the Christmas tree. It was a soft gray day outside, with heavy clouds working across the sky, and occasional squalls of snow. There were always odd jobs to be done about the barn on holidays, and the men were busy until afternoon. Then Jake and I played dominoes, while Otto wrote a long letter home to his mother. He always wrote to her on Christmas Day, he said, no matter where he was, and no matter how long it had been since his last letter. All afternoon he sat in the dining-room. He would write for a while, then sit idle, his clenched fist lying on the table, his eyes following the pattern of the oil-cloth. He spoke and wrote his own language so seldom that it came to him awkwardly. His effort to remember entirely absorbed him.

At about four o'clock a visitor appeared: Mr. Shimerda, wearing his rabbit-skin cap and collar, and new mittens his wife had knitted. He had come to thank us for the presents, and for all grand-mother's kindness to his family. Jake and Otto joined us from the basement and we sat about the stove, enjoying the deepening gray of the winter afternoon and the atmosphere of comfort and secu-rity in my grandfather's house. This feeling seemed completely to take possession of Mr. Shimerda. I suppose, in the crowded clutter of their cave, the old man had come to believe that peace and order had vanished from the earth, or existed only in the old world he had left so far behind. He sat still and passive, his head resting against the back of the wooden rocking-chair, his hands relaxed upon the arms. His face had a look of weariness and pleasure, like that of sick people when they feel relief from pain. Grandmother insisted on his drinking a glass of Virginia apple-brandy after his long walk in the cold, and when a faint flush came up in his cheeks, his features might have been cut out of a shell, they were so transparent. He said almost nothing, and smiled rarely; but as he rested there we all had a sense of his utter content.

As it grew dark, I asked whether I might light the Christmas tree before the lamp was brought. When the candle ends sent up their conical yellow flames, all the colored figures from Austria stood out clear and full of meaning against the green boughs. Mr. Shimerda rose, crossed himself,[1] and quietly knelt down before the tree, his head sunk forward. His long body formed a letter "S." I saw grandmother look apprehensively at grandfather. He was rather narrow in religious matters, and sometimes spoke out and hurt people's feelings. There had been nothing strange about the tree before, but now, with some one kneeling before it,—images, candles, ... Grandfather merely put his finger-tips to his brow and bowed his venerable head, thus Protestantizing the atmosphere.

We persuaded our guest to stay for supper with us. He needed little urging. As we sat down to the table, it occurred to me that he liked to look at us, and that our faces were open books to him. When his deep-seeing eyes rested on me, I felt as if he were look-ing far ahead into the future for me, down the road I would have to travel.

At nine o'clock Mr. Shimerda lighted one of our lanterns and put on his overcoat and fur collar. He stood in the little entry hall, the lantern and his fur cap under his arm, shaking hands with us.

---

1 Made the Catholic sign of the cross with his hand on his forehead, heart, and shoulders.

When he took grandmother's hand, he bent over it as he always did, and said slowly, "Good wo-man!" He made the sign of the cross over me, put on his cap and went off in the dark. As we turned back to the sitting-room, grandfather looked at me searchingly. "The prayers of all good people are good," he said quietly.

XIII

The week following Christmas brought in a thaw, and by New Year's Day all the world about us was a broth of gray slush, and the guttered slope between the windmill and the barn was running black water. The soft black earth stood out in patches along the roadsides. I resumed all my chores, carried in the cobs and wood and water, and spent the afternoons at the barn, watching Jake shell corn with a hand-sheller.

One morning, during this interval of fine weather, Ántonia and her mother rode over on one of their shaggy old horses to pay us a visit. It was the first time Mrs. Shimerda had been to our house, and she ran about examining our carpets and curtains and furniture, all the while commenting upon them to her daughter in an envious, complaining tone. In the kitchen she caught up an iron pot that stood on the back of the stove and said: "You got many, Shimerdas no got." I thought it weak-minded of grandmother to give the pot to her.

After dinner, when she was helping to wash the dishes, she said, tossing her head: "You got many things for cook. If I got all things like you, I make much better."

She was a conceited, boastful old thing, and even misfortune could not humble her. I was so annoyed that I felt coldly even toward Ántonia and listened unsympathetically when she told me her father was not well.

"My papa sad for the old country. He not look good. He never make music any more. At home he play violin all the time; for weddings and for dance. Here never. When I beg him for play, he shake his head no. Some days he take his violin out of his box and make with his fingers on the strings, like this, but never he make the music. He don't like this kawn-tree."

"People who don't like this country ought to stay at home," I said severely. "We don't make them come here."

"He not want to come, nev-er!" she burst out. "My *maminka* make him come. All the time she say: 'America big country; much money, much land for my boys, much husband for my girls.' My papa, he cry for leave his old friends what make music with him. He love very much the man what play the long horn like this"— she indicated a slide trombone. "They go to school together and are friends from boys. But my mama, she want Ambrosch for be rich, with many cattle."

"Your mama," I said angrily, "wants other people's things."

"Your grandfather is rich," she retorted fiercely. "Why he not help my papa? Ambrosch be rich, too, after while, and he pay back. He is very smart boy. For Ambrosch my mama come here."

Ambrosch was considered the important person in the family. Mrs. Shimerda and Ántonia always deferred to him, though he was often surly with them and contemptuous toward his father. Ambrosch and his mother had everything their own way. Though Ántonia loved her father more than she did any one else, she stood in awe of her elder brother.

After I watched Ántonia and her mother go over the hill on their miserable horse, carrying our iron pot with them, I turned to grandmother, who had taken up her darning, and said I hoped that snooping old woman would n't come to see us any more.

Grandmother chuckled and drove her bright needle across a hole in Otto's sock. "She's not old, Jim, though I expect she seems old to you. No, I would n't mourn if she never came again. But, you see, a body never knows what traits poverty might bring out in 'em. It makes a woman grasping to see her children want for things. Now read me a chapter in 'The Prince of the House of David.'[1] Let's forget the Bohemians."

We had three weeks of this mild, open weather. The cattle in the corral ate corn almost as fast as the men could shell it for them, and we hoped they would be ready for an early market. One morning the two big bulls, Gladstone and Brigham Young,[2] thought spring had come, and they began to tease and butt at each other across the barbed wire that separated them. Soon they got angry. They bellowed and pawed up the soft earth with their hoofs, rolling their eyes and tossing their heads. Each withdrew to a far corner of his own corral, and then they made for each other at a gallop. Thud, thud, we could hear the impact of their great heads, and their

---

1   By Joseph Holt Ingraham, this immensely popular novel was published in 1855, and features epistolary, first-hand accounts of Christ's life.
2   William Ewart Gladstone (1809-1898), Prime Minister of Great Britain; Brigham Young (1801-1877), leader of the Mormon migration to the Utah territory.

bellowing shook the pans on the kitchen shelves. Had they not been dehorned, they would have torn each other to pieces. Pretty soon the fat steers took it up and began butting and horning each other. Clearly, the affair had to be stopped. We all stood by and watched admiringly while Fuchs rode into the corral with a pitch-fork and prodded the bulls again and again, finally driving them apart.

The big storm of the winter began on my eleventh birthday, the 20th of January. When I went down to breakfast that morning, Jake and Otto came in white as snow-men, beating their hands and stamping their feet. They began to laugh boisterously when they saw me, calling:—

"You've got a birthday present this time, Jim, and no mistake. They was a full-grown blizzard ordered for you."

All day the storm went on. The snow did not fall this time, it simply spilled out of heaven, like thousands of feather-beds being emptied. That afternoon the kitchen was a carpenter-shop; the men brought in their tools and made two great wooden shovels with long handles. Neither grandmother nor I could go out in the storm, so Jake fed the chickens and brought in a pitiful contribution of eggs.

Next day our men had to shovel until noon to reach the barn— and the snow was still falling! There had not been such a storm in the ten years my grandfather had lived in Nebraska. He said at din-ner that we would not try to reach the cattle—they were fat enough to go without their corn for a day or two; but to-morrow we must feed them and thaw out their water-tap so that they could drink. We could not so much as see the corrals, but we knew the steers were over there, huddled together under the north bank. Our ferocious bulls, subdued enough by this time, were probably warming each other's backs. "This'll take the bile out of 'em!" Fuchs remarked gleefully.

At noon that day the hens had not been heard from. After din-ner Jake and Otto, their damp clothes now dried on them, stretched their stiff arms and plunged again into the drifts. They made a tunnel under the snow to the henhouse, with walls so solid that grandmother and I could walk back and forth in it. We found the chickens asleep; perhaps they thought night had come to stay. One old rooster was stirring about, pecking at the solid lump of ice in their water-tin. When we flashed the lantern in their eyes, the hens set up a great cackling and flew about clumsily, scattering down-feathers. The mottled, pin-headed guinea-hens, always resentful of captivity, ran screeching out into the tunnel and tried to poke their ugly, painted faces through the snow walls. By five o'clock the chores were done—just when it was time to begin them all over again! That was a strange, unnatural sort of day.

XIV

On the morning of the 22d I wakened with a start. Before I opened my eyes, I seemed to know that something had happened. I heard excited voices in the kitchen—grandmother's was so shrill that I knew she must be almost beside herself. I looked forward to any new crisis with delight. What could it be, I wondered, as I hurried into my clothes. Perhaps the barn had burned; perhaps the cattle had frozen to death; perhaps a neighbor was lost in the storm.

Down in the kitchen grandfather was standing before the stove with his hands behind him. Jake and Otto had taken off their boots and were rubbing their woolen socks. Their clothes and boots were steaming, and they both looked exhausted. On the bench behind the stove lay a man, covered up with a blanket. Grandmother motioned me to the dining-room. I obeyed reluctantly. I watched her as she came and went, carrying dishes. Her lips were tightly compressed and she kept whispering to herself: "Oh, dear Saviour!" "Lord, Thou knowest!"

Presently grandfather came in and spoke to me: "Jimmy, we will not have prayers this morning, because we have a great deal to do. Old Mr. Shimerda is dead, and his family are in great distress. Ambrosch came over here in the middle of the night, and Jake and Otto went back with him. The boys have had a hard night, and you must not bother them with questions. That is Ambrosch, asleep on the bench. Come in to breakfast, boys."

After Jake and Otto had swallowed their first cup of coffee, they began to talk excitedly, disregarding grandmother's warning glances. I held my tongue, but I listened with all my ears.

"No, sir," Fuchs said in answer to a question from grandfather, "nobody heard the gun go off. Ambrosch was out with the ox team, trying to break a road, and the women folks was shut up tight in their cave. When Ambrosch come in it was dark and he did n't see nothing, but the oxen acted kind of queer. One of 'em ripped around and got away from him—bolted clean out of the stable. His hands is blistered where the rope run through. He got a lantern and went back and found the old man, just as we seen him."

"Poor soul, poor soul!" grandmother groaned. "I'd like to think he never done it. He was always considerate and un-wishful to give trouble. How could he forget himself and bring this on us!"

"I don't think he was out of his head for a minute, Mrs. Burden," Fuchs declared. "He done everything natural. You know he was always sort of fixy,[1] and fixy he was to the last. He shaved after dinner, and washed hisself all over after the girls was done the dishes. Ántonia heated the water for him. Then he put on a clean shirt and clean socks, and after he was dressed he kissed her and the little one and took his gun and said he was going out to hunt rabbits. He must have gone right down to the barn and done it then. He layed down on that bunk-bed, close to the ox stalls, where he always slept. When we found him, everything was decent except,"—Fuchs wrinkled his brow and hesitated,—"except what he could n't nowise foresee. His coat was hung on a peg, and his boots was under the bed. He'd took off that silk neckcloth he always wore, and folded it smooth and stuck his pin through it. He turned back his shirt at the neck and rolled up his sleeves."

"I don't see how he could do it!" grandmother kept saying.

Otto misunderstood her. "Why, mam, it was simple enough; he pulled the trigger with his big toe. He layed over on his side and put the end of the barrel in his mouth, then he drew up one foot and felt for the trigger. He found it all right!"

"Maybe he did," said Jake grimly. "There's something mighty queer about it."

"Now what do you mean, Jake?" grandmother asked sharply.

"Well, mam, I found Krajiek's axe under the manger, and I picks it up and carries it over to the corpse, and I take my oath it just fit the gash in the front of the old man's face. That there Krajiek had been sneakin' round, pale and quiet, and when he seen me examinin' the axe, he begun whimperin', 'My God, man, don't do that!' 'I reckon I'm a-goin' to look into this,' says I. Then he begun to squeal like a rat and run about wringin' his hands. 'They'll hang me!' says he. 'My God, they'll hang me sure!'"

Fuchs spoke up impatiently. "Krajiek's gone silly, Jake, and so have you. The old man would n't have made all them preparations for Krajiek to murder him, would he? It don't hang together. The gun was right beside him when Ambrosch found him."

"Krajiek could 'a' put it there, could n't he?" Jake demanded.

---

1 Probably "fixed," meaning resolved, intent, or set on something.

Grandmother broke in excitedly: "See here, Jake Marpole, don't you go trying to add murder to suicide. We're deep enough in trouble. Otto reads you too many of them detective stories."

"It will be easy to decide all that, Emmaline," said grandfather quietly. "If he shot himself in the way they think, the gash will be torn from the inside outward."

"Just so it is, Mr. Burden," Otto affirmed. "I seen bunches of hair and stuff sticking to the poles and straw along the roof. They was blown up there by gunshot, no question."

Grandmother told grandfather she meant to go over to the Shimerdas with him.

"There is nothing you can do," he said doubtfully. "The body can't be touched until we get the coroner here from Black Hawk, and that will be a matter of several days, this weather."

"Well, I can take them some victuals, anyway, and say a word of comfort to them poor little girls. The oldest one was his darling, and was like a right hand to him. He might have thought of her. He's left her alone in a hard world." She glanced distrustfully at Ambrosch, who was now eating his breakfast at the kitchen table.

Fuchs, although he had been up in the cold nearly all night, was going to make the long ride to Black Hawk to fetch the priest and the coroner. On the gray gelding, our best horse, he would try to pick his way across the country with no roads to guide him.

"Don't you worry about me, Mrs. Burden," he said cheerfully, as he put on a second pair of socks. "I've got a good nose for directions, and I never did need much sleep. It's the gray I'm worried about. I'll save him what I can, but it'll strain him, as sure as I'm telling you!"

"This is no time to be over-considerate of animals, Otto; do the best you can for yourself. Stop at the Widow Steavens's for dinner. She's a good woman, and she'll do well by you."

After Fuchs rode away, I was left with Ambrosch. I saw a side of him I had not seen before. He was deeply, even slavishly, devout. He did not say a word all morning, but sat with his rosary[1] in his hands, praying, now silently, now aloud. He never looked away from his beads, nor lifted his hands except to cross himself. Several times the poor boy fell asleep where he sat, wakened with a start, and began to pray again.

---

1 A string of beads used to count or keep track of saying prayers by Catholics.

No wagon could be got to the Shimerdas' until a road was broken, and that would be a day's job. Grandfather came from the barn on one of our big black horses, and Jake lifted grandmother up behind him. She wore her black hood and was bundled up in shawls. Grandfather tucked his bushy white beard inside his overcoat. They looked very Biblical as they set off, I thought. Jake and Ambrosch followed them, riding the other black and my pony, carrying bundles of clothes that we had got together for Mrs. Shimerda. I watched them go past the pond and over the hill by the drifted cornfield. Then, for the first time, I realized that I was alone in the house.

I felt a considerable extension of power and authority, and was anxious to acquit myself creditably. I carried in cobs and wood from the long cellar, and filled both the stoves. I remembered that in the hurry and excitement of the morning nobody had thought of the chickens, and the eggs had not been gathered. Going out through the tunnel, I gave the hens their corn, emptied the ice from their drinking-pan, and filled it with water. After the cat had had his milk, I could think of nothing else to do, and I sat down to get warm. The quiet was delightful, and the ticking clock was the most pleasant of companions. I got "Robinson Crusoe" and tried to read, but his life on the island seemed dull compared with ours. Presently, as I looked with satisfaction about our comfortable sitting-room, it flashed upon me that if Mr. Shimerda's soul were lingering about in this world at all, it would be here, in our house, which had been more to his liking than any other in the neighborhood. I remembered his contented face when he was with us on Christmas Day. If he could have lived with us, this terrible thing would never have happened.

I knew it was homesickness that had killed Mr. Shimerda, and I wondered whether his released spirit would not eventually find its way back to his own country. I thought of how far it was to Chicago, and then to Virginia, to Baltimore,—and then the great wintry ocean. No, he would not at once set out upon that long journey. Surely, his exhausted spirit, so tired of cold and crowding and the struggle with the ever-falling snow, was resting now in this quiet house.

I was not frightened, but I made no noise. I did not wish to disturb him. I went softly down to the kitchen which, tucked away so snugly underground, always seemed to me the heart and center of the house. There, on the bench behind the stove, I thought and thought about Mr. Shimerda. Outside I could hear the wind singing over hundreds of miles of snow. It was as if I had let the old man in out of the tormenting winter, and were sitting there with him. I went over all that Ántonia had ever told me about his life before he came to this country; how he used to play the fiddle at weddings and dances. I thought about the friends he had mourned to leave, the trombone-player, the great forest full of game,— belonging, as Ántonia said, to the "nobles,"—from which she and her mother used to steal wood on moonlight nights. There was a white hart that lived in that forest, and if any one killed it, he would be hanged, she said. Such vivid pictures came to me that they might have been Mr. Shimerda's memories, not yet faded out from the air in which they had haunted him.

It had begun to grow dark when my household returned, and grandmother was so tired that she went at once to bed. Jake and I got supper, and while we were washing the dishes he told me in loud whispers about the state of things over at the Shimerdas'. Nobody could touch the body until the coroner came. If any one did, something terrible would happen, apparently. The dead man was frozen through, "just as stiff as a dressed turkey you hang out to freeze," Jake said. The horses and oxen would not go into the barn until he was frozen so hard that there was no longer any smell of blood. They were stabled there now, with the dead man, because there was no other place to keep them. A lighted lantern was kept hanging over Mr. Shimerda's head. Ántonia and Ambrosch and the mother took turns going down to pray beside him. The crazy boy went with them, because he did not feel the cold. I believed he felt cold as much as any one else, but he liked to be thought insensible to it. He was always coveting distinction, poor Marek!

Ambrosch, Jake said, showed more human feeling than he would have supposed him capable of; but he was chiefly concerned about getting a priest, and about his father's soul, which he believed was in a place of torment and would remain there until his family and the priest had prayed a great deal for him. "As I understand it," Jake concluded, "it will be a matter of years to pray his soul out of Purgatory,[1] and right now he's in torment."

"I don't believe it," I said stoutly. "I almost know it is n't true." I did not, of course, say that I believed he had been in that very

---

1 In Catholic theology, a place where sinners are held pending prayers said by loved ones which may liberate them into Heaven (unlike Hell, which is eternal damnation).

kitchen all afternoon, on his way back to his own country. Nevertheless, after I went to bed, this idea of punishment and Purgatory came back on me crushingly. I remembered the account of Dives in torment,[1] and shuddered. But Mr. Shimerda had not been rich and selfish; he had only been so unhappy that he could not live any longer.

XV

Otto Fuchs got back from Black Hawk at noon the next day. He reported that the coroner would reach the Shimerdas' sometime that afternoon, but the missionary priest was at the other end of his parish, a hundred miles away, and the trains were not running. Fuchs had got a few hours' sleep at the livery barn in town, but he was afraid the gray gelding had strained himself. Indeed, he was never the same horse afterward. That long trip through the deep snow had taken all the endurance out of him.

Fuchs brought home with him a stranger, a young Bohemian who had taken a homestead near Black Hawk, and who came on his only horse to help his fellow-countrymen in their trouble. That was the first time I ever saw Anton Jelinek. He was a strapping young fellow in the early twenties then, handsome, warm-hearted, and full of life, and he came to us like a miracle in the midst of that grim business. I remember exactly how he strode into our kitchen in his felt boots and long wolfskin coat, his eyes and cheeks bright with the cold. At sight of grandmother, he snatched off his fur cap, greeting her in a deep, rolling voice which seemed older than he.

"I want to thank you very much, Mrs. Burden, for that you are so kind to poor strangers from my kawn-tree."

He did not hesitate like a farmer boy, but looked one eagerly in the eye when he spoke. Everything about him was warm and spontaneous. He said he would have come to see the Shimerdas before, but he had hired out to husk corn all the fall, and since winter began he had been going to the school by the mill, to learn English, along with the little children. He told me he had a nice "lady-teacher" and that he liked to go to school.

At dinner grandfather talked to Jelinek more than he usually did to strangers.

---

1   See Luke 16:19-31.

"Will they be much disappointed because we cannot get a priest?" he asked.

Jelinek looked serious. "Yes, sir, that is very bad for them. Their father has done a great sin," he looked straight at grandfather. "Our Lord has said that."

Grandfather seemed to like his frankness. "We believe that, too, Jelinek. But we believe that Mr. Shimerda's soul will come to its Creator as well off without a priest. We believe that Christ is our only intercessor."

The young man shook his head. "I know how you think. My teacher at the school has explain. But I have seen too much. I believe in prayer for the dead. I have seen too much."

We asked him what he meant.

He glanced around the table. "You want I shall tell you? When I was a little boy like this one, I begin to help the priest at the altar. I make my first communion very young; what the Church teach seem plain to me. By 'n' by war-times come, when the Prussians fight us.[1] We have very many soldiers in camp near my village, and the cholera break out in that camp, and the men die like flies. All day long our priest go about there to give the Sacrament to dying men, and I go with him to carry the vessels with the Holy Sacrament. Everybody that go near that camp catch the sickness but me and the priest. But we have no sickness, we have no fear, because we carry that blood and that body of Christ, and it preserve us." He paused, looking at grandfather. "That I know, Mr. Burden, for it happened to myself. All the soldiers know, too. When we walk along the road, the old priest and me, we meet all the time soldiers marching and officers on horse. All those officers, when they see what I carry under the cloth, pull up their horses and kneel down on the ground in the road until we pass. So I feel very bad for my kawntree-man to die without the Sacrament, and to die in a bad way for his soul, and I feel sad for his family."

We had listened attentively. It was impossible not to admire his frank, manly faith.

"I am always glad to meet a young man who thinks seriously about these things," said grandfather, "and I would never be the one to say you were not in God's care when you were among the soldiers."

---

1 The Austro-Prussian war concluded in 1866, in Bohemia, a Prussian victory.

After dinner it was decided that young Jelinek should hook our two strong black farmhorses to the scraper and break a road through to the Shimerdas', so that a wagon could go when it was necessary. Fuchs, who was the only cabinet-maker in the neighborhood, was set to work on a coffin.

Jelinek put on his long wolfskin coat, and when we admired it, he told us that he had shot and skinned the coyotes, and the young man who "batched" with him, Jan Bouska, who had been a fur-worker in Vienna, made the coat. From the windmill I watched Jelinek come out of the barn with the blacks, and work his way up the hillside toward the cornfield. Sometimes he was completely hidden by the clouds of snow that rose about him; then he and the horses would emerge black and shining.

Our heavy carpenter's bench had to be brought from the barn and carried down into the kitchen. Fuchs selected boards from a pile of planks grandfather had hauled out from town in the fall to make a new floor for the oats bin. When at last the lumber and tools were assembled, and the doors were closed again and the cold drafts shut out, grandfather rode away to meet the coroner at the Shimerdas', and Fuchs took off his coat and settled down to work. I sat on his work-table and watched him. He did not touch his tools at first, but figured for a long while on a piece of paper, and measured the planks and made marks on them. While he was thus engaged, he whistled softly to himself, or teasingly pulled at his half-ear. Grandmother moved about quietly, so as not to disturb him. At last he folded his ruler and turned a cheerful face to us.

"The hardest part of my job's done," he announced. "It's the head end of it that comes hard with me, especially when I'm out of practice. The last time I made one of these, Mrs. Burden," he continued, as he sorted and tried his chisels, "was for a fellow in The Black Tiger mine, up above Silverton, Colorado. The mouth of that mine goes right into the face of the cliff, and they used to put us in a bucket and run us over on a trolley and shoot us into the shaft. The bucket traveled across a box cañon three hundred feet deep, and about a third full of water. Two Swedes had fell out of that bucket once, and hit the water, feet down. If you'll believe it, they went to work the next day. You can't kill a Swede. But in my time a little Eyetalian[1] tried the high dive, and it turned out different with him. We was snowed in then, like we are now, and I

---

1 Italian.

happened to be the only man in camp that could make a coffin for him. It's a handy thing to know, when you knock about like I've done."

"We'd be hard put to it now, if you did n't know, Otto," grandmother said.

"Yes, 'm," Fuchs admitted with modest pride. "So few folks does know how to make a good tight box that'll turn water. I sometimes wonder if there'll be anybody about to do it for me. However, I'm not at all particular that way."

All afternoon, wherever one went in the house, one could hear the panting wheeze of the saw or the pleasant purring of the plane. They were such cheerful noises, seeming to promise new things for living people: it was a pity that those freshly planed pine boards were to be put underground so soon. The lumber was hard to work because it was full of frost, and the boards gave off a sweet smell of pine woods, as the heap of yellow shavings grew higher and higher. I wondered why Fuchs had not stuck to cabinet-work, he settled down to it with such ease and content. He handled the tools as if he liked the feel of them; and when he planed, his hands went back and forth over the boards in an eager, beneficent way as if he were blessing them. He broke out now and then into German hymns, as if this occupation brought back old times to him.

At four o'clock Mr. Bushy, the postmaster, with another neighbor who lived east of us, stopped in to get warm. They were on their way to the Shimerdas'. The news of what had happened over there had somehow got abroad through the snow-blocked country. Grandmother gave the visitors sugar-cakes and hot coffee. Before these callers were gone, the brother of the Widow Steavens, who lived on the Black Hawk road, drew up at our door, and after him came the father of the German family, our nearest neighbors on the south. They dismounted and joined us in the dining-room. They were all eager for any details about the suicide, and they were greatly concerned as to where Mr. Shimerda would be buried. The nearest Catholic cemetery was at Black Hawk, and it might be weeks before a wagon could get so far. Besides, Mr. Bushy and grandmother were sure that a man who had killed himself could not be buried in a Catholic graveyard. There was a burying-ground over by the Norwegian church, west of Squaw Creek; perhaps the Norwegians would take Mr. Shimerda in.

After our visitors rode away in single file over the hill, we returned to the kitchen. Grandmother began to make the icing for a chocolate cake, and Otto again filled the house with the exciting, expectant song of the plane. One pleasant thing about this time was that everybody talked more than usual. I had never heard the postmaster say anything but "Only papers, to-day," or, "I've got a sackful of mail for ye," until this afternoon. Grandmother always talked, dear woman; to herself or to the Lord, if there was no one else to listen; but grandfather was naturally taciturn, and Jake and Otto were often so tired after supper that I used to feel as if I were surrounded by a wall of silence. Now every one seemed eager to talk. That afternoon Fuchs told me story after story; about the Black Tiger mine, and about violent deaths and casual buryings, and the queer fancies of dying men. You never really knew a man, he said, until you saw him die. Most men were game, and went without a grudge.

The postmaster, going home, stopped to say that grandfather would bring the coroner back with him to spend the night. The officers of the Norwegian church, he told us, had held a meeting and decided that the Norwegian graveyard could not extend its hospitality to Mr. Shimerda.

Grandmother was indignant. "If these foreigners are so clannish, Mr. Bushy, we'll have to have an American graveyard that will be more liberal-minded. I'll get right after Josiah to start one in the spring. If anything was to happen to me, I don't want the Norwegians holding inquisitions over me to see whether I'm good enough to be laid amongst 'em."

Soon grandfather returned, bringing with him Anton Jelinek, and that important person, the coroner. He was a mild, flurried old man, a Civil War veteran, with one sleeve hanging empty. He seemed to find this case very perplexing, and said if it had not been for grandfather he would have sworn out a warrant against Krajiek. "The way he acted, and the way his axe fit the wound, was enough to convict any man."

Although it was perfectly clear that Mr. Shimerda had killed himself, Jake and the coroner thought something ought to be done to Krajiek because he behaved like a guilty man. He was badly frightened, certainly, and perhaps he even felt some stirrings of remorse for his indifference to the old man's misery and loneliness.

At supper the men ate like vikings, and the chocolate cake, which I had hoped would linger on until to-morrow in a mutilated condition, disappeared on the second round. They talked excitedly about where they should bury Mr. Shimerda; I gathered that the neighbors were all disturbed and shocked about something. It developed that Mrs. Shimerda and Ambrosch wanted the old man buried on the southwest corner of their own land; indeed, under the very stake that marked the corner. Grandfather had explained to Ambrosch that some day, when the country was put under fence and the roads were confined to section lines, two roads would cross exactly on that corner. But Ambrosch only said, "It makes no matter."

Grandfather asked Jelinek whether in the old country there was some superstition to the effect that a suicide must be buried at the cross-roads.[1]

Jelinek said he didn't know; he seemed to remember hearing there had once been such a custom in Bohemia. "Mrs. Shimerda is made up her mind," he added. "I try to persuade her, and say it looks bad for her to all the neighbors; but she say so it must be. 'There I will bury him, if I dig the grave myself,' she say. I have to promise her I help Ambrosch make the grave to-morrow."

Grandfather smoothed his beard and looked judicial. "I don't know whose wish should decide the matter, if not hers. But if she thinks she will live to see the people of this country ride over that old man's head, she is mistaken."

XVI

Mr. Shimerda lay dead in the barn four days, and on the fifth they buried him. All day Friday Jelinek was off with Ambrosch digging the grave, chopping out the frozen earth with old axes. On Saturday we breakfasted before daylight and got into the wagon with the coffin. Jake and Jelinek went ahead on horseback to cut the body loose from the pool of blood in which it was frozen fast to the ground.

When grandmother and I went into the Shimerdas' house, we found the women-folk alone; Ambrosch and Marek were at the barn. Mrs. Shimerda sat crouching by the stove, Ántonia was washing dishes. When she saw me she ran out of her dark corner and threw her arms around me. "Oh, Jimmy," she sobbed, "what you tink for my lovely papa!" It seemed to me that I could feel her heart breaking as she clung to me.

Mrs. Shimerda, sitting on the stump by the stove, kept looking over her shoulder toward the door while the neighbors were

---

1 In many parts of the world crossroads are associated with demons and evil spirits generally.

arriving. They came on horseback, all except the postmaster, who brought his family in a wagon over the only broken wagon-trail. The Widow Steavens rode up from her farm eight miles down the Black Hawk road. The cold drove the women into the cave-house, and it was soon crowded. A fine, sleety snow was beginning to fall, and every one was afraid of another storm and anxious to have the burial over with.

Grandfather and Jelinek came to tell Mrs. Shimerda that it was time to start. After bundling her mother up in clothes the neighbors had brought, Ántonia put on an old cape from our house and the rabbit-skin hat her father had made for her. Four men carried Mr. Shimerda's box up the hill; Krajiek slunk along behind them. The coffin was too wide for the door, so it was put down on the slope outside. I slipped out from the cave and looked at Mr. Shimerda. He was lying on his side, with his knees drawn up. His body was draped in a black shawl, and his head was bandaged in white muslin, like a mummy's; one of his long, shapely hands lay out on the black cloth; that was all one could see of him.

Mrs. Shimerda came out and placed an open prayer-book against the body, making the sign of the cross on the bandaged head with her fingers. Ambrosch knelt down and made the same gesture, and after him Ántonia and Marek. Yulka hung back. Her mother pushed her forward, and kept saying something to her over and over. Yulka knelt down, shut her eyes, and put out her hand a little way, but she drew it back and began to cry wildly. She was afraid to touch the bandage. Mrs. Shimerda caught her by the shoulders and pushed her toward the coffin, but grandmother interfered.

"No, Mrs. Shimerda," she said firmly, "I won't stand by and see that child frightened into spasms. She is too little to understand what you want of her. Let her alone."

At a look from grandfather, Fuchs and Jelinek placed the lid on the box, and began to nail it down over Mr. Shimerda. I was afraid to look at Ántonia. She put her arms round Yulka and held the little girl close to her.

The coffin was put into the wagon. We drove slowly away, against the fine, icy snow which cut our faces like a sand-blast. When we reached the grave, it looked a very little spot in that snow-covered waste. The men took the coffin to the edge of the hole and lowered it with ropes. We stood about watching them, and the powdery snow lay without melting on the caps and shoulders of the men and the shawls of the women. Jelinek spoke in a persuasive tone to Mrs. Shimerda, and then turned to grandfather.

"She says, Mr. Burden, she is very glad if you can make some prayer for him here in English, for the neighbors to understand."

Grandmother looked anxiously at grandfather. He took off his hat, and the other men did likewise. I thought his prayer remarkable. I still remember it. He began, "Oh, great and just God, no man among us knows what the sleeper knows, nor is it for us to judge what lies between him and Thee." He prayed that if any man there had been remiss toward the stranger come to a far country, God would forgive him and soften his heart. He recalled the promises to the widow and the fatherless, and asked God to smooth the way before this widow and her children, and to "incline the hearts of men to deal justly with her." In closing, he said we were leaving Mr. Shimerda at "Thy judgment seat, which is also Thy mercy seat."

All the time he was praying, grandmother watched him through the black fingers of her glove, and when he said "Amen," I thought she looked satisfied with him. She turned to Otto and whispered, "Can't you start a hymn, Fuchs? It would seem less heathenish."

Fuchs glanced about to see if there was general approval of her suggestion, then began, "Jesus, Lover of my Soul," and all the men and women took it up after him. Whenever I have heard the hymn since, it has made me remember that white waste and the little group of people; and the bluish air, full of fine, eddying snow, like long veils flying:—

> "While the nearer waters roll,
> While the tempest still is high."

...

Years afterward, when the open-grazing days were over,[1] and the red grass had been ploughed under and under until it had almost disappeared from the prairie; when all the fields were under fence, and the roads no longer ran about like wild things, but followed the surveyed section-lines, Mr. Shimerda's grave was still there, with a sagging wire fence around it, and an unpainted wooden cross. As grandfather had predicted, Mrs. Shimerda never saw

---

1 That is, when the area was settled and fences demarcated private farms throughout the region, eliminating free, open grazing lands.

the roads going over his head. The road from the north curved a little to the east just there, and the road from the west swung out a little to the south; so that the grave, with its tall red grass that was never mowed, was like a little island; and at twilight, under a new moon or the clear evening star, the dusty roads used to look like soft gray rivers flowing past it. I never came upon the place without emotion, and in all that country it was the spot most dear to me. I loved the dim superstition, the propitiatory intent, that had put the grave there; and still more I loved the spirit that could not carry out the sentence—the error from the surveyed lines, the clemency of the soft earth roads along which the home-coming wagons rattled after sunset. Never a tired driver passed the wooden cross, I am sure, without wishing well to the sleeper.

XVII

When spring came, after that hard winter, one could not get enough of the nimble air. Every morning I wakened with a fresh consciousness that winter was over. There were none of the signs of spring for which I used to watch in Virginia, no budding woods or blooming gardens. There was only—spring itself; the throb of it, the light restlessness, the vital essence of it everywhere; in the sky, in the swift clouds, in the pale sunshine, and in the warm, high wind—rising suddenly, sinking suddenly, impulsive and playful like a big puppy that pawed you and then lay down to be petted. If I had been tossed down blindfold on that red prairie, I should have known that it was spring.

Everywhere now there was the smell of burning grass. Our neighbors burned off their pasture before the new grass made a start, so that the fresh growth would not be mixed with the dead stand of last year. Those light, swift fires, running about the country, seemed a part of the same kindling that was in the air.

The Shimerdas were in their new log house by then. The neighbors had helped them to build it in March. It stood directly in front of their old cave, which they used as a cellar. The family were now fairly equipped to begin their struggle with the soil. They had four comfortable rooms to live in, a new windmill,—bought on credit,—a chicken-house and poultry. Mrs. Shimerda had paid grandfather ten dollars for a milk cow, and was to give him fifteen more as soon as they harvested their first crop.

When I rode up to the Shimerdas' one bright windy afternoon in April, Yulka ran out to meet me. It was to her, now, that I gave reading lessons; Ántonia was busy with other things. I tied my pony and went into the kitchen where Mrs. Shimerda was baking bread, chewing poppy seeds as she worked. By this time she could speak enough English to ask me a great many questions about what our men were doing in the fields. She seemed to think that my elders withheld helpful information, and that from me she might get valuable secrets. On this occasion she asked me very craftily when grandfather expected to begin planting corn. I told her, adding that he thought we should have a dry spring and that the corn would not be held back by too much rain, as it had been last year.

She gave me a shrewd glance. "He not Jesus," she blustered; "he not know about the wet and the dry."

I did not answer her; what was the use? As I sat waiting for the hour when Ambrosch and Ántonia would return from the fields, I watched Mrs. Shimerda at her work. She took from the oven a coffee-cake which she wanted to keep warm for supper, and wrapped it in a quilt stuffed with feathers. I have seen her put even a roast goose in this quilt to keep it hot. When the neighbors were there building the new house they saw her do this, and the story got abroad that the Shimerdas kept their food in their feather beds.

When the sun was dropping low, Ántonia came up the big south draw with her team. How much older she had grown in eight months! She had come to us a child, and now she was a tall, strong young girl, although her fifteenth birthday had just slipped by. I ran out and met her as she brought her horses up to the windmill to water them. She wore the boots her father had so thoughtfully taken off before he shot himself, and his old fur cap. Her outgrown cotton dress switched about her calves, over the boot-tops. She kept her sleeves rolled up all day, and her arms and throat were burned as brown as a sailor's. Her neck came up strongly out of her shoulders, like the bole of a tree out of the turf. One sees that draft-horse neck among the peasant women in all old countries.

She greeted me gayly, and began at once to tell me how much ploughing she had done that day. Ambrosch, she said, was on the north quarter, breaking sod with the oxen.

"Jim, you ask Jake how much he ploughed to-day. I don't want that Jake get more done in one day than me. I want we have very much corn this fall."

While the horses drew in the water, and nosed each other, and then drank again, Ántonia sat down on the windmill step and rested her head on her hand. "You see the big prairie fire from your place last night? I hope your grandpa ain't lose no stacks?"[1]

"No, we did n't. I came to ask you something, Tony. Grandmother wants to know if you can't go to the term of school that begins next week over at the sod schoolhouse. She says there's a good teacher, and you'd learn a lot."

Ántonia stood up, lifting and dropping her shoulders as if they were stiff. "I ain't got time to learn. I can work like mans now. My mother can't say no more how Ambrosch do all and nobody to help him. I can work as much as him. School is all right for little boys. I help make this land one good farm."

She clucked to her team and started for the barn. I walked beside her, feeling vexed. Was she going to grow up boastful like her mother, I wondered? Before we reached the stable, I felt something tense in her silence, and glancing up I saw that she was crying. She turned her face from me and looked off at the red streak of dying light, over the dark prairie.

I climbed up into the loft and threw down the hay for her, while she unharnessed her team. We walked slowly back toward the house. Ambrosch had come in from the north quarter, and was watering his oxen at the tank.

Ántonia took my hand. "Sometime you will tell me all those nice things you learn at the school, won't you, Jimmy?" she asked with a sudden rush of feeling in her voice. "My father, he went much to school. He know a great deal; how to make the fine cloth like what you not got here. He play horn and violin, and he read so many books that the priests in Bohemie come to talk to him. You won't forget my father, Jim?"

"No," I said, "I will never forget him."

Mrs. Shimerda asked me to stay for supper. After Ambrosch and Ántonia had washed the field dust from their hands and faces at the wash-basin by the kitchen door, we sat down at the oilcloth-covered table. Mrs. Shimerda ladled meal mush out of an iron pot and poured milk on it. After the mush we had fresh bread and sorghum molasses, and coffee with the cake that had been kept warm in the feathers. Ántonia and Ambrosch were talking in Bohemian; disputing about which of them had done more ploughing that day. Mrs. Shimerda egged them on, chuckling while she gobbled her food.

---

1 Haystacks.

Presently Ambrosch said sullenly in English: "You take them ox to-morrow and try the sod plough. Then you not be so smart."

His sister laughed. "Don't be mad. I know it's awful hard work for break sod. I milk the cow for you to-morrow, if you want."

Mrs. Shimerda turned quickly to me. "That cow not give so much milk like what your grandpa say. If he make talk about fifteen dollars, I send him back the cow."

"He does n't talk about the fifteen dollars," I exclaimed indignantly. "He does n't find fault with people."

"He say I break his saw when we build, and I never," grumbled Ambrosch.

I knew he had broken the saw, and then hid it and lied about it. I began to wish I had not stayed for supper. Everything was disagreeable to me. Ántonia ate so noisily now, like a man, and she yawned often at the table and kept stretching her arms over her head, as if they ached. Grandmother had said, "Heavy field work'll spoil that girl. She'll lose all her nice ways and get rough ones." She had lost them already.

After supper I rode home through the sad, soft spring twilight. Since winter I had seen very little of Ántonia. She was out in the fields from sun-up until sun-down. If I rode over to see her where she was ploughing, she stopped at the end of a row to chat for a moment, then gripped her plough-handles, clucked to her team, and waded on down the furrow, making me feel that she was now grown up and had no time for me. On Sundays she helped her mother make garden or sewed all day. Grandfather was pleased with Ántonia. When we complained of her, he only smiled and said, "She will help some fellow get ahead in the world."

Nowadays Tony could talk of nothing but the prices of things, or how much she could lift and endure. She was too proud of her strength. I knew, too, that Ambrosch put upon her some chores a girl ought not to do, and that the farmhands around the country joked in a nasty way about it. Whenever I saw her come up the furrow, shouting to her beasts, sunburned, sweaty, her dress open at the neck, and her throat and chest dust-plastered, I used to think of the tone in which poor Mr. Shimerda, who could say so little, yet managed to say so much when he exclaimed, "My Án-tonia!"

XVIII

After I began to go to the country school, I saw less of the Bohemians. We were sixteen pupils at the sod schoolhouse, and we all came on horseback and brought our dinner. My schoolmates were none of them very interesting, but I somehow felt that by making comrades of them I was getting even with Ántonia for her indifference. Since the father's death, Ambrosch was more than ever the head of the house and he seemed to direct the feelings as well as the fortunes of his women-folk. Ántonia often quoted his opinions to me, and she let me see that she admired him, while she thought of me only as a little boy. Before the spring was over, there was a distinct coldness between us and the Shimerdas. It came about in this way.

One Sunday I rode over there with Jake to get a horse-collar[1] which Ambrosch had borrowed from him and had not returned. It was a beautiful blue morning. The buffalo-peas were blooming in pink and purple masses along the roadside, and the larks, perched on last year's dried sunflower stalks, were singing straight at the sun, their heads thrown back and their yellow breasts a-quiver. The wind blew about us in warm, sweet gusts. We rode slowly, with a pleasant sense of Sunday indolence.

We found the Shimerdas working just as if it were a week-day. Marek was cleaning out the stable, and Ántonia and her mother were making garden, off across the pond in the draw-head. Ambrosch was up on the windmill tower, oiling the wheel. He

---

1 A part of the harness which fits over the horse's head.

came down, not very cordially. When Jake asked for the collar, he grunted and scratched his head. The collar belonged to grandfather, of course, and Jake, feeling responsible for it, flared up.

"Now, don't you say you have n't got it, Ambrosch, because I know you have, and if you ain't a-going to look for it, I will."

Ambrosch shrugged his shoulders and sauntered down the hill toward the stable. I could see that it was one of his mean days. Presently he returned, carrying a collar that had been badly used— trampled in the dirt and gnawed by rats until the hair was sticking out of it.

"This what you want?" he asked surlily.

Jake jumped off his horse. I saw a wave of red come up under the rough stubble on his face. "That ain't the piece of harness I loaned you, Ambrosch; or if it is, you've used it shameful. I ain't a-going to carry such a looking thing back to Mr. Burden."

Ambrosch dropped the collar on the ground. "All right," he said coolly, took up his oil-can, and began to climb the mill. Jake caught him by the belt of his trousers and yanked him back. Ambrosch's feet had scarcely touched the ground when he lunged out with a vicious kick at Jake's stomach. Fortunately Jake was in such a position that he could dodge it. This was not the sort of thing country boys did when they played at fisticuffs, and Jake was furious. He landed Ambrosch a blow on the head it sounded like the crack of an axe on a cow-pumpkin.[1] Ambrosch dropped over, stunned.

We heard squeals, and looking up saw Ántonia and her mother coming on the run. They did not take the path around the pond, but plunged through the muddy water, without even lifting their skirts. They came on, screaming and clawing the air. By this time Ambrosch had come to his senses and was sputtering with nosebleed. Jake sprang into his saddle. "Let's get out of this, Jim," he called.

Mrs. Shimerda threw her hands over her head and clutched as if she were going to pull down lightning. "Law, law!" she shrieked after us. "Law for knock my Ambrosch down!"

"I never like you no more, Jake and Jim Burden," Ántonia panted. "No friends any more!"

Jake stopped and turned his horse for a second. "Well, you're a damned ungrateful lot, the whole pack of you," he shouted back.

---

1 A pumpkin grown to feed livestock.

"I guess the Burdens can get along without you. You've been a sight of trouble to them, anyhow!"

We rode away, feeling so outraged that the fine morning was spoiled for us. I had n't a word to say, and poor Jake was white as paper and trembling all over. It made him sick to get so angry. "They ain't the same, Jimmy," he kept saying in a hurt tone. "These foreigners ain't the same. You can't trust 'em to be fair. It's dirty to kick a feller. You heard how the women turned on you—and after all we went through on account of 'em last winter! They ain't to be trusted. I don't want to see you get too thick with any of 'em."

"I'll never be friends with them again, Jake," I declared hotly. "I believe they are all like Krajiek and Ambrosch underneath."

Grandfather heard our story with a twinkle in his eye. He advised Jake to ride to town to-morrow, go to a justice of the peace, tell him he had knocked young Shimerda down, and pay his fine. Then if Mrs. Shimerda was inclined to make trouble—her son was still under age—she would be forestalled. Jake said he might as well take the wagon and haul to market the pig he had been fattening. On Monday, about an hour after Jake had started, we saw Mrs. Shimerda and her Ambrosch proudly driving by, looking neither to the right nor left. As they rattled out of sight down the Black Hawk road, grandfather chuckled, saying he had rather expected she would follow the matter up.

Jake paid his fine with a ten-dollar bill grandfather had given him for that purpose. But when the Shimerdas found that Jake sold his pig in town that day, Ambrosch worked it out in his shrewd head that Jake had to sell his pig to pay his fine. This theory afforded the Shimerdas great satisfaction, apparently. For weeks afterward, whenever Jake and I met Ántonia on her way to the post-office, or going along the road with her work-team, she would clap her hands and call to us in a spiteful, crowing voice:—

"Jake-y Jake-y, sell the pig and pay the slap!"

Otto pretended not to be surprised at Ántonia's behavior. He only lifted his brows and said, "You can't tell me anything new about a Czech; I'm an Austrian."[1]

Grandfather was never a party to what Jake called our feud with the Shimerdas. Ambrosch and Ántonia always greeted him respectfully, and he asked them about their affairs and gave them advice as

---

1 See note on page 107. To Otto, the local feud replays Old World animosities.

usual. He thought the future looked hopeful for them. Ambrosch was a far-seeing fellow; he soon realized that his oxen were too heavy for any work except breaking sod, and he succeeded in selling them to a newly arrived German. With the money he bought another team of horses, which grandfather selected for him. Marek was strong, and Ambrosch worked him hard; but he could never teach him to cultivate corn, I remember. The one idea that had ever got through poor Marek's thick head was that all exertion was meritorious. He always bore down on the handles of the cultivator and drove the blades so deep into the earth that the horses were soon exhausted.

In June Ambrosch went to work at Mr. Bushy's for a week, and took Marek with him at full wages. Mrs. Shimerda then drove the second cultivator; she and Ántonia worked in the fields all day and did the chores at night. While the two women were running the place alone, one of the new horses got colic and gave them a terrible fright.

Ántonia had gone down to the barn one night to see that all was well before she went to bed, and she noticed that one of the roans was swollen about the middle and stood with its head hanging.[1] She mounted another horse, without waiting to saddle him, and hammered on our door just as we were going to bed. Grandfather answered her knock. He did not send one of his men, but rode back with her himself, taking a syringe and an old piece of carpet he kept for hot applications when our horses were sick. He found Mrs. Shimerda sitting by the horse with her lantern, groaning and wringing her hands. It took but a few moments to release the gases pent up in the poor beast, and the two women heard the rush of wind and saw the roan visibly diminish in girth.

"If I lose that horse, Mr. Burden," Ántonia exclaimed, "I never stay here till Ambrosch come home! I go drown myself in the pond before morning."

When Ambrosch came back from Mr. Bushy's, we learned that he had given Marek's wages to the priest at Black Hawk, for masses for their father's soul. Grandmother thought Ántonia needed shoes more than Mr. Shimerda needed prayers, but grandfather said tolerantly, "If he can spare six dollars, pinched as he is, it shows he believes what he professes."

---

1 The roan horse's colic has caused its stomach to well.

It was grandfather who brought about a reconciliation with the Shimerdas. One morning he told us that the small grain[1] was coming on so well, he thought he would begin to cut his wheat on the first of July. He would need more men, and if it were agreeable to every one he would engage Ambrosch for the reaping and thrashing, as the Shimerdas had no small grain of their own.

"I think, Emmaline," he concluded, "I will ask Ántonia to come over and help you in the kitchen. She will be glad to earn something, and it will be a good time to end misunderstandings. I may as well ride over this morning and make arrangements. Do you want to go with me, Jim?" His tone told me that he had already decided for me.

After breakfast we set off together. When Mrs. Shimerda saw us coming, she ran from her door down into the draw behind the stable, as if she did not want to meet us. Grandfather smiled to himself while he tied his horse, and we followed her.

Behind the barn we came upon a funny sight. The cow had evidently been grazing somewhere in the draw. Mrs. Shimerda had run to the animal, pulled up the lariat pin, and, when we came upon her, she was trying to hide the cow in an old cave in the bank. As the hole was narrow and dark, the cow held back, and the old woman was slapping and pushing at her hind quarters, trying to spank her into the draw-side.

Grandfather ignored her singular occupation and greeted her politely. "Good-morning, Mrs. Shimerda. Can you tell me where I will find Ambrosch? Which field?"

"He with the sod corn."[2] She pointed toward the north, still standing in front of the cow as if she hoped to conceal it.

"His sod corn will be good for fodder this winter," said grandfather encouragingly. "And where is Ántonia?"

"She go with." Mrs. Shimerda kept wiggling her bare feet about nervously in the dust.

"Very well. I will ride up there. I want them to come over and help me cut my oats and wheat next month. I will pay them wages. Good-morning. By the way, Mrs. Shimerda," he said as he turned up the path, "I think we may as well call it square about the cow."

---

1 Typically oats, rye, barley, and wheat.
2 The name given to the first crop of corn harvested after breaking the sod and plowing new land.

She started and clutched the rope tighter. Seeing that she did not understand, grandfather turned back. "You need not pay me anything more; no more money. The cow is yours."

"Pay no more, keep cow?" she asked in a bewildered tone, her narrow eyes snapping at us in the sunlight.

"Exactly. Pay no more, keep cow." He nodded.

Mrs. Shimerda dropped the rope, ran after us, and crouching down beside grandfather, she took his hand and kissed it. I doubt if he had ever been so much embarrassed before. I was a little startled, too. Somehow, that seemed to bring the Old World very close.

We rode away laughing, and grandfather said: "I expect she thought we had come to take the cow away for certain, Jim. I wonder if she would n't have scratched a little if we'd laid hold of that lariat rope!"

Our neighbors seemed glad to make peace with us. The next Sunday Mrs. Shimerda came over and brought Jake a pair of socks she had knitted. She presented them with an air of great magnanimity, saying, "Now you not come any more for knock my Ambrosch down?"

Jake laughed sheepishly. "I don't want to have no trouble with Ambrosch. If he'll let me alone, I'll let him alone."

"If he slap you, we ain't got no pig for pay the fine," she said insinuatingly.

Jake was not at all disconcerted. "Have the last word, mam," he said cheerfully. "It's a lady's privilege."

XIX

July came on with that breathless, brilliant heat which makes the plains of Kansas and Nebraska the best corn country in the world. It seemed as if we could hear the corn growing in the night; under the stars one caught a faint crackling in the dewy, heavy-odored cornfields where the feathered stalks stood so juicy and green. If all the great plain from the Missouri to the Rocky Mountains had been under glass, and the heat regulated by a thermometer, it could not have been better for the yellow tassels that were ripening and fertilizing the silk day by day. The cornfields were far apart in those times, with miles of wild grazing land between. It took a clear, meditative eye like my grandfather's to foresee that they would enlarge and multiply until they would be, not the Shimerdas' cornfields, or Mr. Bushy's, but the world's cornfields;

that their yield would be one of the great economic facts, like the wheat crop of Russia, which underlie all the activities of men, in peace or war.

The burning sun of those few weeks, with occasional rains at night, secured the corn. After the milky ears were once formed, we had little to fear from dry weather. The men were working so hard in the wheatfields that they did not notice the heat,—though I was kept busy carrying water for them,—and grandmother and Ántonia had so much to do in the kitchen that they could not have told whether one day was hotter than another. Each morning, while the dew was still on the grass, Ántonia went with me up to the garden to get early vegetables for dinner. Grandmother made her wear a sunbonnet, but as soon as we reached the garden she threw it on the grass and let her hair fly in the breeze. I remember how, as we bent over the pea-vines, beads of perspiration used to gather on her upper lip like a little mustache.

"Oh, better I like to work out of doors than in a house!" she used to sing joyfully. "I not care that your grandmother say it makes me like a man. I like to be like a man." She would toss her head and ask me to feel the muscles swell in her brown arm.

We were glad to have her in the house. She was so gay and responsive that one did not mind her heavy, running step, or her clattery way with pans. Grandmother was in high spirits during the weeks that Ántonia worked for us.

All the nights were close and hot during that harvest season. The harvesters slept in the hayloft because it was cooler there than in the house. I used to lie in my bed by the open window, watching the heat lightning play softly along the horizon, or looking up at the gaunt frame of the windmill against the blue night sky. One night there was a beautiful electric storm, though not enough rain fell to damage the cut grain. The men went down to the barn immediately after supper, and when the dishes were washed Ántonia and I climbed up on the slanting roof of the chicken-house to watch the clouds. The thunder was loud and metallic, like the rattle of sheet iron, and the lightning broke in great zigzags across the heavens, making everything stand out and come close to us for a moment. Half the sky was checkered with black thunderheads, but all the west was luminous and clear: in the lightning-flashes it looked like deep blue water, with the sheen of moonlight on it; and the mottled part of the sky was like marble pavement, like the quay of some splendid sea-coast city, doomed to destruction. Great warm splashes of rain fell on our upturned faces. One black cloud,

no bigger than a little boat, drifted out into the clear space unat-
tended, and kept moving westward. All about us we could hear the
felty beat of the raindrops on the soft dust of the farmyard. Grandmother came to the door and said it was late, and we would get
wet out there.

"In a minute we come," Ántonia called back to her. "I like your
grandmother, and all things here," she sighed. "I wish my papa live
to see this summer. I wish no winter ever come again."

"It will be summer a long while yet," I reassured her. "Why are
n't you always nice like this, Tony?"

"How nice?"

"Why, just like this; like yourself. Why do you all the time try to be like Ambrosch?"

She put her arms under her head and lay back, looking up at the sky. "If I live here, like you, that is different. Things will be easy for you. But they will be hard for us."

BOOK II
THE HIRED GIRLS

I

I had been living with my grandfather for nearly three years when he decided to move to Black Hawk. He and grandmother were getting old for the heavy work of a farm, and as I was now thirteen they thought I ought to be going to school. Accordingly our homestead was rented to "that good woman, the Widow Steavens," and her bachelor brother, and we bought Preacher White's house, at the north end of Black Hawk. This was the first town house one passed driving in from the farm, a landmark which told country people their long ride was over.

We were to move to Black Hawk in March, and as soon as grandfather had fixed the date he let Jake and Otto know of his intention. Otto said he would not be likely to find another place that suited him so well; that he was tired of farming and thought he would go back to what he called the "wild West." Jake Marpole, lured by Otto's stories of adventure, decided to go with him. We did our best to dissuade Jake. He was so handicapped by illiteracy and by his trusting disposition that he would be an easy prey to sharpers. Grandmother begged him to stay among kindly, Christian people, where he was known; but there was no reasoning with him. He wanted to be a prospector. He thought a silver mine was waiting for him in Colorado.

Jake and Otto served us to the last. They moved us into town, put down the carpets in our new house, made shelves and cupboards for grandmother's kitchen, and seemed loath to leave us. But at last they went, without warning. Those two fellows had been faithful to us through sun and storm, had given us things that cannot be bought in any market in the world. With me they had been like older brothers; had restrained their speech and manners out of care for me, and given me so much good comradeship. Now they got on the west-bound train one morning, in their Sunday clothes, with their oilcloth valises—and I never saw them again. Months afterward we got a card from Otto, saying that Jake had been down with mountain fever,[1] but now they were both work-

---

1   General term for various malarial or typhoid fevers contracted in mountain regions.

ing in the Yankee Girl mine,[1] and were doing well. I wrote to them at that address, but my letter was returned to me, "unclaimed." After that we never heard from them.

Black Hawk, the new world in which we had come to live, was a clean, well-planted little prairie town, with white fences and good green yards about the dwellings, wide, dusty streets, and shapely little trees growing along the wooden sidewalks. In the center of the town there were two rows of new brick "store" buildings, a brick schoolhouse, the courthouse, and four white churches. Our own house looked down over the town, and from our upstairs windows we could see the winding line of the river bluffs, two miles south of us. That river was to be my compensation for the lost freedom of the farming country.

We came to Black Hawk in March, and by the end of April we felt like town people. Grandfather was a deacon in the new Baptist Church, grandmother was busy with church suppers and missionary societies, and I was quite another boy, or thought I was. Suddenly put down among boys of my own age, I found I had a great deal to learn. Before the spring term of school was over I could fight, play "keeps,"[2] tease the little girls, and use forbidden words as well as any boy in my class. I was restrained from utter savagery only by the fact that Mrs. Harling, our nearest neighbor, kept an eye on me, and if my behavior went beyond certain bounds I was not permitted to come into her yard or to play with her jolly children.

We saw more of our country neighbors now than when we lived on the farm. Our house was a convenient stopping-place for them. We had a big barn where the farmers could put up their teams, and their women-folk more often accompanied them, now that they could stay with us for dinner, and rest and set their bonnets right before they went shopping. The more our house was like a country hotel, the better I liked it. I was glad, when I came home from school at noon, to see a farm wagon standing in the back yard, and I was always ready to run downtown to get beefsteak or baker's bread for unexpected company. All through that first spring and summer I kept hoping that Ambrosch would bring Ántonia and Yulka to see our new house. I wanted to show them our red

---

1   The Yankee Girl Mine was discovered in 1882, in Colorado.
2   A game in which the player who knocks marbles out of the circle gets to keep the marbles. The game was suspect by adults because it was, strictly speaking, gambling.

plush furniture, and the trumpet-blowing cherubs the German paper-hanger had put on our parlor ceiling.

When Ambrosch came to town, however, he came alone, and though he put his horses in our barn, he would never stay for dinner, or tell us anything about his mother and sisters. If we ran out and questioned him as he was slipping through the yard, he would merely work his shoulders about in his coat and say, "They all right, I guess."

Mrs. Steavens, who now lived on our farm, grew as fond of Ántonia as we had been, and always brought us news of her. All through the wheat season, she told us, Ambrosch hired his sister out like a man, and she went from farm to farm, binding sheaves or working with the thrashers.[1] The farmers liked her and were kind to her; said they would rather have her for a hand than Ambrosch. When fall came she was to husk corn for the neighbors until Christmas, as she had done the year before; but grandmother saved her from this by getting her a place to work with our neighbors, the Harlings.

II

Grandmother often said that if she had to live in town, she thanked God she lived next the Harlings. They had been farming people, like ourselves, and their place was like a little farm, with a big barn and a garden, and an orchard and grazing lots,—even a windmill. The Harlings were Norwegians, and Mrs. Harling had lived in Christiania[2] until she was ten years old. Her husband was born in Minnesota. He was a grain merchant and cattle buyer, and was generally considered the most enterprising business man in our county. He controlled a line of grain elevators[3] in the little towns along the railroad to the west of us, and was away from home a great deal. In his absence his wife was the head of the household.

Mrs. Harling was short and square and sturdy-looking, like her house. Every inch of her was charged with an energy that made itself felt the moment she entered a room. Her face was rosy and

---

1 Ántonia is hired out to do heavy farm work, tying the harvested grain into sheaves to be fed into threshing machines. This labor would soon be mechanized, and Jim Burden refers to steam-threshers in Book IV.
2 Renamed Oslo in 1905.
3 Storage structures, in which grain was held along rail lines for loading onto freight cars.

solid, with bright, twinkling eyes and a stubborn little chin. She was quick to anger, quick to laughter, and jolly from the depths of her soul. How well I remember her laugh; it had in it the same sudden recognition that flashed into her eyes, was a burst of humor, short and intelligent. Her rapid footsteps shook her own floors, and she routed lassitude and indifference wherever she came. She could not be negative or perfunctory about anything. Her enthusiasm, and her violent likes and dislikes, asserted themselves in all the every-day occupations of life. Wash-day was interesting, never dreary, at the Harlings'. Preserving-time was a prolonged festival, and house-cleaning was like a revolution. When Mrs. Harling made garden that spring, we could feel the stir of her undertaking through the willow hedge that separated our place from hers.

Three of the Harling children were near me in age. Charley, the only son,—they had lost an older boy,—was sixteen; Julia, who was known as the musical one, was fourteen when I was; and Sally, the tomboy with short hair, was a year younger. She was nearly as strong as I, and uncannily clever at all boys' sports. Sally was a wild thing, with sunburned yellow hair, bobbed about her ears, and a brown skin, for she never wore a hat. She raced all over town on one roller skate, often cheated at "keeps," but was such a quick shot one could n't catch her at it.

The grown-up daughter, Frances, was a very important person in our world. She was her father's chief clerk, and virtually managed his Black Hawk office during his frequent absences. Because of her unusual business ability, he was stern and exacting with her. He paid her a good salary, but she had few holidays and never got away from her responsibilities. Even on Sundays she went to the office to open the mail and read the markets. With Charley, who was not interested in business, but was already preparing for Annapolis, Mr. Harling was very indulgent; bought him guns and tools and electric batteries, and never asked what he did with them.

Frances was dark, like her father, and quite as tall. In winter she wore a sealskin coat and cap, and she and Mr. Harling used to walk home together in the evening, talking about grain-cars and cattle, like two men. Sometimes she came over to see grandfather after supper, and her visits flattered him. More than once they put their wits together to rescue some unfortunate farmer from the clutches of Wick Cutter, the Black Hawk money-lender. Grandfather said Frances Harling was as good a judge of credits as any banker in the county. The two or three men who had tried to take advantage of her in a deal acquired celebrity by their defeat. She knew every farmer for miles about; how much land he had under cultivation, how many cattle he was feeding, what his liabilities were. Her interest in these people was more than a business interest. She carried them all in her mind as if they were characters in a book or a play.

When Frances drove out into the country on business, she would go miles out of her way to call on some of the old people, or to see the women who seldom got to town. She was quick at understanding the grandmothers who spoke no English, and the most reticent and distrustful of them would tell her their story without realizing they were doing so. She went to country funerals and weddings in all weathers. A farmer's daughter who was to be married could count on a wedding present from Frances Harling.

In August the Harlings' Danish cook had to leave them. Grandmother entreated them to try Ántonia. She cornered Ambrosch the next time he came to town, and pointed out to him that any connection with Christian Harling would strengthen his credit and be of advantage to him. One Sunday Mrs. Harling took the long ride out to the Shimerdas' with Frances. She said she wanted to see "what the girl came from" and to have a clear understanding with her mother. I was in our yard when they came driving home, just before sunset. They laughed and waved to me as they passed, and I could see they were in great good humor. After supper, when grandfather set off to church, grandmother and I took my short cut through the willow hedge and went over to hear about the visit to the Shimerdas'.

We found Mrs. Harling with Charley and Sally on the front porch, resting after her hard drive. Julia was in the hammock—she was fond of repose—and Frances was at the piano, playing without a light and talking to her mother through the open window.

Mrs. Harling laughed when she saw us coming. "I expect you left your dishes on the table to-night, Mrs. Burden," she called. Frances shut the piano and came out to join us.

They had liked Ántonia from their first glimpse of her; felt they knew exactly what kind of girl she was. As for Mrs. Shimerda, they found her very amusing. Mrs. Harling chuckled whenever she spoke of her. "I expect I am more at home with that sort of bird than you are, Mrs. Burden. They're a pair, Ambrosch and that old woman!"

They had had a long argument with Ambrosch about Ántonia's allowance for clothes and pocket-money. It was his plan that every cent of his sister's wages should be paid over to him each month, and he would provide her with such clothing as he thought necessary. When Mrs. Harling told him firmly that she would keep fifty dollars a year for Ántonia's own use, he declared they wanted to take his sister to town and dress her up and make a fool of her. Mrs. Harling gave a lively account of Ambrosch's behavior throughout the interview; how he kept jumping up and putting on his cap as if he were through with the whole business, and how his mother tweaked his coat-tail and prompted him in Bohemian. Mrs. Harling finally agreed to pay three dollars a week for Ántonia's services—good wages in those days—and to keep her in shoes. There had been hot dispute about the shoes, Mrs. Shimerda finally saying persuasively that she would send Mrs. Harling three fat geese every year to "make even." Ambrosch was to bring his sister to town next Saturday.

"She'll be awkward and rough at first, like enough," grandmother said anxiously, "but unless she's been spoiled by the hard life she's led, she has it in her to be a real helpful girl."

Mrs. Harling laughed her quick, decided laugh. "Oh, I'm not worrying, Mrs. Burden! I can bring something out of that girl. She's barely seventeen, not too old to learn new ways. She's good-looking, too!" she added warmly.

Frances turned to grandmother. "Oh, yes, Mrs. Burden, you did n't tell us that! She was working in the garden when we got there, barefoot and ragged. But she has such fine brown legs and arms, and splendid color in her cheeks—like those big dark red plums."

We were pleased at this praise. Grandmother spoke feelingly. "When she first came to this country, Frances, and had that genteel old man to watch over her, she was as pretty a girl as ever I saw. But, dear me, what a life she's led, out in the fields with those rough thrashers! Things would have been very different with poor Ántonia if her father had lived."

The Harlings begged us to tell them about Mr. Shimerda's death and the big snowstorm. By the time we saw grandfather coming home from church we had told them pretty much all we knew of the Shimerdas.

"The girl will be happy here, and she'll forget those things," said Mrs. Harling confidently, as we rose to take our leave.

III

On Saturday Ambrosch drove up to the back gate, and Ántonia jumped down from the wagon and ran into our kitchen just as she used to do. She was wearing shoes and stockings, and was breathless and excited. She gave me a playful shake by the shoulders. "You ain't forget about me, Jim?"

Grandmother kissed her. "God bless you, child! Now you've come, you must try to do right and be a credit to us."

Ántonia looked eagerly about the house and admired everything. "Maybe I be the kind of girl you like better, now I come to town," she suggested hopefully.

How good it was to have Ántonia near us again; to see her every day and almost every night! Her greatest fault, Mrs. Harling found, was that she so often stopped her work and fell to playing with the children. She would race about the orchard with us, or take sides in our hay-fights in the barn, or be the old bear that came down from the mountain and carried off Nina. Tony learned English so quickly that by the time school began she could speak as well as any of us.

I was jealous of Tony's admiration for Charley Harling. Because he was always first in his classes at school, and could mend the water-pipes or the door-bell and take the clock to pieces, she seemed to think him a sort of prince. Nothing that Charley wanted was too much trouble for her. She loved to put up lunches for him when he went hunting, to mend his ball-gloves and sew buttons on his shooting-coat, baked the kind of nut-cake he liked, and fed his setter dog when he was away on trips with his father. Ántonia had made herself cloth working-slippers out of Mr. Harling's old coats, and in these she went padding about after Charley, fairly panting with eagerness to please him.

Next to Charley, I think she loved Nina best. Nina was only six, and she was rather more complex than the other children. She was fanciful, had all sorts of unspoken preferences, and was easily offended. At the slightest disappointment or displeasure her velvety brown eyes filled with tears, and she would lift her chin and walk silently away. If we ran after her and tried to appease her, it did no good. She walked on unmollified. I used to think that no eyes in the world could grow so large or hold so many tears as Nina's. Mrs. Harling and Ántonia invariably took her part. We were never given a chance to explain. The charge was simply: "You have made Nina

cry. Now, Jimmy can go home, and Sally must get her arithmetic."
I liked Nina, too; she was so quaint and unexpected, and her eyes
were lovely; but I often wanted to shake her.

We had jolly evenings at the Harlings' when the father was away.
If he was at home, the children had to go to bed early, or they came
over to my house to play. Mr. Harling not only demanded a quiet
house, he demanded all his wife's attention. He used to take her
away to their room in the west ell,[1] and talk over his business with
her all evening. Though we did not realize it then, Mrs. Harling was
our audience when we played, and we always looked to her for
suggestions. Nothing flattered one like her quick laugh.

Mr. Harling had a desk in his bedroom, and his own easy-chair
by the window, in which no one else ever sat. On the nights when
he was at home, I could see his shadow on the blind, and it seemed
to me an arrogant shadow. Mrs. Harling paid no heed to any one
else if he was there. Before he went to bed she always got him a
lunch of smoked salmon or anchovies and beer. He kept an alcohol lamp in his room, and a French coffee-pot, and his wife made
coffee for him at any hour of the night he happened to want it.

Most Black Hawk fathers had no personal habits outside their
domestic ones; they paid the bills, pushed the baby carriage after
office hours, moved the sprinkler about over the lawn, and took
the family driving on Sunday. Mr. Harling, therefore, seemed to me
autocratic and imperial in his ways. He walked, talked, put on his
gloves, shook hands, like a man who felt that he had power. He was
not tall, but he carried his head so haughtily that he looked a commanding figure, and there was something daring and challenging
in his eyes. I used to imagine that the "nobles" of whom Ántonia
was always talking probably looked very much like Christian Harling, wore caped overcoats like his, and just such a glittering dia-
mond upon the little finger.

Except when the father was at home, the Harling house was
never quiet. Mrs. Harling and Nina and Ántonia made as much
noise as a houseful of children, and there was usually somebody at
the piano. Julia was the only one who was held down to regular
hours of practicing, but they all played. When Frances came home
at noon, she played until dinner was ready. When Sally got back
from school, she sat down in her hat and coat and drummed the

---

1   An extension of the house at right angles to the main part.

plantation melodies that negro minstrel troupes brought to town. Even Nina played the Swedish Wedding March.

Mrs. Harling had studied the piano under a good teacher, and somehow she managed to practice every day. I soon learned that if I were sent over on an errand and found Mrs. Harling at the piano, I must sit down and wait quietly until she turned to me. I can see her at this moment; her short, square person planted firmly on the stool, her little fat hands moving quickly and neatly over the keys, her eyes fixed on the music with intelligent concentration.

IV

"I won't have none of your weevily wheat,
and I won't have none of your barley,
But I'll take a measure of fine white flour,
to make a cake for Charley."[1]

We were singing rhymes to tease Ántonia while she was beating up one of Charley's favorite cakes in her big mixing-bowl. It was a crisp autumn evening, just cold enough to make one glad to quit playing tag in the yard, and retreat into the kitchen. We had begun to roll popcorn balls with syrup when we heard a knock at the back door, and Tony dropped her spoon and went to open it. A plump, fair-skinned girl was standing in the doorway. She looked demure and pretty, and made a graceful picture in her blue cashmere dress and little blue hat, with a plaid shawl drawn neatly about her shoulders and a clumsy pocketbook in her hand.

"Hello, Tony. Don't you know me?" she asked in a smooth, low voice, looking in at us archly.

Ántonia gasped and stepped back. "Why, it's Lena! Of course I did n't know you, so dressed up!"

Lena Lingard laughed, as if this pleased her. I had not recognized her for a moment, either. I had never seen her before with a hat on her head—or with shoes and stockings on her feet, for that matter. And here she was, brushed and smoothed and dressed like a town girl, smiling at us with perfect composure.

"Hello, Jim," she said carelessly as she walked into the kitchen and looked about her. "I've come to town to work, too, Tony."

---

1 The lyrics are from a Virginia reel.

"Have you, now? Well, ain't that funny!" Ántonia stood ill at ease, and did n't seem to know just what to do with her visitor.

The door was open into the dining-room, where Mrs. Harling sat crocheting and Frances was reading. Frances asked Lena to come in and join them.

"You are Lena Lingard, are n't you? I've been to see your mother, but you were off herding cattle that day. Mama, this is Chris Lingard's oldest girl."

Mrs. Harling dropped her worsted and examined the visitor with quick, keen eyes. Lena was not at all disconcerted. She sat down in the chair Frances pointed out, carefully arranging her pocketbook and gray cotton gloves on her lap. We followed with our popcorn, but Ántonia hung back—said she had to get her cake into the oven.

"So you have come to town," said Mrs. Harling, her eyes still fixed on Lena. "Where are you working?"

"For Mrs. Thomas, the dressmaker. She is going to teach me to sew. She says I have quite a knack. I'm through with the farm. There ain't any end to the work on a farm, and always so much trouble happens. I'm going to be a dressmaker."

"Well, there have to be dressmakers. It's a good trade. But I would n't run down the farm, if I were you," said Mrs. Harling rather severely. "How is your mother?"

"Oh, mother's never very well; she has too much to do. She'd get away from the farm, too, if she could. She was willing for me to come. After I learn to do sewing, I can make money and help her."

"See that you don't forget to," said Mrs. Harling skeptically, as she took up her crocheting again and sent the hook in and out with nimble fingers.

"No, 'm, I won't," said Lena blandly. She took a few grains of the popcorn we pressed upon her, eating them discreetly and taking care not to get her fingers sticky.

Frances drew her chair up nearer to the visitor. "I thought you were going to be married, Lena," she said teasingly. "Did n't I hear that Nick Svendsen was rushing you pretty hard?"

Lena looked up with her curiously innocent smile. "He did go with me quite a while. But his father made a fuss about it and said he would n't give Nick any land if he married me, so he's going to marry Annie Iverson. I would n't like to be her; Nick's awful sullen, and he'll take it out on her. He ain't spoke to his father since he promised."

Frances laughed. "And how do you feel about it?"

"I don't want to marry Nick, or any other man," Lena murmured. "I've seen a good deal of married life, and I don't care for it. I want to be so I can help my mother and the children at home, and not have to ask lief of anybody."

"That's right," said Frances. "And Mrs. Thomas thinks you can learn dressmaking?"

"Yes, 'm. I've always liked to sew, but I never had much to do with. Mrs. Thomas makes lovely things for all the town ladies. Did you know Mrs. Gardener is having a purple velvet made? The velvet came from Omaha. My, but it's lovely!" Lena sighed softly and stroked her cashmere folds. "Tony knows I never did like out-of-door work," she added.

Mrs. Harling glanced at her. "I expect you'll learn to sew all right, Lena, if you'll only keep your head and not go gadding about to dances all the time and neglect your work, the way some country girls do."

"Yes, 'm. Tiny Soderball is coming to town, too. She's going to work at the Boys' Home Hotel. She'll see lots of strangers," Lena added wistfully.

"Too many, like enough," said Mrs. Harling. "I don't think a hotel is a good place for a girl; though I guess Mrs. Gardener keeps an eye on her waitresses."

Lena's candid eyes, that always looked a little sleepy under their long lashes, kept straying about the cheerful rooms with naïve admiration. Presently she drew on her cotton gloves. "I guess I must be leaving," she said irresolutely.

Frances told her to come again, whenever she was lonesome or wanted advice about anything. Lena replied that she did n't believe she would ever get lonesome in Black Hawk.

She lingered at the kitchen door and begged Ántonia to come and see her often. "I've got a room of my own at Mrs. Thomas's, with a carpet."

Tony shuffled uneasily in her cloth slippers. "I'll come sometime, but Mrs. Harling don't like to have me run much," she said evasively.

"You can do what you please when you go out, can't you?" Lena asked in a guarded whisper. "Ain't you crazy about town, Tony? I don't care what anybody says, I'm done with the farm!" She glanced back over her shoulder toward the dining-room, where Mrs. Harling sat.

When Lena was gone, Frances asked Ántonia why she had n't been a little more cordial to her.

"I did n't know if your mother would like her coming here," said Ántonia, looking troubled. "She was kind of talked about, out there."

"Yes, I know. But mother won't hold it against her if she behaves well here. You need n't say anything about that to the children. I guess Jim has heard all that gossip?"

When I nodded, she pulled my hair and told me I knew too much, anyhow. We were good friends, Frances and I.

I ran home to tell grandmother that Lena Lingard had come to town. We were glad of it, for she had a hard life on the farm.

Lena lived in the Norwegian settlement west of Squaw Creek, and she used to herd her father's cattle in the open country between his place and the Shimerdas'. Whenever we rode over in that direction we saw her out among her cattle, bareheaded and barefooted, scantily dressed in tattered clothing, always knitting as she watched her herd. Before I knew Lena, I thought of her as something wild, that always lived on the prairie, because I had never seen her under a roof. Her yellow hair was burned to a ruddy thatch on her head; but her legs and arms, curiously enough, in spite of constant exposure to the sun, kept a miraculous whiteness which somehow made her seem more undressed than other girls who went scantily clad. The first time I stopped to talk to her, I was astonished at her soft voice and easy, gentle ways. The girls out there usually got rough and mannish after they went to herding. But Lena asked Jake and me to get off our horses and stay awhile, and behaved exactly as if she were in a house and were accustomed to having visitors. She was not embarrassed by her ragged clothes, and treated us as if we were old acquaintances. Even then I noticed the unusual color of her eyes—a shade of deep violet—and their soft, confiding expression.

Chris Lingard was not a very successful farmer, and he had a large family. Lena was always knitting stockings for little brothers and sisters, and even the Norwegian women, who disapproved of her, admitted that she was a good daughter to her mother. As Tony said, she had been talked about. She was accused of making Ole Benson lose the little sense he had—and that at an age when she should still have been in pinafores.[1]

Ole lived in a leaky dugout somewhere at the edge of the

---

1 A collarless, sleeveless garment worn over a dress and fastened in the back.

settlement. He was fat and lazy and discouraged, and bad luck had become a habit with him. After he had had every other kind of misfortune, his wife, "Crazy Mary," tried to set a neighbor's barn on fire, and was sent to the asylum at Lincoln. She was kept there for a few months, then escaped and walked all the way home, nearly two hundred miles, traveling by night and hiding in barns and haystacks by day. When she got back to the Norwegian settlement, her poor feet were as hard as hoofs. She promised to be good, and was allowed to stay at home—though every one realized she was as crazy as ever, and she still ran about barefooted through the snow, telling her domestic troubles to her neighbors.

Not long after Mary came back from the asylum, I heard a young Dane, who was helping us to thrash, tell Jake and Otto that Chris Lingard's oldest girl had put Ole Benson out of his head, until he had no more sense than his crazy wife. When Ole was cultivating his corn that summer, he used to get discouraged in the field, tie up his team, and wander off to wherever Lena Lingard was herding. There he would sit down on the draw-side and help her watch her cattle. All the settlement was talking about it. The Norwegian preacher's wife went to Lena and told her she ought not to allow this; she begged Lena to come to church on Sundays. Lena said she had n't a dress in the world any less ragged than the one on her back. Then the minister's wife went through her old trunks and found some things she had worn before her marriage.

The next Sunday Lena appeared at church, a little late, with her hair done up neatly on her head, like a young woman, wearing shoes and stockings, and the new dress, which she had made over for herself very becomingly. The congregation stared at her. Until that morning no one—unless it were Ole—had realized how pretty she was, or that she was growing up. The swelling lines of her figure had been hidden under the shapeless rags she wore in the fields. After the last hymn had been sung, and the congregation was dismissed, Ole slipped out to the hitch-bar and lifted Lena on her horse. That, in itself, was shocking; a married man was not expected to do such things. But it was nothing to the scene that followed. Crazy Mary darted out from the group of women at the church door, and ran down the road after Lena, shouting horrible threats.

"Look out, you Lena Lingard, look out! I'll come over with a corn-knife one day and trim some of that shape off you. Then you won't sail round so fine, making eyes at the men! ..."

The Norwegian women did n't know where to look. They were

formal housewives, most of them, with a severe sense of decorum.
But Lena Lingard only laughed her lazy, good-natured laugh and
rode on, gazing back over her shoulder at Ole's infuriated wife.

The time came, however, when Lena did n't laugh. More than
once Crazy Mary chased her across the prairie and round and
round the Shimerdas' cornfield. Lena never told her father; perhaps
she was ashamed; perhaps she was more afraid of his anger than of
the corn-knife. I was at the Shimerdas' one afternoon when Lena
came bounding through the red grass as fast as her white legs could
carry her. She ran straight into the house and hid in Ántonia's
feather-bed. Mary was not far behind; she came right up to the
door and made us feel how sharp her blade was, showing us very

graphically just what she meant to do to Lena. Mrs. Shimerda, leaning out of the window, enjoyed the situation keenly, and was sorry when Ántonia sent Mary away, mollified by an apronful of bottle-tomatoes.[1] Lena came out from Tony's room behind the kitchen, very pink from the heat of the feathers, but otherwise calm. She begged Ántonia and me to go with her, and help get her cattle together; they were scattered and might be gorging themselves in somebody's cornfield.

"Maybe you lose a steer and learn not to make somethings with your eyes at married men," Mrs. Shimerda told her hectoringly.

Lena only smiled her sleepy smile. "I never made anything to him with my eyes. I can't help it if he hangs around, and I can't order him off. It ain't my prairie."

V

After Lena came to Black Hawk I often met her downtown, where she would be matching sewing silk or buying "findings"[2] for Mrs. Thomas. If I happened to walk home with her, she told me all about the dresses she was helping to make, or about what she saw and heard when she was with Tiny Soderball at the hotel on Saturday nights.

The Boys' Home was the best hotel on our branch of the Burlington, and all the commercial travelers in that territory tried to get into Black Hawk for Sunday. They used to assemble in the parlor after supper on Saturday nights. Marshall Field's man,[3] Anson Kirkpatrick, played the piano and sang all the latest sentimental songs. After Tiny had helped the cook wash the dishes, she and Lena sat on the other side of the double doors between the parlor and the dining-room, listening to the music and giggling at the jokes and stories. Lena often said she hoped I would be a traveling man when I grew up. They had a gay life of it; nothing to do but ride about on trains all day and go to theaters when they were in big cities. Behind the hotel there was an old store building, where the salesmen opened their big trunks and spread out their samples on the counters. The Black Hawk merchants went to look

---

1 Probably plum tomatoes, with less juice and thus more suitable for canning, or bottling.
2 Dressmaker supplies, including buttons, ribbons, thread, etc.
3 A salesman for Marshall Field's dry goods business.

at these things and order goods, and Mrs. Thomas, though she was "retail trade," was permitted to see them and to "get ideas." They were all generous, these traveling men; they gave Tiny Soderball handkerchiefs and gloves and ribbons and striped stockings, and so many bottles of perfume and cakes of scented soap that she bestowed some of them on Lena.

One afternoon in the week before Christmas I came upon Lena and her funny, square-headed little brother Chris, standing before the drug-store, gazing in at the wax dolls and blocks and Noah's arks arranged in the frosty show window. The boy had come to town with a neighbor to do his Christmas shopping, for he had money of his own this year. He was only twelve, but that winter he had got the job of sweeping out the Norwegian church and making the fire in it every Sunday morning. A cold job it must have been, too!

We went into Duckford's dry-goods store, and Chris unwrapped all his presents and showed them to me—something for each of the six younger than himself, even a rubber pig for the baby. Lena had given him one of Tiny Soderball's bottles of perfume for his mother, and he thought he would get some handkerchiefs to go with it. They were cheap, and he had n't much money left. We found a tableful of handkerchiefs spread out for view at Duckford's. Chris wanted those with initial letters in the corner, because he had never seen any before. He studied them seriously, while Lena looked over his shoulder, telling him she thought the red letters would hold their color best. He seemed so perplexed that I thought perhaps he had n't enough money, after all. Presently he said gravely,—

"Sister, you know mother's name is Berthe. I don't know if I ought to get B for Berthe, or M for Mother."

Lena patted his bristly head. "I'd get the B, Chrissy. It will please her for you to think about her name. Nobody ever calls her by it now."

That satisfied him. His face cleared at once, and he took three reds and three blues. When the neighbor came in to say that it was time to start, Lena wound Chris's comforter about his neck and turned up his jacket collar—he had no overcoat—and we watched him climb into the wagon and start on his long, cold drive. As we walked together up the windy street, Lena wiped her eyes with the back of her woolen glove. "I get awful homesick for them, all the same," she murmured, as if she were answering some remembered reproach.

VI

Winter comes down savagely over a little town on the prairie. The wind that sweeps in from the open country strips away all the leafy screens that hide one yard from another in summer, and the houses seem to draw closer together. The roofs, that looked so far away across the green tree-tops, now stare you in the face, and they are so much uglier than when their angles were softened by vines and shrubs.

In the morning, when I was fighting my way to school against the wind, I could n't see anything but the road in front of me; but in the late afternoon, when I was coming home, the town looked bleak and desolate to me. The pale, cold light of the winter sunset did not beautify—it was like the light of truth itself. When the smoky clouds hung low in the west and the red sun went down behind them, leaving a pink flush on the snowy roofs and the blue drifts, then the wind sprang up afresh, with a kind of bitter song, as if it said: "This is reality, whether you like it or not. All those frivolities of summer, the light and shadow, the living mask of green that trembled over everything, they were lies, and this is what was underneath. This is the truth." It was as if we were being punished for loving the loveliness of summer.

If I loitered on the playground after school, or went to the post-office for the mail and lingered to hear the gossip about the cigar-stand, it would be growing dark by the time I came home. The sun was gone; the frozen streets stretched long and blue before me; the lights were shining pale in kitchen windows, and I could smell the suppers cooking as I passed. Few people were abroad, and each one of them was hurrying toward a fire. The glowing stoves in the houses were like magnets. When one passed an old man, one could see nothing of his face but a red nose sticking out between a frosted beard and a long plush cap. The young men capered along with their hands in their pockets, and sometimes tried a slide on the icy sidewalk. The children, in their bright hoods and comforters, never walked, but always ran from the moment they left their door, beating their mittens against their sides. When I got as far as the Methodist Church, I was about halfway home. I can remember how glad I was when there happened to be a light in the church, and the painted glass window shone out at us as we came along the frozen street. In the winter bleakness a hunger for color came over people, like the Laplander's craving for fats and sugar. Without knowing why, we used to linger on the sidewalk outside the church when the lamps were lighted early for choir practice or prayer-meeting, shivering and talking until our feet were like lumps of ice. The crude reds and greens and blues of that colored glass held us there.

On winter nights, the lights in the Harlings' windows drew me like the painted glass. Inside that warm, roomy house there was color, too. After supper I used to catch up my cap, stick my hands in my pockets, and dive through the willow hedge as if witches were after me. Of course, if Mr. Harling was at home, if his shadow stood out on the blind of the west room, I did not go in, but turned and walked home by the long way, through the street, wondering what book I should read as I sat down with the two old people.

Such disappointments only gave greater zest to the nights when we acted charades, or had a costume ball in the back parlor, with Sally always dressed like a boy. Frances taught us to dance that winter, and she said, from the first lesson, that Ántonia would make the best dancer among us. On Saturday nights, Mrs. Harling used to play the old operas for us,—"Martha," "Norma," "Rigoletto,"— telling us the story while she played.[1] Every Saturday night was like a party. The parlor, the back parlor, and the dining-room were warm and brightly lighted, with comfortable chairs and sofas, and gay pictures on the walls. One always felt at ease there. Ántonia brought her sewing and sat with us—she was already beginning to make pretty clothes for herself. After the long winter evenings on the prairie, with Ambrosch's sullen silences and her mother's complaints, the Harlings' house seemed, as she said, "like Heaven" to her. She was never too tired to make taffy or chocolate cookies for us. If Sally whispered in her ear, or Charley gave her three winks, Tony would rush into the kitchen and build a fire in the range on which she had already cooked three meals that day.

While we sat in the kitchen waiting for the cookies to bake or the taffy to cool, Nina used to coax Ántonia to tell her stories— about the calf that broke its leg, or how Yulka saved her little turkeys from drowning in the freshet,[2] or about old Christmases and weddings in Bohemia. Nina interpreted the stories about the

---

1 The operas are referred to as "old" because they predate Wagnerian opera.
2 A small freshwater stream; a flooding caused by heavy rain or melting snow.

crêche fancifully, and in spite of our derision she cherished a belief that Christ was born in Bohemia a short time before the Shimerdas left that country. We all liked Tony's stories. Her voice had a peculiarly engaging quality; it was deep, a little husky, and one always heard the breath vibrating behind it. Everything she said seemed to come right out of her heart.

One evening when we were picking out kernels for walnut taffy, Tony told us a new story.

"Mrs. Harling, did you ever hear about what happened up in the Norwegian settlement last summer, when I was thrashing there? We were at Iversons', and I was driving one of the grain wagons."

Mrs. Harling came out and sat down among us. "Could you throw the wheat into the bin yourself, Tony?" She knew what heavy work it was.

"Yes, mam, I did. I could shovel just as fast as that fat Andern boy that drove the other wagon. One day it was just awful hot. When we got back to the field from dinner, we took things kind of easy. The men put in the horses and got the machine going, and Ole Iverson was up on the deck, cutting bands. I was sitting against a straw stack, trying to get some shade. My wagon was n't going out first, and somehow I felt the heat awful that day. The sun was so hot like it was going to burn the world up. After a while I see a man coming across the stubble, and when he got close I see it was a tramp. His toes stuck out of his shoes, and he had n't shaved for a long while, and his eyes was awful red and wild, like he had some sickness. He comes right up and begins to talk like he knows me already. He says: 'The ponds in this country is done got so low a man could n't drownd himself in one of 'em.'

"I told him nobody wanted to drownd themselves, but if we did n't have rain soon we'd have to pump water for the cattle.

"'Oh, cattle,' he says, 'you'll all take care of your cattle! Ain't you got no beer here?' I told him he'd have to go to the Bohemians for beer; the Norwegians did n't have none when they thrashed. 'My God!' he says, 'so it's Norwegians now, is it? I thought this was Americy.'

"Then he goes up to the machine and yells out to Ole Iverson, 'Hello, partner, let me up there. I can cut bands, and I'm tired of trampin'. I won't go no farther.'

"I tried to make signs to Ole, 'cause I thought that man was crazy and might get the machine stopped up. But Ole, he was glad to get down out of the sun and chaff—it gets down your neck and sticks to you something awful when it's hot like that. So Ole jumped down and crawled under one of the wagons for shade, and the tramp got on the machine. He cut bands all right for a few minutes, and then, Mrs. Harling, he waved his hand to me and jumped head-first right into the thrashing machine after the wheat.

"I begun to scream, and the men run to stop the horses, but the belt had sucked him down, and by the time they got her stopped he was all beat and cut to pieces. He was wedged in so tight it was a hard job to get him out, and the machine ain't never worked right since."

"Was he clear dead, Tony?" we cried.

"Was he dead? Well, I guess so! There, now, Nina's all upset. We won't talk about it. Don't you cry, Nina. No old tramp won't get you while Tony's here."

Mrs. Harling spoke up sternly. "Stop crying, Nina, or I'll always send you upstairs when Ántonia tells us about the country. Did they never find out where he came from, Ántonia?"

"Never, mam. He had n't been seen nowhere except in a little town they call Conway. He tried to get beer there, but there was n't any saloon. Maybe he came in on a freight, but the brakeman had n't seen him. They could n't find no letters nor nothing on him; nothing but an old penknife in his pocket and the wishbone of a chicken wrapped up in a piece of paper, and some poetry."

"Some poetry?" we exclaimed.

"I remember," said Frances. "It was 'The Old Oaken Bucket,'[1] cut out of a newspaper and nearly worn out. Ole Iverson brought it into the office and showed it to me."

"Now, was n't that strange, Miss Frances?" Tony asked thoughtfully. "What would anybody want to kill themselves in summer for? In thrashing time, too! It's nice everywhere then."

"So it is, Ántonia," said Mrs. Harling heartily. "Maybe I'll go

---

1 A popular nineteenth-century poem, written by Samuel Woodworth.

> How dear to this heart
> Are the scenes of my childhood,
> When fond recollection
> Presents them to view!
>
> *Refrain:*
> The wide spreading pond,
> And the mill that stood by it,
> The bridge and the rock
> Where the cataract fell.

home and help you thrash next summer. Is n't that taffy nearly ready to eat? I've been smelling it a long while."

There was a basic harmony between Ántonia and her mistress. They had strong, independent natures, both of them. They knew what they liked, and were not always trying to imitate other people. They loved children and animals and music, and rough play and digging in the earth. They liked to prepare rich, hearty food and to see people eat it; to make up soft white beds and to see youngsters asleep in them. They ridiculed conceited people and were quick to help unfortunate ones. Deep down in each of them there was a kind of hearty joviality, a relish of life, not over-delicate, but very invigorating. I never tried to define it, but I was distinctly conscious of it. I could not imagine Ántonia's living for a week in any other house in Black Hawk than the Harlings'.

VII

Winter lies too long in country towns; hangs on until it is stale and shabby, old and sullen. On the farm the weather was the great fact, and men's affairs went on underneath it, as the streams creep under the ice. But in Black Hawk the scene of human life was spread out shrunken and pinched, frozen down to the bare stalk.

Through January and February I went to the river with the Harlings on clear nights, and we skated up to the big island and made bonfires on the frozen sand. But by March the ice was rough and choppy, and the snow on the river bluffs was gray and mournful-looking. I was tired of school, tired of winter clothes, of the rutted streets, of the dirty drifts and the piles of cinders that had lain in the yards so long. There was only one break in the dreary

---

The orchard, the meadow,
The deep tangled wildwood,
And ev'ry loved spot
Which my infancy knew.
Refrain

The old oaken bucket,
The ironbound bucket,
The moss-covered bucket
That hung in the well.
Refrain

monotony of that month; when Blind d'Arnault,[1] the negro pianist, came to town. He gave a concert at the Opera House[2] on Monday night, and he and his manager spent Saturday and Sunday at our comfortable hotel. Mrs. Harling had known d'Arnault for years. She told Ántonia she had better go to see Tiny that Saturday evening, as there would certainly be music at the Boys' Home.

Saturday night after supper I ran downtown to the hotel and slipped quietly into the parlor. The chairs and sofas were already occupied, and the air smelled pleasantly of cigar smoke. The parlor had once been two rooms, and the floor was sway-backed[3] where the partition had been cut away. The wind from without made waves in the long carpet. A coal stove glowed at either end of the room, and the grand piano in the middle stood open.

There was an atmosphere of unusual freedom about the house that night, for Mrs. Gardener had gone to Omaha for a week. Johnnie had been having drinks with the guests until he was rather absent-minded. It was Mrs. Gardener who ran the business and looked after everything. Her husband stood at the desk and welcomed incoming travelers. He was a popular fellow, but no manager.

Mrs. Gardener was admittedly the best-dressed woman in Black Hawk, drove the best horse, and had a smart trap[4] and a little white-and-gold sleigh. She seemed indifferent to her possessions, was not half so solicitous about them as her friends were. She was tall, dark, severe, with something Indian-like in the rigid immobility of her face. Her manner was cold, and she talked little. Guests felt that they were receiving, not conferring, a favor when they stayed at her house. Even the smartest traveling men were flattered when Mrs. Gardener stopped to chat with them for a moment. The patrons of the hotel were divided into two classes; those who had seen Mrs. Gardener's diamonds, and those who had not.

When I stole into the parlor Anson Kirkpatrick, Marshall Field's man, was at the piano, playing airs from a musical comedy then

---

1 Likely a composite of Thomas Green Bethune (1849-1908), known as Blind Tom, and John William Boone (1864-1927), known as Blind Boone. (See Appendix G.6.)
2 Many small towns in Nebraska at this time had an Opera House, used for civic events and traveling shows of all kinds.
3 Concave, or warped.
4 A light, usually two-wheeled spring carriage.

running in Chicago. He was a dapper little Irishman, very vain, homely as a monkey, with friends everywhere, and a sweetheart in every port, like a sailor. I did not know all the men who were sitting about, but I recognized a furniture salesman from Kansas City, a drug man, and Willy O'Reilly, who traveled for a jewelry house and sold musical instruments. The talk was all about good and bad hotels, actors and actresses and musical prodigies. I learned that Mrs. Gardener had gone to Omaha to hear Booth and Barrett,[1] who were to play there next week, and that Mary Anderson was having a great success in "A Winter's Tale," in London.

The door from the office opened, and Johnnie Gardener came in, directing Blind d'Arnault,—he would never consent to be led. He was a heavy, bulky mulatto, on short legs, and he came tapping the floor in front of him with his gold-headed cane. His yellow face was lifted in the light, with a show of white teeth, all grinning, and his shrunken, papery eyelids lay motionless over his blind eyes.

"Good-evening, gentlemen. No ladies here? Good-evening, gentlemen. We going to have a little music? Some of you gentlemen going to play for me this evening?" It was the soft, amiable negro voice, like those I remembered from early childhood, with the note of docile subservience in it. He had the negro head, too; almost no head at all; nothing behind the ears but folds of neck under close-clipped wool. He would have been repulsive if his face had not been so kindly and happy. It was the happiest face I had seen since I left Virginia.

He felt his way directly to the piano. The moment he sat down, I noticed the nervous infirmity of which Mrs. Harling had told me. When he was sitting, or standing still, he swayed back and forth incessantly, like a rocking toy. At the piano, he swayed in time to the music, and when he was not playing, his body kept up this motion, like an empty mill grinding on. He found the pedals and tried them, ran his yellow hands up and down the keys a few times, tinkling off scales, then turned to the company.

"She seems all right, gentlemen. Nothing happened to her since the last time I was here. Mrs. Gardener, she always has this piano tuned up before I come. Now, gentlemen, I expect you've all got grand voices. Seems like we might have some good old plantation songs to-night."

---

1 Edwin Booth (1833-1893) and Lawrence Barrett (1838-1891), both very well-known nineteenth-century actors, as was Mary Anderson (1859-1940).

The men gathered round him, as he began to play "My Old Kentucky Home."[1] They sang one negro melody after another, while the mulatto sat rocking himself, his head thrown back, his yellow face lifted, its shriveled eyelids never fluttering.

He was born in the Far South, on the d'Arnault plantation, where the spirit if not the fact of slavery persisted. When he was three weeks old he had an illness which left him totally blind. As soon as he was old enough to sit up alone and toddle about, another affliction, the nervous motion of his body, became apparent. His mother, a buxom young negro wench who was laundress for the d'Arnaults, concluded that her blind baby was "not right" in his head, and she was ashamed of him. She loved him devotedly, but he was so ugly, with his sunken eyes and his "fidgets," that she hid him away from people. All the dainties she brought down from the "Big House" were for the blind child, and she beat and cuffed her other children whenever she found them teasing him or trying to get his chicken-bone away from him. He began to talk early, remembered everything he heard, and his mammy said he "was n't all wrong." She named him Samson,[2] because he was blind, but on the plantation he was known as "yellow Martha's simple child." He was docile and obedient, but when he was six years old he began to run away from home, always taking the same direction. He felt his way through the lilacs, along the boxwood hedge, up to the south wing of the "Big House," where Miss Nellie d'Arnault practiced the piano every morning. This angered his mother more than anything else he could have done; she was so ashamed of his ugliness that she could n't bear to have white folks see him. Whenever she caught him slipping away from the cabin, she whipped him unmercifully, and told him what dreadful things old Mr. d'Arnault would do to him if he ever found him near the "Big House." But the next time Samson had a chance, he ran away again. If Miss d'Arnault stopped practicing for a moment and went toward the window, she saw this hideous little pickaninny,[3] dressed in an old piece of sacking, standing in the open space between the hollyhock rows, his body rocking automatically, his blind face lifted to the sun and wearing an expression of idiotic rapture. Often she was tempted to tell Martha that the child must be kept at home, but some-

---

1 A popular song written by Stephen Foster (1825-1864).
2 See Judges 16.21. Samson was captured by the Philistines and blinded.
3 A small black child; the term is considered offensive as used by whites.

how the memory of his foolish, happy face deterred her. She remembered that his sense of hearing was nearly all he had,— though it did not occur to her that he might have more of it than other children.

One day Samson was standing thus while Miss Nellie was playing her lesson to her music-master. The windows were open. He heard them get up from the piano, talk a little while, and then leave the room. He heard the door close after them. He crept up to the front windows and stuck his head in: there was no one there. He could always detect the presence of any one in a room. He put one foot over the window sill and straddled it. His mother had told him over and over how his master would give him to the big mastiff[1] if he ever found him "meddling." Samson had got too near the mastiff's kennel once, and had felt his terrible breath in his face. He thought about that, but he pulled in his other foot.

Through the dark he found his way to the Thing, to its mouth. He touched it softly, and it answered softly, kindly. He shivered and stood still. Then he began to feel it all over, ran his finger tips along the slippery sides, embraced the carved legs, tried to get some conception of its shape and size, of the space it occupied in primeval night. It was cold and hard, and like nothing else in his black universe. He went back to its mouth, began at one end of the keyboard and felt his way down into the mellow thunder, as far as he could go. He seemed to know that it must be done with the fingers, not with the fists or the feet. He approached this highly artificial instrument through a mere instinct, and coupled himself to it, as if he knew it was to piece him out and make a whole creature of him. After he had tried over all the sounds, he began to finger out passages from things Miss Nellie had been practicing, passages that were already his, that lay under the bones of his pinched, conical little skull, definite as animal desires. The door opened; Miss Nellie and her music-master stood behind it, but blind Samson, who was so sensitive to presences, did not know they were there. He was feeling out the pattern that lay all ready-made on the big and little keys. When he paused for a moment, because the sound was wrong and he wanted another, Miss Nellie spoke softly. He whirled about in a spasm of terror, leaped forward in the dark, struck his head on the open window, and fell screaming and bleeding to the floor. He had what his mother called a fit. The doctor came and gave him opium.

---

1 The watchdog.

When Samson was well again, his young mistress led him back to the piano. Several teachers experimented with him. They found he had absolute pitch, and a remarkable memory. As a very young child he could repeat, after a fashion, any composition that was played for him. No matter how many wrong notes he struck, he never lost the intention of a passage, he brought the substance of it across by irregular and astonishing means. He wore his teachers out. He could never learn like other people, never acquired any finish. He was always a negro prodigy who played barbarously and wonderfully. As piano playing, it was perhaps abominable, but as music it was something real, vitalized by a sense of rhythm that was stronger than his other physical senses,—that not only filled his dark mind, but worried his body incessantly. To hear him, to watch him, was to see a negro enjoying himself as only a negro can. It was as if all the agreeable sensations possible to creatures of flesh and blood were heaped up on those black and white keys, and he were gloating over them and trickling them through his yellow fingers.

In the middle of a crashing waltz d'Arnault suddenly began to play softly, and, turning to one of the men who stood behind him, whispered, "Somebody dancing in there." He jerked his bullet head toward the dining-room. "I hear little feet,—girls, I 'spect."

Anson Kirkpatrick mounted a chair and peeped over the transom. Springing down, he wrenched open the doors and ran out into the dining-room. Tiny and Lena, Ántonia and Mary Dusak, were waltzing in the middle of the floor. They separated and fled toward the kitchen, giggling.

Kirkpatrick caught Tiny by the elbows. "What's the matter with you girls? Dancing out here by yourselves, when there's a roomful of lonesome men on the other side of the partition! Introduce me to your friends, Tiny."

The girls, still laughing, were trying to escape. Tiny looked alarmed. "Mrs. Gardener would n't like it," she protested. "She'd be awful mad if you was to come out here and dance with us."

"Mrs. Gardener's in Omaha, girl. Now, you're Lena, are you?—and you're Tony and you're Mary. Have I got you all straight?"

O'Reilly and the others began to pile the chairs on the tables. Johnnie Gardener ran in from the office.

"Easy, boys, easy!" he entreated them. "You'll wake the cook, and there'll be the devil to pay for me. She won't hear the music, but she'll be down the minute anything's moved in the dining-room."

"Oh, what do you care, Johnnie? Fire the cook and wire Molly to bring another. Come along, nobody'll tell tales."

Johnnie shook his head. "'S a fact, boys," he said confidentially. "If I take a drink in Black Hawk, Molly knows it in Omaha!"

His guests laughed and slapped him on the shoulder. "Oh, we'll make it all right with Molly. Get your back up, Johnnie."

Molly was Mrs. Gardener's name, of course. "Molly Bawn" was painted in large blue letters on the glossy white side of the hotel bus,[1] and "Molly" was engraved inside Johnnie's ring and on his watch-case—doubtless on his heart, too. He was an affectionate little man, and he thought his wife a wonderful woman; he knew that without her he would hardly be more than a clerk in some other man's hotel.

At a word from Kirkpatrick, d'Arnault spread himself out over the piano, and began to draw the dance music out of it, while the perspiration shone on his short wool and on his uplifted face. He looked like some glistening African god of pleasure, full of strong, savage blood. Whenever the dancers paused to change partners or to catch breath, he would boom out softly, "Who's that goin' back on me? One of these city gentlemen, I bet! Now, you girls, you ain't goin' to let that floor get cold?"

Ántonia seemed frightened at first, and kept looking questioningly at Lena and Tiny over Willy O'Reilly's shoulder. Tiny Soderball was trim and slender, with lively little feet and pretty ankles— she wore her dresses very short. She was quicker in speech, lighter in movement and manner than the other girls. Mary Dusak was broad and brown of countenance, slightly marked by smallpox, but handsome for all that. She had beautiful chestnut hair, coils of it; her forehead was low and smooth, and her commanding dark eyes regarded the world indifferently and fearlessly. She looked bold and resourceful and unscrupulous, and she was all of these. They were handsome girls, had the fresh color of their country up-bringing, and in their eyes that brilliancy which is called,—by no metaphor, alas!—"the light of youth."

D'Arnault played until his manager came and shut the piano. Before he left us, he showed us his gold watch which struck the hours, and a topaz ring, given him by some Russian nobleman who delighted in negro melodies, and had heard d'Arnault play in New Orleans. At last he tapped his way upstairs, after bowing to everybody, docile and happy. I walked home with Ántonia. We

---

1 A horse-drawn omnibus used to carry guests to and from the train depot.

were so excited that we dreaded to go to bed. We lingered a long while at the Harlings' gate, whispering in the cold until the restlessness was slowly chilled out of us.

VIII

The Harling children and I were never happier, never felt more contented and secure, than in the weeks of spring which broke that long winter. We were out all day in the thin sunshine, helping Mrs. Harling and Tony break the ground and plant the garden, dig around the orchard trees, tie up vines and clip the hedges. Every morning, before I was up, I could hear Tony singing in the garden rows. After the apple and cherry trees broke into bloom, we ran about under them, hunting for the new nests the birds were building, throwing clods at each other, and playing hide-and-seek with Nina. Yet the summer which was to change everything was coming nearer every day. When boys and girls are growing up, life can't stand still, not even in the quietest of country towns; and they have to grow up, whether they will or no. That is what their elders are always forgetting.

It must have been in June, for Mrs. Harling and Ántonia were preserving cherries, when I stopped one morning to tell them that a dancing pavilion had come to town. I had seen two drays hauling the canvas and painted poles up from the depot.

That afternoon three cheerful-looking Italians strolled about Black Hawk, looking at everything, and with them was a dark, stout woman who wore a long gold watch chain about her neck and carried a black lace parasol. They seemed especially interested in children and vacant lots. When I overtook them and stopped to say a word, I found them affable and confiding. They told me they worked in Kansas City in the winter, and in summer they went out among the farming towns with their tent and taught dancing. When business fell off in one place, they moved on to another.

The dancing pavilion was put up near the Danish laundry, on a vacant lot surrounded by tall, arched cottonwood trees. It was very much like a merry-go-round tent, with open sides and gay flags flying from the poles. Before the week was over, all the ambitious mothers were sending their children to the afternoon dancing class. At three o'clock one met little girls in white dresses and little boys in the round-collared shirts of the time, hurrying along the sidewalk on their way to the tent. Mrs. Vanni received them at the entrance, always dressed in lavender with a great deal of black lace, her important watch chain lying on her bosom. She wore her hair on the top of her head, built up in a black tower, with red coral combs. When she smiled, she showed two rows of strong, crooked yellow teeth. She taught the little children herself, and her husband, the harpist, taught the older ones.

Often the mothers brought their fancy-work and sat on the shady side of the tent during the lesson. The popcorn man wheeled his glass wagon under the big cottonwood by the door, and lounged in the sun, sure of a good trade when the dancing was over. Mr. Jensen, the Danish laundryman, used to bring a chair from his porch and sit out in the grass plot. Some ragged little boys from the depot sold pop and iced lemonade under a white umbrella at the corner, and made faces at the spruce[1] youngsters who came to dance. That vacant lot soon became the most cheerful place in town. Even on the hottest afternoons the cottonwoods made a rustling shade, and the air smelled of popcorn and melted butter, and Bouncing Bets wilting in the sun. Those hardy flowers had run away from the laundryman's garden, and the grass in the middle of the lot was pink with them.

The Vannis kept exemplary order, and closed every evening at the hour suggested by the City Council. When Mrs. Vanni gave the signal, and the harp struck up "Home, Sweet Home,"[2] all Black Hawk knew it was ten o'clock. You could set your watch by that tune as confidently as by the Round House[3] whistle.

At last there was something to do in those long, empty summer evenings, when the married people sat like images on their front porches, and the boys and girls tramped and tramped the board sidewalks—northward to the edge of the open prairie, south to the depot, then back again to the post-office, the ice-cream parlor, the butcher shop. Now there was a place where the girls could wear their new dresses, and where one could laugh aloud without being reproved by the ensuing silence. That silence seemed to ooze out of the ground, to hang under the foliage of the black maple trees with the bats and shadows. Now it was broken by light-hearted sounds. First the deep purring of Mr. Vanni's harp came in silvery ripples through the blackness of the dusty-smelling night; then the

---

1 Dapper, well-dressed.
2 Music adapted from a Sicilian air by Henry Rowley Bishop and set to John Howard Payne's poem about his childhood in New York.
3 A circular repair house for locomotives, with a turntable in the middle.

violins fell in—one of them was almost like a flute. They called so archly, so seductively, that our feet hurried toward the tent of themselves. Why had n't we had a tent before?

Dancing became popular now, just as roller skating had been the summer before. The Progressive Euchre Club[1] arranged with the Vannis for the exclusive use of the floor on Tuesday and Friday nights. At other times any one could dance who paid his money and was orderly; the railroad men, the Round House mechanics, the delivery boys, the iceman, the farmhands who lived near enough to ride into town after their day's work was over.

I never missed a Saturday night dance. The tent was open until midnight then. The country boys came in from farms eight and ten miles away, and all the country girls were on the floor,—Ántonia and Lena and Tiny, and the Danish laundry girls and their friends. I was not the only boy who found these dances gayer than the others. The young men who belonged to the Progressive Euchre Club used to drop in late and risk a tiff with their sweethearts and general condemnation for a waltz with "the hired girls."

IX

There was a curious social situation in Black Hawk. All the young men felt the attraction of the fine, well-set-up country girls who had come to town to earn a living, and, in nearly every case, to help the father struggle out of debt, or to make it possible for the younger children of the family to go to school.

Those girls had grown up in the first bitter-hard times, and had got little schooling themselves. But the younger brothers and sisters, for whom they made such sacrifices and who have had "advantages," never seem to me, when I meet them now, half as interesting or as well educated. The older girls, who helped to break up the wild sod, learned so much from life, from poverty, from their mothers and grandmothers; they had all, like Ántonia, been early awakened and made observant by coming at a tender age from an old country to a new. I can remember a score of these country girls who were in service in Black Hawk during the few years I lived there, and I can member something unusual and

---

1 Progressive euchre is a form of the popular card game in which players
   progress from one table to the next until the winner reaches the Head
   table. Progression from table to table makes it a successful social game.

engaging about each of them. Physically they were almost a race apart, and out-of-door work had given them a vigor which, when they got over their first shyness on coming to town, developed into a positive carriage and freedom of movement, and made them conspicuous among Black Hawk women.

That was before the day of High-School athletics. Girls who had to walk more than half a mile to school were pitied. There was not a tennis court in the town; physical exercise was thought rather inelegant for the daughters of well-to-do families. Some of the High-School girls were jolly and pretty, but they stayed indoors in winter because of the cold, and in summer because of the heat. When one danced with them their bodies never moved inside their clothes; their muscles seemed to ask but one thing—not to be disturbed. I remember those girls merely as faces in the schoolroom, gay and rosy, or listless and dull, cut off below the shoulders, like cherubs, by the ink-smeared tops of the high desks that were surely put there to make us round-shouldered and hollow-chested.

The daughters of Black Hawk merchants had a confident, uninquiring belief that they were "refined," and that the country girls, who "worked out," were not. The American farmers in our county were quite as hard-pressed as their neighbors from other countries. All alike had come to Nebraska with little capital and no knowledge of the soil they must subdue. All had borrowed money on their land. But no matter in what straits the Pennsylvanian or Virginian found himself, he would not let his daughters go out into service. Unless his girls could teach a country school, they sat at home in poverty. The Bohemian and Scandinavian girls could not get positions as teachers, because they had had no opportunity to learn the language. Determined to help in the struggle to clear the homestead from debt, they had no alternative but to go into service. Some of them, after they came to town, remained as serious and as discreet in behavior as they had been when they ploughed and herded on their father's farm. Others, like the three Bohemian Marys, tried to make up for the years of youth they had lost. But every one of them did what she had set out to do, and sent home those hard-earned dollars. The girls I knew were always helping to pay for ploughs and reapers, brood-sows,[1] or steers to fatten.

One result of this family solidarity was that the foreign farmers in our county were the first to become prosperous. After the

---

1 Pigs kept for breeding.

fathers were out of debt, the daughters married the sons of neighbors,—usually of like nationality,—and the girls who once worked
in Black Hawk kitchens are to-day managing big farms and fine
families of their own; their children are better off than the children
of the town women they used to serve.

I thought the attitude of the town people toward these girls
very stupid. If I told my schoolmates that Lena Lingard's grandfather was a clergyman, and much respected in Norway, they looked
at me blankly. What did it matter? All foreigners were ignorant
people who could n't speak English. There was not a man in Black
Hawk who had the intelligence or cultivation, much less the personal distinction, of Ántonia's father. Yet people saw no difference
between her and the three Marys; they were all Bohemians, all
"hired girls."

I always knew I should live long enough to see my country
girls come into their own, and I have. To-day the best that a
harassed Black Hawk merchant can hope for is to sell provisions
and farm machinery and automobiles to the rich farms where that
first crop of stalwart Bohemian and Scandinavian girls are now the
mistresses.

The Black Hawk boys looked forward to marrying Black Hawk
girls, and living in a brand-new little house with best chairs that
must not be sat upon, and hand-painted china that must not be
used. But sometimes a young fellow would look up from his
ledger, or out through the grating of his father's bank, and let his
eyes follow Lena Lingard, as she passed the window with her slow,
undulating walk, or Tiny Soderball, tripping by in her short skirt
and striped stockings.

The country girls were considered a menace to the social order.
Their beauty shone out too boldly against a conventional background. But anxious mothers need have felt no alarm. They mis-
took the mettle of their sons. The respect for respectability was
stronger than any desire in Black Hawk youth.

Our young man of position was like the son of a royal house;
the boy who swept out his office or drove his delivery wagon
might frolic with the jolly country girls, but he himself must sit all
evening in a plush parlor where conversation dragged so percepti-
bly that the father often came in and made blundering efforts to
warm up the atmosphere. On his way home from his dull call, he
would perhaps meet Tony and Lena, coming along the sidewalk
whispering to each other, or the three Bohemian Marys in their
long plush coats and caps, comporting themselves with a dignity

that only made their eventful histories the more piquant. If he went to the hotel to see a traveling man on business, there was Tiny, arching her shoulders at him like a kitten. If he went into the laundry to get his collars, there were the four Danish girls, smiling up from their ironing-boards, with their white throats and their pink cheeks.

The three Marys were the heroines of a cycle of scandalous stories, which the old men were fond of relating as they sat about the cigar-stand in the drug-store. Mary Dusak had been housekeeper for a bachelor rancher from Boston, and after several years in his service she was forced to retire from the world for a short time. Later she came back to town to take the place of her friend, Mary Svoboda, who was similarly embarrassed. The three Marys were considered as dangerous as high explosives to have about the kitchen, yet they were such good cooks and such admirable housekeepers that they never had to look for a place.

The Vannis' tent brought the town boys and the country girls together on neutral ground. Sylvester Lovett, who was cashier in his father's bank, always found his way to the tent on Saturday night. He took all the dances Lena Lingard would give him, and even grew bold enough to walk home with her. If his sisters or their friends happened to be among the onlookers on "popular nights," Sylvester stood back in the shadow under the cottonwood trees, smoking and watching Lena with a harassed expression. Several times I stumbled upon him there in the dark, and I felt rather sorry for him. He reminded me of Ole Benson, who used to sit on the draw-side and watch Lena herd her cattle. Later in the summer, when Lena went home for a week to visit her mother, I heard from Ántonia that young Lovett drove all the way out there to see her, and took her buggy-riding. In my ingenuousness I hoped that Sylvester would marry Lena, and thus give all the country girls a better position in the town.

Sylvester dallied about Lena until he began to make mistakes in his work; had to stay at the bank until after dark to make his books balance. He was daft about her, and every one knew it. To escape from his predicament he ran away with a widow six years older than himself, who owned a half-section. This remedy worked, apparently. He never looked at Lena again, nor lifted his eyes as he ceremoniously tipped his hat when he happened to meet her on the sidewalk.

So that was what they were like, I thought, these white-handed, high-collared clerks and bookkeepers! I used to glare at young

Lovett from a distance and only wished I had some way of showing my contempt for him.

X

It was at the Vannis' tent that Ántonia was discovered. Hitherto she had been looked upon more as a ward of the Harlings than as one of the "hired girls." She had lived in their house and yard and garden; her thoughts never seemed to stray outside that little kingdom. But after the tent came to town she began to go about with Tiny and Lena and their friends. The Vannis often said that Ántonia was the best dancer of them all. I sometimes heard murmurs in the crowd outside the pavilion that Mrs. Harling would soon have her hands full with that girl. The young men began to joke with each other about "the Harlings' Tony" as they did about "the Marshalls' Anna" or "the Gardeners' Tiny."

Ántonia talked and thought of nothing but the tent. She hummed the dance tunes all day. When supper was late, she hurried with her dishes, dropped and smashed them in her excitement. At the first call of the music, she became irresponsible. If she had n't time to dress, she merely flung off her apron and shot out of the kitchen door. Sometimes I went with her; the moment the lighted tent came into view she would break into a run, like a boy. There were always partners waiting for her; she began to dance before she got her breath.

Ántonia's success at the tent had its consequences. The iceman lingered too long now, when he came into the covered porch to fill the refrigerator. The delivery boys hung about the kitchen when they brought the groceries. Young farmers who were in town for Saturday came tramping through the yard to the back door to engage dances, or to invite Tony to parties and picnics. Lena and Norwegian Anna dropped in to help her with her work, so that she could get away early. The boys who brought her home after the dances sometimes laughed at the back gate and wakened Mr. Harling from his first sleep. A crisis was inevitable.

One Saturday night Mr. Harling had gone down to the cellar for beer. As he came up the stairs in the dark, he heard scuffling on the back porch, and then the sound of a vigorous slap. He looked out through the side door in time to see a pair of long legs vaulting over the picket fence. Ántonia was standing there, angry and excited. Young Harry Paine, who was to marry his employer's daughter on Monday, had come to the tent with a crowd of friends and danced all evening. Afterward, he begged Ántonia to let him walk home with her. She said she supposed he was a nice young man, as he was one of Miss Frances's friends, and she did n't mind. On the back porch he tried to kiss her, and when she protested,—because he was going to be married on Monday,—he caught her and kissed her until she got one hand free and slapped him.

Mr. Harling put his beer bottles down on the table. "This is what I've been expecting, Ántonia. You've been going with girls who have a reputation for being free and easy, and now you've got the same reputation. I won't have this and that fellow tramping about my back yard all the time. This is the end of it, to-night. It stops, short. You can quit going to these dances, or you can hunt another place. Think it over."

The next morning when Mrs. Harling and Frances tried to reason with Ántonia, they found her agitated but determined. "Stop going to the tent?" she panted. "I would n't think of it for a minute! My own father could n't make me stop! Mr. Harling ain't my boss outside my work. I won't give up my friends, either. The boys I go with are nice fellows. I thought Mr. Paine was all right, too, because he used to come here. I guess I gave him a red face for his wedding, all right!" she blazed out indignantly.

"You'll have to do one thing or the other, Ántonia," Mrs. Harling told her decidedly. "I can't go back on what Mr. Harling has said. This is his house."

"Then I'll just leave, Mrs. Harling. Lena's been wanting me to get a place closer to her for a long while. Mary Svoboda's going away from the Cutters' to work at the hotel, and I can have her place."

Mrs. Harling rose from her chair. "Ántonia, if you go to the Cutters' to work, you cannot come back to this house again. You know what that man is. It will be the ruin of you."

Tony snatched up the tea-kettle and began to pour boiling water over the glasses, laughing excitedly. "Oh, I can take care of myself! I'm a lot stronger than Cutter is. They pay four dollars there, and there's no children. The work's nothing; I can have every evening, and be out a lot in the afternoons."

"I thought you liked children. Tony, what's come over you?"

"I don't know, something has." Ántonia tossed her head and set her jaw. "A girl like me has got to take her good times when she can. Maybe there won't be any tent next year. I guess I want to have my fling, like the other girls."

Mrs. Harling gave a short, harsh laugh. "If you go to work for the Cutters, you're likely to have a fling that you won't get up from in a hurry."

Frances said, when she told grandmother and me about this scene, that every pan and plate and cup on the shelves trembled when her mother walked out of the kitchen. Mrs. Harling declared bitterly that she wished she had never let herself get fond of Ántonia.

XI

Wick Cutter was the money-lender who had fleeced poor Russian Peter. When a farmer once got into the habit of going to Cutter, it was like gambling or the lottery; in an hour of discouragement he went back.

Cutter's first name was Wycliffe,[1] and he liked to talk about his pious bringing-up. He contributed regularly to the Protestant churches, "for sentiment's sake," as he said with a flourish of the hand. He came from a town in Iowa where there were a great many Swedes, and could speak a little Swedish, which gave him a great advantage with the early Scandinavian settlers.

In every frontier settlement there are men who have come there to escape restraint. Cutter was one of the "fast set" of Black Hawk business men. He was an inveterate gambler, though a poor loser. When we saw a light burning in his office late at night, we knew that a game of poker was going on. Cutter boasted that he never drank anything stronger than sherry, and he said he got his start in life by saving the money that other young men spent for cigars. He was full of moral maxims for boys. When he came to our house on business, he quoted "Poor Richard's Almanack"[2] to me, and told me he was delighted to find a town boy who could milk a cow. He was particularly affable to grandmother, and whenever they met he would begin at once to talk about "the good old times" and simple living. I detested his pink, bald head, and his yellow whiskers, always soft and glistening. It was said he brushed them every night, as a woman does her hair. His white teeth looked factory-made. His skin was red and rough, as if from perpetual sunburn; he often went away to hot springs to take mud baths. He was notoriously

---

1 John Wycliffe was a religious reformer in the fourteenth century.
2 Published in the eighteenth century by Benjamin Franklin, and containing advice in the form of aphorisms.

dissolute with women. Two Swedish girls who had lived in his house were the worse for the experience. One of them he had taken to Omaha and established in the business for which he had fitted her. He still visited her.

Cutter lived in a state of perpetual warfare with his wife, and yet, apparently, they never thought of separating. They dwelt in a fussy, scroll-work house, painted white and buried in thick evergreens, with a fussy white fence and barn. Cutter thought he knew a great deal about horses, and usually had a colt which he was training for the track. On Sunday mornings one could see him out at the fair grounds, speeding around the race-course in his trotting-buggy, wearing yellow gloves and a black-and-white-check traveling cap, his whiskers blowing back in the breeze. If there were any boys about, Cutter would offer one of them a quarter to hold the stop-watch, and then drive off, saying he had no change and would "fix it up next time." No one could cut his lawn or wash his buggy to suit him. He was so fastidious and prim about his place that a boy would go to a good deal of trouble to throw a dead cat into his back yard, or to dump a sackful of tin cans in his alley. It was a peculiar combination of old-maidishness and licentiousness that made Cutter seem so despicable.

He had certainly met his match when he married Mrs. Cutter. She was a terrifying looking person; almost a giantess in height, raw-boned, with iron-gray hair, a face always flushed, and prominent, hysterical eyes. When she meant to be entertaining and agreeable, she nodded her head incessantly and snapped her eyes at one. Her teeth were long and curved, like a horse's; people said babies always cried if she smiled at them. Her face had a kind of fascination for me; it was the very color and shape of anger. There was a gleam of something akin to insanity in her full, intense eyes. She was formal in manner, and made calls in rustling, steel-gray brocades[1] and a tall bonnet with bristling aigrettes.[2]

Mrs. Cutter painted china so assiduously that even her washbowls and pitchers, and her husband's shaving-mug, were covered with violets and lilies. Once when Cutter was exhibiting some of his wife's china to a caller, he dropped a piece. Mrs. Cutter put her handkerchief to her lips as if she were going to faint and said

---

1 A fabric woven with raised patterns.
2 An egret's plume, a tuft of feathers, or other ornament worn on the head.

grandly: "Mr. Cutter, you have broken all the Commandments—spare the finger-bowls!"

They quarreled from the moment Cutter came into the house until they went to bed at night, and their hired girls reported these scenes to the town at large. Mrs. Cutter had several times cut paragraphs about unfaithful husbands out of the newspapers and mailed them to Cutter in a disguised handwriting. Cutter would come home at noon, find the mutilated journal in the paper-rack, and triumphantly fit the clipping into the space from which it had been cut. Those two could quarrel all morning about whether he ought to put on his heavy or his light underwear, and all evening about whether he had taken cold or not.

The Cutters had major as well as minor subjects for dispute. The chief of these was the question of inheritance: Mrs. Cutter told her husband it was plainly his fault they had no children. He insisted that Mrs. Cutter had purposely remained childless, with the determination to outlive him and to share his property with her "people," whom he detested. To this she would reply that unless he changed his mode of life, she would certainly outlive him. After listening to her insinuations about his physical soundness, Cutter would resume his dumb-bell practice for a month, or rise daily at the hour when his wife most liked to sleep, dress noisily, and drive out to the track with his trotting-horse.

Once when they had quarreled about household expenses, Mrs. Cutter put on her brocade and went among their friends soliciting orders for painted china, saying that Mr. Cutter had compelled her "to live by her brush." Cutter was n't shamed as she had expected; he was delighted!

Cutter often threatened to chop down the cedar trees which half-buried the house. His wife declared she would leave him if she were stripped of the "privacy" which she felt these trees afforded her. That was his opportunity, surely; but he never cut down the trees. The Cutters seemed to find their relations to each other interesting and stimulating, and certainly the rest of us found them so. Wick Cutter was different from any other rascal I have ever known, but I have found Mrs. Cutters all over the world; sometimes founding new religions, sometimes being forcibly fed[1]—easily recognizable, even when superficially tamed.

---

1   A person on a hungerstrike, protesting conditions or treatment, might be "forcibly fed" to counter the action. Mrs. Cutters possesses, to the narrator, a radical or oppositional temperament.

After Ántonia went to live with the Cutters, she seemed to care about nothing but picnics and parties and having a good time. When she was not going to a dance, she sewed until midnight. Her new clothes were the subject of caustic comment. Under Lena's direction she copied Mrs. Gardener's new party dress and Mrs. Smith's street costume so ingeniously in cheap materials that those ladies were greatly annoyed, and Mrs. Cutter, who was jealous of them, was secretly pleased.

Tony wore gloves now, and high-heeled shoes and feathered bonnets, and she went downtown nearly every afternoon with Tiny and Lena and the Marshalls' Norwegian Anna. We High-School boys used to linger on the playground at the afternoon recess to watch them as they came tripping down the hill along the board sidewalk, two and two. They were growing prettier every day, but as they passed us, I used to think with pride that Ántonia, like Snow-White in the fairy tale, was still "fairest of them all."

Being a Senior now, I got away from school early. Sometimes I overtook the girls downtown and coaxed them into the ice-cream parlor, where they would sit chattering and laughing, telling me all the news from the country. I remember how angry Tiny Soderball made me one afternoon. She declared she had heard grandmother was going to make a Baptist preacher of me. "I guess you'll have to stop dancing and wear a white necktie then. Won't he look funny, girls?"

Lena laughed. "You'll have to hurry up, Jim. If you're going to be a preacher, I want you to marry me. You must promise to marry us all, and then baptize the babies."

Norwegian Anna, always dignified, looked at her reprovingly.

"Baptists don't believe in christening babies,[1] do they, Jim?"

I told her I did n't know what they believed, and did n't care, and that I certainly was n't going to be a preacher.

"That's too bad," Tiny simpered. She was in a teasing mood. "You'd make such a good one. You're so studious. Maybe you'd like to be a professor. You used to teach Tony, did n't you?"

Ántonia broke in. "I've set my heart on Jim being a doctor. You'd be good with sick people, Jim. Your grandmother's trained you up so nice. My papa always said you were an awful smart boy."

---

1 Baptists practice adult baptism.

I said I was going to be whatever I pleased. "Won't you be surprised, Miss Tiny, if I turn out to be a regular devil of a fellow?"

They laughed until a glance from Norwegian Anna checked them; the High-School Principal had just come into the front part of the shop to buy bread for supper. Anna knew the whisper was going about that I was a sly one. People said there must be something queer about a boy who showed no interest in girls of his own age, but who could be lively enough when he was with Tony and Lena or the three Marys.

The enthusiasm for the dance, which the Vannis had kindled, did not at once die out. After the tent left town, the Euchre Club became the Owl Club, and gave dances in the Masonic Hall[1] once a week. I was invited to join, but declined. I was moody and restless that winter, and tired of the people I saw every day. Charley Harling was already at Annapolis, while I was still sitting in Black Hawk, answering to my name at roll-call every morning, rising from my desk at the sound of a bell and marching out like the grammar-school children. Mrs. Harling was a little cool toward me, because I continued to champion Ántonia. What was there for me to do after supper? Usually I had learned next day's lessons by the time I left the school building, and I could n't sit still and read forever.

In the evening I used to prowl about, hunting for diversion. There lay the familiar streets, frozen with snow or liquid with mud. They led to the houses of good people who were putting the babies to bed, or simply sitting still before the parlor stove, digesting their supper. Black Hawk had two saloons. One of them was admitted, even by the church people, to be as respectable as a saloon could be. Handsome Anton Jelinek, who had rented his homestead and come to town, was the proprietor. In his saloon there were long tables where the Bohemian and German farmers could eat the lunches they brought from home while they drank their beer. Jelinek kept rye bread on hand, and smoked fish and strong imported cheeses to please the foreign palate. I liked to drop into his bar-room and listen to the talk. But one day he overtook me on the street and clapped me on the shoulder.

---

1 Masons are a fraternal organization.

"Jim," he said, "I am good friends with you and I always like to see you. But you know how the church people think about saloons. Your grandpa has always treated me fine, and I don't like to have you come into my place, because I know he don't like it, and it puts me in bad with him."

So I was shut out of that.

One could hang about the drug-store, and listen to the old men who sat there every evening, talking politics and telling raw stories. One could go to the cigar factory and chat with the old German who raised canaries for sale, and look at his stuffed birds. But whatever you began with him, the talk went back to taxidermy. There was the depot, of course; I often went down to see the night train come in, and afterward sat awhile with the disconsolate telegrapher who was always hoping to be transferred to Omaha or Denver, "where there was some life." He was sure to bring out his pictures of actresses and dancers. He got them with cigarette coupons, and nearly smoked himself to death to possess these desired forms and faces. For a change, one could talk to the station agent; but he was another malcontent; spent all his spare time writing letters to officials requesting a transfer. He wanted to get back to Wyoming where he could go trout-fishing on Sundays. He used to say "there was nothing in life for him but trout streams, ever since he'd lost his twins."

These were the distractions I had to choose from. There were no other lights burning downtown after nine o'clock. On starlight nights I used to pace up and down those long, cold streets, scowling at the little, sleeping houses on either side, with their storm-windows and covered back porches. They were flimsy shelters, most of them poorly built of light wood, with spindle porch-posts horribly mutilated by the turning-lathe. Yet for all their frailness, how much jealousy and envy and unhappiness some of them managed to contain! The life that went on in them seemed to me made up of evasions and negations; shifts to save cooking, to save washing and cleaning, devices to propitiate the tongue of gossip. This guarded mode of existence was like living under a tyranny. People's speech, their voices, their very glances, became furtive and repressed. Every individual taste, every natural appetite, was bridled by caution. The people asleep in those houses, I thought, tried to live like the mice in their own kitchens; to make no noise, to leave no trace, to slip over the surface of things in the dark. The growing piles of ashes and cinders in the back yards were the only evidence that the wasteful, consuming process of life went on at all.

On Tuesday nights the Owl Club danced; then there was a little stir in the streets, and here and there one could see a lighted window until midnight. But the next night all was dark again.

After I refused to join "the Owls," as they were called, I made a bold resolve to go to the Saturday night dances at Firemen's Hall. I knew it would be useless to acquaint my elders with any such plan. Grandfather did n't approve of dancing anyway; he would only say that if I wanted to dance I could go to the Masonic Hall, among "the people we knew." It was just my point that I saw altogether too much of the people we knew.

My bedroom was on the ground floor, and as I studied there, I had a stove in it. I used to retire to my room early on Saturday night, change my shirt and collar and put on my Sunday coat. I waited until all was quiet and the old people were asleep, then raised my window, climbed out, and went softly through the yard. The first time I deceived my grandparents I felt rather shabby, perhaps even the second time, but I soon ceased to think about it.

The dance at the Firemen's Hall was the one thing I looked forward to all the week. There I met the same people I used to see at the Vannis' tent. Sometimes there were Bohemians from Wilber, or German boys who came down on the afternoon freight from Bismarck. Tony and Lena and Tiny were always there, and the three Bohemian Marys, and the Danish laundry girls.

The four Danish girls lived with the laundryman and his wife in their house behind the laundry, with a big garden where the clothes were hung out to dry. The laundryman was a kind, wise old fellow, who paid his girls well, looked out for them, and gave them a good home. He told me once that his own daughter died just as she was getting old enough to help her mother, and that he had been "trying to make up for it ever since." On summer afternoons he used to sit for hours on the sidewalk in front of his laundry, his newspaper lying on his knee, watching his girls through the big open window while they ironed and talked in Danish. The clouds of white dust that blew up the street, the gusts of hot wind that withered his vegetable garden, never disturbed his calm. His droll expression seemed to say that he had found the secret of contentment. Morning and evening he drove about in his spring wagon,[1]

---

1 A horse-drawn wagon with elliptical springs and removable seats to transport passengers or products.

distributing freshly ironed clothes, and collecting bags of linen that cried out for his suds and sunny drying-lines. His girls never looked so pretty at the dances as they did standing by the ironing-board, or over the tubs, washing the fine pieces, their white arms and throats bare, their cheeks bright as the brightest wild roses, their gold hair moist with the steam or the heat and curling in little damp spirals about their ears. They had not learned much English, and were not so ambitious as Tony or Lena; but they were kind, simple girls and they were always happy. When one danced with them, one smelled their clean, freshly ironed clothes that had been put away with rosemary leaves from Mr. Jensen's garden.

There were never girls enough to go round at those dances, but every one wanted a turn with Tony and Lena. Lena moved without exertion, rather indolently, and her hand often accented the rhythm softly on her partner's shoulder. She smiled if one spoke to her, but seldom answered. The music seemed to put her into a soft, waking dream, and her violet-colored eyes looked sleepily and confidingly at one from under her long lashes. When she sighed she exhaled a heavy perfume of sachet powder. To dance "Home, Sweet Home," with Lena was like coming in with the tide. She danced every dance like a waltz, and it was always the same waltz—the waltz of coming home to something, of inevitable, fated return. After a while one got restless under it, as one does under the heat of a soft, sultry summer day.

When you spun out into the floor with Tony, you did n't return to anything. You set out every time upon a new adventure: I liked to schottische[1] with her; she had so much spring and variety, and was always putting in new steps and slides. She taught me to dance against and around the hard-and-fast beat of the music. If, instead of going to the end of the railroad, old Mr. Shimerda had stayed in New York and picked up a living with his fiddle, how different Ántonia's life might have been!

Ántonia often went to the dances with Larry Donovan, a passenger conductor who was a kind of professional ladies' man, as we said. I remember how admiringly all the boys looked at her the night she first wore her velveteen dress, made like Mrs. Gardener's black velvet. She was lovely to see, with her eyes shining, and her lips always a little parted when she danced. That constant, dark color in her cheeks never changed.

---

1 A dance resembling a polka.

One evening when Donovan was out on his run, Ántonia came to the hall with Norwegian Anna and her young man, and that night I took her home. When we were in the Cutters' yard, sheltered by the evergreens, I told ·her she must kiss me good-night.

"Why, sure, Jim." A moment later she drew her face away and whispered indignantly, "Why, Jim! You know you ain't right to kiss me like that. I'll tell your grandmother on you!"

"Lena Lingard lets me kiss her," I retorted, "and I'm not half as fond of her as I am of you."

"Lena does?" Tony gasped. "If she's up to any of her nonsense with you, I'll scratch her eyes out!" She took my arm again and we walked out of the gate and up and down the sidewalk. "Now, don't you go and be a fool like some of these town boys. You're not going to sit around here and whittle store-boxes and tell stories all your life. You are going away to school and make something of yourself. I'm just awful proud of you. You won't go and get mixed up with the Swedes, will you?"

"I don't care anything about any of them but you," I said. "And you'll always treat me like a kid, I suppose."

She laughed and threw her arms around me. "I expect I will, but you're a kid I'm awful fond of, anyhow! You can like me all you want to, but if I see you hanging round with Lena much, I'll go to your grandmother, as sure as your name's Jim Burden! Lena's all right, only—well, you know yourself she's soft that way. She can't help it. It's natural to her."

If she was proud of me, I was so proud of her that I carried my head high as I emerged from the dark cedars and shut the Cutters' gate softly behind me. Her warm, sweet face, her kind arms, and the true heart in her; she was, oh, she was still my Ántonia! I looked with contempt at the dark, silent little houses about me as I walked home, and thought of the stupid young men who were asleep in some of them. I knew where the real women were, though I was only a boy; and I would not be afraid of them, either!

I hated to enter the still house when I went home from the dances, and it was long before I could get to sleep. Toward morning I used to have pleasant dreams: sometimes Tony and I were out in the country, sliding down straw stacks as we used to do; climbing up the yellow mountains over and over, and slipping down the smooth sides into soft piles of chaff.

One dream I dreamed a great many times, and it was always the same. I was in a harvest-field full of shocks, and I was lying against one of them. Lena Lingard came across the stubble barefoot, in a short skirt, with a curved reaping-hook[1] in her hand, and she was flushed like the dawn, with a kind of luminous rosiness all about her. She sat down beside me, turned to me with a soft sigh and said, "Now they are all gone, and I can kiss you as much as I like."

I used to wish I could have this flattering dream about Ántonia, but I never did.

XIII

I noticed one afternoon that grandmother had been crying. Her feet seemed to drag as she moved about the house, and I got up from the table where I was studying and went to her, asking if she did n't feel well, and if I could n't help her with her work.

"No, thank you, Jim. I'm troubled, but I guess I'm well enough. Getting a little rusty in the bones, maybe," she added bitterly.

I stood hesitating. "What are you fretting about, grandmother? Has grandfather lost any money?"

"No, it ain't money. I wish it was. But I've heard things. You must 'a' known it would come back to me sometime." She dropped into a chair, and covering her face with her apron, began to cry. "Jim," she said, "I was never one that claimed old folks could bring up their grandchildren. But it came about so, there was n't any other way for you, it seemed like."

I put my arms around her. I could n't bear to see her cry.

"What is it, grandmother? Is it the Firemen's dances?"

She nodded.

"I'm sorry I sneaked off like that. But there's nothing wrong about the dances, and I have n't done anything wrong. I like all those country girls, and I like to dance with them. That's all there is to it."

"But it ain't right to deceive us, son, and it brings blame on us. People say you are growing up to be a bad boy, and that ain't just to us."

"I don't care what they say about me, but if it hurts you, that settles it. I won't go to the Firemen's Hall again."

I kept my promise, of course, but I found the spring months dull enough. I sat at home with the old people in the evenings now, reading Latin that was not in our High-School course. I had made

1 A sickle.

up my mind to do a lot of college requirement work in the summer, and to enter the freshman class at the University without conditions[1] in the fall. I wanted to get away as soon as possible.

Disapprobation hurt me, I found,—even that of people whom I did not admire. As the spring came on, I grew more and more lonely, and fell back on the telegrapher and the cigar-maker and his canaries for companionship. I remember I took a melancholy pleasure in hanging a May-basket[2] for Nina Harling that spring. I bought the flowers from an old German woman who always had more window plants than any one else, and spent an afternoon trimming a little work-basket. When dusk came on, and the new moon hung in the sky, I went quietly to the Harlings' front door with my offering, rang the bell, and then ran away as was the custom. Through the willow hedge I could hear Nina's cries of delight, and I felt comforted.

On those warm, soft spring evenings I often lingered downtown to walk home with Frances, and talked to her about my plans and about the reading I was doing. One evening she said she thought Mrs. Harling was not seriously offended with me.

"Mama is as broad-minded as mothers ever are, I guess. But you know she was hurt about Ántonia, and she can't understand why you like to be with Tiny and Lena better than with the girls of your own set."

"Can you?" I asked bluntly.

Frances laughed. "Yes, I think I can. You knew them in the country, and you like to take sides. In some ways you're older than boys of your age. It will be all right with mama after you pass your college examinations and she sees you're in earnest."

"If you were a boy," I persisted, "you would n't belong to the Owl Club, either. You'd be just like me."

She shook her head. "I would and I would n't. I expect I know the country girls better than you do. You always put a kind of glamour over them. The trouble with you, Jim, is that you're romantic. Mama's going to your Commencement. She asked me the other

---

1 High schools in small prairie towns at this time often did not have academic programs sufficient for college preparation, and graduates would be required to take an examination to gain admission. Jim is studying for the entrance exam.
2 A small basket containing flowers, or a gift, hung on the door of a favored person, like a Valentine, on May 1.

day if I knew what your oration is to be about. She wants you to do well."

I thought my oration very good. It stated with fervor a great many things I had lately discovered. Mrs. Harling came to the Opera House to hear the Commencement exercises, and I looked at her most of the time while I made my speech. Her keen, intelligent eyes never left my face. Afterward she came back to the dressing-room where we stood, with our diplomas in our hands, walked up to me, and said heartily: "You surprised me, Jim. I did n't believe you could do as well as that. You did n't get that speech out of books." Among my graduation presents there was a silk umbrella from Mrs. Harling, with my name on the handle.

I walked home from the Opera House alone. As I passed the Methodist Church, I saw three white figures ahead of me, pacing up and down under the arching maple trees, where the moonlight filtered through the lush June foliage. They hurried toward me; they were waiting for me—Lena and Tony and Anna Hansen.

"Oh, Jim, it was splendid!" Tony was breathing hard, as she always did when her feelings outran her language. "There ain't a lawyer in Black Hawk could make a speech like that. I just stopped your grandpa and said so to him. He won't tell you, but he told us he was awful surprised himself, did n't he, girls?"

Lena sidled up to me and said teasingly. "What made you so solemn? I thought you were scared. I was sure you'd forget."

Anna spoke wistfully. "It must make you happy, Jim, to have fine thoughts like that in your mind all the time, and to have words to put them in. I always wanted to go to school, you know."

"Oh, I just sat there and wished my papa could hear you! Jim,"—Ántonia took hold of my coat lapels,—"there was something in your speech that made me think so about my papa!"

"I thought about your papa when I wrote my speech, Tony," I said. "I dedicated it to him."

She threw her arms around me, and her dear face was all wet with tears.

I stood watching their white dresses glimmer smaller and smaller down the sidewalk as they went away. I have had no other success that pulled at my heartstrings like that one.

XIV

The day after Commencement I moved my books and desk upstairs, to an empty room where I should be undisturbed, and I fell to studying in earnest. I worked off a year's trigonometry that summer, and began Virgil alone. Morning after morning I used to pace up and down my sunny little room, looking off at the distant river bluffs and the roll of the blond pastures between, scanning the Æneid[1] aloud and committing long passages to memory. Sometimes in the evening Mrs. Harling called to me as I passed her gate, and asked me to come in and let her play for me. She was lonely for Charley, she said, and liked to have a boy about. Whenever my grandparents had misgivings, and began to wonder whether I was not too young to go off to college alone, Mrs. Harling took up my cause vigorously. Grandfather had such respect for her judgment that I knew he would not go against her.

I had only one holiday that summer. It was in July. I met Ántonia downtown on Saturday afternoon, and learned that she and Tiny and Lena were going to the river next day with Anna Hansen—the elder was all in bloom now, and Anna wanted to make elder-blow wine.

"Anna's to drive us down in the Marshalls' delivery wagon, and we'll take a nice lunch and have a picnic. Just us; nobody else. Could n't you happen along, Jim? It would be like old times."

I considered a moment. "Maybe I can, if I won't be in the way."

On Sunday morning I rose early and got out of Black Hawk while the dew was still heavy on the long meadow grasses. It was the high season for summer flowers. The pink bee-bush stood tall along the sandy roadsides, and the cone-flowers and rose mallow grew everywhere. Across the wire fence, in the long grass, I saw a clump of flaming orange-colored milkweed, rare in that part of the State. I left the road and went around through a stretch of pasture that was always cropped short in summer, where the gaillardia came up year after year and matted over the ground with the deep, velvety red that is in Bokhara[2] carpets. The country was empty and solitary except for the larks that Sunday morning, and it seemed to lift itself up to me and to come very close.

The river was running strong for midsummer; heavy rains to the west of us had kept it full. I crossed the bridge and went upstream along the wooded shore to a pleasant dressing-room I knew among the dogwood bushes, all overgrown with wild grapevines. I began

---

1 Used to teach Latin, Virgil's epic poem recalls the legend of the founding of Rome.
2 Turkish.

to undress for a swim. The girls would not be along yet. For the first time it occurred to me that I would be homesick for that river after I left it. The sandbars, with their clean white beaches and their little groves of willows and cottonwood seedlings, were a sort of No Man's Land, little newly-created worlds that belonged to the Black Hawk boys. Charley Harling and I had hunted through these woods, fished from the fallen logs, until I knew every inch of the river shores and had a friendly feeling for every bar and shallow.

After my swim, while I was playing about indolently in the water, I heard the sound of hoofs and wheels on the bridge. I struck downstream and shouted, as the open spring wagon came into view on the middle span. They stopped the horse, and the two girls in the bottom of the cart stood up, steadying themselves by the shoulders of the two in front, so that they could see me better. They were charming up there, huddled together in the cart and peering down at me like curious deer when they come out of the thicket to drink. I found bottom near the bridge and stood up, waving to them.

"How pretty you look!" I called.

"So do you!" they shouted altogether, and broke into peals of laughter. Anna Hansen shook the reins and they drove on, while I zigzagged back to my inlet and clambered up behind an over-hanging elm. I dried myself in the sun, and dressed slowly, reluc-tant to leave that green enclosure where the sunlight flickered so bright through the grapevine leaves and the woodpecker ham-mered away in the crooked elm that trailed out over the water. As I went along the road back to the bridge I kept picking off little pieces of scaly chalk from the dried water gullies, and breaking them up in my hands.

When I came upon the Marshalls' delivery horse, tied in the shade, the girls had already taken their baskets and gone down the east road which wound through the sand and scrub. I could hear them calling to each other. The elder bushes did not grow back in the shady ravines between the bluffs, but in the hot, sandy bottoms along the stream, where their roots were always in moisture and their tops in the sun. The blossoms were unusually luxuriant and beautiful that summer.

I followed a cattle path through the thick underbrush until I came to a slope that fell away abruptly to the water's edge. A great chunk of the shore had been bitten out by some spring freshet, and the scar was masked by elder bushes, growing down to the water in flowery terraces. I did not touch them. I was overcome by content and drowsiness and by the warm silence about me. There was no sound but the high, sing-song buzz of wild bees and the sunny gurgle of the water underneath. I peeped over the edge of the bank to see the little stream that made the noise; it flowed along perfectly clear over the sand and gravel, cut off from the muddy main current by a long sandbar. Down there, on the lower shelf of the bank, I saw Ántonia, seated alone under the pagoda-like elders. She looked up when she heard me, and smiled, but I saw that she had been crying. I slid down into the soft sand beside her and asked her what was the matter.

"It makes me homesick, Jimmy, this flower, this smell," she said softly. "We have this flower very much at home, in the old country. It always grew in our yard and my papa had a green bench and a table under the bushes. In summer, when they were in bloom, he used to sit there with his friend that played the trombone. When I was little I used to go down there to hear them talk—beautiful talk, like what I never hear in this country."

"What did they talk about?" I asked her.

She sighed and shook her head. "Oh, I don't know! About music, and the woods, and about God, and when they were young." She turned to me suddenly and looked into my eyes. "You think, Jimmy, that maybe my father's spirit can go back to those old places?"

I told her about the feeling of her father's presence I had on that winter day when my grandparents had gone over to see his dead body and I was left alone in the house. I said I felt sure then that he was on his way back to his own country, and that even now, when I passed his grave, I always thought of him as being among the woods and fields that were so dear to him.

Ántonia had the most trusting, responsive eyes in the world; love and credulousness seemed to look out of them with open faces. "Why did n't you ever tell me that before? It makes me feel more sure for him." After a while she said: "You know, Jim, my father was different from my mother. He did not have to marry my mother, and all his brothers quarreled with him because he did. I used to hear the old people at home whisper about it. They said he could have paid my mother money, and not married her. But he was older than she was, and he was too kind to treat her like that. He lived in his mother's house, and she was a poor girl come in to do the work. After my father married her, my grandmother never let my mother come into her house again. When I went to my grandmother's funeral was the only time I was ever in my grandmother's house. Don't that seem strange?"

While she talked, I lay back in the hot sand and looked up at the blue sky between the flat bouquets of elder. I could hear the bees humming and singing, but they stayed up in the sun above the flowers and did not come down into the shadow of the leaves. Ántonia seemed to me that day exactly like the little girl who used to come to our house with Mr. Shimerda.

"Some day, Tony, I am going over to your country, and I am going to the little town where you lived. Do you remember all about it?"

"Jim," she said earnestly, "if I was put down there in the middle of the night, I could find my way all over that little town; and along the river to the next town, where my grandmother lived. My feet remember all the little paths through the woods, and where the big roots stick out to trip you. I ain't never forgot my own country."

There was a crackling in the branches above us, and Lena Lingard peered down over the edge of the bank.

"You lazy things!" she cried. "All this elder, and you two lying there! Did n't you hear us calling you?" Almost as flushed as she had been in my dream, she leaned over the edge of the bank and began to demolish our flowery pagoda. I had never seen her so energetic; she was panting with zeal, and the perspiration stood in drops on her short, yielding upper lip. I sprang to my feet and ran up the bank.

It was noon now, and so hot that the dogwoods and scrub-oaks began to turn up the silvery under-side of their leaves, and all the foliage looked soft and wilted. I carried the lunch-basket to the top of one of the chalk bluffs,[1] where even on the calmest days there was always a breeze. The flat-topped, twisted little oaks threw light shadows on the grass. Below us we could see the windings of the river, and Black Hawk, grouped among its trees, and, beyond, the rolling country, swelling gently until it met the sky. We could recognize familiar farmhouses and windmills. Each of the girls pointed out to me the direction in which her father's farm lay, and told me how many acres were in wheat that year and how many in corn.

"My old folks," said Tiny Soderball, "have put in twenty acres of rye. They get it ground at the mill, and it makes nice bread. It seems

---

1 Probably limestone.

like my mother ain't been so homesick, ever since father's raised rye flour for her."

"It must have been a trial for our mothers," said Lena, "coming out here and having to do everything different. My mother had always lived in town. She says she started behind in farm-work, and never has caught up."

"Yes, a new country's hard on the old ones, sometimes," said Anna thoughtfully. "My grandmother's getting feeble now, and her mind wanders. She's forgot about this country, and thinks she's at home in Norway. She keeps asking mother to take her down to the waterside and the fish market. She craves fish all the time. Whenever I go home I take her canned salmon and mackerel."

"Mercy, it's hot!" Lena yawned. She was supine under a little oak, resting after the fury of her elder-hunting, and had taken off the high-heeled slippers she had been silly enough to wear. "Come here, Jim. You never got the sand out of your hair." She began to draw her fingers slowly through my hair.

Ántonia pushed her away. "You'll never get it out like that," she said sharply. She gave my head a rough touzling and finished me off with something like a box on the ear. "Lena, you ought n't to try to wear those slippers any more. They're too small for your feet. You'd better give them to me for Yulka."

"All right," said Lena good-naturedly, tucking her white stockings under her skirt. "You get all Yulka's things, don't you? I wish father did n't have such bad luck with his farm machinery; then I could buy more things for my sisters. I'm going to get Mary a new coat this fall, if the sulky plough's[1] never paid for!"

Tiny asked her why she did n't wait until after Christmas, when coats would be cheaper. "What do you think of poor me?" she added; "with six at home, younger than I am? And they all think I'm rich, because when I go back to the country I'm dressed so fine!" She shrugged her shoulders. "But, you know, my weakness is playthings. I like to buy them playthings better than what they need."

"I know how that is," said Anna. "When we first came here, and I was little, we were too poor to buy toys. I never got over the loss

---

1 A plough that its operator rides, as opposed to a plough one walks behind.

of a doll somebody gave me before we left Norway. A boy on the boat broke her, and I still hate him for it."

"I guess after you got here you had plenty of live dolls to nurse, like me!" Lena remarked cynically.

"Yes, the babies came along pretty fast, to be sure. But I never minded. I was fond of them all. The youngest one, that we did n't any of us want, is the one we love best now."

Lena sighed. "Oh, the babies are all right; if only they don't come in winter. Ours nearly always did. I don't see how mother stood it. I tell you what, girls," she sat up with sudden energy; "I'm going to get my mother out of that old sod house where she's lived so many years. The men will never do it. Johnnie, that's my oldest brother, he's wanting to get married now, and build a house for his girl instead of his mother. Mrs. Thomas says she thinks I can move to some other town pretty soon, and go into business for myself. If I don't get into business, I'll maybe marry a rich gambler."

"That would be a poor way to get on," said Anna sarcastically. "I wish I could teach school, like Selma Kronn. Just think! She'll be the first Scandinavian girl to get a position in the High School. We ought to be proud of her."

Selma was a studious girl, who had not much tolerance for giddy things like Tiny and Lena; but they always spoke of her with admiration.

Tiny moved about restlessly, fanning herself with her straw hat. "If I was smart like her, I'd be at my books day and night. But she was born smart—and look how her father's trained her! He was something high up in the old country."

"So was my mother's father," murmured Lena, "but that's all the good it does us! My father's father was smart, too, but he was wild. He married a Lapp. I guess that's what's the matter with me, they say Lapp blood will out."

"A real Lapp, Lena?" I exclaimed. "The kind that wear skins?"

"I don't know if she wore skins, but she was a Lapp all right, and his folks felt dreadful about it. He was sent up north on some Government job he had, and fell in with her. He would marry her."

"But I thought Lapland women were fat and ugly, and had squint eyes, like Chinese?" I objected.

"I don't know, maybe. There must be something mighty taking about the Lapp girls, though; mother says the Norwegians up north are always afraid their boys will run after them."

In the afternoon, when the heat was less oppressive, we had a

lively game of "Pussy Wants a Corner,"[1] on the flat bluff-top, with
the little trees for bases. Lena was Pussy so often that she finally said
she would n't play any more. We threw ourselves down on the
grass, out of breath.

"Jim," Ántonia said dreamily, "I want you to tell the girls about
how the Spanish first came here, like you and Charley Harling used
to talk about. I've tried to tell them, but I leave out so much."

They sat under a little oak, Tony resting against the trunk and
the other girls leaning against her and each other, and listened to
the little I was able to tell them about Coronado[2] and his search
for the Seven Golden Cities. At school we were taught that he
had not got so far north as Nebraska, but had given up his quest
and turned back somewhere in Kansas. But Charley Harling and
I had a strong belief that he had been along this very river. A
farmer in the county north of ours, when he was breaking sod,
had turned up a metal stirrup of fine workmanship, and a sword
with a Spanish inscription on the blade. He lent these relics to
Mr. Harling, who brought them home with him. Charley and I
scoured them, and they were on exhibition in the Harling office
all summer. Father Kelly, the priest, had found the name of the
Spanish maker on the sword, and an abbreviation that stood for
the city of Cordova.[3]

"And that I saw with my own eyes," Ántonia put in triumphantly. "So Jim and Charley were right, and the teachers were
wrong!"

The girls began to wonder among themselves. Why had the
Spaniards come so far? What must this country have been like,
then? Why had Coronado never gone back to Spain, to his riches
and his castles and his king? I could n't tell them. I only knew the
school books said he "died in the wilderness, of a broken heart."

"More than him has done that," said Ántonia sadly, and the girls
murmured assent.

We sat looking off across the country, watching the sun go
down. The curly grass about us was on fire now. The bark of the

---

1   A game where each player except the one designated "Puss" occupies a
    base, or corner. Players exchange places while Puss tries to steal a corner
    spot, at which time the evicted player becomes Puss.
2   Francisco Vásquez de Coronado (1510-1554) explored the American
    southwest in 1540 in search of the Seven Golden Cities of Cibola.
3   A metalworking city in the south of Spain.

oaks turned red as copper. There was a shimmer of gold on the brown river. Out in the stream the sandbars glittered like glass, and the light trembled in the willow thickets as if little flames were leaping among them. The breeze sank to stillness. In the ravine a ringdove mourned plaintively, and somewhere off in the bushes an owl hooted. The girls sat listless, leaning against each other. The long fingers of the sun touched their foreheads.

Presently we saw a curious thing: There were no clouds, the sun was going down in a limpid, gold-washed sky. Just as the lower edge of the red disc rested on the high fields against the horizon, a great black figure suddenly appeared on the face of the sun. We sprang to our feet, straining our eyes toward it. In a moment we realized what it was. On some upland farm, a plough had been left standing in the field. The sun was sinking just behind it. Magnified across the distance by the horizontal light, it stood out against the sun, was exactly contained within the circle of the disc; the handles, the tongue, the share—black against the molten red. There it was, heroic in size, a picture writing on the sun.

Even while we whispered about it, our vision disappeared; the ball dropped and dropped until the red tip went beneath the earth. The fields below us were dark, the sky was growing pale, and that forgotten plough had sunk back to its own littleness somewhere on the prairie.

XV

Late in August the Cutters went to Omaha for a few days, leaving Ántonia in charge of the house. Since the scandal about the Swedish girl, Wick Cutter could never get his wife to stir out of Black Hawk without him.

The day after the Cutters left, Ántonia came over to see us. Grandmother noticed that she seemed troubled and distracted. "You've got something on your mind, Ántonia," she said anxiously.

"Yes, Mrs. Burden. I could n't sleep much last night." She hesitated, and then told us how strangely Mr. Cutter had behaved before he went away. He put all the silver in a basket and placed it under her bed, and with it a box of papers which he told her were valuable. He made her promise that she would not sleep away from the house, or be out late in the evening, while he was gone. He strictly forbade her to ask any of the girls she knew to stay with her at night. She would be perfectly safe, he said, as he had just put a new Yale lock on the front door.

Cutter had been so insistent in regard to these details that now she felt uncomfortable about staying there alone. She had n't liked the way he kept coming into the kitchen to instruct her, or the way he looked at her. "I feel as if he is up to some of his tricks again, and is going to try to scare me, somehow."

Grandmother was apprehensive at once. "I don't think it's right for you to stay there, feeling that way. I suppose it would n't be right for you to leave the place alone, either, after giving your word. Maybe Jim would be willing to go over there and sleep, and you could come here nights. I'd feel safer, knowing you were under my own roof. I guess Jim could take care of their silver and old usury notes as well as you could."

Ántonia turned to me eagerly. "Oh, would you, Jim? I'd make up my bed nice and fresh for you. It's a real cool room, and the bed's right next the window. I was afraid to leave the window open last night."

I liked my own room, and I did n't like the Cutters' house under any circumstances; but Tony looked so troubled that I consented to try this arrangement. I found that I slept there as well as anywhere, and when I got home in the morning, Tony had a good breakfast waiting for me. After prayers she sat down at the table with us, and it was like old times in the country.

The third night I spent at the Cutters', I awoke suddenly with the impression that I had heard a door open and shut. Everything was still, however, and I must have gone to sleep again immediately.

The next thing I knew, I felt some one sit down on the edge of the bed. I was only half awake, but I decided that he might take the Cutters' silver, whoever he was. Perhaps if I did not move, he would find it and get out without troubling me. I held my breath and lay absolutely still. A hand closed softly on my shoulder, and at the same moment I felt something hairy and cologne-scented brushing my face. If the room had suddenly been flooded with electric light, I could n't have seen more clearly the detestable bearded countenance that I knew was bending over me. I caught a handful of whiskers and pulled, shouting something. The hand that held my shoulder was instantly at my throat. The man became insane; he stood over me, choking me with one fist and beating me in the face with the other, hissing and chuckling and letting out a flood of abuse.

"So this is what she's up to when I'm away, is it? Where is she, you nasty whelp, where is she? Under the bed, are you, hussy? I know your tricks! Wait till I get at you! I'll fix this rat you've got in here. He's caught, all right!"

So long as Cutter had me by the throat, there was no chance for me at all. I got hold of his thumb and bent it back, until he let go with a yell. In a bound, I was on my feet, and easily sent him sprawling to the floor. Then I made a dive for the open window, struck the wire screen, knocked it out, and tumbled after it into the yard.

Suddenly I found myself running across the north end of Black Hawk in my nightshirt, just as one sometimes finds one's self behaving in bad dreams. When I got home I climbed in at the kitchen window. I was covered with blood from my nose and lip, but I was too sick to do anything about it. I found a shawl and an overcoat on the hatrack, lay down on the parlor sofa, and in spite of my hurts, went to sleep.

Grandmother found me there in the morning. Her cry of fright awakened me. Truly, I was a battered object. As she helped me to my room, I caught a glimpse of myself in the mirror. My lip was cut and stood out like a snout. My nose looked like a big blue plum, and one eye was swollen shut and hideously discolored. Grandmother said we must have the doctor at once, but I implored her, as I had never begged for anything before, not to send for him. I could stand anything, I told her, so long as nobody saw me or knew what had happened to me. I entreated her not to let grandfather, even, come into my room. She seemed to understand, though I was too faint and miserable to go into explanations. When she took off my nightshirt, she found such bruises on my chest and shoulders that she began to cry. She spent the whole morning bathing and poulticing[1] me, and rubbing me with arnica.[2] I heard Ántonia sobbing outside my door, but I asked grandmother to send her away. I felt that I never wanted to see her again. I hated her almost as much as I hated Cutter. She had let me in for all this disgustingness. Grandmother kept saying how thankful we ought to be that I had been there instead of Ántonia. But I lay with my disfigured face to the wall and felt no particular gratitude. My one concern was that grandmother should keep every one away from me. If the story once got abroad, I would never hear the last of it. I could well imagine what the old men down at the drugstore would do with such a theme.

---

1 Applying warm materials to wounds, to ease pain and stimulate circulation.

2 A medicinal tincture prepared from the arnica plant.

While grandmother was trying to make me comfortable, grandfather went to the depot and learned that Wick Cutter had come home on the night express from the east, and had left again on the six o'clock train for Denver that morning. The agent said his face was striped with court-plaster,[1] and he carried his left hand in a sling. He looked so used up, that the agent asked him what had happened to him since ten o'clock the night before; whereat Cutter began to swear at him and said he would have him discharged for incivility.

That afternoon, while I was asleep, Ántonia took grandmother with her, and went over to the Cutters' to pack her trunk. They found the place locked up, and they had to break the window to get into Ántonia's bedroom. There everything was in shocking disorder. Her clothes had been taken out of her closet, thrown into the middle of the room, and trampled and torn. My own garments had been treated so badly that I never saw them again; grandmother burned them in the Cutters' kitchen range.

While Ántonia was packing her trunk and putting her room in order, to leave it, the front-door bell rang violently. There stood Mrs. Cutter,—locked out, for she had no key to the new lock—her head trembling with rage. "I advised her to control herself, or she would have a stroke," grandmother said afterwards.

Grandmother would not let her see Ántonia at all, but made her sit down in the parlor while she related to her just what had occurred the night before. Ántonia was frightened, and was going home to stay for a while, she told Mrs. Cutter; it would be useless to interrogate the girl, for she knew nothing of what had happened.

Then Mrs. Cutter told her story. She and her husband had started home from Omaha together the morning before. They had to stop over several hours at Waymore Junction to catch the Black Hawk train. During the wait, Cutter left her at the depot and went to the Waymore bank to attend to some business. When he returned, he told her that he would have to stay overnight there, but she could go on home. He bought her ticket and put her on the train. She saw him slip a twenty-dollar bill into her handbag with her ticket. That bill, she said, should have aroused her suspicions at once—but did not.

---

1   A salve, to dress wounds.

The trains are never called at little junction towns; everybody knows when they come in. Mr. Cutter showed his wife's ticket to the conductor, and settled her in her seat before the train moved off. It was not until nearly nightfall that she discovered she was on the express bound for Kansas City, that her ticket was made out to that point, and that Cutter must have planned it so. The conductor told her the Black Hawk train was due at Waymore twelve minutes after the Kansas City train left. She saw at once that her husband had played this trick in order to get back to Black Hawk without her. She had no choice but to go on to Kansas City and take the first fast train for home.

Cutter could have got home a day earlier than his wife by any one of a dozen simpler devices; he could have left her in the Omaha hotel, and said he was going on to Chicago for a few days. But apparently it was part of his fun to outrage her feelings as much as possible.

"Mr. Cutter will pay for this, Mrs. Burden. He will pay!" Mrs. Cutter avouched, nodding her horselike head and rolling her eyes.

Grandmother said she had n't a doubt of it.

Certainly Cutter liked to have his wife think him a devil. In some way he depended upon the excitement he could arouse in her hysterical nature. Perhaps he got the feeling of being a rake more from his wife's rage and amazement than from any experiences of his own. His zest in debauchery might wane, but never Mrs. Cutter's belief in it. The reckoning with his wife at the end of an escapade was something he counted on—like the last powerful liqueur after a long dinner. The one excitement he really could n't do without was quarreling with Mrs. Cutter!

BOOK III
LENA LINGARD

I

At the University[1] I had the good fortune to come immediately under the influence of a brilliant and inspiring young scholar. Gaston Cleric had arrived in Lincoln only a few weeks earlier than I, to begin his work as head of the Latin Department. He came West at the suggestion of his physicians, his health having been enfeebled by a long illness in Italy. When I took my entrance examinations he was my examiner, and my course was arranged under his supervision.

I did not go home for my first summer vacation, but stayed in Lincoln, working off a year's Greek, which had been my only condition on entering the Freshman class.[2] Cleric's doctor advised against his going back to New England, and except for a few weeks in Colorado, he, too, was in Lincoln all that summer. We played tennis, read, and took long walks together. I shall always look back on that time of mental awakening as one of the happiest in my life. Gaston Cleric introduced me to the world of ideas; when one first enters that world everything else fades for a time, and all that went before is as if it had not been. Yet I found curious survivals; some of the figures of my old life seemed to be waiting for me in the new.

In those days there were many serious young men among the students who had come up to the University from the farms and the little towns scattered over the thinly settled State. Some of those boys came straight from the cornfields with only a summer's wages in their pockets, hung on through the four years, shabby and underfed, and completed the course by really heroic self-sacrifice. Our instructors were oddly assorted; wandering pioneer schoolteachers, stranded ministers of the Gospel, a few enthusiastic young men just out of graduate schools. There was an atmosphere of endeavor, of expectancy and bright hopefulness about the young college that had lifted its head from the prairie only a few years before.

---

1 The University of Nebraska, at Lincoln, established in 1871.
2 As a result of his performance on entrance examinations, Jim is required to take one year of pre-college Greek.

Our personal life was as free as that of our instructors. There were no college dormitories; we lived where we could and as we could. I took rooms with an old couple, early settlers in Lincoln, who had married off their children and now lived quietly in their house at the edge of town, near the open country. The house was inconveniently situated for students, and on that account I got two rooms for the price of one. My bedroom, originally a linen closet, was unheated and was barely large enough to contain my cot bed, but it enabled me to call the other room my study. The dresser, and the great walnut wardrobe which held all my clothes, even my hats and shoes, I had pushed out of the way, and I considered them non-existent, as children eliminate incongruous objects when they are playing house. I worked at a commodious green-topped table placed directly in front of the west window which looked out over the prairie. In the corner at my right were all my books, in shelves I had made and painted myself. On the blank wall at my left the dark, old-fashioned wall-paper was covered by a large map of ancient Rome, the work of some German scholar. Cleric had ordered it for me when he was sending for books from abroad. Over the bookcase hung a photograph of the Tragic Theater at Pompeii, which he had given me from his collection.

When I sat at work I half faced a deep, upholstered chair which stood at the end of my table, its high back against the wall. I had bought it with great care. My instructor sometimes looked in upon me when he was out for an evening tramp, and I noticed that he was more likely to linger and become talkative if I had a comfortable chair for him to sit in, and if he found a bottle of Bénédictine[1] and plenty of the kind of cigarettes he liked, at his elbow. He was, I had discovered, parsimonious about small expenditures—a trait absolutely inconsistent with his general character. Sometimes when he came he was silent and moody, and after a few sarcastic remarks went away again, to tramp the streets of Lincoln, which were almost as quiet and oppressively domestic as those of Black Hawk. Again, he would sit until nearly midnight, talking about Latin and English poetry, or telling me about his long stay in Italy.

I can give no idea of the peculiar charm and vividness of his talk. In a crowd he was nearly always silent. Even for his classroom he had no platitudes, no stock of professorial anecdotes. When he was tired his lectures were clouded, obscure, elliptical; but when he

---

1 A brandy liqueur made originally by Benedictine monks.

was interested they were wonderful. I believe that Gaston Cleric narrowly missed being a great poet, and I have sometimes thought that his bursts of imaginative talk were fatal to his poetic gift. He squandered too much in the heat of personal communication. How often I have seen him draw his dark brows together, fix his eyes upon some object on the wall or a figure in the carpet, and then flash into the lamplight the very image that was in his brain. He could bring the drama of antique life before one out of the shadows—white figures against blue backgrounds. I shall never forget his face as it looked one night when he told me about the solitary day he spent among the sea temples at Paestum:[1] the soft wind blowing through the roofless columns, the birds flying low over the flowering marsh grasses, the changing lights on the silver, cloud-hung mountains. He had willfully stayed the short summer night there, wrapped in his coat and rug, watching the constellations on their path down the sky until "the bride of old Tithonus"[2] rose out of the sea, and the mountains stood sharp in the dawn. It was there he caught the fever which held him back on the eve of his departure for Greece and of which he lay ill so long in Naples. He was still, indeed, doing penance for it.

I remember vividly another evening, when something led us to talk of Dante's veneration for Virgil.[3] Cleric went through canto after canto of the "Commedia," repeating the discourse between Dante and his "sweet teacher," while his cigarette burned itself out unheeded between his long fingers. I can hear him now, speaking the lines of the poet Statius,[4] who spoke for Dante: "*I was famous on earth with the name which endures longest and honors most. The seeds of my ardor were the sparks from that divine flame whereby more than a thousand have kindled; I speak of the Æneid, mother to me and nurse to me in poetry.*"

Although I admired scholarship so much in Cleric, I was not deceived about myself; I knew that I should never be a scholar. I could never lose myself for long among impersonal things. Mental excitement was apt to send me with a rush back to my own naked land and the figures scattered upon it. While I was in the very act of yearning toward the new forms that Cleric brought up before

---

1   The site of Greek ruins, on the Italian coast south of Naples.
2   A reference to Aurora, or dawn, common in Virgil and Homer.
3   In *The Divine Comedy*, Virgil is Dante's guide through hell and purgatory.
4   Dante and Virgil meet Statius in purgatory.

me, my mind plunged away from me, and I suddenly found myself thinking of the places and people of my own infinitesimal past. They stood out strengthened and simplified now, like the image of the plough against the sun. They were all I had for an answer to the new appeal. I begrudged the room that Jake and Otto and Russian Peter took up in my memory, which I wanted to crowd with other things. But whenever my consciousness was quickened,[1] all those early friends were quickened within it, and in some strange way they accompanied me through all my new experiences. They were so much alive in me that I scarcely stopped to wonder whether they were alive anywhere else, or how.

II

One March evening in my Sophomore year I was sitting alone in my room after supper. There had been a warm thaw all day, with mushy yards and little streams of dark water gurgling cheerfully into the streets out of old snow-banks. My window was open, and the earthy wind blowing through made me indolent. On the edge of the prairie, where the sun had gone down, the sky was turquoise blue, like a lake, with gold light throbbing in it. Higher up, in the utter clarity of the western slope, the evening star hung like a lamp suspended by silver chains— like the lamp engraved upon the title-page of old Latin texts, which is always appearing in new heavens, and waking new desires in men. It reminded me, at any rate, to shut my window and light my wick in answer. I did so regretfully, and the dim objects in the room emerged from the shadows and took their place about me with the helpfulness which custom breeds.

I propped my book open and stared listlessly at the page of the Georgics[2] where tomorrow's lesson began. It opened with the melancholy reflection that, in the lives of mortals, the best days are the first to flee. "Optima dies ... prima fugit."[3] I turned back to the beginning of the third book, which we had read in class that morning. "Primus ego in patriam mecum ... deducam Musas"; "for

---

1 Less-often used today, "quicken" in Cather's time meant to come to life, become living, or to revive.
2 Virgil's pastoral poem, celebrating the virtues of agricultural life.
3 See the novel's title page; this phrase is the book's epigraph.

I shall be the first, if I live, to bring the Muse[1] into my country."
Cleric had explained to us that "patria" here meant, not a nation
or even a province, but the little rural neighborhood on the Mincio[2] where the poet was born. This was not a boast, but a hope, at
once bold and devoutly humble, that he might bring the Muse (but
lately come to Italy from her cloudy Grecian mountains), not to
the capital, the *palatia Romana,* but to his own little "country"; to
his father's fields, "sloping down to the river and to the old beech
trees with broken tops."

Cleric said he thought Virgil, when he was dying at Brindisi,[3]
must have remembered that passage. After he had faced the bitter
fact that he was to leave the Æneid unfinished, and had decreed
that the great canvas, crowded with figures of gods and men, should
be burned rather than survive him unperfected, then his mind must
have gone back to the perfect utterance of the Georgics, where the
pen was fitted to the matter as the plough is to the furrow; and he
must have said to himself with the thankfulness of a good man, "I
was the first to bring the Muse into my country."

We left the classroom quietly, conscious that we had been
brushed by the wing of a great feeling, though perhaps I alone
knew Cleric intimately enough to guess what that feeling was. In
the evening, as I sat staring at my book, the fervor of his voice
stirred through the quantities on the page before me. I was wondering whether that particular rocky strip of New England coast
about which he had so often told me was Cleric's *patria.* Before I
had got far with my reading I was disturbed by a knock. I hurried
to the door and when I opened it saw a woman standing in the
dark hall.

"I expect you hardly know me, Jim."

The voice seemed familiar, but I did not recognize her until she
stepped into the light of my doorway and I beheld—Lena Lingard!
She was so quietly conventionalized by city clothes that I might
have passed her on the street without seeing her. Her black suit fitted her figure smoothly, and a black lace hat, with pale-blue forget-
me-nots, sat demurely on her yellow hair.

---

1 The Greek Muses, nine daughters of Zeus and Mnemosyne (Memory),
  are the sources of inspiration and learning in the arts, especially music
  and literature.
2 Virgil was born to farmers near the city of Mantua on the Mincio River.
3 A city in southern Italy, far from Virgil's birthplace.

I led her toward Cleric's chair, the only comfortable one I had, questioning her confusedly.

She was not disconcerted by my embarrassment. She looked about her with the naïve curiosity I remembered so well. "You are quite comfortable here, are n't you? I live in Lincoln now, too, Jim. I'm in business for myself. I have a dressmaking shop in the Raleigh Block, out on O Street. I've made a real good start."

"But, Lena, when did you come?"

"Oh, I've been here all winter. Did n't your grandmother ever write you? I've thought about looking you up lots of times. But we've all heard what a studious young man you've got to be, and I felt bashful. I did n't know whether you'd be glad to see me." She laughed her mellow, easy laugh, that was either very artless or very comprehending, one never quite knew which. "You seem the same, though,—except you're a young man, now, of course. Do you think I've changed?"

"Maybe you're prettier—though you were always pretty enough. Perhaps it's your clothes that make a difference."

"You like my new suit? I have to dress pretty well in my business." She took off her jacket and sat more at ease in her blouse, of some soft, flimsy silk. She was already at home in my place, had slipped quietly into it, as she did into everything. She told me her business was going well, and she had saved a little money.

"This summer I'm going to build the house for mother I've talked about so long. I won't be able to pay up on it at first, but I want her to have it before she is too old to enjoy it. Next summer I'll take her down new furniture and carpets, so she'll have something to look forward to all winter."

I watched Lena sitting there so smooth and sunny and well cared-for, and thought of how she used to run barefoot over the prairie until after the snow began to fly, and how Crazy Mary chased her round and round the cornfields. It seemed to me wonderful that she should have got on so well in the world. Certainly she had no one but herself to thank for it.

"You must feel proud of yourself, Lena," I said heartily. "Look at me, I've never earned a dollar, and I don't know that I'll ever be able to."

"Tony says you're going to be richer than Mr. Harling some day. She's always bragging about you, you know."

"Tell me, how *is* Tony?"

"She's fine. She works for Mrs. Gardener at the hotel now. She's housekeeper. Mrs. Gardener's health is n't what it was, and she can't see after everything like she used to. She has great confidence in Tony. Tony's made it up with the Harlings, too. Little Nina is so fond of her that Mrs. Harling kind of overlooked things."

"Is she still going with Larry Donovan?"

"Oh, that's on, worse than ever! I guess they're engaged. Tony talks about him like he was president of the railroad. Everybody laughs about it, because she was never a girl to be soft. She won't hear a word against him. She's so sort of innocent."

I said I did n't like Larry, and never would.

Lena's face dimpled. "Some of us could tell her things, but it would n't do any good. She'd always believe him. That's Ántonia's failing, you know; if she once likes people, she won't hear anything against them."

"I think I'd better go home and look after Ántonia," I said.

"I think you had." Lena looked up at me in frank amusement. "It's a good thing the Harlings are friendly with her again. Larry's afraid of them. They ship so much grain, they have influence with the railroad people. What are you studying?" She leaned her elbows on the table and drew my book toward her. I caught a faint odor of violet sachet.[1] "So that's Latin, is it? It looks hard. You do go to the theater sometimes, though, for I've seen you there. Don't you just love a good play, Jim? I can't stay at home in the evening if there's one in town. I'd be willing to work like a slave, it seems to me, to live in a place where there are theaters."

"Let's go to a show together sometime. You are going to let me come to see you, are n't you?"

"Would you like to? I'd be ever so pleased. I'm never busy after six o'clock, and I let my sewing girls go at half-past five. I board, to save time, but sometimes I cook a chop for myself, and I'd be glad to cook one for you. Well,"—she began to put on her white gloves,—"it's been awful good to see you, Jim."

"You need n't hurry, need you? You've hardly told me anything yet."

"We can talk when you come to see me. I expect you don't often have lady visitors. The old woman downstairs did n't want to let me come up very much. I told her I was from your home town, and had promised your grandmother to come and see you. How surprised Mrs. Burden would be!" Lena laughed softly as she rose.

---

1 A small bag or packet containing dried perfume, placed among clothing; also a small scented bag for carrying handkerchiefs.

When I caught up my hat she shook her head. "No, I don't want you to go with me. I'm to meet some Swedes at the drug-store. You would n't care for them. I wanted to see your room so I could write Tony all about it, but I must tell her how I left you right here with your books. She's always so afraid some one will run off with you!" Lena slipped her silk sleeves into the jacket I held for her, smoothed it over her person, and buttoned it slowly. I walked with her to the door. "Come and see me sometimes when you're lonesome. But maybe you have all the friends you want. Have you?" She turned her soft cheek to me. "Have you?" she whispered teasingly in my ear. In a moment I watched her fade down the dusky stairway.

When I turned back to my room the place seemed much pleasanter than before. Lena had left something warm and friendly in the lamplight. How I loved to hear her laugh again! It was so soft and unexcited and appreciative—gave a favorable interpretation to everything. When I closed my eyes I could hear them all laughing—the Danish laundry girls and the three Bohemian Marys. Lena had brought them all back to me. It came over me, as it had never done before, the relation between girls like those and the poetry of Virgil. If there were no girls like them in the world, there would be no poetry. I understood that clearly, for the first time. This revelation seemed to me inestimably precious. I clung to it as if it might suddenly vanish.

As I sat down to my book at last, my old dream about Lena coming across the harvest field in her short skirt seemed to me like the memory of an actual experience. It floated before me on the page like a picture, and underneath it stood the mournful line: *Optima dies ... prima fugit.*

III

In Lincoln the best part of the theatrical season came late, when the good companies stopped off there for one-night stands, after their long runs in New York and Chicago. That spring Lena went with me to see Joseph Jefferson in "Rip Van Winkle," and to a war play called "Shenandoah." She was inflexible about paying for her own seat; said she was in business now, and she would n't have a schoolboy spending his money on her. I liked to watch a play with Lena; everything was wonderful to her, and everything was true. It was like going to revival meetings with some one who was always being converted. She handed her feelings over to the actors with a kind of fatalistic resignation. Accessories of costume and scene meant much more to her than to me. She sat entranced through "Robin Hood" and hung upon the lips of the contralto who sang, "Oh, Promise Me!"

Toward the end of April, the billboards, which I watched anxiously in those days, bloomed out one morning with gleaming white posters on which two names were impressively printed in blue Gothic letters: the name of an actress of whom I had often heard, and the name "Camille."[1]

I called at the Raleigh Block for Lena on Saturday evening, and we walked down to the theater. The weather was warm and sultry and put us both in a holiday humor. We arrived early, because Lena liked to watch the people come in. There was a note on the programme, saying that the "incidental music" would be from the opera "Traviata," which was made from the same story as the play. We had neither of us read the play, and we did not know what it was about—though I seemed to remember having heard it was a piece in which great actresses shone. "The Count of Monte Cristo," which I had seen James O'Neill play that winter, was by the only Alexandre Dumas I knew. This play, I saw, was by his son, and I expected a family resemblance. A couple of jack-rabbits, run in off the prairie, could not have been more innocent of what awaited them than were Lena and I.

Our excitement began with the rise of the curtain, when the moody Varville,[2] seated before the fire, interrogated Nanine. Decidedly, there was a new tang about this dialogue. I had never heard in the theater lines that were alive, that presupposed and took for granted, like those which passed between Varville and Marguerite in the brief encounter before her friends entered. This introduced the most brilliant, worldly, the most enchantingly gay scene I had ever looked upon. I had never seen champagne bottles opened on the stage before—indeed, I had never seen them

---

1　Alexandre Dumas' play, *Camille* (1852), concerns the great love of Armand Duval, a man from a respectable family, and Marguerite Gautier, a courtesan. Armand's father intervenes in the affair, and convinces Marguerite to give up Armand for the good of his family. The two are reunited at the end of the play, but by then Marguerite is dying of tuberculosis.

2　The various characters referred to in the play are: Varville, Armand's amorous rival; Nanine, Marguerite's maid; Gaston, a womanizing man; Olympe, a mistress; and Prudence, a friend of Armand.

opened anywhere. The memory of that supper makes me hungry now; the sight of it then, when I had only a students' boarding-house dinner behind me, was delicate torment. I seem to remember gilded chairs and tables (arranged hurriedly by footmen in white gloves and stockings), linen of dazzling whiteness, glittering glass, silver dishes, a great bowl of fruit, and the reddest of roses. The room was invaded by beautiful women and dashing young men, laughing and talking together. The men were dressed more or less after the period in which the play was written; the women were not. I saw no inconsistency. Their talk seemed to open to one the brilliant world in which they lived; every sentence made one older and wiser, every pleasantry enlarged one's horizon. One could experience excess and satiety without the inconvenience of learning what to do with one's hands in a drawing-room! When the characters all spoke at once and I missed some of the phrases they flashed at each other, I was in misery. I strained my ears and eyes to catch every exclamation.

The actress who played Marguerite was even then old-fashioned, though historic. She had been a member of Daly's famous New York company,[1] and afterward a "star" under his direction. She was a woman who could not be taught, it is said, though she had a crude natural force which carried with people whose feelings were accessible and whose taste was not squeamish. She was already old, with a ravaged countenance and a physique curiously hard and stiff. She moved with difficulty—I think she was lame— I seem to remember some story about a malady of the spine. Her Armand was disproportionately young and slight, a handsome youth, perplexed in the extreme. But what did it matter? I believed devoutly in her power to fascinate him, in her dazzling loveliness. I believed her young, ardent, reckless, disillusioned, under sentence, feverish, avid of pleasure. I wanted to cross the footlights and help the slim-waisted Armand in the frilled shirt to convince her that there was still loyalty and devotion in the world. Her sudden illness, when the gayety was at its height, her pallor, the handkerchief she crushed against her lips, the cough she smothered under the laughter while Gaston kept playing the piano lightly—it all wrung my heart. But not so much as her cynicism in the long dialogue with her lover which followed. How far was I from questioning her unbelief! While the charmingly sincere young man pleaded

---

1 A Fifth Avenue, New York, theater company.

with her—accompanied by the orchestra in the old "Traviata" duet, "misterioso, misterios' altero,"[1]—she maintained her bitter skepticism, and the curtain fell on her dancing recklessly with the others, after Armand had been sent away with his flower.

Between the acts we had no time to forget. The orchestra kept sawing away at the "Traviata" music, so joyous and sad, so thin and far-away, so clap-trap and yet so heart-breaking. After the second act I left Lena in tearful contemplation of the ceiling, and went out into the lobby to smoke. As I walked about there I congratulated myself that I had not brought some Lincoln girl who would talk during the waits about the Junior dances, or whether the cadets would camp at Plattsmouth.[2] Lena was at least a woman, and I was a man.

Through the scene between Marguerite and the elder Duval, Lena wept unceasingly, and I sat helpless to prevent the closing of that chapter of idyllic love, dreading the return of the young man whose ineffable happiness was only to be the measure of his fall.

I suppose no woman could have been further in person, voice, and temperament from Dumas' appealing heroine than the veteran actress who first acquainted me with her. Her conception of the character was as heavy and uncompromising as her diction; she bore hard on the idea and on the consonants. At all times she was highly tragic, devoured by remorse. Lightness of stress or behavior was far from her. Her voice was heavy and deep: "Ar-r-r-mond!" she would begin, as if she were summoning him to the bar of Judgment. But the lines were enough. She had only to utter them. They created the character in spite of her.

The heartless world which Marguerite re-entered with Varville had never been so glittering and reckless as on the night when it gathered in Olympe's salon for the fourth act. There were chandeliers hung from the ceiling, I remember, many servants in livery, gaming-tables where the men played with piles of gold, and a staircase down which the guests made their entrance. After all the others had gathered round the card tables, and young Duval had been warned by Prudence, Marguerite descended the staircase with Varville; such a cloak, such a fan, such jewels—and her face! One knew at a glance how it was with her. When Armand, with the terrible words, "Look, all of you, I owe this woman nothing!" flung

---

1 In Verdi's opera, "mysterious and noble, / Both cross and ecstasy."
2 Where the Platte and Missouri Rivers meet.

the gold and bank notes at the half-swooning Marguerite, Lena cowered beside me and covered her face with her hands.

The curtain rose on the bedroom scene. By this time there was n't a nerve in me that had n't been twisted. Nanine alone could have made me cry. I loved Nanine tenderly; and Gaston, how one clung to that good fellow! The New Year's presents were not too much; nothing could be too much now. I wept unrestrainedly. Even the handkerchief in my breast-pocket, worn for elegance and not at all for use, was wet through by the time that moribund woman sank for the last time into the arms of her lover.

When we reached the door of the theater, the streets were shining with rain. I had prudently brought along Mrs. Harling's useful Commencement present, and I took Lena home under its shelter. After leaving her, I walked slowly out into the country part of the town where I lived. The lilacs were all blooming in the yards, and the smell of them after the rain, of the new leaves and the blossoms together, blew into my face with a sort of bitter sweetness. I tramped through the puddles and under the showery trees, mourning for Marguerite Gautier as if she had died only yesterday, sighing with the spirit of 1840, which had sighed so much, and which had reached me only that night, across long years and several languages, through the person of an infirm old actress. The idea is one that no circumstances can frustrate. Wherever and whenever that piece is put on, it is April.

IV

How well I remember the stiff little parlor where I used to wait for Lena: the hard horsehair furniture, bought at some auction sale, the long mirror, the fashion-plates on the wall. If I sat down even for a moment I was sure to find threads and bits of colored silk clinging to my clothes after I went away. Lena's success puzzled me. She was so easy-going; had none of the push and self-assertiveness that get people ahead in business. She had come to Lincoln, a country girl, with no introductions except to some cousins of Mrs. Thomas who lived there, and she was already making clothes for the women of "the young married set." She evidently had great natural aptitude for her work. She knew, as she said, "what people looked well in." She never tired of poring over fashion books. Sometimes in the evening I would find her alone in her workroom, draping folds of satin on a wire figure, with a quite blissful expression of countenance. I could n't help thinking that the years when Lena literally had n't enough clothes to cover herself might have something to do with her untiring interest in dressing the human figure. Her clients said that Lena "had style," and overlooked her habitual inaccuracies. She never, I discovered, finished anything by the time she had promised, and she frequently spent more money on materials than her customer had authorized. Once, when I arrived at six o'clock, Lena was ushering out a fidgety mother and her awkward, overgrown daughter. The woman detained Lena at the door to say apologetically:—

"You'll try to keep it under fifty for me, won't you, Miss Lingard? You see, she's really too young to come to an expensive dressmaker, but I knew you could do more with her than anybody else."

"Oh, that will be all right, Mrs. Herron. I think we'll manage to get a good effect," Lena replied blandly.

I thought her manner with her customers very good, and wondered where she had learned such self-possession.

Sometimes after my morning classes were over, I used to encounter Lena downtown, in her velvet suit and a little black hat, with a veil tied smoothly over her face, looking as fresh as the spring morning. Maybe she would be carrying home a bunch of jonquils or a hyacinth plant. When we passed a candy store her footsteps would hesitate and linger. "Don't let me go in," she would murmur. "Get me by if you can." She was very fond of sweets, and was afraid of growing too plump.

We had delightful Sunday breakfasts together at Lena's. At the back of her long work-room was a bay-window, large enough to hold a box-couch and a reading-table. We breakfasted in this recess, after drawing the curtains that shut out the long room, with cutting-tables and wire women and sheet-draped garments on the walls. The sunlight poured in, making everything on the table shine and glitter and the flame of the alcohol lamp disappear altogether. Lena's curly black water-spaniel, Prince, breakfasted with us. He sat beside her on the couch and behaved very well until the Polish violin-teacher across the hall began to practice, when Prince would growl and sniff the air with disgust. Lena's landlord, old Colonel Raleigh, had given her the dog, and at first she was not at all pleased. She had spent too much of her life taking care of animals to have much sentiment about them. But Prince was a knowing little beast, and she grew fond of him. After breakfast I made him do his lessons; play dead dog, shake hands, stand up like a soldier. We used to put my cadet cap on his head—I had to take military drill at the University—and give him a yard-measure to hold with his front leg. His gravity made us laugh immoderately.

Lena's talk always amused me. Ántonia had never talked like the people about her. Even after she learned to speak English readily there was always something impulsive and foreign in her speech. But Lena had picked up all the conventional expressions she heard at Mrs. Thomas's dressmaking shop. Those formal phrases, the very flower of small-town proprieties, and the flat commonplaces, nearly all hypocritical in their origin, became very funny, very engaging, when they were uttered in Lena's soft voice, with her caressing intonation and arch naiveté. Nothing could be more diverting than to hear Lena, who was almost as candid as Nature, call a leg a "limb" or a house a "home."

We used to linger a long while over our coffee in that sunny corner. Lena was never so pretty as in the morning; she wakened fresh with the world every day, and her eyes had a deeper color then, like the blue flowers that are never so blue as when they first open. I could sit idle all through a Sunday morning and look at her. Ole Benson's behavior was now no mystery to me.

"There was never any harm in Ole," she said once. "People need n't have troubled themselves. He just liked to come over and sit on the draw-side and forget about his bad luck. I liked to have him. Any company's welcome when you're off with cattle all the time."

"But was n't he always glum?" I asked. "People said he never talked at all."

"Sure he talked, in Norwegian. He'd been a sailor on an English boat and had seen lots of queer places. He had wonderful tattoos. We used to sit and look at them for hours; there was n't much to look at out there. He was like a picture book. He had a ship and a strawberry girl on one arm, and on the other a girl standing before a little house, with a fence and gate and all, waiting for her sweetheart. Farther up his arm, her sailor had come back and was kissing her. 'The Sailor's Return,' he called it."

I admitted it was no wonder Ole liked to look at a pretty girl once in a while, with such a fright at home.

"You know," Lena said confidentially, "he married Mary because he thought she was strong-minded and would keep him straight. He never could keep straight on shore. The last time he landed in Liverpool he'd been out on a two years' voyage. He was paid off one morning, and by the next he had n't a cent left, and his watch and compass were gone. He'd got with some women, and they'd taken everything. He worked his way to this country on a little passenger boat. Mary was a stewardess, and she tried to convert him on the way over. He thought she was just the one to keep him steady. Poor Ole! He used to bring me candy from town, hidden in his feed-bag. He could n't refuse anything to a girl. He'd have given away his tattoos long ago, if he could. He's one of the people I'm sorriest for."

If I happened to spend an evening with Lena and stayed late, the Polish violin-teacher across the hall used to come out and watch me descend the stairs, muttering so threateningly that it would have been easy to fall into a quarrel with him. Lena had told him once that she liked to hear him practice, so he always left his door open, and watched who came and went.

There was a coolness between the Pole and Lena's landlord on her account. Old Colonel Raleigh had come to Lincoln from Kentucky and invested an inherited fortune in real estate, at the time of inflated prices. Now he sat day after day in his office in the Raleigh Block, trying to discover where his money had gone and how he could get some of it back. He was a widower, and found very little congenial companionship in this casual Western city. Lena's good looks and gentle manners appealed to him. He said her voice reminded him of Southern voices, and he found as many opportunities of hearing it as possible. He painted and papered her rooms for her that spring, and put in a porcelain bathtub in place of the tin one that had satisfied the former tenant. While these repairs were being made, the old gentleman often dropped in to consult Lena's preferences. She told me with amusement how Ordinsky, the Pole, had presented himself at her door one evening, and said that if the landlord was annoying her by his attentions, he would promptly put a stop to it.

"I don't exactly know what to do about him," she said, shaking her head, "he's so sort of wild all the time. I would n't like to have him say anything rough to that nice old man. The Colonel is long-winded, but then I expect he's lonesome. I don't think he cares much for Ordinsky, either. He said once that if I had any complaints to make of my neighbors, I must n't hesitate."

One Saturday evening when I was having supper with Lena we heard a knock at her parlor door, and there stood the Pole, coat-less, in a dress shirt and collar. Prince dropped on his paws and began to growl like a mastiff, while the visitor apologized, saying that he could not possibly come in thus attired, but he begged Lena to lend him some safety pins.

"Oh, you'll have to come in, Mr. Ordinsky, and let me see what's the matter." She closed the door behind him. "Jim, won't you make Prince behave?"

I rapped Prince on the nose, while Ordinsky explained that he had not had his dress clothes on for a long time, and to-night, when he was going to play for a concert, his waistcoat had split down the back. He thought he could pin it together until he got it to a tailor.

Lena took him by the elbow and turned him round. She laughed when she saw the long gap in the satin. "You could never pin that, Mr. Ordinsky. You've kept it folded too long, and the goods is all gone along the crease. Take it off. I can put a new piece of lining-silk in there for you in ten minutes." She disappeared into her work-room with the vest, leaving me to confront the Pole, who stood against the door like a wooden figure. He folded his arms and glared at me with his excitable, slanting brown eyes. His head was the shape of a chocolate drop, and was covered with dry, straw-colored hair that fuzzed up about his pointed crown. He had never done more than mutter at me as I passed him, and I was surprised when he now addressed me.

"Miss Lingard," he said haughtily, "is a young woman for whom I have the utmost, the utmost respect."

"So have I," I said coldly.

He paid no heed to my remark, but began to do rapid finger-exercises on his shirt-sleeves, as he stood with tightly folded arms.

"Kindness of heart," he went on, staring at the ceiling, "sentiment, are not understood in a place like this. The noblest qualities are ridiculed. Grinning college boys, ignorant and conceited, what do they know of delicacy!"

I controlled my features and tried to speak seriously.

"If you mean me, Mr. Ordinsky, I have known Miss Lingard a long time, and I think I appreciate her kindness. We come from the same town, and we grew up together."

His gaze traveled slowly down from the ceiling and rested on me. "Am I to understand that you have this young woman's interests at heart? That you do not wish to compromise her?"

"That's a word we don't use much here, Mr. Ordinsky. A girl who makes her own living can ask a college boy to supper without being talked about. We take some things for granted."

"Then I have misjudged you, and I ask your pardon,"—he bowed gravely. "Miss Lingard," he went on, "is an absolutely trustful heart. She has not learned the hard lessons of life. As for you and me, *noblesse oblige*,"—he watched me narrowly.

Lena returned with the vest. "Come in and let us look at you as you go out, Mr. Ordinsky. I've never seen you in your dress suit," she said as she opened the door for him.

A few moments later he reappeared with his violin case—a heavy muffler about his neck and thick woolen gloves on his bony hands. Lena spoke encouragingly to him, and he went off with such an important, professional air, that we fell to laughing as soon as we had shut the door. "Poor fellow," Lena said indulgently, "he takes everything so hard."

After that Ordinsky was friendly to me, and behaved as if there were some deep understanding between us. He wrote a furious article, attacking the musical taste of the town, and asked me to do him a great service by taking it to the editor of the morning paper. If the editor refused to print it, I was to tell him that he would be answerable to Ordinsky "in person." He declared that he would never retract one word, and that he was quite prepared to lose all his pupils. In spite of the fact that nobody ever mentioned his article to him after it appeared—full of typographical errors which he thought intentional—he got a certain satisfaction from believing that the citizens of Lincoln had meekly accepted the epithet "coarse barbarians." "You see how it is," he said to me, "where there is no chivalry, there is no *amour propre*." When I met him on his rounds now, I thought he carried his head more disdainfully than ever, and strode up the steps of front porches and rang doorbells with more assurance. He told Lena he would never forget how I had stood by him when he was "under fire."

All this time, of course, I was drifting. Lena had broken up my serious mood. I was n't interested in my classes. I played with Lena and Prince, I played with the Pole, I went buggy-riding with the old Colonel, who had taken a fancy to me and used to talk to me about Lena and the "great beauties" he had known in his youth. We were all three in love with Lena.

Before the first of June, Gaston Cleric was offered an instructorship at Harvard College, and accepted it. He suggested that I should follow him in the fall, and complete my course at Harvard. He had found out about Lena—not from me—and he talked to me seriously.

"You won't do anything here now. You should either quit school and go to work, or change your college and begin again in earnest. You won't recover yourself while you are playing about with this handsome Norwegian. Yes, I've seen her with you at the theater. She's very pretty, and perfectly irresponsible, I should judge."

Cleric wrote my grandfather that he would like to take me East with him. To my astonishment, grandfather replied that I might go if I wished. I was both glad and sorry on the day when the letter came. I stayed in my room all evening and thought things over; I even tried to persuade myself that I was standing in Lena's way—it is so necessary to be a little noble!—and that if she had not me to play with, she would probably marry and secure her future.

The next evening I went to call on Lena. I found her propped up on the couch in her bay window, with her foot in a big slipper. An awkward little Russian girl whom she had taken into her work-room had dropped a flat-iron on Lena's toe. On the table beside her there was a basket of early summer flowers which the Pole had left after he heard of the accident. He always managed to know what went on in Lena's apartment.

Lena was telling me some amusing piece of gossip about one of her clients, when I interrupted her and picked up the flower basket.

"This old chap will be proposing to you some day, Lena."

"Oh, he has—often!" she murmured.

"What! After you've refused him?"

"He does n't mind that. It seems to cheer him to mention the subject. Old men are like that, you know. It makes them feel important to think they're in love with somebody."

"The Colonel would marry you in a minute. I hope you won't marry some old fellow; not even a rich one."

Lena shifted her pillows and looked up at me in surprise. "Why, I'm not going to marry anybody. Did n't you know that?"

"Nonsense, Lena. That's what girls say, but you know better. Every handsome girl like you marries, of course."

She shook her head. "Not me."

"But why not? What makes you say that?" I persisted.

Lena laughed. "Well, it's mainly because I don't want a husband. Men are all right for friends, but as soon as you marry them they turn into cranky old fathers, even the wild ones. They begin to tell you what's sensible and what's foolish, and want you to stick at home all the time. I prefer to be foolish when I feel like it, and be accountable to nobody."

"But you'll be lonesome. You'll get tired of this sort of life, and you'll want a family."

"Not me. I like to be lonesome. When I went to work for Mrs. Thomas I was nineteen years old, and I had never slept a night in

my life when there were n't three in the bed. I never had a minute
to myself except when I was off with the cattle."

Usually, when Lena referred to her life in the country at all, she
dismissed it with a single remark, humorous or mildly cynical. But
to-night her mind seemed to dwell on those early years. She told
me she could n't remember a time when she was so little that she
was n't lugging a heavy baby about, helping to wash for babies, trying to keep their little chapped hands and faces clean. She remembered home as a place where there were always too many children,
a cross man, and work piling up around a sick woman.

"It was n't mother's fault. She would have made us comfortable
if she could. But that was no life for a girl! After I began to herd
and milk I could never get the smell of the cattle off me. The few
underclothes I had I kept in a cracker box. On Saturday nights,
after everybody was in bed, then I could take a bath if I was n't too
tired. I could make two trips to the windmill to carry water, and
heat it in the wash-boiler on the stove. While the water was heat-
ing, I could bring in a washtub out of the cave, and take my bath
in the kitchen. Then I could put on a clean nightgown and get into
bed with two others, who likely had n't had a bath unless I'd given
it to them. You can't tell me anything about family life. I've had
plenty to last me."

"But it's not all like that," I objected.

"Near enough. It's all being under somebody's thumb. What's on
your mind, Jim? Are you afraid I'll want you to marry me some
day?"

Then I told her I was going away.

"What makes you want to go away, Jim? Have n't I been nice
to you?"

"You've been just awfully good to me, Lena," I blurted. "I don't
think about much else. I never shall think about much else while
I'm with you. I'll never settle down and grind if I stay here. You
know that." I dropped down beside her and sat looking at the floor.
I seemed to have forgotten all my reasonable explanations.

Lena drew close to me, and the little hesitation in her voice that
had hurt me was not there when she spoke again.

"I ought n't to have begun it, ought I?" she murmured. "I ought
n't to have gone to see you that first time. But I did want to. I guess
I've always been a little foolish about you. I don't know what first
put it into my head, unless it was Ántonia, always telling me I must
n't be up to any of my nonsense with you. I let you alone for a long
while, though, did n't I?"

She was a sweet creature to those she loved, that Lena Lingard! At last she sent me away with her soft, slow, renunciatory kiss. "You are n't sorry I came to see you that time?" she whispered. "It seemed so natural. I used to think I'd like to be your first sweetheart. You were such a funny kid!" She always kissed one as if she were sadly and wisely sending one away forever.

We said many good-byes before I left Lincoln, but she never tried to hinder me or hold me back. "You are going, but you have n't gone yet, have you?" she used to say.

My Lincoln chapter closed abruptly. I went home to my grandparents for a few weeks, and afterward visited my relatives in Virginia until I joined Cleric in Boston. I was then nineteen years old.

BOOK IV
THE PIONEER WOMAN'S STORY

I

Two years after I left Lincoln I completed my academic course at Harvard. Before I entered the Law School I went home for the summer vacation. On the night of my arrival Mrs. Harling and Frances and Sally came over to greet me. Everything seemed just as it used to be. My grandparents looked very little older. Frances Harling was married now, and she and her husband managed the Harling interests in Black Hawk. When we gathered in grandmother's parlor, I could hardly believe that I had been away at all. One subject, however, we avoided all evening.

When I was walking home with Frances, after we had left Mrs. Harling at her gate, she said simply, "You know, of course, about poor Ántonia."

Poor Ántonia! Every one would be saying that now, I thought bitterly. I replied that grandmother had written me how Ántonia went away to marry Larry Donovan at some place where he was working; that he had deserted her, and that there was now a baby. This was all I knew.

"He never married her," Frances said. "I have n't seen her since she came back. She lives at home, on the farm, and almost never comes to town. She brought the baby in to show it to mama once. I'm afraid she's settled down to be Ambrosch's drudge for good."

I tried to shut Ántonia out of my mind. I was bitterly disappointed in her. I could not forgive her for becoming an object of pity, while Lena Lingard, for whom people had always foretold trouble, was now the leading dressmaker of Lincoln, much respected in Black Hawk. Lena gave her heart away when she felt like it, but she kept her head for her business and had got on in the world.

Just then it was the fashion to speak indulgently of Lena and severely of Tiny Soderball, who had quietly gone West to try her fortune the year before. A Black Hawk boy, just back from Seattle, brought the news that Tiny had not gone to the coast on a venture, as she had allowed people to think, but with very definite plans. One of the roving promoters that used to stop at Mrs. Gardener's hotel owned idle property along the water front in Seattle, and he had offered to set Tiny up in business in one of his empty buildings. She was now conducting a sailors' lodging-house. This, every one said, would be the end of Tiny. Even if she had begun by running a decent place, she could n't keep it up; all sailors' boarding-houses were alike.

When I thought about it, I discovered that I had never known Tiny as well as I knew the other girls. I remembered her tripping briskly about the dining-room on her high heels, carrying a big tray full of dishes, glancing rather pertly at the spruce traveling men, and contemptuously at the scrubby ones—who were so afraid of her that they did n't dare to ask for two kinds of pie. Now it occurred to me that perhaps the sailors, too, might be afraid of Tiny. How astonished we would have been, as we sat talking about her on Frances Harling's front porch, if we could have known what her future was really to be! Of all the girls and boys who grew up together in Black Hawk, Tiny Soderball was to lead the most adventurous life and to achieve the most solid worldly success.

This is what actually happened to Tiny: While she was running her lodging-house in Seattle, gold was discovered in Alaska. Miners and sailors came back from the North with wonderful stories and pouches of gold. Tiny saw it and weighed it in her hands. That daring which nobody had ever suspected in her, awoke. She sold her business and set out for Circle City, in company with a carpenter and his wife whom she had persuaded to go along with her. They reached Skaguay in a snowstorm, went in dog sledges over the Chilkoot Pass, and shot the Yukon in flatboats. They reached Circle City on the very day when some Siwash[1] Indians came into the settlement with the report that there had been a rich gold strike farther up the river, on a certain Klondike Creek. Two days later Tiny and her friends, and nearly every one else in Circle City, started for the Klondike fields on the last steamer that went up the Yukon before it froze for the winter. That boatload of people founded Dawson City. Within a few weeks there were fifteen hundred homeless men in camp. Tiny and the carpenter's wife began to cook for them, in a tent. The miners gave her a lot, and the carpenter put up a log hotel for her. There she sometimes fed a hundred and fifty men a day. Miners came in on snowshoes from their placer[2] claims twenty miles away to buy fresh bread from her, and paid for it in gold.

---

1 A derogatory term of Chinook origin for Indians in the American northwest and Pacific coast territories. There is no tribe called Siwash; the term is akin to "redskin."

2 A placer is a place where a deposit of sand, gravel, or earth in a stream is washed for gold or other valuable minerals.

That winter Tiny kept in her hotel a Swede whose legs had been frozen one night in a storm when he was trying to find his way back to his cabin. The poor fellow thought it great good fortune to be cared for by a woman, and a woman who spoke his own tongue. When he was told that his feet must be amputated, he said he hoped he would not get well; what could a working-man do in this hard world without feet? He did, in fact, die from the operation, but not before he had deeded Tiny Soderball his claim on Hunker Creek. Tiny sold her hotel, invested half her money in Dawson building lots, and with the rest she developed her claim. She went off into the wilds and lived on it. She bought other claims from discouraged miners, traded or sold them on percentages.[1]

After nearly ten years in the Klondike, Tiny returned, with a considerable fortune, to live in San Francisco. I met her in Salt Lake City in 1908. She was a thin, hard-faced woman, very well-dressed, very reserved in manner. Curiously enough, she reminded me of Mrs. Gardener, for whom she had worked in Black Hawk so long ago. She told me about some of the desperate chances she had taken in the gold country, but the thrill of them was quite gone. She said frankly that nothing interested her much now but making money. The only two human beings of whom she spoke with any feeling were the Swede, Johnson, who had given her his claim, and Lena Lingard. She had persuaded Lena to come to San Francisco and go into business there.

"Lincoln was never any place for her," Tiny remarked. "In a town of that size Lena would always be gossiped about. Frisco's the right field for her. She has a fine class of trade. Oh, she's just the same as she always was! She's careless, but she's level-headed. She's the only person I know who never gets any older. It's fine for me to have her there; somebody who enjoys things like that. She keeps an eye on me and won't let me be shabby. When she thinks I need a new dress, she makes it and sends it home—with a bill that's long enough, I can tell you!"

Tiny limped slightly when she walked. The claim on Hunker Creek took toll from its possessors. Tiny had been caught in a sudden turn of weather, like poor Johnson. She lost three toes from one of those pretty little feet that used to trip about Black Hawk

---

1 I.e., she traded or sold them for a base price plus a percentage of the claim's proceeds.

in pointed slippers and striped stockings. Tiny mentioned this mutilation quite casually—did n't seem sensitive about it. She was satisfied with her success, but not elated. She was like some one in whom the faculty of becoming interested is worn out.

II

Soon after I got home that summer I persuaded my grandparents to have their photographs taken, and one morning I went into the photographer's shop to arrange for sittings. While I was waiting for him to come out of his developing-room, I walked about trying to recognize the likenesses on his walls: girls in Commencement dresses, country brides and grooms holding hands, family groups of three generations. I noticed, in a heavy frame, one of those depressing "crayon enlargements"[1] often seen in farmhouse parlors, the subject being a round-eyed baby in short dresses. The photographer came out and gave a constrained, apologetic laugh.

"That's Tony Shimerda's baby. You remember her; she used to be the Harlings' Tony. Too bad! She seems proud of the baby, though; would n't hear to a cheap frame for the picture. I expect her brother will be in for it Saturday."

I went away feeling that I must see Ántonia again. Another girl would have kept her baby out of sight, but Tony, of course, must have its picture on exhibition at the town photographer's, in a great gilt frame. How like her! I could forgive her, I told myself, if she had n't thrown herself away on such a cheap sort of fellow.

Larry Donovan was a passenger conductor, one of those train-crew aristocrats who are always afraid that some one may ask them to put up a car-window, and who, if requested to perform such a menial service, silently point to the button that calls the porter. Larry wore this air of official aloofness even on the street, where there were no car-windows to compromise his dignity. At the end of his run he stepped indifferently from the train along with the passengers, his street hat on his head and his conductor's cap in an alligator-skin bag, went directly into the station and changed his clothes. It was a matter of the utmost importance to him never to be seen in his blue trousers away from his train. He was usually cold and distant with men, but with all women he had a silent, grave familiarity, a special handshake accompanied by a significant,

---

1 Photographic images enlarged and traced with crayons.

deliberate look. He took women, married or single, into his confidence; walked them up and down in the moonlight, telling them what a mistake he had made by not entering the office branch of the service, and how much better fitted he was to fill the post of General Passenger Agent in Denver than the roughshod man who then bore that title. His unappreciated worth was the tender secret Larry shared with his sweethearts, and he was always able to make some foolish heart ache over it.

As I drew near home that morning, I saw Mrs. Harling out in her yard, digging round her mountain-ash tree. It was a dry summer, and she had now no boy to help her. Charley was off in his battleship, cruising somewhere on the Caribbean sea.[1] I turned in at the gate—it was with a feeling of pleasure that I opened and shut that gate in those days; I liked the feel of it under my hand. I took the spade away from Mrs. Harling, and while I loosened the earth around the tree, she sat down on the steps and talked about the oriole family that had a nest in its branches.

"Mrs. Harling," I said presently, "I wish I could find out exactly how Ántonia's marriage fell through."

"Why don't you go out and see your grandfather's tenant, the Widow Steavens? She knows more about it than anybody else. She helped Ántonia get ready to be married, and she was there when Ántonia came back. She took care of her when the baby was born. She could tell you everything. Besides, the Widow Steavens is a good talker, and she has a remarkable memory."

III

On the first or second day of August I got a horse and cart and set out for the high country, to visit the Widow Steavens. The wheat harvest was over, and here and there along the horizon I could see black puffs of smoke from the steam thrashing-machines. The old pasture land was now being broken up into wheatfields and corn-fields, the red grass was disappearing, and the whole face of the country was changing. There were wooden houses where the old sod dwellings used to be, and little orchards, and big red barns; all this meant happy children, contented women, and men who saw their lives coming to a fortunate issue. The windy springs and the blazing summers, one after another, had enriched and mellowed

---

1 Probably in service in the Spanish-American War.

that flat tableland; all the human effort that had gone into it was coming back in long, sweeping lines of fertility. The changes seemed beautiful and harmonious to me; it was like watching the growth of a great man or of a great idea. I recognized every tree and sandbank and rugged draw. I found that I remembered the conformation of the land as one remembers the modeling of human faces.

When I drew up to our old windmill, the Widow Steavens came out to meet me. She was brown as an Indian woman, tall, and very strong. When I was little, her massive head had always seemed to me like a Roman senator's. I told her at once why I had come.

"You'll stay the night with us, Jimmy? I'll talk to you after supper. I can take more interest when my work is off my mind. You've no prejudice against hot biscuit for supper? Some have, these days."

While I was putting my horse away I heard a rooster squawking. I looked at my watch and sighed; it was three o'clock, and I knew that I must eat him at six.

After supper Mrs. Steavens and I went upstairs to the old sitting-room, while her grave, silent brother remained in the basement to read his farm papers.[1] All the windows were open. The white summer moon was shining outside, the windmill was pumping lazily in the light breeze. My hostess put the lamp on a stand in the corner, and turned it low because of the heat. She sat down in her favorite rocking-chair and settled a little stool comfortably under her tired feet. "I'm troubled with callouses, Jim; getting old," she sighed cheerfully. She crossed her hands in her lap and sat as if she were at a meeting of some kind.

"Now, it's about that dear Ántonia you want to know? Well, you've come to the right person. I've watched her like she'd been my own daughter.

"When she came home to do her sewing that summer before she was to be married, she was over here about every day. They've never had a sewing machine at the Shimerdas', and she made all her things here. I taught her hemstitching, and I helped her to cut and fit. She used to sit there at that machine by the window, pedaling the life out of it—she was so strong—and always singing them queer Bohemian songs, like she was the happiest thing in the world.

---

1 Newspapers and periodicals about developments in farming, including new techniques and ideas to increase productivity.

"'Ántonia,' I used to say, 'don't run that machine so fast. You won't hasten the day none that way.'

"Then she'd laugh and slow down for a little, but she'd soon forget and begin to pedal and sing again. I never saw a girl work harder to go to housekeeping right and well-prepared. Lovely table linen the Harlings had given her, and Lena Lingard had sent her nice things from Lincoln. We hemstitched all the tablecloths and pillow-cases, and some of the sheets. Old Mrs. Shimerda knit yards and yards of lace for her underclothes. Tony told me just how she meant to have everything in her house. She'd even bought silver spoons and forks, and kept them in her trunk. She was always coaxing brother to go to the post-office. Her young man did write her real often, from the different towns along his run.

"The first thing that troubled her was when he wrote that his run had been changed, and they would likely have to live in Denver. 'I'm a country girl,' she said, 'and I doubt if I'll be able to manage so well for him in a city. I was counting on keeping chickens, and maybe a cow.' She soon cheered up, though.

"At last she got the letter telling her when to come. She was shaken by it; she broke the seal and read it in this room. I suspected then that she'd begun to get faint-hearted, waiting; though she'd never let me see it.

"Then there was a great time of packing. It was in March, if I remember rightly, and a terrible muddy, raw spell, with the roads bad for hauling her things to town. And here let me say, Ambrosch did the right thing. He went to Black Hawk and bought her a set of plated silver in a purple velvet box, good enough for her station. He gave her three hundred dollars in money; I saw the check. He'd collected her wages all those first years she worked out, and it was but right. I shook him by the hand in this room. 'You're behaving like a man, Ambrosch,' I said, 'and I'm glad to see it, son.'

"'T was a cold, raw day he drove her and her three trunks into Black Hawk to take the night train for Denver—the boxes had been shipped before. He stopped the wagon here, and she ran in to tell me good-bye. She threw her arms around me and kissed me, and thanked me for all I'd done for her. She was so happy she was crying and laughing at the same time, and her red cheeks was all wet with rain.

"'You're surely handsome enough for any man,' I said, looking her over.

"She laughed kind of flighty like, and whispered, 'Good-bye, dear house!' and then ran out to the wagon. I expect she meant that for you and your grandmother, as much as for me, so I'm particular to tell you. This house had always been a refuge to her.

"Well, in a few days we had a letter saying she got to Denver safe, and he was there to meet her. They were to be married in a few days. He was trying to get his promotion before he married, she said. I did n't like that, but I said nothing. The next week Yulka got a postal card, saying she was 'well and happy.' After that we heard nothing. A month went by, and old Mrs. Shimerda began to get fretful. Ambrosch was as sulky with me as if I'd picked out the man and arranged the match.

"One night brother William came in and said that on his way back from the fields he had passed a livery team from town, driving fast out the west road. There was a trunk on the front seat with the driver, and another behind. In the back seat there was a woman all bundled up; but for all her veils, he thought 't was Ántonia Shimerda, or Ántonia Donovan, as her name ought now to be.

"The next morning I got brother to drive me over. I can walk still, but my feet ain't what they used to be, and I try to save myself. The lines outside the Shimerdas' house was full of washing, though it was the middle of the week. As we got nearer I saw a sight that made my heart sink—all those underclothes we'd put so much work on, out there swinging in the wind. Yulka came bringing a dishpanful of wrung clothes, but she darted back into the house like she was loath to see us. When I went in, Ántonia was standing over the tubs, just finishing up a big washing. Mrs. Shimerda was going about her work, talking and scolding to herself. She did n't so much as raise her eyes. Tony wiped her hand on her apron and held it out to me, looking at me steady but mournful. When I took her in my arms she drew away. 'Don't, Mrs. Steavens,' she says, 'you'll make me cry, and I don't want to.'

"I whispered and asked her to come out of doors with me. I knew she could n't talk free before her mother. She went out with me, bareheaded, and we walked up toward the garden.

"'I'm not married, Mrs. Steavens,' she says to me very quiet and natural-like, 'and I ought to be.'

"'Oh, my child,' says I, 'what's happened to you? Don't be afraid to tell me!'

"She sat down on the draw-side, out of sight of the house. 'He's run away from me,' she said. 'I don't know if he ever meant to marry me.'

"'You mean he's thrown up his job and quit the country?' says I.

"'He did n't have any job. He'd been fired; blacklisted for knocking down fares. I did n't know. I thought he had n't been treated right. He was sick when I got there. He'd just come out of the hospital. He lived with me till my money gave out, and afterwards I found he had n't really been hunting work at all. Then he just did n't come back. One nice fellow at the station told me, when I kept going to look for him, to give it up. He said he was afraid Larry'd gone bad and would n't come back any more. I guess he's gone to Old Mexico. The conductors get rich down there, collecting half-fares off the natives and robbing the company. He was always talking about fellows who had got ahead that way.'

"I asked her, of course, why she did n't insist on a civil marriage at once—that would have given her some hold on him. She leaned her head on her hands, poor child, and said, 'I just don't know, Mrs. Steavens. I guess my patience was wore out, waiting so long. I thought if he saw how well I could do for him, he'd want to stay with me.'

"Jimmy, I sat right down on that bank beside her and made lament. I cried like a young thing. I could n't help it. I was just about heart-broke. It was one of them lovely warm May days, and the wind was blowing and the colts jumping around in the pastures; but I felt bowed with despair. My Ántonia, that had so much good in her, had come home disgraced. And that Lena Lingard, that was always a bad one, say what you will, had turned out so well, and was coming home here every summer in her silks and her satins, and doing so much for her mother. I give credit where credit is due, but you know well enough, Jim Burden, there is a great difference in the principles of those two girls. And here it was the good one that had come to grief! I was poor comfort to her. I marveled at her calm. As we went back to the house, she stopped to feel of her clothes to see if they was drying well, and seemed to take pride in their whiteness—she said she'd been living in a brick block, where she did n't have proper conveniences to wash them.

"The next time I saw Ántonia, she was out in the fields ploughing corn. All that spring and summer she did the work of a man on the farm; it seemed to be an understood thing. Ambrosch did n't get any other hand to help him. Poor Marek had got violent and been sent away to an institution a good while back. We never even saw any of Tony's pretty dresses. She did n't take them out of her trunks. She was quiet and steady. Folks respected her industry and tried to treat her as if nothing had happened. They talked, to be sure; but not like they would if she'd put on airs. She was so crushed and quiet that nobody seemed to want to humble her. She never went anywhere. All that summer she never once came to see me. At first I was hurt, but I got to feel that it was because this house reminded her of too much. I went over there when I could, but the times when she was in from the fields were the times when I was busiest here. She talked about the grain and the weather as if she'd never had another interest, and if I went over at night she always looked dead weary. She was afflicted with toothache; one tooth after another ulcerated, and she went about with her face swollen half the time. She would n't go to Black Hawk to a dentist for fear of meeting people she knew. Ambrosch had got over his good spell long ago, and was always surly. Once I told him he ought not to let Ántonia work so hard and pull herself down. He said, 'If you put that in her head, you better stay home.' And after that I did.

"Ántonia worked on through harvest and thrashing, though she was too modest to go out thrashing for the neighbors, like when she was young and free. I did n't see much of her until late that fall when she begun to herd Ambrosch's cattle in the open ground north of here, up toward the big dog town. Sometimes she used to bring them over the west hill, there, and I would run to meet her and walk north a piece with her. She had thirty cattle in her bunch; it had been dry, and the pasture was short, or she would n't have brought them so far.

"It was a fine open fall, and she liked to be alone. While the steers grazed, she used to sit on them grassy banks along the draws and sun herself for hours. Sometimes I slipped up to visit with her, when she had n't gone too far.

"'It does seem like I ought to make lace, or knit like Lena used to,' she said one day, 'but if I start to work, I look around and forget to go on. It seems such a little while ago when Jim Burden and I was playing all over this country. Up here I can pick out the very places where my father used to stand. Sometimes I feel like I'm not going to live very long, so I'm just enjoying every day of this fall.'

"After the winter begun she wore a man's long overcoat and boots, and a man's felt hat with a wide brim. I used to watch her coming and going, and I could see that her steps were getting heavier. One day in December, the snow began to fall. Late in the afternoon I saw Ántonia driving her cattle homeward across the hill. The snow was flying round her and she bent to face it, looking more lonesome-like to me than usual. 'Deary me,' I says to myself, 'the girl's stayed out too late. It'll be dark before she gets them cattle put into the corral.' I seemed to sense she'd been feeling too miserable to get up and drive them.

"That very night, it happened. She got her cattle home, turned them into the corral, and went into the house, into her room behind the kitchen, and shut the door. There, without calling to anybody, without a groan, she lay down on the bed and bore her child.

"I was lifting supper when old Mrs. Shimerda came running down the basement stairs, out of breath and screeching:—

"'Baby come, baby come!' she says, 'Ambrosch much like devil!'

"Brother William is surely a patient man. He was just ready to sit down to a hot supper after a long day in the fields. Without a word he rose and went down to the barn and hooked up his team. He got us over there as quick as it was humanly possible. I went right in, and began to do for Ántonia; but she laid there with her eyes shut and took no account of me. The old woman got a tubful of warm water to wash the baby. I overlooked what she was doing and I said out loud:—

"'Mrs. Shimerda, don't you put that strong yellow soap near that baby. You'll blister its little skin.' I was indignant.

"'Mrs. Steavens,' Ántonia said from the bed, 'if you'll look in the top tray of my trunk, you'll see some fine soap.' That was the first word she spoke.

"After I'd dressed the baby, I took it out to show it to Ambrosch. He was muttering behind the stove and would n't look at it.

"'You'd better put it out in the rain barrel,' he says.

"'Now, see here, Ambrosch,' says I, 'there's a law in this land, don't forget that. I stand here a witness that this baby has come into the world sound and strong, and I intend to keep an eye on what befalls it.' I pride myself I cowed him.

"Well, I expect you're not much interested in babies, but Ántonia's got on fine. She loved it from the first as dearly as if she'd had a ring on her finger, and was never ashamed of it. It's a year and eight months old now, and no baby was ever better cared-for.

WT Benda

Ántonia is a natural-born mother. I wish she could marry and raise a family, but I don't know as there's much chance now."

I slept that night in the room I used to have when I was a little boy, with the summer wind blowing in at the windows, bringing the smell of the ripe fields. I lay awake and watched the moonlight shining over the barn and the stacks and the pond, and the windmill making its old dark shadow against the blue sky.

IV

The next afternoon I walked over to the Shimerdas'. Yulka showed me the baby and told me that Ántonia was shocking wheat on the southwest quarter. I went down across the fields, and Tony saw me from a long way off. She stood still by her shocks, leaning on her pitchfork, watching me as I came. We met like the people in the old song, in silence, if not in tears.[1] Her warm hand clasped mine.

"I thought you'd come, Jim. I heard you were at Mrs. Steavens's last night. I've been looking for you all day."

She was thinner than I had ever seen her, and looked, as Mrs. Steavens said, "worked down," but there was a new kind of strength in the gravity of her face, and her color still gave her that look of deep-seated health and ardor. Still? Why, it flashed across me that though so much had happened in her life and in mine, she was barely twenty-four years old.

Ántonia stuck her fork in the ground, and instinctively we walked toward that unploughed patch at the crossing of the roads as the fittest place to talk to each other. We sat down outside the sagging wire fence that shut Mr. Shimerda's plot off from the rest of the world. The tall red grass had never been cut there. It had died down in winter and come up again in the spring until it was as thick and shrubby as some tropical garden-grass. I found myself telling her everything: why I had decided to study law and to go into the law office of one of my mother's relatives in New York City; about Gaston Cleric's death from pneumonia last winter, and the difference it had made in my life. She wanted to know about my friends and my way of living, and my dearest hopes.

"Of course it means you are going away from us for good," she said with a sigh. "But that don't mean I'll lose you. Look at my papa here; he's been dead all these years, and yet he is more real to me than almost anybody else. He never goes out of my life. I talk to him and consult him all the time. The older I grow, the better I know him and the more I understand him."

She asked me whether I had learned to like big cities. "I'd always be miserable in a city. I'd die of lonesomeness. I liked to be where I know every stack and tree, and where all the ground is friendly. I want to live and die here. Father Kelly says everybody's put into this world for something, and I know what I've got to do. I'm

---

1 An allusion to Lord Byron's poem, "When We Two Parted."

going to see that my little girl has a better chance than ever I had. I'm going to take care of that girl, Jim."

I told her I knew she would. "Do you know, Ántonia, since I've been away, I think of you more often than of any one else in this part of the world. I'd have liked to have you for a sweetheart, or a wife, or my mother or my sister—anything that a woman can be to a man. The idea of you is a part of my mind; you influence my likes and dislikes, all my tastes, hundreds of times when I don't realize it. You really are a part of me."

She turned her bright, believing eyes to me, and the tears came up in them slowly. "How can it be like that, when you know so many people, and when I've disappointed you so? Ain't it wonderful, Jim, how much people can mean to each other? I'm so glad we had each other when we were little. I can't wait till my little girl's old enough to tell her about all the things we used to do. You'll always remember me when you think about old times, won't you? And I guess everybody thinks about old times, even the happiest people."

As we walked homeward across the fields, the sun dropped and lay like a great golden globe in the low west. While it hung there, the moon rose in the east, as big as a cartwheel, pale silver and streaked with rose color, thin as a bubble or a ghost-moon. For five, perhaps ten minutes, the two luminaries confronted each other across the level land, resting on opposite edges of the world. In that singular light every little tree and shock of wheat, every sunflower stalk and clump of snow-on-the-mountain,[1] drew itself up high and pointed; the very clods and furrows in the fields seemed to stand up sharply. I felt the old pull of the earth, the solemn magic that comes out of those fields at nightfall. I wished I could be a little boy again, and that my way could end there.

We reached the edge of the field, where our ways parted. I took her hands and held them against my breast, feeling once more how strong and warm and good they were, those brown hands, and remembering how many kind things they had done for me. I held them now a long while, over my heart. About us it was growing darker and darker, and I had to look hard to see her face, which I meant always to carry with me; the closest, realest face,

---

1 Common name for *euphorbia marginata*, so named for its green and white leaves.

under all the shadows of women's faces, at the very bottom of my memory.

"I'll come back," I said earnestly, through the soft, intrusive darkness.

"Perhaps you will"—I felt rather than saw her smile. "But even if you don't, you're here, like my father. So I won't be lonesome."

As I went back alone over that familiar road, I could almost believe that a boy and girl ran along beside me, as our shadows used to do, laughing and whispering to each other in the grass.

BOOK V
CUZAK'S BOYS

I

I told Ántonia I would come back, but life intervened, and it was twenty years before I kept my promise. I heard of her from time to time; that she married, very soon after I last saw her, a young Bohemian, a cousin of Anton Jelinek; that they were poor, and had a large family. Once when I was abroad I went into Bohemia, and from Prague I sent Ántonia some photographs of her native village. Months afterward came a letter from her, telling me the names and ages of her many children, but little else; signed, "Your old friend, Ántonia Cuzak." When I met Tiny Soderball in Salt Lake, she told me that Ántonia had not "done very well"; that her husband was not a man of much force, and she had had a hard life. Perhaps it was cowardice that kept me away so long. My business took me West several times every year, and it was always in the back of my mind that I would stop in Nebraska some day and go to see Ántonia. But I kept putting it off until the next trip. I did not want to find her aged and broken; I really dreaded it. In the course of twenty crowded years one parts with many illusions. I did not wish to lose the early ones. Some memories are realities, and are better than anything that can ever happen to one again.

I owe it to Lena Lingard that I went to see Ántonia at last. I was in San Francisco two summers ago when both Lena and Tiny Soderball were in town. Tiny lives in a house of her own, and Lena's shop is in an apartment house just around the corner. It interested me, after so many years, to see the two women together. Tiny audits Lena's accounts occasionally, and invests her money for her; and Lena, apparently, takes care that Tiny does n't grow too miserly. "If there's anything I can't stand," she said to me in Tiny's presence, "it's a shabby rich woman." Tiny smiled grimly and assured me that Lena would never be either shabby or rich. "And I don't want to be," the other agreed complacently.

Lena gave me a cheerful account of Ántonia and urged me to make her a visit.

"You really ought to go, Jim. It would be such a satisfaction to her. Never mind what Tiny says. There's nothing the matter with Cuzak. You'd like him. He is n't a hustler, but a rough man would never have suited Tony. Tony has nice children—ten or eleven of them by this time, I guess. I should n't care for a family of that size myself, but somehow it's just right for Tony. She'd love to show them to you."

On my way East I broke my journey at Hastings, in Nebraska, and set off with an open buggy and a fairly good livery team to find the Cuzak farm. At a little past midday, I knew I must be nearing my destination. Set back on a swell of land at my right, I saw a wide farmhouse, with a red barn and an ash grove, and cattle yards in front that sloped down to the high road. I drew up my horses and was wondering whether I should drive in here, when I heard low voices. Ahead of me, in a plum thicket beside the road, I saw two boys bending over a dead dog. The little one, not more than four or five, was on his knees, his hands folded, and his close-clipped, bare head drooping forward in deep dejection. The other stood beside him, a hand on his shoulder, and was comforting him in a language I had not heard for a long while. When I stopped my horses opposite them, the older boy took his brother by the hand and came toward me. He, too, looked grave. This was evidently a sad afternoon for them.

"Are you Mrs. Cuzak's boys?" I asked.

The younger one did not look up; he was submerged in his own feelings, but his brother met me with intelligent gray eyes. "Yes, sir."

"Does she live up there on the hill? I am going to see her. Get in and ride up with me."

He glanced at his reluctant little brother. "I guess we'd better walk. But we'll open the gate for you."

I drove along the side-road and they followed slowly behind. When I pulled up at the windmill, another boy, barefooted and curly-headed, ran out of the barn to tie my team for me. He was a handsome one, this chap, fair-skinned and freckled, with red cheeks and a ruddy pelt as thick as a lamb's wool, growing down on his neck in little tufts. He tied my team with two flourishes of his hands, and nodded when I asked him if his mother was at home. As he glanced at me, his face dimpled with a seizure of irrelevant merriment, and he shot up the windmill tower with a lightness that struck me as disdainful. I knew he was peering down at me as I walked toward the house.

Ducks and geese ran quacking across my path. White cats were sunning themselves among yellow pumpkins on the porch steps. I looked through the wire screen into a big, light kitchen with a white floor. I saw a long table, rows of wooden chairs against the wall, and a shining range in one corner. Two girls were washing dishes at the sink, laughing and chattering, and a little one, in a short pinafore, sat on a stool playing with a rag baby. When I asked for their mother, one of the girls dropped her towel, ran across the floor with noiseless bare feet, and disappeared. The older one, who wore shoes and stockings, came to the door to admit me. She was a buxom girl with dark hair and eyes, calm and self-possessed.

"Won't you come in? Mother will be here in a minute."

Before I could sit down in the chair she offered me, the miracle happened; one of those quiet moments that clutch the heart, and take more courage than the noisy, excited passages in life. Ántonia came in and stood before me; a stalwart, brown woman, flat-chested, her curly brown hair a little grizzled. It was a shock, of course. It always is, to meet people after long years, especially if they have lived as much and as hard as this woman had. We stood looking at each other. The eyes that peered anxiously at me were— simply Ántonia's eyes. I had seen no others like them since I looked into them last, though I had looked at so many thousands of human faces. As I confronted her, the changes grew less apparent to me, her identity stronger. She was there, in the full vigor of her personality, battered but not diminished, looking at me, speaking to me in the husky, breathy voice I remembered so well.

"My husband's not at home, sir. Can I do anything?"

"Don't you remember me, Ántonia? Have I changed so much?"

She frowned into the slanting sunlight that made her brown hair look redder than it was. Suddenly her eyes widened, her whole face seemed to grow broader. She caught her breath and put out two hard-worked hands.

"Why, it's Jim! Anna, Yulka, it's Jim Burden!" She had no sooner caught my hands than she looked alarmed. "What's happened? Is anybody dead?"

I patted her arm. "No. I did n't come to a funeral this time. I got off the train at Hastings and drove down to see you and your family."

She dropped my hand and began rushing about. "Anton, Yulka, Nina, where are you all? Run, Anna, and hunt for the boys. They're off looking for that dog, somewhere. And call Leo. Where is that Leo!" She pulled them out of corners and came bringing them like a mother cat bringing in her kittens. "You don't have to go right off, Jim? My oldest boy's not here. He's gone with papa to the street fair at Wilber. I won't let you go! You've got to stay and see Rudolph and our papa." She looked at me imploringly, panting with excitement.

While I reassured her and told her there would be plenty of time, the barefooted boys from outside were slipping into the kitchen and gathering about her.

"Now, tell me their names, and how old they are."

As she told them off in turn, she made several mistakes about ages, and they roared with laughter. When she came to my light-footed friend of the windmill, she said, "This is Leo, and he's old enough to be better than he is."

He ran up to her and butted her playfully with his curly head, like a little ram, but his voice was quite desperate. "You've forgot! You always forget mine. It's mean! Please tell him, mother!" He clenched his fists in vexation and looked up at her impetuously.

She wound her forefinger in his yellow fleece and pulled it, watching him. "Well, how old are you?"

"I'm twelve," he panted, looking not at me but at her; "I'm twelve years old, and I was born on Easter day!"

She nodded to me. "It's true. He was an Easter baby."

The children all looked at me, as if they expected me to exhib-it astonishment or delight at this information. Clearly, they were proud of each other, and of being so many. When they had all been introduced, Anna, the eldest daughter, who had met me at the door, scattered them gently, and came bringing a white apron which she tied round her mother's waist.

"Now, mother, sit down and talk to Mr. Burden. We'll finish the dishes quietly and not disturb you."

Ántonia looked about, quite distracted. "Yes, child, but why don't we take him into the parlor, now that we've got a nice par-lor for company?"

The daughter laughed indulgently, and took my hat from me. "Well, you're here, now, mother, and if you talk here, Yulka and I can listen, too. You can show him the parlor after while." She smiled at me, and went back to the dishes, with her sister. The little girl with the rag doll found a place on the bottom step of an enclosed back stairway, and sat with her toes curled up, looking out at us expectantly.

"She's Nina, after Nina Harling," Ántonia explained. "Ain't her eyes like Nina's? I declare, Jim, I loved you children almost as much as I love my own. These children know all about you and Charley and Sally, like as if they'd grown up with you. I can't think of what I want to say, you've got me so stirred up. And then, I've forgot my English so. I don't often talk it any more. I tell the children I used to speak real well." She said they always spoke Bohemian at home.

The little ones could not speak English at all—did n't learn it until they went to school.

"I can't believe it's you, sitting here, in my own kitchen. You would n't have known me, would you, Jim? You've kept so young, yourself. But it's easier for a man. I can't see how my Anton looks any older than the day I married him. His teeth have kept so nice. I have n't got many left. But I feel just as young as I used to, and I can do as much work. Oh, we don't have to work so hard now! We've got plenty to help us, papa and me. And how many have you got, Jim?"

When I told her I had no children she seemed embarrassed. "Oh, ain't that too bad! Maybe you could take one of my bad ones, now? That Leo; he's the worst of all." She leaned toward me with a smile. "And I love him the best," she whispered.

"Mother!" the two girls murmured reproachfully from the dishes.

Ántonia threw up her head and laughed. "I can't help it. You know I do. Maybe it's because he came on Easter day, I don't know. And he's never out of mischief one minute!"

I was thinking, as I watched her, how little it mattered—about her teeth, for instance. I know so many women who have kept all the things that she had lost, but whose inner glow has faded. Whatever else was gone, Ántonia had not lost the fire of life. Her skin, so brown and hardened, had not that look of flabbiness, as if the sap beneath it had been secretly drawn away.

While we were talking, the little boy whom they called Jan came in and sat down on the step beside Nina, under the hood of the stairway. He wore a funny long gingham apron, like a smock, over his trousers, and his hair was clipped so short that his head looked white and naked. He watched us out of his big, sorrowful gray eyes.

"He wants to tell you about the dog, mother. They found it dead," Anna said, as she passed us on her way to the cupboard.

Ántonia beckoned the boy to her. He stood by her chair, leaning his elbows on her knees and twisting her apron strings in his slender fingers, while he told her his story softly in Bohemian, and the tears brimmed over and hung on his long lashes. His mother listened, spoke soothingly to him, and in a whisper promised him something that made him give her a quick, teary smile. He slipped away and whispered his secret to Nina, sitting close to her and talking behind his hand.

When Anna finished her work and had washed her hands, she

came and stood behind her mother's chair. "Why don't we show Mr. Burden our new fruit cave?" she asked.

We started off across the yard with the children at our heels. The boys were standing by the windmill, talking about the dog; some of them ran ahead to open the cellar door. When we descended, they all came down after us, and seemed quite as proud of the cave as the girls were. Ambrosch, the thoughtful-looking one who had directed me down by the plum bushes, called my attention to the stout brick walls and the cement floor. "Yes, it is a good way from the house," he admitted. "But, you see, in winter there are nearly always some of us around to come out and get things."

Anna and Yulka showed me three small barrels; one full of dill pickles, one full of chopped pickles, and one full of pickled watermelon rinds.

"You would n't believe, Jim, what it takes to feed them all!" their mother exclaimed. "You ought to see the bread we bake on Wednesdays and Saturdays! It's no wonder their poor papa can't get rich, he has to buy so much sugar for us to preserve with. We have our own wheat ground for flour,—but then there's that much less to sell."

Nina and Jan, and a little girl named Lucie, kept shyly pointing out to me the shelves of glass jars. They said nothing, but glancing at me, traced on the glass with their finger-tips the outline of the cherries and strawberries and crab-apples within, trying by a blissful expression of countenance to give me some idea of their deliciousness.

"Show him the spiced plums, mother. Americans don't have those," said one of the older boys. "Mother uses them to make kolaches,"[1] he added.

Leo, in a low voice, tossed off some scornful remark in Bohemian.

I turned to him. "You think I don't know what *kolaches* are, eh? You're mistaken, young man. I've eaten your mother's *kolaches* long before that Easter day when you were born."

"Always too fresh, Leo," Ambrosch remarked with a shrug.

Leo dived behind his mother and grinned out at me.

We turned to leave the cave; Ántonia and I went up the stairs first, and the children waited. We were standing outside talking, when they all came running up the steps together, big and little,

---

1 Traditional Czech pastry, filled with poppy seed or fruit preserves, similar to an American "Danish" pastry.

tow heads and gold heads and brown, and flashing little naked legs; a veritable explosion of life out of the dark cave into the sunlight. It made me dizzy for a moment.

The boys escorted us to the front of the house, which I had n't yet seen; in farmhouses, somehow, life comes and goes by the back door. The roof was so steep that the eaves were not much above the forest of tall hollyhocks, now brown and in seed. Through July, Ántonia said, the house was buried in them; the Bohemians, I remembered, always planted hollyhocks. The front yard was enclosed by a thorny locust hedge, and at the gate grew two silvery, moth-like trees of the mimosa family. From here one looked down over the cattle yards, with their two long ponds, and over a wide stretch of stubble which they told me was a rye-field in summer.

At some distance behind the house were an ash grove and two orchards; a cherry orchard, with gooseberry and currant bushes between the rows, and an apple orchard, sheltered by a high hedge from the hot winds. The older children turned back when we reached the hedge, but Jan and Nina and Lucie crept through it by a hole known only to themselves and hid under the low-branching mulberry bushes.

As we walked through the apple orchard, grown up in tall blue-grass, Ántonia kept stopping to tell me about one tree and another. "I love them as if they were people," she said, rubbing her hand over the bark. "There was n't a tree here when we first came. We planted every one, and used to carry water for them, too—after we'd been working in the fields all day. Anton, he was a city man, and he used to get discouraged. But I could n't feel so tired that I would n't fret about these trees when there was a dry time. They were on my mind like children. Many a night after he was asleep I've got up and come out and carried water to the poor things. And now, you see, we have the good of them. My man worked in the orange groves in Florida, and he knows all about grafting. There ain't one of our neighbors has an orchard that bears like ours."

In the middle of the orchard we came upon a grape-arbor, with seats built along the sides and a warped plank table. The three children were waiting for us there. They looked up at me bashfully and made some request of their mother.

"They want me to tell you how the teacher has the school picnic here every year. These don't go to school yet, so they think it's all like the picnic."

After I had admired the arbor sufficiently, the youngsters ran away to an open place where there was a rough jungle of French pinks, and squatted down among them, crawling about and measuring with a string. "Jan wants to bury his dog there," Ántonia explained. "I had to tell him he could. He's kind of like Nina Harling; you remember how hard she used to take little things? He has funny notions, like her."

We sat down and watched them. Ántonia leaned her elbows on the table. There was the deepest peace in that orchard. It was surrounded by a triple enclosure; the wire fence, then the hedge of thorny locusts, then the mulberry hedge which kept out the hot winds of summer and held fast to the protecting snows of winter. The hedges were so tall that we could see nothing but the blue sky above them, neither the barn roof nor the windmill. The afternoon sun poured down on us through the drying grape leaves. The orchard seemed full of sun, like a cup, and we could smell the ripe apples on the trees. The crabs hung on the branches as thick as beads on a string, purple-red, with a thin silvery glaze over them. Some hens and ducks had crept through the hedge and were pecking at the fallen apples. The drakes were handsome fellows, with pinkish gray bodies, their heads and necks covered with iridescent green feathers which grew close and full, changing to blue like a peacock's neck. Ántonia said they always reminded her of soldiers—some uniform she had seen in the old country, when she was a child.

"Are there any quail left now?" I asked. I reminded her how she used to go hunting with me the last summer before we moved to town. "You were n't a bad shot, Tony. Do you remember how you used to want to run away and go for ducks with Charley Harling and me?"

"I know, but I'm afraid to look at a gun now." She picked up one of the drakes and ruffled his green capote[1] with her fingers. "Ever since I've had children, I don't like to kill anything. It makes me kind of faint to wring an old goose's neck. Ain't that strange, Jim?"

"I don't know. The young Queen of Italy[2] said the same thing

---

1 A capote is a long-hooded cloak worn by soldiers; Jim is applying Ántonia's soldier imagery to the duck's neck.
2 Elena, wife of Vittorio Emmanuele III, was a Slav from Montenegro who reportedly gave up hunting when she became a mother.

once, to a friend of mine. She used to be a great huntswoman, but now she feels as you do, and only shoots clay pigeons."

"Then I'm sure she's a good mother," Ántonia said warmly.

She told me how she and her husband had come out to this new country when the farm land was cheap and could be had on easy payments. The first ten years were a hard struggle. Her husband knew very little about farming and often grew discouraged. "We'd never have got through if I had n't been so strong. I've always had good health, thank God, and I was able to help him in the fields until right up to the time before my babies came. Our children were good about taking care of each other. Martha, the one you saw when she was a baby, was such a help to me, and she trained Anna to be just like her. My Martha's married now, and has a baby of her own. Think of that, Jim!

"No, I never got down-hearted. Anton's a good man, and I loved my children and always believed they would turn out well. I belong on a farm. I'm never lonesome here like I used to be in town. You remember what sad spells I used to have, when I did n't know what was the matter with me? I've never had them out here. And I don't mind work a bit, if I don't have to put up with sadness." She leaned her chin on her hand and looked down through the orchard, where the sunlight was growing more and more golden.

"You ought never to have gone to town, Tony," I said, wondering at her.

She turned to me eagerly. "Oh, I'm glad I went! I'd never have known anything about cooking or housekeeping if I had n't. I learned nice ways at the Harlings', and I've been able to bring my children up so much better. Don't you think they are pretty well-behaved for country children? If it had n't been for what Mrs. Harling taught me, I expect I'd have brought them up like wild rabbits. No, I'm glad I had a chance to learn; but I'm thankful none of my daughters will ever have to work out. The trouble with me was, Jim, I never could believe harm of anybody I loved."

While we were talking, Ántonia assured me that she could keep me for the night. "We've plenty of room. Two of the boys sleep in the haymow till cold weather comes, but there's no need for it. Leo always begs to sleep there, and Ambrosch goes along to look after him."

I told her I would like to sleep in the haymow, with the boys.

"You can do just as you want to. The chest is full of clean blankets, put away for winter. Now I must go, or my girls will be doing all the work, and I want to cook your supper myself."

As we went toward the house, we met Ambrosch and Anton, starting off with their milking-pails to hunt the cows. I joined them, and Leo accompanied us at some distance, running ahead and starting up at us out of clumps of ironweed, calling, "I'm a jack rabbit," or, "I'm a big bull-snake."

I walked between the two older boys—straight, well-made fellows, with good heads and clear eyes. They talked about their school and the new teacher, told me about the crops and the harvest, and how many steers they would feed that winter. They were easy and confidential with me, as if I were an old friend of the family—and not too old. I felt like a boy in their company, and all manner of forgotten interests revived in me. It seemed, after all, so natural to be walking along a barbed-wire fence beside the sunset, toward a red pond, and to see my shadow moving along at my right, over the close-cropped grass.

"Has mother shown you the pictures you sent her from the old country?" Ambrosch asked. "We've had them framed and they're hung up in the parlor. She was so glad to get them. I don't believe I ever saw her so pleased about anything." There was a note of simple gratitude in his voice that made me wish I had given more occasion for it.

I put my hand on his shoulder. "Your mother, you know, was very much loved by all of us. She was a beautiful girl."

"Oh, we know!" They both spoke together; seemed a little surprised that I should think it necessary to mention this. "Everybody liked her, did n't they? The Harlings and your grandmother, and all the town people."

"Sometimes," I ventured, "it does n't occur to boys that their mother was ever young and pretty."

"Oh, we know!" they said again, warmly. "She's not very old now," Ambrosch added. "Not much older than you."

"Well," I said, "if you were n't nice to her, I think I'd take a club and go for the whole lot of you. I could n't stand it if you boys were inconsiderate, or thought of her as if she were just somebody who looked after you. You see I was very much in love with your mother once, and I know there's nobody like her."

The boys laughed and seemed pleased and embarrassed. "She never told us that," said Anton. "But she's always talked lots about you, and about what good times you used to have. She has a picture of you that she cut out of the Chicago paper once, and Leo says he recognized you when you drove up to the windmill. You can't tell about Leo, though; sometimes he likes to be smart."

We brought the cows home to the corner nearest the barn, and the boys milked them while night came on. Everything was as it should be: the strong smell of sunflowers and ironweed in the dew, the clear blue and gold of the sky, the evening star, the purr of the milk into the pails, the grunts and squeals of the pigs fighting over their supper. I began to feel the loneliness of the farm-boy at evening, when the chores seem everlastingly the same, and the world so far away.

What a tableful we were at supper; two long rows of restless heads in the lamplight, and so many eyes fastened excitedly upon Ántonia as she sat at the head of the table, filling the plates and starting the dishes on their way. The children were seated according to a system; a little one next an older one, who was to watch over his behavior and to see that he got his food. Anna and Yulka left their chairs from time to time to bring fresh plates of *kolaches* and pitchers of milk.

After supper we went into the parlor, so that Yulka and Leo could play for me. Ántonia went first, carrying the lamp. There were not nearly chairs enough to go round, so the younger children sat down on the bare floor. Little Lucie whispered to me that they were going to have a parlor carpet if they got ninety cents for their wheat. Leo, with a good deal of fussing, got out his violin. It was old Mr. Shimerda's instrument, which Ántonia had always kept, and it was too big for him. But he played very well for a self-taught boy. Poor Yulka's efforts were not so successful. While they were playing, little Nina got up from her corner, came out into the middle of the floor, and began to do a pretty little dance on the boards with her bare feet. No one paid the least attention to her, and when she was through she stole back and sat down by her brother.

Ántonia spoke to Leo in Bohemian. He frowned and wrinkled up his face. He seemed to be trying to pout, but his attempt only brought out dimples in unusual places. After twisting and screwing the keys, he played some Bohemian airs, without the organ to hold him back, and that went better. The boy was so restless that I had not had a chance to look at his face before. My first impression was right; he really was faun-like. He had n't much head behind his ears, and his tawny fleece grew down thick to the back of his neck. His eyes were not frank and wide apart like those of the other boys, but were deep-set, gold-green in color, and seemed sensitive to the light. His mother said he got hurt oftener than all the others put together. He was always trying to ride the colts before they were broken, teasing the turkey gobbler, seeing just how much red the bull would stand for, or how sharp the new axe was.

After the concert was over Ántonia brought out a big boxful of photographs; she and Anton in their wedding clothes, holding hands; her brother Ambrosch and his very fat wife, who had a farm of her own, and who bossed her husband, I was delighted to hear; the three Bohemian Marys and their large families.

"You would n't believe how steady those girls have turned out," Ántonia remarked. "Mary Svoboda's the best butter-maker in all this country, and a fine manager. Her children will have a grand chance."

As Ántonia turned over the pictures the young Cuzaks stood behind her chair, looking over her shoulder with interested faces. Nina and Jan, after trying to see round the taller ones, quietly brought a chair, climbed up on it, and stood close together, looking. The little boy forgot his shyness and grinned delightedly when familiar faces came into view. In the group about Ántonia I was conscious of a kind of physical harmony. They leaned this way and that, and were not afraid to touch each other. They contemplated the photographs with pleased recognition; looked at some admiringly, as if these characters in their mother's girlhood had been remarkable people. The little children, who could not speak English, murmured comments to each other in their rich old language.

Ántonia held out a photograph of Lena that had come from San Francisco last Christmas. "Does she still look like that? She has n't been home for six years now." Yes, it was exactly like Lena, I told her; a comely woman, a trifle too plump, in a hat a trifle too large, but with the old lazy eyes, and the old dimpled ingenuousness still lurking at the corners of her mouth.

There was a picture of Frances Harling in a be-frogged[1] riding costume that I remembered well. "Is n't she fine!" the girls murmured. They all assented. One could see that Frances had come down as a heroine in the family legend. Only Leo was unmoved.

"And there's Mr. Harling, in his grand fur coat. He was awfully rich, was n't he, mother?"

---

1 Ornamental coat-fastening, originally forming part of military dress, consisting of a spindle-shaped button covered with silk or similar material and a loop through which it is passed.

"He was n't any Rockefeller," put in Master Leo, in a very low tone, which reminded me of the way in which Mrs. Shimerda had once said that my grandfather "was n't Jesus." His habitual skepticism was like a direct inheritance from that old woman.

"None of your smart speeches," said Ambrosch severely.

Leo poked out a supple red tongue at him, but a moment later broke into a giggle at a tintype[1] of two men, uncomfortably seated, with an awkward-looking boy in baggy clothes standing between them; Jake and Otto and I! We had it taken, I remembered, when we went to Black Hawk on the first Fourth of July I spent in Nebraska. I was glad to see Jake's grin again, and Otto's ferocious mustaches. The young Cuzaks knew all about them.

"He made grandfather's coffin, did n't he?" Anton asked.

"Was n't they good fellows, Jim?" Ántonia's eyes filled. "To this day I'm ashamed because I quarreled with Jake that way. I was saucy and impertinent to him, Leo, like you are with people sometimes, and I wish somebody had made me behave."

"We are n't through with you, yet," they warned me. They produced a photograph taken just before I went away to college; a tall youth in striped trousers and a straw hat, trying to look easy and jaunty.

"Tell us, Mr. Burden," said Charley, "about the rattler you killed at the dog town. How long was he? Sometimes mother says six feet and sometimes she says five."

These children seemed to be upon very much the same terms with Ántonia as the Harling children had been so many years before. They seemed to feel the same pride in her, and to look to her for stories and entertainment as we used to do.

It was eleven o'clock when I at last took my bag and some blankets and started for the barn with the boys. Their mother came to the door with us, and we tarried for a moment to look out at the white slope of the corral and the two ponds asleep in the moonlight, and the long sweep of the pasture under the star-sprinkled sky.

The boys told me to choose my own place in the haymow, and I lay down before a big window, left open in warm weather, that looked out into the stars. Ambrosch and Leo cuddled up in a haycave, back under the eaves, and lay giggling and whispering. They tickled each other and tossed and tumbled in the hay; and then, all

---

1 A photograph taken as a positive on a tin plate.

at once, as if they had been shot, they were still. There was hardly a minute between giggles and bland slumber.

I lay awake for a long while, until the slow-moving moon passed my window on its way up the heavens. I was thinking about Ántonia and her children; about Anna's solicitude for her, Ambrosch's grave affection, Leo's jealous, animal little love. That moment, when they all came tumbling out of the cave into the light, was a sight any man might have come far to see. Ántonia had always been one to leave images in the mind that did not fade—that grew stronger with time. In my memory there was a succession of such pictures, fixed there like the old woodcuts of one's first primer: Ántonia kicking her bare legs against the sides of my pony when we came home in triumph with our snake; Ántonia in her black shawl and fur cap, as she stood by her father's grave in the snowstorm; Ántonia coming in with her work-team along the evening sky-line. She lent herself to immemorial human attitudes which we recognize by instinct as universal and true. I had not been mistaken. She was a battered woman now, not a lovely girl; but she still had that something which fires the imagination, could still stop one's breath for a moment by a look or gesture that somehow revealed the meaning in common things. She had only to stand in the orchard, to put her hand on a little crab tree and look up at the apples, to make you feel the goodness of planting and tending and harvesting at last. All the strong things of her heart came out in her body, that had been so tireless in serving generous emotions.

It was no wonder that her sons stood tall and straight. She was a rich mine of life, like the founders of early races.

II

When I awoke in the morning long bands of sunshine were coming in at the window and reaching back under the eaves where the two boys lay. Leo was wide awake and was tickling his brother's leg with a dried cone-flower he had pulled out of the hay. Ambrosch kicked at him and turned over. I closed my eyes and pretended to be asleep. Leo lay on his back, elevated one foot, and began exercising his toes. He picked up dried flowers with his toes and brandished them in the belt of sunlight. After he had amused himself thus for some time, he rose on one elbow and began to look at me, cautiously, then critically, blinking his eyes in the light. His expression was droll; it dismissed me lightly. "This old fellow is no different from other people. He does n't know my secret." He seemed conscious of possessing a keener power of enjoyment than other people; his quick recognitions made him frantically impatient of deliberate judgments. He always knew what he wanted without thinking.

After dressing in the hay, I washed my face in cold water at the windmill. Breakfast was ready when I entered the kitchen, and Yulka was baking griddle-cakes. The three older boys set off for the fields early. Leo and Yulka were to drive to town to meet their father, who would return from Wilber on the noon train.

"We'll only have a lunch at noon," Ántonia said, "and cook the geese for supper, when our papa will be here. I wish my Martha could come down to see you. They have a Ford car now, and she don't seem so far away from me as she used to. But her husband's crazy about his farm and about having everything just right, and they almost never get away except on Sundays. He's a handsome boy, and he'll be rich some day. Everything he takes hold of turns out well. When they bring that baby in here, and unwrap him, he looks like a little prince; Martha takes care of him so beautiful. I'm reconciled to her being away from me now, but at first I cried like I was putting her into her coffin."

We were alone in the kitchen, except for Anna, who was pouring cream into the churn. She looked up at me. "Yes, she did. We were just ashamed of mother. She went round crying, when Martha was so happy, and the rest of us were all glad. Joe certainly was patient with you, mother."

Ántonia nodded and smiled at herself. "I know it was silly, but I could n't help it. I wanted her right here. She'd never been away from me a night since she was born. If Anton had made trouble about her when she was a baby, or wanted me to leave her with my mother, I would n't have married him. I could n't. But he always loved her like she was his own."

"I did n't even know Martha was n't my full sister until after she was engaged to Joe," Anna told me.

Toward the middle of the afternoon the wagon drove in, with the father and the eldest son. I was smoking in the orchard, and as I went out to meet them, Ántonia came running down from the house and hugged the two men as if they had been away for months.

"Papa" interested me, from my first glimpse of him. He was shorter than his older sons; a crumpled little man, with run-over boot heels, and he carried one shoulder higher than the other. But he moved very quickly, and there was an air of jaunty liveliness about him. He had a strong, ruddy color, thick black hair, a little grizzled, a curly mustache, and red lips. His smile showed the strong teeth of which his wife was so proud, and as he saw me his lively, quizzical eyes told me that he knew all about me. He looked like a humorous philosopher who had hitched up one shoulder under the burdens of life, and gone on his way having a good time when he could. He advanced to meet me and gave me a hard hand, burned red on the back and heavily coated with hair. He wore his Sunday clothes, very thick and hot for the weather, an unstarched white shirt, and a blue necktie with big white dots, like a little boy's, tied in a flowing bow. Cuzak began at once to talk about his holiday—from politeness he spoke in English.

"Mama, I wish you had see the lady dance on the slack-wire[1] in the street at night. They throw a bright light on her and she float through the air something beautiful, like a bird! They have a dancing bear, like in the old country, and two three merry-go-around, and people in balloons, and what you call the big wheel, Rudolph?"

"A Ferris wheel," Rudolph entered the conversation in a deep baritone voice. He was six foot two, and had a chest like a young blacksmith. "We went to the big dance in the hall behind the saloon last night, mother, and I danced with all the girls, and so did father. I never saw so many pretty girls. It was a Bohunk[2] crowd, for sure. We did n't hear a word of English on the street, except from the show people, did we, papa?"

Cuzak nodded. "And very many send word to you, Ántonia. You will excuse"—turning to me—"if I tell her." While we walked toward the house he related incidents and delivered messages in the tongue he spoke fluently, and I dropped a little behind, curious to know what their relations had become—or remained. The two seemed to be on terms of easy friendliness, touched with humor. Clearly, she was the impulse, and he the corrective. As they went up the hill he kept glancing at her sidewise, to see whether she got his point, or how she received it. I noticed later that he always looked at people sidewise, as a work-horse does at its yoke-mate. Even when he sat opposite me in the kitchen, talking, he would

---

1 A loosely-stretched rope, the opposite of a tight-rope, for acrobatic performance.
2 Slang term for Bohemian.

turn his head a little toward the clock or the stove and look at me from the side, but with frankness and good-nature. This trick did not suggest duplicity or secretiveness, but merely long habit, as with the horse.

He had brought a tintype of himself and Rudolph for Ántonia's collection, and several paper bags of candy for the children. He looked a little disappointed when his wife showed him a big box of candy I had got in Denver—she had n't let the children touch it the night before. He put his candy away in the cupboard, "for when she rains," and glanced at the box, chuckling. "I guess you must have hear about how my family ain't so small," he said.

Cuzak sat down behind the stove and watched his women-folk and the little children with equal amusement. He thought they were nice, and he thought they were funny, evidently. He had been off dancing with the girls and forgetting that he was an old fellow, and now his family rather surprised him; he seemed to think it a joke that all these children should belong to him. As the younger ones slipped up to him in his retreat, he kept taking things out of his pockets; penny dolls, a wooden clown, a balloon pig that was inflated by a whistle. He beckoned to the little boy they called Jan, whispered to him, and presented him with a paper snake, gently, so as not to startle him. Looking over the boy's head he said to me, "This one is bashful. He gets left."

Cuzak had brought home with him a roll of illustrated Bohemian papers. He opened them and began to tell his wife the news, much of which seemed to relate to one person. I heard the name Vasakova, Vasakova, repeated several times with lively interest, and presently I asked him whether he were talking about the singer, Maria Vasak.

"You know? You have heard, maybe?" he asked incredulously. When I assured him that I had heard her, he pointed out her picture and told me that Vasak had broken her leg, climbing in the Austrian Alps, and would not be able to fill her engagements. He seemed delighted to find that I had heard her sing in London and in Vienna; got out his pipe and lit it to enjoy our talk the better. She came from his part of Prague. His father used to mend her shoes for her when she was a student. Cuzak questioned me about her looks, her popularity, her voice; but he particularly wanted to know whether I had noticed her tiny feet, and whether I thought she had saved much money. She was extravagant, of course, but he hoped she would n't squander everything, and have nothing left when she was old. As a young man, working in Wien,[1] he had seen a good many artists who were old and poor, making one glass of beer last all evening, and "it was not very nice, that."

When the boys came in from milking and feeding, the long table was laid, and two brown geese, stuffed with apples, were put down sizzling before Ántonia. She began to carve, and Rudolph, who sat next his mother, started the plates on their way. When everybody was served, he looked across the table at me.

"Have you been to Black Hawk lately, Mr. Burden? Then I wonder if you've heard about the Cutters?"

No, I had heard nothing at all about them.

"Then you must tell him, son, though it's a terrible thing to talk about at supper. Now, all you children be quiet, Rudolph is going to tell about the murder."

"Hurrah! The murder!" the children murmured, looking pleased and interested.

Rudolph told his story in great detail, with occasional promptings from his mother or father.

Wick Cutter and his wife had gone on living in the house that Ántonia and I knew so well, and in the way we knew so well. They grew to be very old people. He shriveled up, Ántonia said, until he looked like a little old yellow monkey, for his beard and his fringe of hair never changed color. Mrs. Cutter remained flushed and wild-eyed as we had known her, but as the years passed she became afflicted with a shaking palsy which made her nervous nod continuous instead of occasional. Her hands were so uncertain that she could no longer disfigure china, poor woman! As the couple grew older, they quarreled more and more about the ultimate disposition of their "property." A new law was passed in the State, securing the surviving wife a third of her husband's estate under all conditions. Cutter was tormented by the fear that Mrs. Cutter would live longer than he, and that eventually her "people," whom he had always hated so violently, would inherit. Their quarrels on this subject passed the boundary of the close-growing cedars, and were heard in the street by whoever wished to loiter and listen.

One morning, two years ago, Cutter went into the hardware store and bought a pistol, saying he was going to shoot a dog, and adding that he "thought he would take a shot at an old cat while

1 Vienna.

he was about it." (Here the children interrupted Rudolph's narrative by smothered giggles.)

Cutter went out behind the hardware store, put up a target, practiced for an hour or so, and then went home. At six o'clock that evening, when several men were passing the Cutter house on their way home to supper, they heard a pistol shot. They paused and were looking doubtfully at one another, when another shot came crashing through an upstairs window. They ran into the house and found Wick Cutter lying on a sofa in his upstairs bedroom, with his throat torn open, bleeding on a roll of sheets he had placed beside his head.

"Walk in, gentlemen," he said weakly. "I am alive, you see, and competent. You are witnesses that I have survived my wife. You will find her in her own room. Please make your examination at once, so that there will be no mistake."

One of the neighbors telephoned for a doctor, while the others went into Mrs. Cutter's room. She was lying on her bed, in her nightgown and wrapper, shot through the heart. Her husband must have come in while she was taking her afternoon nap and shot her, holding the revolver near her breast. Her nightgown was burned from the powder.

The horrified neighbors rushed back to Cutter. He opened his eyes and said distinctly, "Mrs. Cutter is quite dead, gentlemen, and I am conscious. My affairs are in order." Then, Rudolph said, "he let go and died."

On his desk the coroner found a letter, dated at five o'clock that afternoon. It stated that he had just shot his wife; that any will she might secretly have made would be invalid, as he survived her. He meant to shoot himself at six o'clock and would, if he had strength, fire a shot through the window in the hope that passers-by might come in and see him "before life was extinct," as he wrote.

"Now, would you have thought that man had such a cruel heart?" Ántonia turned to me after the story was told. "To go and do that poor woman out of any comfort she might have from his money after he was gone!"

"Did you ever hear of anybody else that killed himself for spite, Mr. Burden?" asked Rudolph.

I admitted that I hadn't. Every lawyer learns over and over how strong a motive hate can be, but in my collection of legal anecdotes I had nothing to match this one. When I asked how much the estate amounted to, Rudolph said it was a little over a hundred thousand dollars.

Cuzak gave me a twinkling, sidelong glance. "The lawyers, they got a good deal of it, sure," he said merrily.

A hundred thousand dollars; so that was the fortune that had been scraped together by such hard dealing, and that Cutter himself had died for in the end!

After supper Cuzak and I took a stroll in the orchard and sat down by the windmill to smoke. He told me his story as if it were my business to know it.

His father was a shoemaker, his uncle a furrier, and he, being a younger son, was apprenticed to the latter's trade. You never got anywhere working for your relatives, he said, so when he was a journeyman he went to Vienna and worked in a bog fur shop, earning good money. But a young fellow who liked a good time did n't save anything in Vienna; there were too many pleasant ways of spending every night what he'd made in the day. After three years there, he came to New York. He was badly advised and went to work on furs during a strike, when the factories were offering big wages. The strikers won, and Cuzak was blacklisted. As he had a few hundred dollars ahead, he decided to go to Florida and raise oranges. He had always thought he would like to raise oranges! The second year a hard frost killed his young grove, and he fell ill with malaria. He came to Nebraska to visit his cousin, Anton Jelinek, and to look about. When he began to look about, he saw Ántonia, and she was exactly the kind of girl he had always been hunting for. They were married at once, though he had to borrow money from his cousin to buy the wedding-ring.

"It was a pretty hard job, breaking up this place and making the first crops grow," he said, pushing back his hat and scratching his grizzled hair. "Sometimes I git awful sore on this place and want to quit, but my wife she always say we better stick it out. The babies come along pretty fast, so it look like it be hard to move, anyhow. I guess she was right, all right. We got this place clear now. We pay only twenty dollars an acre then, and I been offered a hundred. We bought another quarter ten years ago, and we got it most paid for. We got plenty boys; we can work a lot of land. Yes, she is a good wife for a poor man. She ain't always so strict with me, neither. Sometimes maybe I drink a little too much beer in town, and when I come home she don't say nothing. She don't ask me no questions. We always get along fine, her and me, like at first. The children don't make trouble between us, like sometimes happens." He lit another pipe and pulled on it contentedly.

I found Cuzak a most companionable fellow. He asked me a

great many questions about my trip through Bohemia, about Vienna and the Ringstrasse[1] and the theaters.

"Gee! I like to go back there once, when the boys is big enough to farm the place. Sometimes when I read the papers from the old country, I pretty near run away," he confessed with a little laugh. "I never did think how I would be a settled man like this."

He was still, as Ántonia said, a city man. He liked theaters and lighted streets and music and a game of dominoes after the day's work was over. His sociability was stronger than his acquisitive instinct. He liked to live day by day and night by night, sharing in the excitement of the crowd.—Yet his wife had managed to hold him here on a farm, in one of the loneliest countries in the world.

I could see the little chap, sitting here every evening by the windmill, nursing his pipe and listening to the silence; the wheeze of the pump, the grunting of the pigs, an occasional squawking when the hens were disturbed by a rat. It did rather seem to me that Cuzak had been made the instrument of Ántonia's special mission. This was a fine life, certainly, but it was n't the kind of life he had wanted to live. I wondered whether the life that was right for one was ever right for two!

I asked Cuzak if he did n't find it hard to do without the gay company he had always been used to. He knocked out his pipe against an upright, sighed, and dropped it into his pocket.

"At first I near go crazy with lonesomeness," he said frankly, "but my woman is got such a warm heart. She always make it as good for me as she could. Now it ain't so bad; I can begin to have some fun with my boys, already!"

As we walked toward the house, Cuzak cocked his hat jauntily over one ear and looked up at the moon. "Gee!" he said in a hushed voice, as if he had just wakened up, "it don't seem like I am away from there twenty-six year!"

III

After dinner the next day I said good-bye and drove back to Hastings to take the train for Black Hawk. Ántonia and her children gathered round my buggy before I started, and even the little ones looked up at me with friendly faces. Leo and Ambrosch ran ahead to open the lane gate. When I reached the bottom of the hill, I

---

1 The boulevard around the heart of Vienna.

glanced back. The group was still there by the windmill. Ántonia was waving her apron.

At the gate Ambrosch lingered beside my buggy, resting his arm on the wheel-rim. Leo slipped through the fence and ran off into the pasture.

"That's like him," his brother said with a shrug. "He's a crazy kid. Maybe he's sorry to have you go, and maybe he's jealous. He's jealous of anybody mother makes a fuss over, even the priest."

I found I hated to leave this boy, with his pleasant voice and his fine head and eyes. He looked very manly as he stood there without a hat, the wind rippling his shirt about his brown neck and shoulders.

"Don't forget that you and Rudolph are going hunting with me up on the Niobrara[1] next summer," I said. "Your father's agreed to let you off after harvest."

He smiled. "I won't likely forget. I've never had such a nice thing offered to me before. I don't know what makes you so nice to us boys," he added, blushing.

"Oh, yes you do!" I said, gathering up my reins.

He made no answer to this, except to smile at me with unabashed pleasure and affection as I drove away.

My day in Black Hawk was disappointing. Most of my old friends were dead or had moved away. Strange children, who meant nothing to me, were playing in the Harlings' big yard when I passed; the mountain ash had been cut down, and only a sprouting stump was left of the tall Lombardy poplar that used to guard the gate. I hurried on. The rest of the morning I spent with Anton Jelinek, under a shady cottonwood tree in the yard behind his saloon. While I was having my mid-day dinner at the hotel, I met one of the old lawyers who was still in practice, and he took me up to his office and talked over the Cutter case with me. After that, I scarcely knew how to put in the time until the night express was due.

I took a long walk north of the town, out into the pastures where the land was so rough that it had never been ploughed up, and the long red grass of early times still grew shaggy over the draws and hillocks. Out there I felt at home again. Overhead the sky was that indescribable blue of autumn; bright and shadowless,

---

1 A river in northern Nebraska.

hard as enamel. To the south I could see the dun-shaded river bluffs that used to look so big to me, and all about stretched drying corn-fields, of the pale-gold color I remembered so well. Russian this-tles were blowing across the uplands and piling against the wire fences like barricades. Along the cattle paths the plumes of golden-rod were already fading into sun-warmed velvet, gray with gold threads in it. I had escaped from the curious depression that hangs over little towns, and my mind was full of pleasant things; trips I meant to take with the Cuzak boys, in the Bad Lands[1] and up on the Stinking Water.[2] There were enough Cuzaks to play with for a long while yet. Even after the boys grew up, there would always be Cuzak himself! I meant to tramp along a few miles of lighted streets with Cuzak.

As I wandered over those rough pastures, I had the good luck to stumble upon a bit of the first road that went from Black Hawk out to the north country; to my grandfather's farm, then on to the Shimerdas' and to the Norwegian settlement. Everywhere else it had been ploughed under when the highways were surveyed; this half-mile or so within the pasture fence was all that was left of that old road which used to run like a wild thing across the open prairie, clinging to the high places and circling and doubling like a rabbit before the hounds. On the level land the tracks had almost disappeared—were mere shadings in the grass, and a stranger would not have noticed them. But wherever the road had crossed a draw, it was easy to find. The rains had made channels of the wheel-ruts and washed them so deep that the sod had never healed over them. They looked like gashes torn by a grizzly's claws, on the slopes where the farm wagons used to lurch up out of the hollows with a pull that brought curling muscles on the smooth hips of the horses. I sat down and watched the haystacks turn rosy in the slant-ing sunlight.

This was the road over which Ántonia and I came on that night when we got off the train at Black Hawk and were bedded down in the straw, wondering children, being taken we knew not whither. I had only to close my eyes to hear the rumbling of the wagons in the dark, and to be again overcome with that obliter-ating strangeness. The feelings of that night were so near that I could reach out and touch them with my hand. I had the sense of

---

1 Grasslands in South Dakota, east of the Black Hills.
2 There are two Stinking Water creeks in the Badlands.

coming home to myself, and of having found out what a little circle man's experience is. For Ántonia and for me, this had been the road of Destiny; had taken us to those early accidents of fortune which predetermined for us all that we can ever be. Now I understood that the same road was to bring us together again. Whatever we had missed, we possessed together the precious, the incommunicable past.

THE END

Appendix A: Cather's Revised Introduction to the 1926 Edition of My Ántonia

[A revised Introduction to the novel was prepared by Willa Cather for the 1926 edition of *My Ántonia*. In this revision, Cather made drastic cuts to the original Introduction leaving, we might assume, what she considered in 1926 to be its most significant components.]

Last summer, in a season of intense heat, Jim Burden and I happened to be crossing Iowa on the same train. He and I are old friends, we grew up together in the same Nebraska town, and we had a great deal to say to each other. While the train flashed through never-ending miles of ripe wheat, by country towns and bright-flowered pastures and oak groves wilting in the sun, we sat in the observation car, where the woodwork was hot to the touch and red dust lay deep over everything. The dust and heat, the burning wind, reminded us of many things. We were talking about what it is like to spend one's childhood in little towns like these, buried in wheat and corn, under stimulating extremes of climate: burning summer when the world lies green and billowy beneath a brilliant sky, when one is fairly stifled in vegetation, in the colour and smell of strong weeds and heavy harvests; blustery winters with little snow, when the whole country is stripped bare and grey as sheet-iron. We agreed that no one who had not grown up in a little prairie town could know anything about it. It was a kind of freemasonry, we said.

Although Jim Burden and I both live in New York, I do not see much of him there. He is legal counsel for one of the great Western railways and is often away from his office for weeks together. That is one reason why we seldom meet. Another is that I do not like his wife. She is handsome, energetic, executive, but to me she seems unimpressionable and temperamentally incapable of enthusiasm. Her husband's quiet tastes irritate her, I think, and she finds it worth while to play the patroness to a group of young poets and painters of advanced ideas and mediocre ability. She has her own fortune and lives her own life. For some reason, she wishes to remain Mrs. James Burden.

As for Jim, disappointments have not changed him. The romantic disposition which often made him seem very funny as a boy, has been one of the strongest elements in his success. He loves with a personal passion the great country through which his railway runs and branches. His faith in it and his knowledge of it have played an important part in its development.

During that burning day when we were crossing Iowa, our talk kept returning to a central figure, a Bohemian girl whom we had both known long ago. More than any other person we remembered, this girl seemed to mean to us the country, the conditions, the whole adventure of our childhood. I had lost sight of her altogether, but Jim had found her again after long years, and had renewed a friendship that meant a great deal to him. His mind was full of her that day. He made me see her again, feel her presence, revived all my old affection for her.

"From time to time I've been writing down what I remember about Ántonia," he told me. "On my long trips across the country, I amuse myself like that, in my stateroom."

When I told him that I would like to read his account of her, he said I should certainly see it—if it were ever finished.

Months afterward, Jim called at my apartment one stormy winter afternoon, carrying a legal portfolio. He brought it into the sitting-room with him, and said, as he stood warming his hands,

"Here is the thing about Ántonia. Do you still want to read it? I finished it last night. I didn't take time to arrange it; I simply wrote down pretty much all that her name recalls to me. I suppose it hasn't any form. It hasn't any title, either." He went into the next room, sat down at my desk and wrote across the face of the portfolio the word "Ántonia." He frowned at this a moment, then prefixed another word, making it "My Ántonia." That seemed to satisfy him.

Appendix B: Cather's "Mesa Verde Wonderland is Easy to Reach"

[Although Cather's experience in Mesa Verde is often and rightly associated with her novel, *The Professor's House*, it gave rise immediately to the composition of *My Ántonia*. We hear the genesis of *My Ántonia* in Cather's observation about the mesa people, "They seem not to have struggled to overcome their environment. They accommodated themselves to it, interpreted it and made it personal; lived in a dignified relation with it. In more senses than one they built themselves into it." See Appendix G.1 and G.2 for Nebraskans who "built themselves into" their environment.]

Twenty-five years ago an adventurous young Swede, the Baron Nordenskjold, started on a trip around the world, sailing westward. When he got to Denver he heard rumors about certain cliff dweller remains that had been found in the extreme southwest corner of Colorado. He went down to the Mesa Verde and got no farther on his trip around the world. He stayed on the mesa for some months and then went back to Stockholm and wrote and published the book which first made the Mesa Verde known to the world. Later the book was translated but the English edition also was published in Stockholm. There is no American edition.

The journey to the Mesa Verde, which was a hard one in Nordenskjold's time, is now a very easy one, and the railway runs within thirty miles of the mesa. You leave Denver in the evening, over the Denver & Rio Grande. From the time when your train crawls out of La Veta pass at about 4 in the morning, until you reach Durango at nightfall, there is not a dull moment. All day you are among high mountains, swinging back and forth between Colorado and New Mexico, with the Sangre de Cristo and the Culebra ranges always in sight until you cross the continental divide at the Cumbres and begin the wild scurry down the westward slope.

That particular branch of the Denver & Rio Grande is called the Whiplash, and most of the way you can signal to the engineer from the rear car. You stay all night in Durango. In the morning you take another train for Mancos; a friendly train with invariably friendly passengers and a conductor who has been on that run for fourteen years and who can give you all sorts of helpful information. When you reach Mancos you find the station agent, the hotel people and the camp outfitters quite as cordial as the train crew. Your business transactions become of minor importance, and before you know it you are staying on in Mancos because you like the people.

I expected to find Mancos a railway station and had planned to stay one night there. I stayed in all six days. The town lies at the foot of the La Plata (Silver) mountains, in a richly irrigated valley. The Mancos river, clear as glass and bordered with poplars and water willows, runs thru the middle of the town. The streets are lined with trees, the yards are a riot of giant sage and Indian paintbrush, shaded with cedars; the wheat fields are veritable cloth of gold and the whole town is buried in sweet clover. It grows in tall hedges along the water ditches and in the low ground along the river. Not once while I was in Mancos, indoors or out, was there a moment when I could not smell the sweet clover.

From the streets of Mancos and from the hills about it one can always see the green mesa—not green at that distance but a darkish purple, a rather grim mass bulking up in the West. It sits like a cheese box in the plain, the deep canons with which it is slashed imperceptible from far away. The mesa is forty-five miles long and twenty-five wide, and its sides are so steep that it is accessible from only one point. The government wagon road is recent. Until within a few years there was only a difficult horse trail. Charles Kelly, who now takes travelers out to the mesa by wagon or motor, is the same guide who formerly provided mounts and provisions and pack horses for people who came to see ruins on the mesa. There is now a very comfortable tent camp on the mesa, just above the fine spring at Spruce Tree house, and the wife of the forest ranger provides excellent food. Anyone can be very comfortable there for several weeks.

Any approach to the Mesa Verde is impressive, but one must always think with envy of the entrada of Richard Wetherill, the first white man who discovered the ruins in its canyons forty-odd years ago. Until that time the mesa was entirely unexplored, and was known only as a troublesome place into which cattle wandered off, and from which they never came back. All the country about it was open range. The Wetherills had a ranch west of Mancos. One December day a boy brought word to the ranch house that a bunch of cattle had got away and gone up into the mesa. The same thing had happened before, and young Richard Wetherill said that this time he was going after his beasts. He rode off with one of his cow men and they entered the mesa by a deep canyon from the Mancos river, which flows at its base. They followed the canyon toward the heart of the mesa until they could go no farther with horses. They tied their mounts and went on foot up a side canyon, now called Cliff canyon. After a long stretch of hard climbing young Wetherill happened to glance up at the great cliffs above him, and there, thru a veil of lightly falling snow, he saw practically as it stands today and as it had stood for 800 years before, the cliff palace—not a cliff dwelling, but a cliff village; houses, courts, terraces and towers, a place large enough to house 300 people, lying in a natural archway let back into the cliff. It stood as if it had been deserted yesterday; undisturbed and undesecrated, preserved by the dry atmosphere and by its great inacessibility.

That is what the Mesa Verde means; its ruins are the highest achievement of stone-age man—preserved in bright, dry sunshine, like a fly in amber—sheltered by great canyon walls and hidden away in a difficult mesa into which no one had ever found a trail. When Wetherill rode in after his cattle no later civilization blurred the outlines there. Life had been extinct upon the mesa since the days of the Cliff Dwellers. Not only their building, but their pottery, linen cloth, feather cloth, sandals, stone and bone tools, dried pumpkins, corn and onions, remained as they had been left. There were even a few well-preserved mummies—not many, for the cliff dwellers cremated their dead.

Altho only three groups of buildings have been excavated and made easily accessible to travelers, there are ruins everywhere— perched about like swallow's nests. The whole mesa, indeed, is one vast ruin. Eight hundred years ago the mesa was hung with villages, as the hills above Amalfi are today. There must have been about 10,000 people living there. The villages were all built back in these gracious natural arches in the cliffs; with such an outlook, such a setting as men have never found for their dwellings anywhere else in the world. The architecture is like that of most southern countries— of Palestine, northern Africa, southern Spain—absolutely harmonious with its site and setting. On the way from New York to the Montezuma valley one goes thru hundreds of ugly little American towns, but when you once reach the mesa, all that is behind you. The stone villages in the cliff arches are a successful evasion of ugliness— perhaps an indolent evasion. Color, simplicity, space, an absence of clutter, the houses of the Pueblo Indians today and of their ancestors on the Mesa Verde are a reproach to the messiness in which we live.

Everything in the cliff dweller villages points to a tempered, settled, ritualistic life, where generations went on gravely and reverently repeating the past, rather than battling for anything new. Their lives were so full of ritual and symbolism that all their common actions were ceremonial—planting, harvesting, hunting, feasting, fasting. The great drama of the weather and the seasons occupied their minds a good deal, and they seem to have ordered their behavior according to the moon and sun and stars. The windows in the towers were arranged with regard for astronomical observations. Their strong habitations, their settled mode of living, their satisfying ritual, seem to have made this people conservative and aristocratic. The most plausible theory as to their extinction is that the dwellers on the Mesa Verde were routed and driven out by their vulgar, pushing neighbors of the plains, who were less comfortable, less satisfied, and consequently more energetic.

The mesa people may have been somewhat enslaved by their strongholds, and their temper may have been softened by their comparative comfort and their attention to order and detail. They worked out a mode of life which satisfied them, and they were absolutely unenterprising in the modern American sense. Their architecture and their religion were their national purpose. Their religion was largely a personal recognition and interpretation of nature. They seem not to have struggled to overcome their environment. They accommodated themselves to it, interpreted it and made it personal; lived in a dignified relation with it. In more senses than one they built themselves into it. They were living by hurrying and concentrating natural conditions and processes just a little. They supplemented the rainfall by building reservoirs and irrigating. House building, in those great natural arches of stone, was but carrying out a suggestion that stared them in the face; often they used a great rock that had fallen down into the archway as a cornerstone and anchor for their own lighter masonry. When they felled cedars with stone axes they were but accelerating a natural process; the ends of their roof rafters looked as if they had been gnawed thru by a beaver.

Dr. Johnson declared that man is an historical animal. Certainly it is the human record, however slight, that stirs us most deeply, and a country without such a record is dumb, no matter how beautiful. The Mesa Verde is not, as many people think, an inconveniently situated museum. It is the story of an early race, of the social and religious life of a people indigenous to that soil and to its rocky splendors. It is the human expression of that land of sharp contours, brutal contrasts, glorious color and blinding light. The human consciousness, as we know it today, dwelt there, and a feeling for beauty and order was certainly not absent. There are in those stone villages no suggestions revolting to our sensibilities. No sinister ideas lurk in the sun-drenched ruins hung among the crags. One has only to go down into Hopiland to find the same life going on today on other mesa tops; houses like these, kivas like these, ceremonial and religious implements like these—every detail preserved with the utmost fidelity. When you see those ancient, pyramidal pueblos once more brought nearer by the sunset light that beats on them like gold-beaters' hammers, when the aromatic piñon smoke begins to curl in the still air and the boys bring in the cattle and the old Indians come out in their white burnouses and take their accustomed grave positions upon the housetops, you begin to feel that custom, ritual, integrity of tradition have a reality that goes deeper than the bustling business of the world.

The Denver Times, January 31, 1916.

Appendix C: Cather's "Nebraska: The End of the First Cycle"

[Published five years after the first edition of *My Ántonia*, this essay provides a gloss on the people and situations depicted in the novel, as well as a major statement of Cather's sense of Nebraska as a social, economic, and political force in American history.]

The State of Nebraska is part of the great plain which stretches west of the Missouri River, gradually rising until it reaches the Rocky Mountains. The character of all this country between the river and the mountains is essentially the same throughout its extent: a rolling, alluvial plain, growing gradually more sandy toward the west, until it breaks into the white sand-hills of western Nebraska and Kansas and eastern Colorado. From east to west this plain measures something over five hundred miles; in appearance it resembles the wheat lands of Russia, which fed the continent of Europe for so many years. Like Little Russia it is watered by slow-flowing, muddy rivers, which run full in the spring, often cutting into the farm lands along their banks; but by midsummer they lie low and shrunken, their current split by glistening white sand-bars half overgrown with scrub willows.

The climate, with its extremes of temperature, gives to this plateau the variety which, to the casual eye at least, it lacks. There we have short, bitter winters; windy, flower-laden springs; long, hot summers; triumphant autumns that last until Christmas—a season of perpetual sunlight, blazing blue skies, and frosty nights. In this newest part of the New World autumn is the season of beauty and sentiment, as spring is in the Old World.

Nebraska is a newer State than Kansas. It was a State before there were people in it. Its social history falls easily within a period of sixty years, and the first stable settlements of white men were made within the memory of old folk now living. The earliest of these settlements—Bellevue, Omaha, Brownville, Nebraska City— were founded along the Missouri River, which was at that time a pathway for small steamers. In 1855-60 these four towns were straggling groups of log houses, hidden away along the wooded river banks.

Before 1860 civilization did no more than nibble at the eastern edge of the State, along the river bluffs. Lincoln, the present capital, was open prairie; and the whole of the great plain to the westward was still a sunny wilderness, where the tall red grass and the buffalo and the Indian hunter were undisturbed. Fremont,[1] with Kit Carson, the famous scout, had gone across Nebraska in 1842, exploring the valley of the Platte. In the days of the Mormon persecution fifteen thousand Mormons camped for two years, 1845-46, six miles north of Omaha, while their exploring parties went farther west, searching for fertile land outside of government jurisdiction. In 1847 the entire Mormon sect, under the leadership of Brigham Young, went with their wagons through Nebraska and on to that desert beside the salty sea which they have made so fruitful.

In forty-nine and the early fifties, gold hunters, bound for California, crossed the State in thousands, always following the old Indian trail along the Platte valley. The State was a highway for dreamers and adventurers; men who were in quest of gold or grace, freedom or romance.[2] With all these people the road led out, but never back again.

While Nebraska was a camping-ground for seekers outward bound, the wooden settlements along the Missouri were growing into something permanent. The settlers broke the ground and began to plant the fine orchards which have ever since been the pride of Otoe and Nemaha counties. It was at Brownville that the first telegraph wire was brought across the Missouri River. When I was a child I heard ex-Governor Furness relate how he stood with other pioneers in the log cabin where the Morse instrument had been installed, and how, when it began to click, the men took off their hats as if they were in church. The first message across the river into Nebraska was not a market report, but a line of poetry: "Westward the course of empire takes its way."[3] The Old West was like that.

---

1 John C. Fremont, known as "The Pathfinder."
2 See Appendix H.4.
3 "Westward the course of empire takes its way.
         The four first acts already past,
   A fifth shall close the drama with the day.
         Time's noblest offspring is the last."

   George Berkeley (1685-1753), "On the Prospect of Planting Arts and Learning in America." The first line of Berkeley's poem is also the title of a famous printing by Emanuel Leutze, commissioned in 1861.

The first back-and-forth travel through the State was by way of the Overland Mail, a monthly passenger-and-mail-stage service across the plains from Independence to the newly founded colony at Salt Lake—a distance of twelve hundred miles.

When silver ore was discovered in the mountains of Colorado near Cherry Creek—afterward Camp Denver and later the city of Denver—a picturesque form of commerce developed across the great plain of Nebraska: the transporting of food and merchandise from the Missouri to the Colorado mining camps, and on to the Mormon settlement at Salt Lake. One of the largest freighting companies, operating out of Nebraska City, in the six summer months of 1860 carried nearly three million pounds of freight across Nebraska, employing 515 wagons, 5,687 oxen, and 600 drivers.

The freighting began in the early spring, usually about the middle of April, and continued all summer and through the long, warm autumns. The oxen made from ten to twenty miles a day. I have heard the old freighters say that, after embarking on their six-hundred mile trail, they lost count of the days of the week and the days of the month. While they were out in that sea of waving grass, one day was like another; and, if one can trust the memory of these old men, all the days were glorious. The buffalo trails still ran north and south then; deep, dusty paths the bison wore when, single file, they came north in the spring for the summer grass, and went south again in the autumn. Along these trails were the buffalo "wallows"—shallow depressions where the rain water gathered when it ran off the tough prairie sod. These wallows the big beasts wore deeper and packed hard when they rolled about and bathed in the pools, so that they held water like a cement bottom. The freighters lived on game and shot the buffalo for their hides. The grass was full of quail and prairie chickens, and flocks of wild ducks swam about on the lagoons. These lagoons have long since disappeared, but they were beautiful things in their time; long stretches where the rain water gathered and lay clear on a grassy bottom without mud. From the lagoons the first settlers hauled water to their homesteads, before they had dug their wells. The freighters could recognize the lagoons from afar by the clouds of golden coreopsis which grew up out of the water and waved delicately above its surface. Among the pioneers the coreopsis was known simply as "the lagoon flower."

As the railroads came in, the freighting business died out. Many a freight-driver settled down upon some spot he had come to like on his journeys to and fro, homesteaded it, and wandered no more. The Union Pacific, the first transcontinental railroad, was completed in 1869. The Burlington entered Nebraska in the same year, at Platsmouth, and began construction westward. It finally reached Denver by an indirect route, and went on extending and ramifying through the State. With the railroads came the home-seeking people from overseas.

When the first courageous settlers came straggling out through the waste with their oxen and covered wagons, they found open range all the way from Lincoln to Denver; a continuous, undulating plateau, covered with long, red, shaggy grass. The prairie was green only where it had been burned off in the spring by the new settlers or by the Indians, and toward autumn even the new grass became a coppery brown. This sod, which had never been broken by the plow, was so tough and strong with the knotted grass roots of many years, that the home-seekers were able to peel it off the earth like peat, cut it up into bricks, and make of it warm, comfortable, durable houses.[1] Some of these sod houses lingered on until the open range was gone and the grass was gone, and the whole face of the country had been changed.

Even as late as 1885 the central part of the State, and everything to the westward, was, in the main, raw prairie. The cultivated fields and broken land seemed mere scratches in the brown, running steppe that never stopped until it broke against the foothills of the Rockies. The dugouts and sod farm-houses were three or four miles apart, and the only means of communication was the heavy farm wagon, drawn by heavy work horses. The early population of Nebraska was largely transatlantic. The county in which I grew up, in the south-central part of the State, was typical. On Sunday we could drive to a Norwegian church and listen to a sermon in that language, or to a Danish or a Swedish church. We could go to the French Catholic settlement in the next county and hear a sermon in French, or into the Bohemian township and hear one in Czech, or we could go to church with the German Lutherans. There were, of course, American congregations also.

There is a Prague in Nebraska as well as in Bohemia. Many of our Czech immigrants are people of a very superior type. The political emigration resulting from the revolutionary disturbances of 1848 was distinctly different from the emigration resulting from

---

1 See Appendix G.2.

economic causes, and brought to the United States brilliant young men both from Germany and Bohemia.[1] In Nebraska our Czech settlements were large and very prosperous. I have walked about the streets of Wilber, the country seat of Saline County, for a whole day without hearing a word of English spoken. In Wilber, in the old days, behind the big, friendly, brick saloon—it was not a "saloon," properly speaking, but a beer garden, where the farmers ate their lunch when they came to town—there was a pleasant little theater where the boys and girls were trained to give the masterpieces of Czech drama in the Czech language. "Americanization" has doubtless done away with all this. Our lawmakers have a rooted conviction that a boy can be a better American if he speaks only one language than if he speaks two. I could name a dozen Bohemian towns in Nebraska where one used to be able to go into a bakery and buy better pastry than is to be had anywhere except in the best pastry shops of Prague or Vienna. The American lard pie never corrupted the Czech.

Cultivated, restless young men from Europe made incongruous figures among the hard-handed breakers of the soil. Frederick Amiel's nephew lived for many years and finally died among the Nebraska farmers. Amiel's letters to his kinsman were published in the *Atlantic Monthly* of March, 1921, under the title "Amiel in Nebraska." Camille Saint-Saëns's cousin lived just over the line, in Kansas. Knut Hamsun, the Norwegian writer who was awarded the Nobel Prize for 1920, was a "hired hand" on a Dakota farm to the north of us. Colonies of European people, Slavonic, Germanic, Scandinavian, Latin, spread across our bronze prairies like the daubs of color on a painter's palette. They brought with them something that this neutral new world needed even more than the immigrants needed land.

Unfortunately, their American neighbors were seldom open-minded enough to understand the Europeans, or to profit by their older traditions. Our settlers from New England, cautious and convinced of their own superiority, kept themselves insulated as much as possible from foreign influences. The incomers from the South—from Missouri, Kentucky, the two Virginias—were provincial and utterly without curiosity.[2] They were kind neighbors— lent a hand to help a Swede when he was sick or in trouble. But I

---

1 See Appendix H.1.
2 Cather herself was an immigrant to Nebraska from Virginia.

am quite sure that Knut Hamsun might have worked a year for any one of our Southern farmers, and his employer would never have discovered that there was anything unusual about the Norwegian. A New England settler might have noticed that his chore-boy had a kind of intelligence, but he would have distrusted and stonily disregarded it. If the daughter of a shiftless West Virginia mountaineer married the nephew of a professor at the University of Upsala, the native family felt disgraced by such an alliance.

Nevertheless, the thrift and intelligence of its preponderant European population have been potent factors in bringing about the present prosperity of the State. The census of 1910 showed that there were then 228,648 foreign-born and native-born Germans living in Nebraska; 103,503 Scandinavians; 50,680 Czechs. The total foreign population of the State was then 900,571, while the entire population was 1,192,214. That is, in round numbers, there were about nine hundred thousand foreign Americans in the State, to three hundred thousand native stock. With such a majority of foreign stock, nine to three, it would be absurd to say that the influence of the European does not cross the boundary of his own acres, and has had nothing to do with shaping the social ideals of the commonwealth.

When I stop at one of the graveyards in my own country, and see on the headstones the names of fine old men I used to know, "*Eric Ericson, born Bergen, Norway … died Nebraska,*" "*Anton Pucelik, born Prague, Bohemia … died Nebraska,*" I have always the hope that something went into the ground with those pioneers that will one day come out again. Something that will come out not only in sturdy traits of character, but in elasticity of mind, in an honest attitude toward the realities of life, in certain qualities of feeling and imagination. Some years ago a professor at the University of Nebraska happened to tell me about a boy in one of his Greek classes who had a very unusual taste for the classics—intuitions and perceptions in literature. This puzzled him, he said, as they boy's parents had no interest in such things. I knew what the professor did not: that, though this boy had an American name, his grandfather was a Norwegian, a musician of high attainment, a fellow-student and life-long friend of Edvard Grieg.[1] It is in that great cosmopolitan country known as the Middle West that we may hope to see the hard molds of American provincialism broken up; that

---

1 Edvard Hagerup Grieg (1843-1907), Norwegian composer.

we may hope to find young talent which will challenge the pale proprieties, the insincere, conventional optimism of our art and thought.

The rapid industrial development of Nebraska, which began in the latter eighties, was arrested in the years 1893-97 by a succession of crop failures and by the financial depression which spread over the whole country at that time—the depression which produced the People's Party and the Free Silver agitation.[1] These years of trial, as everyone now realizes, had a salutary effect upon the new State. They winnowed out the settlers with a purpose from the drifting malcontents who are ever seeking a land where man does not live by the sweat of his brow. The slack farmer moved on. Superfluous banks failed, and money lenders who drove hard bargains with desperate men came to grief. The strongest stock survived, and within ten years those who had weathered the storm came into their reward. What that reward is, you can see for yourself if you motor through the State from Omaha to the Colorado line. The country has no secrets; it is as open as an honest human face.

The old, isolated farms have come together. They rub shoulders. The whole State is a farm. Now it is the pasture lands that look little and lonely, crowded in among so much wheat and corn. It is scarcely an exaggeration to say that every farmer owns an automobile. I believe the last estimate showed that there is one motor car for every six inhabitants in Nebraska. The great grain fields are plowed by tractors. The old farm houses are rapidly being replaced by more cheerful dwellings, with bathrooms and hardwood floors, heated by furnaces or hot-water plants. Many of them are lighted by electricity, and every farm house has its telephone. The country towns are clean and well kept. On Saturday night the main street is a long black line of parked motor cars; the farmers have brought their families to town to see the moving-picture show. When the school bell rings on Monday morning, crowds of happy looking children, well nourished—for the most part well mannered, too,—

---

1   At the end of the nineteenth century the United States moved to adopt the gold standard, a transition which produced temporary economic turmoil. The People's Party, led by William Jennings Bryan (unsuccessful in the 1896 presidential election), incorporated the Free Silver movement (advocating a return to bimetallist—gold and silver—currency) into a populist platform which included female suffrage, income tax, and anti-imperialist policies.

flock along the shady streets. They wear cheerful, modern clothes, and the girls, like the boys, are elastic and vigorous in their movements. These thousands and thousands of children—in the little towns and in the country schools—these, of course, ten years from now, will be the State.

In this time of prosperity any farmer boy who wishes to study at the State University can do so. A New York lawyer who went out to Lincoln to assist in training the university students for military service in war time exclaimed when he came back: "What splendid young men! I would not have believed that any school in the world could get together so many boys physically fit, and so few unfit."

Of course, there is the other side of the medal, stamped with the ugly crest of materialism, which has set its seal upon all of our most productive commonwealths. Too much prosperity, too many moving-picture shows, too much gaudy fiction have colored the taste and manners of so many of these Nebraskans of the future. There, as elsewhere, one finds the frenzy to be show; farmer boys who wish to be spenders before they are earners, girls who try to look like the heroines of the cinema screen; a coming generation which tries to cheat its aesthetic sense by buying things instead of making anything. There is even danger that that fine institution, the University of Nebraska, may become a gigantic trade school. The men who control its destiny, the regents and the lawmakers, wish their sons and daughters to study machines, mercantile processes, "the principles of business"; everything that has to do with the game of getting on in the world—and nothing else. The classics, the humanities, are having their dark hour. They are in eclipse. Studies that develop taste and enrich personality are not encouraged. But the "Classics" have a way of revenging themselves. One may venture to hope that the children, or the grandchildren of a generation that goes to a university to select only the most utilitarian subjects in the course of study—among them, salesmanship and dressmaking—will revolt against all the heaped-up, machine-made materialism about them. They will go back to the old sources of culture and wisdom—not as a duty, but with burning desire.

In Nebraska, as in so many other States, we must face the fact that the splendid story of the pioneers is finished, and that no new story worthy to take its place has yet begun. The generation that subdued the wild land and broke up the virgin prairie is passing, but it is still there, a group of rugged figures in the background which inspire respect, compel admiration. With these old men and women the attainment of material prosperity was a moral victory, because it was wrung from hard conditions, was the result of a struggle that tested character. They can look out over those broad stretches of fertility and say: "We made this, with our backs and hands." The sons, the generation now in middle life, were reared amid hardships, and it is perhaps natural that they should be very interested in material comfort, in buying whatever is expensive and ugly. Their fathers came into a wilderness and had to make everything, had to be as ingenious as shipwrecked sailors. The generation now in the driver's seat hates to make anything, wants to live and die in an automobile, scudding past those acres where the old men used to follow the long corn-rows up and down. They want to buy everything ready-made: clothes, food, education, music, pleasure. Will the third generation—the full-blooded, joyous one just coming over the hill—will it be fooled? Will it believe that to live easily is to live happily?

The wave of generous idealism, of noble seriousness, which swept over the State of Nebraska in 1917 and 1918,[1] demonstrated how fluid and flexible is any living, growing, expanding society. If such "conversions" do not last, they at least show of what men and women are capable. Surely the materialism and showy extravagance of this hour are a passing phase! They will mean no more in half a century from now than will the "hard times" of twenty-five years ago—which are already forgotten. The population is as clean and full of vigor as the soil; there are no old grudges, no heritages of disease or hate. The belief that snug success and easy money are the real aims of human life has settled down over our prairies, but it has not yet hardened into molds and crusts. The people are warm, mercurial, impressionable, restless, over-fond of novelty and change. These are not the qualities which make the dull chapters of history.

The Nation, September 5, 1923, pp. 236–38.

1 Cather refers here to the years of sacrifice during the Great War, or World War I.

Appendix D: Cather's "Peter"

[This short story, published when Cather was nineteen years old and in college, contains the germ of the first book of *My Ántonia*, "The Shimerdas," the story of Mr. Shimerda's suicide. Many details would remain, while the cumbersome prose would disappear entirely. Cather published two subsequent versions of the story, one later in 1892, in *The Hesperian*, and another, in 1900, in *The Library*—she served as editor at both magazines.]

"No, Antone, I have told thee many times, no, thou shalt not sell it until I am gone."

"But I need money; what good is that old fiddle to thee? The very crows laugh at thee when thou art trying to play. Thy hand trembles so thou canst scarce hold the bow. Thou shalt go with me to the Blue to cut wood tomorrow. See to it thou art up early."

"What, on the Sabbath, Antone, when it is so cold? I get so very cold, my son, let us not go tomorrow."

"Yes, tomorrow, thou lazy old man. Do not I cut wood upon the Sabbath? Care I how cold it is? Wood thou shalt cut, and haul it too, and as for the fiddle, I tell thee I will sell it yet." Antone pulled his ragged cap down over his low heavy brow, and went out. The old man drew his stool up nearer the fire, and sat stroking his violin with trembling fingers and muttering, "Not while I live, not while I live."

Five years ago they had come here, Peter Sadelack, and his wife, and oldest son Antone, and countless smaller Sadelacks, here to the dreariest part of southwestern Nebraska, and had taken up a homestead. Antone was the acknowledged master of the premises, and people said he was a likely youth, and would do well. That he was mean and untrustworthy every one knew, but that made little difference. His corn was better tended than any in the county, and his wheat always yielded more than other men's.

Of Peter no one knew much, nor had any one a good word to say for him. He drank whenever he could get out of Antone's sight long enough to pawn his hat or coat for whisky. Indeed there were but two things he would not pawn, his pipe and his violin. He was a lazy, absentminded old fellow, who liked to fiddle better than to plow, though Antone surely got work enough out of them all, for that matter. In the house of which Antone was master there was no one, from the little boy three years old, to the old man of sixty, who did not earn his bread. Still people said that Peter was worthless, and was a great drag on Antone, his son, who never drank, and was a much better man than his father had ever been. Peter did not care what people said. He did not like the country, nor the people, least of all he liked the plowing. He was very homesick for Bohemia. Long ago, only eight years ago by the calendar, but it seemed eight centuries to Peter, he had been a second violinist in the great theatre at Prague. He had gone into the theatre very young, and had been there all his life, until he had a stroke of paralysis, which made his arm so weak that his bowing was uncertain. Then they told him he could go. Those were great days at the theatre. He had plenty to drink then, and wore a dress coat every evening, and there were always parties after the play. He could play in those days, ay, that he could! He could never read the notes well, so he did not play first; but his touch, he had a touch indeed, so Herr Mikilsdoff, who led the orchestra, had said. Sometimes now Peter thought he could plow better if he could only bow as he used to. He had seen all the lovely women in the world there, all the great singers and the great players. He was in the orchestra when Rachel played, and he heard Liszt play when the Countess d'Agoult sat in the stage box and threw the master white lilies. Once, a French woman came and played for weeks, he did not remember her name now. He did not remember her face very well either, for it changed so, it was never twice the same. But the beauty of it, and the great hunger men felt at the sight of it, that he remembered. Most of all he remembered her voice. He did not know French, and could not understand a word she said, but it seemed to him that she must be talking the music of Chopin. And her voice, he thought he should know that in the other world. The last night she played a play in which a man touched her arm, and she stabbed him. As Peter sat among the smoking gas jets down below the footlights with his fiddle on his knee, and looked up at her, he thought he would like to die too, if he could touch her arm once, and have her stab him so. Peter went home to his wife very drunk that night. Even in those days he was a foolish fellow, who cared for nothing but music and pretty faces.

It was all different now. He had nothing to drink and little to eat, and here, there was nothing but sun, and grass, and sky. He had forgotten almost everything, but some things he remembered well enough. He loved his violin and the holy Mary, and above all else he feared the Evil One, and his son Antone.

The fire was low, and it grew cold. Still Peter sat by the fire remembering. He dared not throw more cobs on the fire; Antone would be angry. He did not want to cut wood tomorrow, it would be Sunday, and he wanted to go to mass. Antone might let him do that. He held his violin under his wrinkled chin, his white hair fell over it, and he began to play "Ave Maria." His hand shook more than ever before, and at last refused to work the bow at all. He sat stupefied for a while, then arose, and taking his violin with him, stole out into the old sod stable. He took Antone's shotgun down from its peg, and loaded it by the moonlight which streamed in through the door. He sat down on the dirt floor, and leaned back against the dirt wall. He heard the wolves howling in the distance, and the night wind screaming as it swept over the snow. Near him he heard the regular breathing of the horses in the dark. He put his crucifix above his heart, and folding his hands said brokenly all the Latin he had ever known, "*Pater noster, qui in coelum est.*"[1] Then he raised his head and sighed, "Not one kreutzer will Antone pay them to pray for my soul, not one kreutzer,[2] he is so careful of his money, is Antone, he does not waste it in drink, he is a better man than I, but hard sometimes. He works the girls too hard, women were not made to work so. But he shall not sell thee, my fiddle, I can play thee no more, but they shall not part us. We have seen it all together, and we will forget it together, the French woman and all." He held his fiddle under his chin a moment, where it had lain so often, then put it across his knee and broke it through the middle. He pulled off his old boot, held the gun between his knees with the muzzle against his forehead, and pressed the trigger with his toe.

In the morning, Antone found him stiff, frozen fast in a pool of blood. They could not straighten him out enough to fit a coffin, so they buried him in a pine box. Before the funeral Antone carried to town the fiddlebow which Peter had forgotten to break. Antone was very thrifty, and a better man than his father had been.

The Mahogany Tree, May 21, 1892, pp. 323–24.

---

1 This is the first line of the Lord's Prayer, "Our Father, who art in heaven."

2 A small silver or copper coin, originally stamped with a cross, in use in parts of Germany and in Austria in the nineteenth century.

Appendix E: Interviews and Commentary by Cather on My Ántonia

[This appendix includes feature articles from the literary and popular press in which Willa Cather is quoted or interviewed about *My Ántonia*.]

1. Latrobe Carroll, "Willa Sibert Cather"

Miss Cather's most recent novel, "My Antonia", is a fuller evocation of the "old, old west" than was "O Pioneers!" The descriptions of the western prairie, brief, poignant, lift us from our easy chairs and set us down on those high plains. The book is ruthless, poetical, tremendously alive. It is the first thing Miss Cather has written.[1] H.L. Mencken laid it down with the conviction that it is the best piece of fiction done by any woman in America.[2] The portrayal of Ántonia is masterly.

"She was a Bohemian girl," Miss Cather said, "who was good to me when I was a child. I saw a great deal of her from the time I was eight until I was twelve. She was big-hearted and essentially romantic."

Willa Cather's foreigners are true to type. August Brunius, after noting the Swede, as presented by writers outside his own country, usually seems absurd to a Swedish reader, goes on to say that in "O Pioneers!" and "The Song of the Lark", Swedes are presented with true insight and art. Small wonder that all Miss Cather's books have been translated into the Scandinavian and are to be translated into French.

Her latest volume, "Youth and the Bright Medusa", is a collection of eight short stories. Simply and vividly told, they are studies of the artistic temperament. In them, there is none of the usual sentimentalizing about the artist. They are widely recognized as works of distinction. An anonymous critic in "The Nation" slyly

---

1 The meaning of this statement is not clear, as Carroll also identifies *O Pioneers!* as a work of art, later in the essay. Carroll probably means to stress the "fuller evocation" mentioned in his first sentence.
2 See Appendix E.10 for Mencken's review.

remarks that the collection "represents the triumph of mind over Nebraska".

Willa Cather's best work is satisfying because it is sincere. In her books, there is none of the sweet reek that pervades the pages of so many "lady novelists". Love, to her, is "not a simple state, like measles". Her treatment of sex is without either squeamishness or sensuality. She loves the west, and the arts, particularly music, and she had sought to express feelings and convictions on these subjects. She tried, failed, and kept on trying until she succeeded. For example, we have her word for it that at college she attempted to tell about immigrants in rough sketches.[1] She drew them more skillfully in "The Bohemian Girl", a short story which appeared in "McClure's Magazine" in 1912. Then came "O Pioneers!", a work of art. In "My Ántonia", she reached what she had been advancing toward for many years. Similarly in her exploration of the minds and emotions of artists, she has striven to tell the truth—the truth stripped of sentimentality. She experimented in "The Troll Garden", succeeded partially in "Youth and the Bright Medusa", grasped fully what she had sought in "The Song of the Lark". It would, of course, be unfair to speak of the books and stories that led up to this novel and to "My Ántonia" as preliminary studies, for there is too much in them not touched upon in the two later novels. But there is a certain summing up, in these books, of two subjects which have interested Miss Cather profoundly: the life of foreigners in the west, and the mind and heart of the artist. Of the books, the author herself said: "I think 'My Ántonia' is the most successfully done. 'The Song of the Lark' was the most interesting to write."

"I work from two and a half to three hours a day," Miss Cather went on to say. "I don't hold myself to longer hours; if I did, I wouldn't gain by it. The only reason I write is because it interests me more than any other activity I've ever found. I like riding, going to operas and concerts, travel in the west; but on the whole writing interests me more than anything else. If I made a chore of it, my enthusiasm would die. I make it an adventure every day. I get more entertainment from it than any I could buy, except the privilege of hearing a few great musicians and singers. To listen to them interests me as much as a good morning's work.

---

1 See Appendix D for one example.

"For me, the morning is the best time to write. During the other hours of the day I attend to my housekeeping, take walks in Central Park, go to concerts, and see something of my friends. I try to keep myself fit, fresh: one has to be in as good form to write as to sing. When not working, I shut work from my mind."

At present Miss Cather is writing a new novel—she says of it:

"What I always want to do is to make the 'writing' count for less and less and the people for more. In this new novel I'm trying to cut out all analysis, observation, description, even the picture-making quality, in order to make things and people tell their own story simply by juxtaposition, without any persuasion or explanation on my part.

"Just as if I put here on the table a green vase, and beside it a yellow orange. Now, those two things affect each other. Side by side, they produce a reaction which neither of them will produce alone. Why should I try to say anything clever, or by any colorful rhetoric detract attention from those two objects, the relation they have to each other and the effect they have upon each other? I want the reader to see the orange and the vase—beyond that, *I* am out of it. Mere cleverness must go. I'd like the writing to be so lost in the object, that it doesn't exist for the reader—except for the reader who knows how difficult it is to lose writing in the object. One must choose one's audience, and the audience I try to write for is the one interested in the effect the green vase brings out in the orange, and the orange in the green vase."

Miss Cather has never sought publicity, or quick success. It took her three years to write "The Song of the Lark", and three to write "My Ántonia". Of the two paths of art—give the public what it wants, or make your work so fine that the public will want it—she has consistently chosen the path of fine work. She is moving unhurriedly toward a richer self-expression.

Bookman, 3 May 1921.

2. "A Talk with Miss Cather"

[Red Cloud, in Webster County, Nebraska, was Cather's childhood home; the *Argus*, the county newspaper.]

It always gives us much pleasure when some reader of the *Argus* here on a visit calls us at the office for a friendly chat because of the feeling that those who read the paper and those who are charged with its preparation belong to one big family. Naturally we were especially pleased when last Friday Miss Willa Cather, whose address is New York City, but who is at home in Red Cloud, New York, London, Paris, or any other city on earth in which she happens to be, called at this office for that reason. Miss Cather is enjoying a several weeks' visit with her parents, Mr. and Mrs. C.F. Cather.

While her work has called to her other scenes Miss Cather told us that there is not any place in this world that is more interesting to her than Red Cloud. She came here from Virginia with her parents when a child, and here grew to womanhood, graduating from the local high school. During part of her course she wrote school items for the *Argus*, which may have been her first contributions to the public press. In those days she was often called upon to stay in her father's office while he was at the court house making abstracts or was out of the city on other business. She had her own desk in the office, and here she did much studying and writing. But the matter which she deems of greatest importance in this connection was the acquaintances formed with the leaders in the life of the community who, calling to transact business with her father, remained to visit with her, telling her of personal affairs in the way that grownups will disclose to a child matters which they would not discuss with a mature person. Often she accompanied Dr. Damerall or Dr. McKeeby on their long trips into the country, and listened with childish admiration as they talked on a variety of subjects from their personal experiences. There were no trained nurses here in those days, so sometimes she was called upon to assist them with surgical operations. In the best homes of the city she was always a welcome visitor. Red Cloud had many men and women of exceptional ability. Miss Cather looks back to her association with these as one of the brightest and most helpful periods of her life.

But the time came when it was necessary that she leave her home and friends. Greater opportunities in other places called her. Times were hard in Nebraska. Her father had acquired large holdings of land, but these were not producing enough revenue to pay the taxes. She could not be contented to stay here and depend on her parents for support. But the thought of leaving her family and friends who meant so much to her was almost too much, and she confessed during her visit the other day that at one time she was actually on the point of giving up, when some words of timely counsel from Mr. and Mrs. O.C. Case gave her new courage and led her to go on with her plans for self improvement.

The interest which has been felt by Red Cloud people in *My Ántonia*, many of the scenes of which are laid in this city, led us to turn the conversation to that subject. Three characters of the story, Miss Cather said, were intended as comparatively faithful pictures of citizens of Red Cloud about 1888 or 1889. These were the author's grandparents, whose characteristics made a deep impression upon her youthful mind when she first came here from Virginia, and Mrs. J.L. Miner—the Mrs. Harling of the book, in whose home she was a frequent guest. In the first draft of the story the picture of Mrs. Harling was of a very different character. While the manuscript was being revised by the author, news came to her of Mrs. Miner's death. So profound an impression did this make upon her, and so active were her memories of old times brought to mind by the news that she made changes in some parts of the book in honor of her friend of early days.

Another character in the book, she informed us, was in part a picture of a former Red Cloud man, and in part of a man she had known in the east. For some reason, she said, this treatment of a character is a very natural one for an author to give. We inquired if these were not because the life of the average person is so commonplace that a faithful delineation of him alone would not make interesting reading. Miss Cather wholly disagreed with this view. She contended that the average person has just as interesting emotions and experiences as public personages. She knew Red Cloud people whose experiences were no less intense and thrilling than those of the public personages with whom she was well acquainted. She found people here just as interesting as those she met in London and Paris, although in a different way. She summed up the matter by saying that if a person is wide awake and not self-centered he can see those interesting things in the life of those about him.

My Ántonia has been translated into a number of different languages, and has a very large sale. Miss Cather is very familiar with the French tongue, and was able to revise the manuscript after the translator had completed his work in that language. This gentleman was a very scholarly man and in the main did excellent work, but he was a little handicapped by never having lived in the prairie states. Miss Cather found that when he came to the word "gopher" at various places in the book he had used the French word meaning "mole." This might have passed among the French readers had it not been for a passage where the gophers were spoken of as playing about in the sun.

Miss Cather writes of Nebraska, not from any sense of duty, but because her early life was so bound up with this commonwealth that this part of the world is of greatest interest to her. She has just completed a new book, some of the scenes of which are laid in this part of the state. That it is bound to be one of her greatest successes is indicated by a telegram received from her publisher, after reading the last installment of the manuscript.

> Just finished the book. Congratulations. It is masterly, a perfectly gorgeous novel, far ahead of anything you have ever yet done, and far ahead of anything I have read in a very long while. With it your position should be secure forever. I shall be proud to have my name associated with it.

Webster County Argus, 29 September 1921.

3. Eleanor Hinman, "Willa Cather"

"The old-fashioned farmer's wife is nearer to the type of the true artist and the prima donna than is the culture enthusiast," declared Miss Willa Cather, author of *The Song of the Lark, O Pioneers!, My Ántonia, Youth and the Bright Medusa*, who has earned the title of one of the foremost American novelists by her stories of prima donnas and pioneers. She was emphasizing that the two are not so far apart in type as most people seem to imagine.

Miss Cather had elected to take her interview out-of-doors in the autumnal sunshine, walking. The fact is characteristic. She is an outdoor person, not far different in type from the pioneers and prima donnas whom she exalts.

She walks with the gait of one who has been used to the saddle. Her complexion is firm with an outdoor wholesomeness. The red in her cheeks is the red that comes from the bite of the wind. Her voice is deep, rich, and full of color; she speaks with her whole body, like a singer.

"Downright" is the word that comes most often to the mind in thinking of her. Whatever she does is done with every fibre. There is no pretense in her, and no conventionality. In conversation she is more stimulating than captivating. She has ideas and is not afraid to express them. Her mind scintillates and sends rays of light down many avenues of thought.

When the interviewer was admitted to her, she was pasting press clippings on a huge sheet of brown wrapping paper, as whole-heartedly as though it were the most important action of her life.

"This way you get them all together," she explained, "and you can see who it is that really likes you, who that really hates you, and who that actually hates you but pretends to like you. I don't mind the ones that hate me; I don't doubt they have good reasons; but I despise the ones that pretend."

When she had finished, she went to her room and almost immediately came out of it again, putting on her hat and coat as she came down the stairs, and going out without a glance at the mirror. She dresses well, yet she is clearly one of the women to whom the chief requirement of clothes is that they should be clean and comfortable.

Although she is very fond of walking, it is evidently strictly subordinate in her mind to conversation. The stroll was perpetually slowing down to a crawl and stopping short at some point which required emphasis. She has a characteristic gesture to bring out a cardinal point; it commences as though it would be a hearty clap upon the shoulder of the person whom she is addressing, but it checks itself and ends without even a touch.

I had intended to interview her on how she gathers the material for her writings; but walking leads to discursiveness and it would be hard to assemble the whole interview under any more definite topic than that bugbear of authors, "an author's views on art." But the longer Miss Cather talks, the more one is filled with the conviction that life is a fascinating business and one's own experience more fascinating than one had ever suspected of it being. Some persons have this gift of infusing their own abundant vitality into the speaker, as Roosevelt is said to have done.

"I don't gather the material for my stories," declared Miss Cather. "All my stories have been written with material that was gathered—no, God save us! not gathered but absorbed—before I was fifteen years old. Other authors tell me it is the same way with them. Sarah Orne Jewett insisted to me that she has used nothing in all her short stories which she did not remember before she was eight years old.

"People will tell you that I come west to get ideas for a new novel, or material for a new novel, as though a novel could be conceived by running around with a pencil and [paper] and jotting down phrases and suggestions. I don't even come west for local color.

"I could not say, however, that I don't come west for inspiration. I do get freshened up by coming out here. I like to go back to my home town, Red Cloud, and get out among the folk who like me for myself, who don't know and don't care a thing about my books, and who treat me just as they did before I published any of them. It makes me feel just like a kid!" cried Willa Cather, writer of finely polished prose.

"The ideas for all my novels have come from things that happened around Red Cloud when I was a child. I was all over the country then, on foot, on horseback and in our farm wagons. My nose went poking into nearly everything. It happened that my mind was constructed for the particular purpose of absorbing impressions and retaining them. I seldom had much idea of the plot or the other characters, but I used my eyes and my ears."

Miss Cather described in detail the way in which the book *My Ántonia* took form in her mind. This is the most recent of her novels; its scene is laid in Nebraska, and it is evidently a favorite of hers.

"One of the people who interested me most as a child was the Bohemian hired girl of one of our neighbors, who was so good to me. She was one of the truest artists I ever knew in the keenness and sensitiveness of her enjoyment, in her love of people and in her willingness to take pains. I did not realize all this as a child, but Annie fascinated me, and I always had it in mind to write a story about her.

"But from what point of view should I write it up? I might give her a lover and write from his standpoint. However, I thought my Ántonia deserved something better than the *Saturday Evening Post* sort of stuff in her book.[1] Finally I concluded that I would write from the point of a detached observer, because that was what I had always been.

"Then, I noticed that much of what I knew about Annie came from the talks I had with young men. She had a fascination for them, and they used to be with her whenever they could. They had

---

1 *The Saturday Evening Post* was one of the most widely read magazines in the United States at this time, and published much popular, and one might say formulaic fiction.

to manage it on the sly, because she was only a hired girl. But they respected and admired her, and she meant a good deal to some of them. So I decided to make my observer a young man.

"There was the material in that book for a lurid melodrama. But I decided in writing it I would dwell very lightly upon those things that a novelist would ordinarily emphasize and make up my story of the little, every-day happenings and occurrences that form the greatest parts of everyone's life and happiness.

"After all, it is the little things that really matter most, the unfinished things, the things that never quite come to birth. Sometimes a man's wedding day is the happiest day in his life; but usually he likes most of all to look back upon some quite simple, quite uneventful day when nothing in particular happened but all the world seemed touched with gold. Sometimes it is a man's wife who sums up to him his ideal of all a woman can be; but how often it is some girl whom he scarcely knows, whose beauty and kindliness have caught at his imagination without cloying it!"

It was many years after the conception of the story that it was written. This story of Nebraska was finally brought to birth in the White Mountains.[1] And Miss Cather's latest novel, which will be published next fall, and which alone of all her prairie stories deals with the Nebraska of the present, was written largely on the Mediterranean coast in southern France, where its author has been during the past spring and summer.

It is often related that Miss Cather draws the greater part of her characters from the life, that they are actual portraits of individual people. This statement she absolutely denies.

"I have never drawn but one portrait of an actual person. That was the mother of the neighbor family in *My Ántonia*. She was the mother of my childhood chums in Red Cloud. I used her so for this reason: while I was getting under way with the book in the White Mountains, I received the word of her death. One clings to one's friends so—I don't know why it was—but the resolve came over me that I would put her into my book as nearly drawn from the life as I could do it. I had not seen her for years.

"I have always been so glad that I did so, because her daughters were so deeply touched. When the book was published it

---

1   Major portions of *My Ántonia* were written in Jaffrey, New Hampshire, where Cather rented rooms at the Shattuck Inn, with a view of Mount Monadnock.

recalled to them little traits of hers that they had not remembered of themselves—as, for example, that when she was vexed she used to dig her heels into the floor as she walked and go clump! clump! clump! across the floor. They cannot speak of the book without weeping.

"All my other characters are drawn from life, but they are all composites of three or four persons. I do not quite understand it, but certain persons seem to coalesce naturally when one is working up a story. I believe most authors shrink from actual portrait painting. It seems so cold-blooded, so heartless, so indecent almost, to present an actual person in that intimate fashion, stripping his very soul."

Although Miss Cather's greatest novels all deal with Nebraska, and although it has been her work which has first put Nebraska upon the literary map, this seems to have been more a matter of necessity with her than of choice. For when she was asked to give her reflections about Nebraska as a storehouse of literary or artistic material, her answer was not altogether conciliatory.

"Of course Nebraska is a storehouse of literary material. Everywhere is a storehouse of literary material. If a true artist was born in a pigpen and raised in a sty, he would still find plenty of inspiration for his work. The only need is the eye to see.

"Generally speaking, the older and more established the civilization, the better a subject it is for art. In an old community, there has been time for associations to gather and for interesting types to develop. People do not feel that they all must be exactly alike.

"At present in the west there seems to be an idea that we all must be like somebody else, as much as if we had all been cast in the same mold. We wear exactly similar clothes, drive the same make of car, live in the same part of town, in the same style of house. It's deadly! Not long ago one of my dear friends said to me that she was about to move.

"'Oh,' I cried, 'how can you leave this beautiful old house!'

"'Well,' she said, 'I don't really want to go, but all our friends have moved to the other end of town, and we have lived in this house for forty years.'

"What better reason can you want for staying in a house than that you have lived there for forty years?

"New things are always ugly. New clothes are always ugly. A prima donna will never wear a new gown upon the stage. She wears it first around her apartment until it shapes itself to her figure; or if she hasn't time to do that, she hires an understudy to wear it. A house can never be beautiful until it has been lived in for a long time. An old house built and furnished in miserable taste is more beautiful than a new house built and furnished in correct taste. The beauty lies in the associations that cluster around it, the way in which the house has fitted itself to the people.

"This rage for newness and conventionality is one of the things which I deplore in the present-day Nebraska. The second is the prevalence of a superficial culture. These women who run about from one culture club to another studying Italian art out of a textbook and an encyclopedia and believing that they are learning something about it by memorizing a string of facts, are fatal to the spirit of art. The nigger boy who plays by ear on his fiddle airs from *Traviata* without knowing what he is playing, or why he likes it, has more real understanding of Italian art than these esthetic creatures with a head and a larynx, and no organs that they get any use of, who reel you off the life of Leonardo da Vinci.

"Art is a matter of enjoyment through the five senses. Unless you can see the beauty all around you everywhere, and enjoy it, you can never comprehend art. Take the cottonwood, for example, the most beautiful tree on the plains. The people of Paris go crazy about them. They have planted long boulevards with them. They hold one of their fetes when the cotton begins to fly; they call it 'summer snow.' But people of Red Cloud and Hastings chop them down.

"Take our Nebraska wild flowers. There is no place in the world that has more beautiful ones. But they have no common names. In England, in any European country, they would all have beautiful names like eglantine, primrose, and celandine. As a child I gave them all names of my own. I used to gather great armfuls of them and sit and cry over them. They were so lovely, and no one seemed to care for them at all! There is one book that I would rather have produced than all my novels. That is the Clemens botany dealing with the wild flowers of the west.[1]

"But why am I taking so many examples from one sense? Esthetic appreciation begins with the enjoyment of the morning bath. It should include all the activities of life. There is real art in

---

1 Probably Frederic E. Clements and Edith S. Clements, *Rocky Mountain Flowers; an Illustrated Guide for Plant Lovers and Plant-Users*. New York: H. W. Wilson, 1914.

cooking a roast just right, so that it is brown and dripping and odorous and 'saignant.'[1]

"The farmer's wife who raises a large family and cooks for them and makes their clothes and keeps house and on the side runs a truck garden and a chicken farm and a canning establishment, and thoroughly enjoys doing it all, and doing it well, contributes more to art than all the culture clubs. Often you find such a woman with all the appreciation of the beautiful bodies of her children, of the order and harmony of her kitchen, of the real creative joy of all her activities, which marks the great artist.

"Most of the women artists I have known—the prima donnas, novelists, poets, sculptors—have been women of this same type. The very best cooks I have ever known have been prima donnas. When I visited them the way to their hearts was the same as to the hearts of the pioneer rancher's wife in my childhood—I must eat a great deal, and enjoy it.

"Many people seem to think that art is a luxury to be imported and tacked on to life. Art springs out of the very stuff that life is made of. Most of our young authors start to write a story and make a few observations from nature to add local color. The results are invariably false and hollow. Art must spring out of the fullness and richness of life."

This glorification of the old-fashioned housewife came very naturally from Willa Cather, chronicler of women with careers. What does Miss Cather think of the present movement of women into business and the arts?

"It cannot help but be good," was her reply. "It at least keeps the woman interested in something real.

"As for the choice between a woman's home and her career, is there any reason why she cannot have both? In France the business is regarded as a family affair. It is taken for granted that Madame will be the business partner of her husband; his bookkeeper, cashier or whatever she fits best. Yet the French women are famous housekeepers and their children do not suffer for lack of care.

"The situation is similar if the woman's business is art. Her family life will be a help rather than a hinderance to her; and if she has a quarter of the vitality of her prototype on the farm she will be able to fulfill the claims of both."

---

1   "Bleeding."

Miss Cather, however, deplores heartily the drift of the present generation away from the land.

"All the farmer's sons and daughters seem to want to get into the professions where they think they may find a soft place. 'I'm sure not going to work the way the old man did,' seems to be the slogan of today. Soon only the Swedes and Germans will be left to uphold the prosperity of the country."

She contrasts the university of the present with that in the lean days of the nineties, "when," as she says, "the ghosts walked in this country." She came to Lincoln, a child barely in her teens, with her own way to make absolutely. She lived on thirty dollars a month, worked until 1 or 2 o'clock every night, ate no breakfast in the morning by way of saving time and money, never really had enough to eat, and carried full college work. "And many of the girls I was with were much worse off than I." Yet the large majority of the famous alumni of the university date from precisely this period of hard work and little cash.

In making her way into the literary world she never had, she declares, half the hardships that she endured in this battle for an education. Her first book of short stories, to be sure, was a bitter disappointment. Few people bought it, and her Nebraska friends could find no words bad enough for it. "They wanted me to write propaganda for the commercial club," she explained.

"An author is seldom sensitive except about his first volume. Any criticism of that hurts. Not criticism of its style—that only spurs one on to improve it. But the root-and-branch kind of attack is hard to forget. Nearly all very young authors write sad stories and very many of them write their first stories in revolt against everything. Humor, kindliness, tolerance come later."

Some of the stories from this unsuccessful volume, *The Troll Garden*, were reprinted in *Youth and the Bright Medusa*, the recent volume which has had a wide success.

Miss Cather spent Monday, Tuesday, and Wednesday, with Mrs. Max Westerman, going from here to Omaha to deliver a lecture before the fine arts club.

Lincoln Sunday Star, 6 November 1921.

4. Rose C. Field, "Restlessness Such as Ours Does Not Make for Beauty"

Tea with Willa Sibert Cather is a rank failure. The fault is entirely hers. You get so highly interested in what she had to say and how she says it that you ask for cream when you prefer lemon and let the butter on your hot toast grow cold and smeary. It is vastly more important to you to watch her eyes and lips which betray her when she seems to be giving voice to a serious concept, but is really poking fun at the world—or at your own foolish question. For Willa Sibert Cather has a rare good sense, homespun sense, if you will— and that is rare enough—which she drives home with a well-wrought mallet of humor.

It started with the question of books and the overwhelming quantities which the American public of today is buying. What exactly was the explanation of that? Did it mean that we were becoming a more cultured people, a more artistic people? Miss Cather was suffering from neuritis[1] that day. It was difficult to understand, therefore, whether the twinge that crossed her face was caused by the pain we gave her or that of her temporary illness.

"Don't confuse reading with culture or art," she said, when her face cleared. There was laughter in her blue eyes. "Not in this country, at any rate. So many books are sold today because of the economic condition of this country, not the cultural. We have a prosperous middle class, in cities, in suburbs, in small towns, on farms, to whom the expediture of $2 for a book imposes no suffering. What's more, they have to read it. They want a book which will fill up commuting boredom every morning and evening; they want a book to read mornings after breakfast when the maid takes care of the apartment housework; they want a book to keep in the automobile while they're waiting for tardy friends or relatives; they want fillers-in, in a word, something to take off the edge of boredom and empty leisure. Publishers, who are, after all, business men, recognize the demand and pour forth their supply. It's good sense; it's good psychology. It's the same thing that is responsible for the success of the cinema. It is, as a matter of fact, the cinema public for whom this reading material is published. But it has no more to do with culture than with anarchy or philosophy. You might with

---

1 An inflammation of peripheral nerves; Cather suffered this ailment in her wrist and writing hand.

equal reason ask whether we are becoming a more cultured people because so many more of us are buying chiffoniers[1] and bureaus and mirrors and toilet sets. Forty or fifty years ago these things were not to be found in the average home. Forty or fifty years ago we couldn't afford them, and today we can. As a result, every home has an increased modicum of comfort and luxury. But, carrying the thought a step further, every home has not increased in beauty.

"Not so long ago I was speaking to William Dean Howells[2] about this subject of book reading and book publication. He said something which was of interest to me and which may be of interest to you. Forty years ago, he maintained, we were in the midst of a great literary period. Then, only good books were published, only cultivated people read. The others didn't read at all, or if they did it was the newspapers, the almanac, and the Bible on Sundays. This public doesn't exist today any more than the cinema public existed then. Fine books were written for fine people. Fine books are still written for fine people. Sometimes the others read them, too, and if they can stand it, it doesn't hurt them."

Her lips twitched in a smile she tried to suppress. She shook her head at a wayward thought.

"That discrimination is not a snobbish one," she went on. "Don't think that. By the fine reader I don't necessarily mean the man or woman with a cultivated background, an academic, or a wealthy background. I mean the person with quickness and richness of mentality, fineness of spirituality. You found it often in a carpenter or a blacksmith, who went to his few books for recreation and inspiration. The son of a long line of college presidents may be nothing but a dolt and idiot in spite of the fact that he knows how to enter a room properly or to take off a lady's wraps. It's the shape of the head that's of importance; it's the something that's in it that can bring an ardor and an honesty to a masterpiece and make it over until it becomes a personal possession.

"I am not making generalities, I hope. I hate generalities. There's no sense to them. They're superficial; they're easy. People in talking of art and art appreciation make the generality, for instance, that all

---

1 A movable low cupboard with a sideboard top.
2 Howells (1837-1920) was a highly influential author, editor, and critic. He exerted enormous influence on American literary history as editor of the *Atlantic Monthly* in the late nineteenth century

singers come out of the mud. Mud has nothing to do with it, just as being a carpenter has nothing to do with the accident of a good mind. Art requires a vast amount of character. It's a whole lot more than talent. It demonstrates itself in relationships the artist thinks important. I am not speaking of morality. It means great, good sense, as well as the gift of expression. The singer who is born in the mud doesn't arrive unless he's very good; there are so many obstacles which he must surmount. It requires a very little effort for a person with a mediocre voice and a deep, lined purse to get a hearing; it requires unusual ability for the poor man. When the latter arrives, it is because he has proved his genius. Mud had nothing to do with it; it only made his progress more difficult.

"Because of this vast amount of writing and reading, there are many among us who make the mistake of thinking we are an artistic people. Talking about it won't make us that. We can build excellent bridges; we can put up beautiful office buildings, factories; in time, it may be, we shall be known for the architecture which our peculiar industrial progress has fostered here, but literary art, painting, culture, no. We haven't yet acquired the good sense of discrimination possessed by the French, for instance. They have a great purity of tradition; they all but murder originality, and yet they worship it. The taste of the nation is represented by the Academy; it is a corrective rod which the young artist ever dreads. He revolts against it, but he cannot free himself from it. He cannot pull the wool over the eyes of the academy by saying his is a new movement, an original movement, a breaking away from the old. His work is judged on its merits, and if it isn't good, he gets spanked. Here in America, on the other hand, every little glimmer of color calls itself art; every youth that misuses a brush calls himself an artist, and an adoring group of admirers flatter and gush over him. It's rather pathetic.

"Read the life of Manet and Monet,[1] both great artists, great masters. The French people had to be sure of their genius before it would acclaim them. Death almost took them before acknowledgment of their power was given them. It is good sense, deliberation, and an eagerness for the beautiful that keeps up the fine front of French art. That is true of her literature as well as of her painting.

"France is sensitive; we are not. It may be that our youth has something to do with it, and yet I don't know whether that is it. It's our

---

1   Edouard Manet (1832-83) and Claude Monet (1840-1926), French impressionist painters.

prosperity, our judging success in terms of dollars. Life not only gives us wages for our toil but a bonus besides. It makes for nice, easy family life but not for art. The French people, on the other hand, have had no bonus. Their minds have been formed by rubbing up cruelly with the inescapable realities of life; they've played a close game, wresting their wages from a miserly master. Mrs. Wharton[1] expressed it very well in a recent article when she said that the Frenchman elected to live at home and use his wits to make his condition happy. He don't want an easier land. He chose France, above all, as the home of his family and his children after him. There you are.

"The Frenchman doesn't talk nonsense about art, about self-expression; he is too greatly occupied with building the things that make his home. His house, his garden, his vineyards, these are the things that fill his mind. He creates something beautiful, something lasting. And what happens? When a French painter wants to paint a picture he makes a copy of a garden, a home, a village. The art in them inspires his brush. And twenty, thirty, forty years later you'll come to see the original of that picture, and you'll find it, changed only by the mellowness of time.

"Restlessness such as ours, success such as ours, striving such as ours, do not make for beauty. Other things must come first: good cookery; cottages that are homes, not playthings; gardens; repose. These are first-rate things, and out of first-rate stuff is art made. It is possible that machinery has finished us as far as this is concerned. Nobody stays at home any more; nobody makes anything beautiful any more. Quick transportation is the death of art. We can't keep still because it is so easy to move about.

"Yet it isn't always a question of one country being artistic and another not. The world goes through periods or waves of art. Between these periods come great resting places. We may be resting right now. Older countries have their wealth of former years to fall back upon. We haven't. But, like older countries, we have a few individuals who have caught the flame of former years and are carrying the torch into the next period. Whistler was one of these; Whitman was another."[2]

---

1 Edith Wharton (1862-1937), American novelist. Cather is likely referring to Wharton's essay, "French Ways and their Meaning" (1919).
2 James Abbott McNeil Whistler (1834-1903), American painter and printmaker; Walt Whitman (1819-92), American poet. The title of Cather's novel O Pioneers! is taken from a Whitman poem.

Miss Cather poured some tea into a cup and diluted it with the cream we asked for but didn't want. We let it stand on the arm of the chair and proceeded with a question that her words had awakened.

"If we have no tradition of years behind us, the people who come to live here have. Are they contributing anything to the artistic expression of the country?"

Again that twinge crossed her face. This time it was plain that the question had started it.

"Contribute? What shall they contribute? They are not peddlers with something to sell; they are not gypsies. They have come here to live in the sense that they lived in the Old World, and if they were let alone their lives might turn into the beautiful ways of their homeland. But they are not let alone. Social workers, missionaries—call them what you will—go after them, hound them pursue them and devote their days and nights toward the great task of turning them into stupid replicas of smug American citizens. This passion for Americanizing everything and everybody is a deadly disease with us. We do it the way we build houses. Speed, uniformity, dispatch, nothing else matters.

"It wasn't so years ago. When I was a child, all our neighbors were foreigners. Nobody paid any attention to them outside of the attention they wanted. We let them alone. Work was assigned them, and they made good houseworkers and splendid craftsmen. They furnished their houses as they had in the countries from which they came. Beauty was there and charm. Nobody investigated them; nobody regarded them as laboratory specimens. Everybody had a sort of protective air toward them, but nobody interfered with them. A 'foreigner' was a person foreign to our manners or custom of living, not possible prey for reform. Nobody ever cheated a foreigner. A man lost everything in the esteem of the community when he was discovered in a crime of false barter. It was very much better that way. I hate this poking into personal affairs by social workers, and I know the people hate it, too. Yet settlement work is a mark of progress, our progress. That's that. I know there's much to be said for it, but nevertheless, I hate it."

We spoke about *My Ántonia*, Miss Cather's story about the immigrant family of Czechs.

"Is *My Ántonia* a good book because it is the story of the soil?" we asked. She shook her head.

"No, no, decidedly no. There is no formula; there is no reason. It was the story of people I knew. I expressed a mood, the core of which was like a folksong, a thing Grieg could have written. That it was powerfully tied to the soil had nothing to do with it. Ántonia was tied to the soil. But I might have written the tale of a Czech baker in Chicago, and it would have been the same. It was nice to have her in the country; it was more simple to handle, but Chicago could have told the same story. It would have been smearier, joltier, noisier, less sugar and more sand, but still a story that had as its purpose the desire to express the quality of these people. No, the country has nothing to do with it; the city has nothing to do with it; nothing contributes consciously. The thing worth while is always unplanned. Any art that is a result of pre-concerted plans is a dead baby."

Miss Cather is now writing a new novel which will come out next Autumn. "There will be no theories, no panaceas, no generalizations. It will be a story about people in a prosperous provincial-city in the Middle West. Nothing new or strange, you see."

New York Times Book Review, 21 December 1924.

Appendix F: Contemporary Reviews of the Novel

1. Randolph Bourne, "Morals and Art from the West"

Willa Cather has already shown herself an artist in that beautiful story of Nebraska immigrant life, *O Pioneers!* Her digression into *The Song of the Lark* took her into a field that neither her style nor her enthusiasm really fitted her for. Now in *My Ántonia* (Houghton Mifflin; $1.60) she has returned to the Nebraska countryside with an enriched feeling and an even more golden charm of style. Here at last is an American novel, redolent of the Western prairie that our most irritated and exacting preconceptions can be content with. It is foolish to be captious about American fiction when the same year gives us two so utterly unlike, and yet equally artistic, novels as Mr. Fuller's *On the Stairs* and Miss Cather's *My Ántonia*. She is also of the brevity school, and beside William Allen White's swollen bulk she makes you realize anew how much art is suggestion and not transcription. One sentence from Miss Cather's pages is more vivid than paragraphs of Mr. White's stale brightness of conversation.[1] The reflections she does not make upon her characters are more convincing than all his moralizing. Her purpose is neither to illustrate eternal truths nor to set before us the crowded gallery of a whole society. Yet in these simple pictures of the struggling pioneer life, of the comfortable middle classes of the bleak little towns, there is an understanding of what these people have to contend with and grope for that goes to the very heart of their lives.

Miss Cather convinces because she knows her story and carries it along with the surest touch. It has all the artistic simplicity of

---

1   William Allen White (1868-1944) was best known as a journalist, the "Sage of Emporia," the voice of Kansas. The book alluded to here may be *In the Heart of a Fool* (1918), published at a hefty 615 pages. White rose to national prominence with his 1896 editorial, "What's the Matter with Kansas?," claiming that the Populists were an embarrassment to the state. The editorial was picked up by newspapers throughout the country and reprinted by the Republican party organization. White later retracted many of his conservative ideas and came to support some aspects of Populist politics.

material that has been patiently shaped until everything irrelevant has been scraped away. The story has a flawless tone of candor, a naive charm, that seems quite artless until we realize that no spontaneous narrative could possibly have the clean pertinence and grace which this story has. It would be cluttered, as Mr. White's novel is cluttered; it would have uneven streaks of self-consciousness, as most of the younger novelists' work, done impromptu with a mistaken ideal of "saturation," is both cluttered and self-conscious. But Miss Cather's even novel has that serenity of the story that is telling itself, of people who are living through their own spontaneous charm.

The story purports to be the memories of a successful man as he looks back over his boyhood on the Nebraska farm and in the little town. Of that boyhood Ántonia was the imaginative center, the little Bohemian immigrant, his playmate and wistful sweetheart. His vision is romantic, but no more romantic than anyone would be towards so free and warm and glorious a girl. He goes to the University, and it is only twenty years later that he hears the story of her pathetic love and desertion, and her marriage to a simple Bohemian farmer, strong and good like herself.

> She was a battered woman now, not a lovely girl; but she still had that something which fires the imagination, could still stop one's breath for a moment by a look or gesture that somehow revealed the meaning in common things. She had only to stand in the orchard, to put her hand on a little crab tree and look up at the apples to make you feel the goodness of planting and tending and harvesting at last. All the strong things of her heart came out in her body, that had been so tireless in serving generous emotions. It was no wonder that her sons stood tall and straight. She was a rich mine of life, like the founders of early races.

My Ántonia has the indestructible fragrance of youth: the prairie girls and the dances; the softly alluring Lena, who so unaccountably fails to go wrong; the rich flowered prairie, with its drowsy heats and stinging colds. The book, in its different way, is as fine as the Irishman Corkery's *The Threshold of Quiet*,[1] that other

---

1 Daniel Corkery, *The Threshold of Quiet* (1917), published in Ireland. By distinguishing Cather from William Allen White and comparing her to Corkery, the reviewer means to align Cather's work with those of the highest forms of literary art rather than with works of journalism or popular fiction.

recent masterpiece of wistful youth. But this story lives with the hopefulness of the West. It is poignant and beautiful, but it is not sad. Miss Cather, I think, in this book has taken herself out of the rank of provincial writers and given us something we can fairly class with the modern literary art the world over that is earnestly and richly interpreting the sprit of youth. In her work the stiff moral molds are fortunately broken, and she writes what we can wholly understand.

The Dial, 14 December 1918, pp. 556–57.

2. H.W. Boynton, "All Sorts"

To Miss Cather's new story, "My Ántonia", ... tribute must first of all be paid. It is true to the Nebraskan soil of her own childhood, and therefore true to America and the world. On the surface it also might be called artless and deficient in action. But here in fact it differs sharply from a chronicle like "The Manse at Barren Rocks".[1] Miss Cather is an accomplished artist. Her method is that of the higher realism; it rests not at all upon the machinery of dramatic action which is so right and essential for romance. Her "Song of the Lark", a triumphal story if there ever was one, lacked the rounded artifice that lures a big public—lacked, above all, the conventional "happy ending". So does "My Ántonia", which, even more frankly a portrait than its predecessor, is a portrait of a woman.

Miss Cather has owned as among the most vivid of her experiences on the Nebraska ranch of her childhood, her impression of the Scandinavian and Bohemian settlers who were among her neighbors. Thea Kronborg in "The Song of the Lark" was of Swedish parentage. Ántonia is a Bohemian girl on a Nebraska ranch. Her father, a musician and dreamer, has no heart in the new life and presently kills himself as the only way out. The mother and the elder son are ambitious and unscrupulous. Ántonia is the one well-rounded member of the family: somehow she joins her father's sensitiveness to the sturdiness of her mother, and con-

---

1 By Albert Benjamin Cunningham (1918).

tributes that magic something of her own that is necessary to transmute mere characteristics into personality.

She is not infallible or protected by a special Providence, does not push forward to an obvious success or happiness. On the contrary she passes her first years of grown girlhood as a farm worker, becomes a "hired girl" in the neighboring town, runs away with a flashy drummer[1] who deserts her before the birth of her child, and later marries an undistinguished and not especially successful farmer of her own race.[2] But she is unconquerable; and she lives through everything to transmit that superb health and courage of mind and body to a great family who are bound to make their worthy contribution to America. It is in the guise, as "a rich mine of life, like the founders of early races", that we see her fulfilled and justified.

Clearly, the effectiveness of such a portrait depends in an unusual sense upon the skill of the painter. Casual as her touches seem, no stroke is superfluous or wrongly emphasized; and we may be hardly conscious how much of the total effect of the portrait is owing to the quiet beauty and purity of the artist's style.

Bookman, December 1918, pp. 489-95.

3. C.L.H., "Struggles With the Soil"

Ántonia is not the conventional heroine. She never becomes an heiress, she uncovers no spy plot for the government, she never even dreams of the life of a Red Cross nurse, and she is no adventuress. She is a stalwart Bohemian peasant girl, grows up on a windy and barren Nebraska farm and helps her parents till the soil and make it fruitful.

We follow her through a difficult and picturesque childhood, see her emerge into a glowing and vital young womanhood, and in the end find her where such a vigorous and elemental person should be—on her farm, surrounded by a family of nine or ten children.

---

1 A traveling salesman.
2 That is, her same nationality, or ethnicity. The term "race" was used for such distinctions at this time.

No less vivid and stirring than Ántonia herself is the physical background of the story. The long and bitter winters, the scorching summers, the vast stretches of uncultivated prairies, the hard struggle against poverty and actual starvation—these things are described with a simplicity and directness that give us a real feeling of the actuality. We read much of the struggles of the foreigners in our big cities; this book gives us a picture of the grim and determined fight for life and prosperity of the vigorous foreigners who have settled in the West and helped to make it a land of fruitfulness. The story is a fresh and sincere piece of work.

New York Call, 13 November 1918, p. 10.

4. Anon. Rev. of *My Ántonia*, by Willa Cather

The prairie is the background for this narrative of the fortunes of a Bohemian girl as they were observed by an American boy who grew up on a neighboring farm and in the little Nebraska village. Stark realism gives a haunting quality to two grim scenes; others are not so grim but just as vivid. The whole gives an intimate friendship for the quiet, strong, simple Ántonia with her own charm and power from childhood to contented middle age as the mother of her prairie children. It will not appeal to as many readers as *The Song of the Lark* (*Booklist*, 12:136, D 15). Illustrated by W. Benda.

A.L.A. Booklist 15.3 (1918), p. 107.

5. Anon. Rev. of *My Ántonia*, by Willa Cather

The story of Ántonia is told by one of the friends of her childhood, a man who thru all his years of worldly success has never forgotten his fine Bohemian girl who had been one of the strongest influences in his early life. Ántonia is the child of immigrant parents who have come from Bohemia to wrest a living from the rich but untamed prairie soil. In the struggle the sensitive tempered father loses his grip and goes under, and Ántonia is called on to do a man's work on the farm. Later she becomes a town hired girl, is betrayed, deserted and left with a child. She marries, bears many children and, thru all vicissitudes, preserves a valor of spirit that no hardship can daunt or break. When Jim Burden sees her again after many years, he finds her battered but not broken. Surrounded by her thrifty, fruitful acres, her rugged, happy children, she is a woman who has triumphed over life.

Book Review Digest 14 (1918), p. 85.

6. Anon. Rev. of *My Ántonia*, by Willa Cather

To those who appreciate style in fiction, and for that quality alone can enjoy a story that has neither exciting plot nor swift action, Miss Cather's new book, *My Ántonia*, will make strong appeal. With sympathy and understanding she tells a tale of youth and courage in the red grass region of Nebraska, when that part of our country was being settled by a large foreign immigration. The simple tale of growth centers about a Bohemian girl and an American lad, but Ántonia is the main character. The story of her development thru the hardships of frontier life is full of human appeal and the fascination of the making of Americans from the foreign born.

Independent, 25 January 1919, p. 131.

7. Anon. Rev. of *My Ántonia*, by Willa Cather

Nebraska is the scene of Willa S. Cather's new novel, the central character being a young Bohemian girl, Ántonia Shimerda, the daughter of immigrants. Her father and mother came to Nebraska, where they had bought a farm out in the prairie from a fellow-countryman who cheated them badly. Jim Burden, who tells the story, is an American boy, living with his prosperous grandparents in their big farm, which, as distances go in that country, is not so very far from the Shimerdas' place. Jim's grandparents befriend the Shimerdas, and it is Jim himself who teaches Ántonia English. A large part of the book is given over to an account of the work and play of these two during the year when Jim was about 10 and Ántonia about 14.

There is a carefully detailed picture of daily existence on a Nebraska farm, and indeed the whole book is a carefully detailed picture rather than a story. Presently Jim's grandparents decide that they are getting too old to run the farm, and move to the little town of Black Hawk. Then we are told all about the long Summer days, the bitter cold of Winter, the games and music at the Hastings' [Harlings'], and the arrival of the dance tent which made so pronounced a change in the own. Ántonia, who had come to live with the Hastings as their "hired girl," was fascinated by the dancing, and presently quarreled with her employers because of it. But she was a born countrywoman, and after a very unfortunate experience she returned to the country and the farm. The book is full of sketches of farm life, of plowing, reaping and thrashing, of the difficulties of feeding cattle in Winter, and all the troubles of husbandry. Ántonia is a true daughter of the soil, thus described: "She had only to stand in the orchard, to put her hand on a little crab tree and look up at the apples, to make you feel the goodness of planting and tending and harvesting as last." There are other immigrants in the book besides the Shimerdas, Norwegians, Danes, Russians, &c., and the ways of all of them are more or less fully described. They are all, to some extent, pioneers, the period of the book being that in which the first foreign immigrants came to Nebraska.

New York Times, 6 October 1918, sec. 7, p. 429.

8. Anon. "Two Portraits." Rev. of *Camilla* and *My Ántonia*, by Elizabeth Robins and Willa Cather

Miss Robins[1] affects the deliberate, elliptical, smooth-spoken post-Jacobite manner that appears to attract so many of the current women story-tellers, Mrs. Wharton leading the way. It touches snobbishness at both ends. It is too niggling and high-heeled for much real usefulness on this side of the water. A writer like Miss Cather is as clear of it as of the man-in-the-street patter of the

---

1   Elizabeth Robins (1862-1952) was a major figure in Cather's time. Novelist, feminist activist, suffragette, literary critic and historian, she exemplified the kind of public life and devotion to political causes Cather eschewed. Cather would surely have known of her career and writing. Although only ten years older than Cather, the reviewer sees her as a representative of an older style of writing. Robins' novels based on her adventures in Alaska may have influenced Cather's imagination of the character Tiny Soderball, in *My Ántonia*.

magazine story-tellers (snobbishness at its nadir). Her style has distinction, no manner; and it is the style of an artist whose imagination is at home in her own land, among her own people, which happens to be a democratic land and a plain people. She has a strong feeling about this—that we cannot get away from our sources. One recalls how this is enforced in "The Song of the Lark"—how we were made to understand that Thea Kronborg's genius sprang from the soil of her birthplace. And one recognizes how discreetly this story, like "The Song of the Lark," springs from Miss Cather's own soil. She was born in Virginia, but her childhood was passed on her father's ranch in Nebraska. During her most receptive years her nature was responding to the charm and mystery of the prairie, and also to her human setting. The pioneer neighborhood was mainly peopled by Scandinavians and Bohemians. Their exotic character and ways became a part of the child's America. Her three novels are stories of women: two of them Swedish-American girls, and the third, Ántonia, the child of a Bohemian immigrant. This is and professes to be (despite the publishers who inconceivably declare it a "love-story") nothing more or less than a portrait of a woman. The Shimerdas are a poor Bohemian family who have taken up a little Nebraskan farm. The father, a man of sensitive feeling, devoted to his own land, has come to America at the insistence of the vulgar and ambitious mother. He finds nothing to live for here, and takes his own life not long after their arrival. The girl Ántonia has his fineness of nature but a vigor and steadfastness also, of body and spirit, which fit her for conquest of life. Not in Thea Kronborg's way, by genius infallibly journeying upward, but by the commoner road of a strong and simple character not to be submerged by circumstance. We do not so much hear her story told as go with her upon her humble triumphant way, as farmhand, hired girl, woman befooled and deserted by the father of her first child, and at last as happy wife and drudge of a commonplace good little man of her own race, and mother of a great brood of healthy and rewarding offspring. Our guide upon this quiet pilgrimage is the American who has been Ántonia's neighbor and playmate in childhood, and whose love for her, in his years of "success" in the great world, remains a feeling of peculiar depth and unlessening inspiration. In some sense, after all that has come between them, she is still "his Ántonia." "She was a battered woman now, not a lovely girl; but she still had that something which fires the imagination, could still stop one's breath for a moment by a look or gesture that somehow revealed the meaning in common things ... It was no wonder that her sons stood tall and straight. She was a rich mine of life, like the founders of early races." A notable portrait, rendered too quietly perhaps, to catch the eye of the seeker for color and movement of the picturesque or dramatic order, but worthy to stand with "The Song of the Lark" among the best of our recent interpretations of American life.

Nation, 2 November 1918, pp. 522-23.

9. N.P.D. "The New Books"

Verily, some authors make the life of the reviewer a very pleasant one. Last week it was Mr. Hergeshelmer; this week it is Willa Sibert Cather. In "My Ántonia," Miss Cather multiplies many times the genius of one of her first novels, "O Pioneers!"—another story of Nebraska and the middle west, with the American pioneers and foreign settlers. It has the fascination of Mr. Hudson's "Far Away and Long Ago,"[1] and the striking originality of Conrad's "A Personal Record."[2] The only book we can recall that approaches it in the truthfulness and charm of its descriptions of the prairie country is a book published some years ago called "A Stepdaughter of the Prairie."[3]

But here we are writing of Miss Cather's book as if it were autobiography and not a story. Like most works of art, it is probably both. Miss Cather has the gift of remembering, and the equally important gift of forgetting, what is not important. She is a genuine realist. Her passion for the truth is apparently as great as her aversion for mere writing. If she is ever tempted to indulge in fine writing, she seems to follow the advice of the one who said, "be bold and murder all your darlings." Nor does this mean that Miss Cather's narrative has any of the dulness and flatness and ugliness generally associated with realistic writing. With manifest fidelity to scene and characters, and apparent simplicity and naturalness in the telling of the story, it is at the same time shimmering with romance

---

1 William Henry Hudson, *Far Away and Long Ago; A History of My Early Life* (1918).
2 Joseph Conrad, *A Personal Record* (1912).
3 Margaret Lynn, A *Stepdaughter of the Prairie* (1914).

and excitement. She can tell a bigger snake story, and a more horrifying one, than Mr. Hudson; while her story of the Russian bride thrown to the wolves is as picturesque, shall we say, as Mr. Conrad's story of his heroic great-uncle who was with Napoleon and ate the Lithuanian dog. There are stories within stories, all as neatly unfolding as a set of Chinese boxes. There are many characters, living, breathing people.

But it is the description of the country itself that will perhaps most impress the reader, especially the reader who knows. It may be wondered if there is something in what Miss Cather says in her opening chapter about the freemasonry of people who come from the same parts of the country. If this is true, as we are inclined to think it is, some fears may well be felt for the new internationalism. A child's idea of Heaven is a place just like home. In an introduction, in which she cleverly and with art explains the male medium of her story-telling, Miss Cather says:

"We were talking about what it is like to spend one's childhood in little towns like these, buried in wheat and corn, under stimulating extremes of climate: burning summers when the world lies green and billowy, beneath a brilliant sky, when one is fairly stifled in vegetation, in the color and smell of strong weeds and heavy harvest; blustery winters with little snow, when the whole country is stripped bare and gray as sheet iron. We agreed that no one who had not grown up in a little prairie town could know anything about it. It was a kind of freemasonry, we said."

Well, the country is here in all its variety: hot summer nights when "you can hear the corn grow," and not only winters that bluster, but winters that are real with the "big blizzard," when the snow is "spilled out of heaven like thousands of feather beds being emptied"—such feather beds as Mrs. Shimerda, the Bohemian woman, used to keep her roast goose hot in.

On the train carrying the small boy from Virginia to Nebraska to make his home with his grandparents—the same train bringing the Bohemian family with "My Ántonia," we read that "the only thing very noticeable about Nebraska was that it was still all day long Nebraska." There was nothing but land. In fact, it seemed "not a country at all, but the material out of which countries are made." The grass was the country, "as the water is the sea," and the grass had "so much motion in it that the whole country seemed, somehow, to be running."

Bits of description such as these are not only wonderfully vivid, but are poetic and excite the imagination. The second half of the story moves to town where the husky farm girls who had followed a plough become "hired girls," and wear pretty clothes and know the traveling men and train conductors and go to dances. "My Ántonia" goes to town also, where she is "hired girl" for the Harlings, and gets acquainted with a train conductor, "one of those train-crew aristocrats who are always afraid that some one may ask them to put up a car window."

But Ántonia's apotheosis must be left for the reader to behold for himself; the chapter called "Cuzak's Boy's" gives the picture, and there are considerably more than two cherubs in it. It is a story of great truth and greater art; more than this, it is interesting, and will be enjoyed by those who never heard the corn grow or saw a prairie-dog town either.

The Globe and Commercial Advertiser, 11 January 1919.

10. H.L. Mencken, "Mainly Fiction"

The Cather story, "My Ántonia" (*Houghton-Mifflin*), was reviewed somewhat briefly in this place last month. It well deserves another notice, for it is not an isolated phenomenon, an extraordinary single book like Cahan's "The Rise of David Levinsky,"[1] or Master's "Spoon River Anthology,"[2] but merely one more step upward in the career of a writer who has labored with the utmost patience and industry, and won every foot of the way by hard work. She began, setting aside certain early experiments, with "Alexander's Bridge" in 1912—a book strongly suggesting the influence of Edith Wharton and yet thoroughly individual and newly thought out. Its defect was one of locale and people: one somehow got the feeling that Miss Cather was dealing with things at second-hand, that she knew her personages a bit less intimately than she should have known them. This defect, I venture to guess, impressed itself upon the author herself. At all events, she abandoned New England, in her next novel, for the Middle West, and in particular for the Middle West of the last great immigrations—a region far better known to her. The result was "O Pioneers" (1913), a book of very fine achievement and of even finer promise. Then came "The

---

1 Abraham Cahan, *The Rise of David Levinsky* (1917).
2 Edgar Lee Masters, *Spoon River Anthology* (1914).

Song of the Lark" in 1915—still more competent, more searching and convincing, better in every way. And now, after three years, comes "My Ántonia," a work in which improvement takes a sudden leap—a novel, indeed, that is not only the best done by Miss Cather herself, but also one of the best that any American has ever done, East or West, early or late. It is simple; it is honest; it is intelligent; it is moving. The means that appear in it are means perfectly adapted to its end. Its people are unquestionably real. Its background is brilliantly vivid. It has form, grace, good literary manners. In a word, it is a capital piece of writing, and it will be heard of long after the baroque balderdash now touted on the "book pages" is forgotten.

It goes without saying that all the machinery customary to that balderdash is charmingly absent. There is, in the ordinary sense, no plot. There is no hero. There is, save as a momentary flash, no love affair. There is no apparent hortatory purpose, no show of theory, no visible aim to improve the world. The whole enchantment is achieved by the simplest of all possible devices. One follows a poor Bohemian farm girl from her earliest teens to middle age, looking closely at her narrow world, mingling with her friends, observing the gradual widening of her experience, her point of view—and that is all. Intrinsically, the thing is sordid—the life is almost horrible, the horizon is leaden, the soul within is pitifully shrunken and dismayed. But what Miss Cather tries to reveal is the true romance that lies even there— the grim tragedy at the heart of all that dull, cow-like existence—the fineness that lies deeply buried beneath the peasant shell. Dreiser tried to do the same thing with both Carrie Meeber and Jennie Gerhardt,[1] and his success was unmistakable. Miss Cather succeeds quite as certainly, but in an altogether different way. Dreiser's method was that of tremendous particularity—he built up his picture with an infinity of little strokes, many of them superficially meaningless. Miss Cather's method inclines more to suggestion and indirection. Here a glimpse, there a turn of phrase, and suddenly the thing stands out, suddenly it is as real as real can be—and withal moving, arresting, beautiful with a strange and charming beauty ... I commend the book to your attention, and the author no less. There is no other American author of her sex, now in view, whose future promises so much....

The Smart Set, 17 February 1919, pp. 140-41.

---

1 Theodore Dreiser, *Sister Carrie* (1900) and *Jennie Gerhardt* (1911).

Appendix G: Photographs of Nebraska

[Historical photographs contemporaneous to the events depicted in *My Ántonia*.]

1. Primitive Dugout

[The Shimerda family, like many Great Plains immigrants, lived their first year in America in a dugout—literally, a cave-like dwelling dug into the landscape. Over the first year wood would be gathered for a house, while the family constructed a temporary sod house (Appendix G.2) and began working on a wood-frame home. Prairies are largely treeless, and families had to travel great distances to gather or purchase wood for construction. See Appendix H.1 for the unofficial "six year plan" from dugout to farm. After abandoning the dugout, it might be used as a smoke-house and storm cellar. Courtesy of the Nebraska State Historical Society, Item RG3464-45.]

2. Sod House, second-stage of prairie housing

[While taking shelter in a dugout (Appendix G.1), the immigrant family on the prairie would construct a sod house, made from cutting sod from the ground in squares and assembling from this organic material the walls of a house. Courtesy of the Nebraska State Historical Society, Item RG2608-2023.]

3. Threshing Scene

[Ántonia describes the suicide during threshing season of a wandering man, who throws himself into the threshing machine. This
machine threshes, or separates the grain from the husk and straw.
It could also do significant damage to a human body. Courtesy of
the Nebraska State Historical Society, Item NSHS 2608-3134.]

4. The Pavelka Farm

[This is the actual homestead of Anna Pavelka's family, located in Webster County; or, Ántonia's homestead as depicted in the last book of the novel, "Cuzak's Boys." It now belongs to the Willa Cather Pioneer Memorial and Educational Foundation, and is maintained as a historical site. Courtesy of the Nebraska State Historical Society, Item NSHS RG1951-386.]

5. Anna Sadilek

[Anna Sadilek (Mrs. Anna Pavelka) is the prototype of Ántonia Shimerda. This photograph was taken around 1886. Courtesy of the Nebraska State Historical Society, Item NSHS RG1951-208.]

6. Blind Boone

[Cather had knowledge of at least two blind black musicians upon which she could draw to create the character of Blind D'Arnault, the child prodigy whose story is told in Book II, "The Hired Girls": Thomas Green Bethune (1849–1908), known as Blind Tom, a pianist and composer who was born a slave near Columbus, Georgia; and John William Boone (1864–1927), known as Blind Boone, a black pianist and composer, born in Missouri. Cather reviewed a performance by Blind Tom in the *Nebraska State Journal* in 1894. Blind Boone performed in Red Cloud several times in the late 1880s, before Cather left for the University of Nebraska. Blind Boone's photograph is used by permission, State Historical Society of Missouri, Columbia.]

7. The University of Nebraska, c. 1900

[Jim Burden attends the University of Nebraska in Book III, "Lena Lingard." Cather attended the University of Nebraska from 1890 to 1895. Courtesy of the Nebraska State Historical Society, Item NSHS RG2758:2-15.]

Appendix H: Immigration to and Migration Across America

1. Nebraska Land Company, Czech Language Immigration Poster

[Posters such as these were distributed throughout Europe to attract immigrants to America. Note the pictorial "six-year plan" from dugout to sod house to farm. This poster is in Czech, and would have been seen by people such as the Shimerda family, to enable them to visualize the American dream in a six-step program. Courtesy of the Nebraska State Historical Society, Item RG 1600-10.]

2. Welcome to the Land of Freedom

[This somewhat romanticized scene on the steerage deck of an unidentified ocean steamer, passing the Statue of Liberty on its way to Ellis Island in New York, was drawn by a staff artist. Courtesy of the Library of Congress, Item LC-USZ62-113735.]

3. Emigrants Coming to the "Land of Promise"

[Images such as these were common during the Great Migration, 1880-1920, when over 20 million people emigrated from their homelands to America. About half went back after various periods of time, and many made repeated crossings before either settling in a new country or returning to origins. America, known as the "Land of Promise," was indeed that for millions of people, such as Ántonia Shimerda, but for millions of others, like Ántonia's father, emigration could be disastrous. Of note is the crowded, "huddled" arrangement of human beings, transported at maximum profit by land and sea companies, and romanticized by the Statue of Liberty's call for the world's "huddled masses" to come to America for secular renewal. Courtesy of the Library of Congress, Item LC-USZ62-7307.]

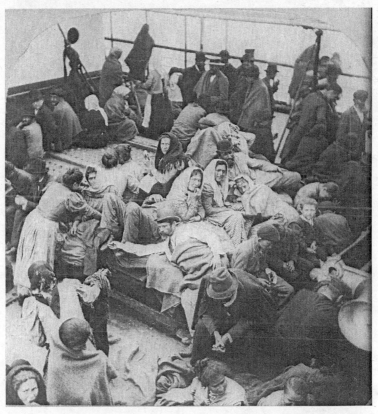

4. Crossing the Great American Desert in Nebraska

[This caravan of emigrants is bound for California. The image makes clear that Nebraska was not, at first glance, a place considered ideal for human habitation. Indeed, during the nineteenth century it was known as "the great American desert," although it is not, properly speaking, a desert. Settling in frontier Nebraska was nothing at all like settling in colonial New England, Virginia, the northeast or south, or west. *My Ántonia* is entirely accurate, if somewhat romanticized, in its depiction of the amount of labor necessary to settle this landscape. Courtesy of the Library of Congress, Item LC-USZC4-2635.]

Appendix I: Music from My Ántonia

1. "Oh, Promise Me"

[This song from the 1891 comic opera, *Robin Hood*, written by the popular songwriting team of Reginald de Koven and Harry B. Smith, was among Lena Lingard's favorites when she and Jim Burden were dating in Lincoln. Comic operas, especially those of Gilbert and Sullivan, were immensely popular in this era. Gilbert and Sullivan gave rise to domestic imitations of their formulaic operettas, and de Koven and Smith were among the more successful of their time.]

Oh, Promise Me

Words by Clement Scott
Music by R. de Koven

new,   And find the hol-lows where those flow-ers grew, _____   Those

first sweet vi - o-lets of   ear - ly spring,   which come in whis-pers, thrill us

both,   and sing O   love un - speak - a - ble that   is   to be;   Oh

pro - mise me! oh pro - mise   me!

2. "O Bury Me Not on the Lone Prairie"

[One of the songs Jim Burden recalls the cowboy Otto Fuchs singing, this one has an interesting history and is not an insignificant choice for Cather. The song was adapted from a traditional sailor's lament. The metaphoric connection between crossing the ocean and crossing the American plains is emphasized in the adaptation of the sailor's song for use by American cowboys.]

17. O BURY ME NOT ON THE LONE PRAIRIE

"O bur-y me not___ on the lone prai-rie." ___ These words came low___

___ and mourn-ful - ly, ___ From the pal - lid lips___ of a youth who

lay___ On his dy - ing bed ___ at the close of day.___

1. "O bury me not on the lone prairie."
   These words came low and mournfully,
   From the pallid lips of a youth who lay
   On his dying bed at the close of day.

2. He had wasted and pined till o'er his brow
   Death's shades were slowly gathering now.
   He thought of home and loved ones nigh,
   As the cowboys gathered to see him die.

3. "O bury me not on the lone prairie,
   Where the coyotes howl and the wind blows free.
   In a narrow grave just six by three—
   O bury me not on the lone prairie."

4. "It matters not, I've oft been told,
   Where the body lies when the heart grows cold.
   Yet grant, o grant, this wish to me,
   O bury me not on the lone prairie."

5. "I've always wished to be laid when I died
   In a little churchyard on the green hillside.
   By my father's grave there let me be,
   O bury me not on the lone prairie."

6. "I wish to lie where a mother's prayer
   And a sister's tear will mingle there.
   Where friends can come and weep o'er me.
   O bury me not on the lone prairie."

7. "For there's another whose tears will shed
   For the one who lies in a prairie bed.
   It breaks my heart to think of her now,
   She has curled these locks; she has kissed this brow."

8. "O bury me not . . ." And his voice failed there.
   But they took no heed to his dying prayer.
   In a narrow grave, just six by three,
   They buried him there on the lone prairie.

9. And the cowboys now as they roam the plain,
   For they marked the spot where his bones were lain,
   Fling a handful of roses o'er his grave
   With a prayer to God, his soul to save.

Select Bibliography

Books by Willa Cather

Alexander's Bridge. New York: Houghton Mifflin, 1912.

April Twilights (1903). Lincoln: U of Nebraska P, 1962.

The Autobiography of S.S. McClure (1914). Ed. with Introduction by Robert Thacker. Lincoln: U of Nebraska P, 1997.

Death Comes for the Archbishop. New York: Knopf, 1927.

The Life of Mary Baker G. Eddy and the History of Christian Science (1909). With Georgine Milmine. Ed. with Introduction and Afterword by David Stouck. Lincoln: U of Nebraska P, 1993.

A Lost Lady. New York: Knopf, 1923.

Lucy Gayheart. New York: Knopf, 1935.

My Mortal Enemy. New York: Knopf, 1926.

O Pioneers! New York: Knopf, 1913.

Obscure Destinies. New York: Knopf, 1932.

The Old Beauty, and Others. New York: Knopf, 1948.

One of Ours. New York, Knopf, 1922.

The Professor's House. New York: Knopf, 1925.

Sapphira and the Slave Girl. New York: Knopf, 1940.

Shadows on the Rock. New York: Knopf, 1931.

The Song of the Lark. New York: Houghton Mifflin, 1915.

The Troll Garden. New York: S.S. McClure, 1905.

Youth and the Bright Medusa. New York: Knopf, 1920.

Books and Articles about Willa Cather

Acocella, Joan Ross. *Willa Cather and the Politics of Criticism.* Lincoln: U of Nebraska P, 2000.

Ambrose, Jamie. *Willa Cather: Writing at the Frontier.* New York: St. Martin's Press, 1988.

Bennett, Mildred R. *The World of Willa Cather.* Lincoln. U of Nebraska P, 1961.

Bloom, Edward Alan, and Bloom, Lillian. *Willa Cather's Gift of Sympathy.* Carbondale: Southern Illinois UP, 1962.

Bloom, Harold, ed. *Willa Cather's My Ántonia.* New York: Chelsea

House, 1987.

Bloom, Harold, ed. *Willa Cather: Modern Critical Views*. New York: Chelsea House, 1985.

Bohlke, Brent L., ed. *Willa Cather in Person: Interviews, Speeches, and Letters*. Lincoln: U of Nebraska P, 1986.

Brown, E.K. *Willa Cather: A Critical Biography* (1953). Lincoln: U of Nebraska P, 1987.

Carlin, Deborah. *Cather, Canon, and the Politics of Reading*. Amherst: U of Massachusetts P, 1992.

Cather Studies, U of Nebraska P, an annual since 1990.

Gerber, Philip. *Willa Cather*. New York: Twayne, 1995.

Giannone, Richard. *Music in Willa Cather's Fiction*. Lincoln: U of Nebraska P, 1968.

Goldberg, Jonathan. *Willa Cather and Others*. Durham, NC: Duke UP, 2001.

Harrell, David. *From Mesa Verde to The Professor's House*. Albuquerque: U of New Mexico P, 1992.

Harvey, Sally Peltier. *Redefining the American Dream: The Novels of Willa Cather*. Rutherford, NJ: Associated University Presses, 1995.

Hively, Evelyn Helmick. *Sacred Fire: Willa Cather's Novel Cycle*. Lanham, MD: UP of America, 1994.

Kaye, Frances W. *Isolation and Masquerade: Willa Cather's Women*. New York: Peter Lang, 1993.

Lee, Hermione. *Willa Cather: Double Lives*. NY: Pantheon Books, 1989.

Lewis, Edith. *Willa Cather Living: A Personal Record* (1953). Lincoln: U of Nebraska P, 2000.

Lindemann, Marilee. *Willa Cather, Queering America*. New York: Columbia UP, 1999.

McDonald, Joyce. *The Stuff of Our Forbears: Willa Cather's Southern Heritage*. Tuscaloosa: U of Alabama P, 1998.

Middleton, Jo Ann. *Willa Cather's Modernism: A Study of Style and Technique*. Rutherford: Fairleigh Dickinson UP, 1990.

Murphy, John J. *My Ántonia: The Road Home*. Boston: Twayne, 1989.

Murphy, John J. et al., eds. *Willa Cather: Family, Community, and History* (The BYU Symposium). Provo, UT: Brigham Young University Humanities Publications Center (and Willa Cather Education Foundation), 1990.

O'Brien, Sharon, ed. "Chronology" *Willa Cather: Stories, Poems, and Other Writings*. New York: Library of America, 1992, pp.

983-1002.

O'Brien, Sharon, ed., *New Essays on Cather's My Ántonia*. New York: Cambridge UP, 1998.

O'Brien, Sharon. *Willa Cather: The Emerging Voice*. New York: Oxford UP, 1987.

O'Connor, Margaret Anne, ed. *Willa Cather: The Contemporary Reviews*. New York: Cambridge UP, 2001.

Reynolds, Guy. *Willa Cather in Context: Progress, Race, Empire*. New York: St. Martin's Press, 1996.

Robinson, Phyllis C. *Willa: The Life of Willa Cather*. New York: Holt, Rinehart and Winston, 1983.

Romines, Ann. *The Home Plot: Women, Writing, and Domestic Ritual*. Amherst: U of Massachusetts P, 1992.

Romines, Ann, ed. *Willa Cather's Southern Connections: New Essays on Cather and the South*. Charlottesville: UP of Virginia, 2000.

Ronning, Kari. "The University of Nebraska in the 1890s." in *Willa Cather's University Days*. Lincoln: Center for the Great Plains Studies, U of Nebraska-Lincoln, 1995, pp. 10-13.

Rosowski, Susan J., ed. *Approaches to Teaching Cather's My Ántonia*. New York: Modern Language Association, 1989.

Rosowski, Susan J. *The Voyage Perilous: Willa Cather's Romanticism*. Lincoln: U of Nebraska P, 1986.

Rosowski, Susan, and Bernice Slote. "Willa Cather's 1916 Mesa Verde Essay: The Genesis of *The Professor's House*," *Prairie Schooner* 58:4 (1984): 81-92.

Sergeant, Elizabeth Shepley. *Willa Cather: A Memoir*. Lincoln: U of Nebraska P, 1953.

Skaggs, Merrill. *After the World Broke in Two: The Later Novels of Willa Cather*. Charlottesville: UP of Virginia, 1990.

Skaggs, Merrill, ed. *Willa Cather's New York: New Essays on Cather in the City*. Madison, NJ: Fairleigh Dickinson UP, 2000.

Stouck, David, *Willa Cather's Imagination*. Lincoln: U of Nebraska P, 1975.

Stout, Janis P. *Willa Cather: The Writer and Her World*. Charlottesville: UP of Virginia, 2000.

Swift, John N. and Joseph R. Urgo, eds. *Willa Cather and the American Southwest*. Lincoln: U of Nebraska P, 2002.

Thomas, Susie. *Willa Cather*. Totowa, NJ: Barnes & Noble Books, 1990.

Urgo, Joseph R. *Willa Cather and the Myth of American Migration*. Urbana: U of Illinois P, 1995.

Winters, Laura. *Willa Cather: Landscape and Exile*. Selinsgrove, PA:

Susquehanna UP, 1993.

Woodress, James. *Willa Cather: A Literary Life*. Lincoln: U of Nebraska P, 1987.